PRINTHOUSE BOOKS PRESENTS:

MADE II

Fall of a Family; Rise of a Boss.

FICTION, *Inspired by True Events...*

To YARD
Thank you for the support
God Bless!
Ant Bank$
6-24-13

An Organized Crime Novel.

ANTWAN 'ANT' BANK$

1

PrintHouse Books, Atlanta, GA.   Published 3-12-13

www.PrintHouseBooks.com

VIP INK Publishing Group; Incorporated

This novel is fiction but also has been inspired by true events, most characters are fictitious no matter how true the event. Some characters remained the same as the events have been documented to the public and are on public record.

Cover art, designed by SK7.

ISBN – 978-0-9886428-4-3 Paperback

Library of Congress Cataloging-in-Publication Data

ANTWAN 'ANT' BANK$

MADE II; Fall of A Family; Rise of A Boss.

1. Crime Thriller 2.Mystery 3.Erotica 4.Urban Literature

5. Organized Crime 6. ANTWAN 'ANT' BANK$

Printed in the United States of America

Hello Reader;

I know you've been waiting to see what happened in regards to the ending of book one. So wait no longer; the time is here. Get comfortable, grab your cup of coffee, wine, smoke or whatever you do; now it's time to get back to some Gangster Sh**. In book two of the Epic MADE Trilogy; AC, Manny and Duck come face to face with Sabrina's kidnappers. Nina, Denna, Loon and Big Will have bigger shoes to fill in their new roles, while Chief Espinoza suspicions escalates as Sin City crime rise's along with Hector's body count.

Monica's back and has plans on picking up from where she left off. Cash flow is at an all-time high with Coop at the helms as Crime continues to pay big for the new Sin City Boss. The recipe of Sex, Drugs and Murder prove to be the perfect mix, as one family falls and the next Boss is donned; King of the Devils playground.

Dedicated to the Street Life; A necessary evil.

ANTWAN BANK$

MADE II

Fall of a Family, Rise of A Boss.

VIP INK Publishing Group, Incorporated

Atlanta, GA.

Table of Contents

CHAPTER 1, Adulation

The Vegas strip is now empty; tons and tons of trash, party favors, drunks and empty champagne bottles cover the streets and sidewalks from the night before. A new year was now here and the morning sun was every ones worst enemy, especially the city workers who just arrived on the scene to clean the big mess. Coops balcony door is still open from the night before; while Duck, Loon and Will lay out on the deck in a deep sleep. Inside; Hector, Nina, Denna, Manny and AC sit at the kitchen table, drinking on fresh cups of hot coffee. No one said a word as the sun rays beam through the deck window and lit up the front room.

Chino and the others still lay asleep in the bedroom, Nina couldn't take the silence any longer; she had to speak up. Ok God dammit, what the fuck are we gonna do about Sabrina? AC sat his coffee down on the table then looked over at her. I'm still trying to decide on that sis. Well; you need to hurry up and make a decision; because you only have like 12 hours bro! Yeah I know. Do you want to know what I think bro? What do you think Denna? I say we let them have her ass! The way I see it, she's the damn reason we're in all this craziness anyway. Let them have that bitch man; we got the business on lock, why do we need her? You have a point Denna, but I think she still can be of some use to us. We are just now putting things in place and she can be a big help.

Aww man; your ass is pussy whip, aint you poppi? Hell nah, I whips the pussy Denna, not the other way around! Shiiitttt; I can't tell! Ha-Ha-Ha. Fuck you Nina! I'm just saying man, look at you! Look at you! Hector just sat there silent, the entire time watching them go back and forth. Yo, what do you have to say Hector; should we let them kill that bitch cuz? Denna, I'm in no position to make that decision cuz but if it was me. I would play the shit out; see what them punta's do next. Coop points at Hector, then speaks softly while in thought. Right; let them show their hand. Yep!

So that's what I think. Good Morning people, what yall fools in here talking about, early in the damn morning? Morning Loon! They all shouted. We're debating over what to do with Sabrina! AC do you really want to know what I think brother! No Loon, but go ahead and tell me anyway. We should give them fools the money and get your girl back bruh. Really! Yep! I'm looking at you right now and you look like a sad puppy that just lost his milk. Ha-Ha-Ha! Fuck you Loon! Man I'm serious; go get your bitch dawg. A Happy Boss is a good Boss; you dig. Well homies; give me a call if you need me, I'm about to be going, I have some business to handle at the shop. Alright Hector; we will be in contact! Alright AC, remember I'm only a phone call away. For sho! They give each other a pound.

Hector gives his cousins Nina and Denna a hug then head to the bedroom to get his people. Alright cuz, I will call you later. Ok Nina, Denna, talk to you guys in a bit. Manny; you're my Capo; what do you have to say? I say give them the cash but let's see if we can find a way, to find out who they are too. We can't afford to have a bull's eye on our backs while we're running Sin City; that will definitely be a problem. You got a point there Capo, hold on a minute. Will! Wake your ass up and get in here! Duck you too! AC shouted out to them as he walked towards the balcony. Will and Duck sat up from their sleeping positions, stretched then stood up.

Damn Coop, do you have some aspirin; my head is throbbing! Yeah Will; look in my bathroom medicine cabinet. Pow! Pow! Yo Duck! What the fuck are you shooting at boy! Oh it's a New Year brother; I always let off two shots on the first day of a new one man. Bro if you don't put that thing up with your crazy ass; come in here and join this meeting. I'm coming; I'm coming, give me a minute to wash off my face AC. Alright hurry it up. Denna, Nina, AC, Manny, Will and Loon gather around the kitchen table waiting on Duck so they could put together a plan to get Sabrina back. Hey Honey; I'm going to head home while you guys handle your business, call me if you need anything. Ok babe! Sophie walks over to the table and kisses Manny on the cheek before leaving. See you guys later! Alright; bye Sophie! They all shouted.

Duck makes his way back to the front room. Alright folks! What's the plan? Hold on Duck, give me a second; I'm working on it. OK Coop! AC picks up his cup of coffee and takes another sip while the others watch him; awaiting a response. Coop sat his mug down on the table; leaned back in his chair then placed his right hand on his chin. Ok gang; this is the move. Nina; go to the Mansion and pick up 2 million from the vault; Duck I'm gonna need a brief case with a six digit combination code; put your special touch on it! Got it Boss! Nina; you good? Yep I got you AC! Oh Duck! Yeah what's up? Sixty minutes and 11pm! Say no more; I'm on it! Duck grabs his coat then head out the door.

Nina; meet up with him after you pick up the loot, then head to the agency to open for business. Alright; I got you bro! Nina gathers her things then proceed to handle the mission. Denna; head out to the ranch to make sure the girls are ok and call me when you get there; we need to hire some people. Ok cool; I'm on it! Loon! Yeah Bro! Take care of the video store and the peep show girls, let them know we're in charge now and we mean business. No problem brother; I'm on that shit! Cool! Loon daps Coop up then leaves the Condo. Will! Yes sir! Get over to Dolls, meet with Red and have her stock up for today, everyone else will fall in place when they clock in; I will be there after I get Sabrina back. You sure you don't want me to go with you! I'm good player; Manny will be with me. Ok family; you guys be safe and I will see yall later tonight. Alright bro!

So Capo; what's your next move my man? I'm all in AC; you know what it is. Manny stands up from the table then pats Coop on the shoulder. Where you going Capo? Relax brother; I'll be right back; I have some chronic in my inside coat pocket. Shit boy; that's why you my motherfucker! He makes his way over to the closet to retrieve his jacket. Oh yeah, here it is, you got a light? Yep! AC reaches in his pocket for a lighter. Manny takes a seat at the table then passes Coop the blunt. The flame from the lighter caught the tip; its bright orange flicker began to burn slowly, releasing a strong soothing aroma as AC inhaled from the opposite end. Yeeaaahhhhhh, the chronic, this is more like it Capo. He passes the spliff to Manny. We have to make sure we handle this business correctly with this Brina shit; there can't be any signs of weakness Capo! Don't worry AC; I'm sure Duck is going to be extra careful on this job.

Oh no doubt; I know that. It's just that these cats hating already and we haven't even gotten the first damn day of the New Year in yet! Yeah I feel you on that Boss man; they're plenty of jealous fools out there; I'm sure this won't be the last time we have to deal with them. That may be true, but these fools that kidnapped Sabrina are going to be sorry they ever fucked with us! Smack! They give each other high five. Damn right! They both shouted. Yo; did you speak with the Towers about resigning yet? Yeah; I gave them a weeks-notice; I'm training David; starting tomorrow. Hmm, you think he can handle everything; even the dirty part of it? Yeah, he has a good head on his shoulders, we're going to need him on the team anyway; you dig. Alright Capo; if you say so! Man I'm hungry as hell, who's working the kitchen today? I have no idea bruh; I didn't check the schedule yet.

Well; I'm about to order something; did you want anything? Yeah; get me a steak and a fully loaded baked potato! Cool; how did you want that steak? Medium well! Ok! AC picks up the phone to call room service. Ring-Ring-Ring. Hello; room service; how can I help you? Hi; this is Mr. Cooper; I wanted to place two orders. Hi Mr. Cooper; go ahead; order when you're ready! For the first; let me get a fully loaded baked potato with a Medium Well T-bone. The second will be a half rack of hickory smoked ribs with garlic mashed potatoes. Ok; that's one T-bone; medium well with a fully loaded baked potato and a half rack of Hickory smoked ribs with garlic mashed potatoes.

Yep; that's it! Thanks for your order Mr. Cooper; it will be up in one hour. Ok thanks! Hey they said it will be up in a hour, you got anymore of that chronic. I have enough for one more blunt. That's what's up, let me have it, I'll roll it up. Might as well burn it while we wait.

As Nina pulled up to the Spanish Trails Mansion; there were two black 3 Series BMW's parked along-side the curb. The huge wooden front door was ajar and she could see inside through the glass of the screen door. Nina shifted her car to park; turned off the engine and stepped out; making sure to grab the Nine millimeter from under her seat. The adrenalin rushed through her body as she approached the steps; gun cocked and held down by her side; finger on the trigger, while in her right hand. Ha-Ha-Ha. Nina could hear laughter as she got closer to the front door. She took a peep inside before entering. Sitting on the couch was two white females, both with blond hair, wearing blue sweats and white t-shirts. She could hear them talking, then noticed that they were speaking with a German accent. Tap-Tap-Tap! Nina knocked on the glass door with the butt of her gun.

Yes! Who is it! It's Nina! Nina! Yes Nina! Who Nina! I work for your Boss; AC! Oh AC! Come in Nina! Come in! She enters the Mansion as the tall Blonde female approached her. Hi Nina, I'm ILona; nice to meet you! Nice to meet you too ILona! That is Vicky over there watching TV. Hi Vicky! Hi! The other lady waved to Nina. Well; I just came to pick up something; don't mind me! Ok Nina! Did you want something to drink? No I'm fine; go ahead continue what you were doing. Ok! ILona headed back over to the couch to join Vicky. Nina made her way over to the statue, pushed down the arm then entered the elevator. A few seconds later, she exited into the vault, picked up the two million dollars then placed it in an empty duffle bag. She jumped on the elevator and headed back upstairs then hurried to her car then dialed Coop's number from her car phone.

Ring-Ring-Ring. Hello! Hey bro.; it's Nina! Hey sis, you get it? Yep! Cool, take it over to Ducks place then head over to the agency to get them girls working. Alright bro, I will holler at you later then. For sho; I will call you and keep you posted on Brina's situation. Ok; be safe man! No doubt sis!

Beep! Beep! Damn esse'! All this traffic, it's making me crazy. Calm down Chino before you hit someone. I'm good Hector; I aint gonna hit nobody. Yo, just pull over to that liquor store real quick! Ok Homes; hold on; let me get over. Hurry up Chino! He whipped the impala over to the left turning lane of Tropicana Avenue then swung a left into the strip mall parking lot, just before Maryland parkway. Chino parked the car; then he and Hector jump out and walk inside the store. Girls we'll be right back! Ok Hector! Hey esse'; grab a bottle of Vodka; I will get the Tequila! Alright Hector! Chino walked to the rear of the store to get a bottle of Goose as Hector picked up the Jose' from the front row. The store attendant noticed the two gentlemen; then walked from behind the counter to keep a close eye on them.

Chino picked up the bottle of vodka and attempted to slip it in his khaki's. Hey you! Hey you! The Korean store clerk; shouted at him repeatedly. You no steal here! Get out! Get out now! What the fuck! Hector shouted; as he noticed the clerk rapidly approaching Chino. He placed the Jose' back on the shelf then reached for his piece. Pow! Pow! The clerk fell to the floor; two shots to the back. Pow!Pow!

17

Two more shots let out from Chino's 357. The clerk lay there in a puddle of blood as the two esse's grabbed all the liquor they could hold and high tailed it to the car. What the fuck Homes! Why you had to steal that shit! Now we got a motherfucking body for nothing; you ass hole! Damn! Let's go; start the car already; what the hell are you waiting on! Get the fuck out of here! Vrooom! Vrooom! Skrrrrrtt! Chino peeled out the lot at a high speed and back onto Maryland Parkway. The two ladies sat in the car puzzled. What's wrong Hector? Nothing baby; everything's cool!

Bullshit Hector! What did you fools do? I said it was cool baby; now mind your damn business chica! She folded her arms then sat back in her seat with an angry look on her face. Chino; speed this fucker up esse'! I'm speeding homes; I'm speeding! The white Impala cruised in and out of traffic as they got further and further away; from the scene of another crime. So does that one count bro? What are you talking about Chino? The chink homes; can I add it to my bodies? Fool; keep driving; you can be a dumb ass sometimes homes; I swear esse'! I'm just asking homes; that fool is dead! Yeah because I shot him; not you punta!

Whatever esse'! Chino just shut the hell up and drive; speed this fucker up! We need to drop these girls off so we can get to the shop. There are five cars coming in, four hours from now. Four hours! Yeah homes, four! Hector, that's a long time, we can make it. Chino just speed up; so we can handle business. Ok esse', ok!

Damn, what time is it? Will looked down at his watch as he turned off of Industrial and onto Dolls parking lot; the staff was all standing out front waiting on someone to let them in; he could see the frustration in their faces as he stepped out of his truck. Will; this isn't cool man! I know Red; I'm running a little behind baby; it won't happen again. Ok; I hear you man! The crew stood there restless as he unlocked the front doors. Beep! Beep! Beep! The alarm sounded as they entered. Hey Debbie; can you get that alarm baby? Sure; I got you man. Red went to disarm the alarm as the wait staff headed to the locker room to get ready for first shift. A strong aroma of cigarette and cigar smoke was left in the air from the night before. Dozens of hand prints; splatter the mirrors through-out the club from the dancers that worked New Year's Eve. Will turned on the white lights so the staff could clean the club before it was time to open for business.

Happy New Year Everybody! A soft female voice shouted from the entrance. Heyyy Malibu! Happy New Year baby! Thanks Red; did you have fun last night? Yes Ma'am; I did! Girl; you have to tell me all about it! Me and China went over to Asia's parent's, that party was crazy! Really; well hurry up and get dressed so we can talk then! Ok baby; have me a double shot of Henn waiting. Girl you crazy; go ahead; I got you covered.

Dylan, Remy and Gia walk in the club next. Hello ladies; Happy New Year! Happy New Year Red! Thanks girls; did you guys have fun last night? Bitch; my damn head is killing me; I don't know about them two but I need a BC, Goodie Powder or something! I got some Tylenol back here Dylan; did you want that? Hell yeah; I'll take it; thanks Red! Your welcome baby! Remy and Gia; dressed in sweats with hoodies over their heads and shades on, just kept walking to the dressing room. The wait staff came out of the locker room to clean the mirror's, tables and vacuum the floors. Big Will stepped out of his office and on to the main floor.   Alright people; hurry up; we only have 20 minutes before the doors open.

 He walks over to have a seat at the bar. Hey Red; did you need anything from the stock room? Yeah; I'm gone need a ton of stuff; give me a sec; making the list now. Ok baby. Hey yall; Happy New Year. Hey Barbie; Happy New Year to you too baby. Hey Will! Hey Barbie! Red leans over the bar to write her list on a bar napkin. Ok; here you go Boss! Thanks Red; I will have one of the security guards bring it up for you. Thanks Will! He gets up from the bar and takes the list over to one of the bouncers. Hey Bruh, go get these items from the stock room for me then take them to Red. Ok sir; no problem! The floors were now spotless, mirror's and tables cleaned. Hey! Hey! Happy New Year Motherfuckers! Hey Tru; Happy New Year Baby! Dj Tru; rushed in pass the bar and up the stairs to the Dj Booth.

 The bouncer rolled the loaded dolly over to the bar and unloaded the stock for Red. Will turned off the white lights. Alright people; look sharp! It's show time and we already have several customers in the lot waiting to come in! Tru turned on the stage lights and fluorescents then played some music from Dominoe's cd. "Here we go here we go as the tunes starts to bloom." Hey Red; do you have everything baby? Yes Will; I'm all good. Ok; I'm turning on the open sign. Will wave to the door man to turn on the sign and let the patrons in. "Saturday Morning just getting up" "With a hangover smellin like fuck."

Happy New Year People! Hey China; Happy New Year baby; slow down! I'm late Red! You're fine girl; don't hurt yourself rushing. China walked in; hastily pass the bar; heading to the dressing room. What's up bitches! She shouted to the other ladies as she entered the dressing room. Hey Chica; where did you go last night? Oh, I had to leave the party and pick up a package from a friend that was in town; why? Did you miss me Malibu? Hell nah; what was the package? Did you get a car? Your ass need one! Ha-Ha-ha. Shut up Dylan; mind your business! Ahhhh; don't get mad pookie! Pop! Dylan walked over to her then smacked her butt. Whatever! China took a seat at the make-up table, opened her back pack and pulled out a baby blue shrink wrapped package. China; what the hell is that? What do you think it is Malibu?

Bam! She slammed it on the table. That's $100,000.00 bitch; Uncut! What the fuck! The ladies shouted; jumped up and ran over to where she was sitting. Damn girl, who in the hell is going to buy that! Relax Remy; you know your man can't afford this; don't even ask. Bitch; you don't know what we can afford! Well this is 100 grams of pure powder baby; tell D if he can come up with 100 g's by tomorrow it's all his. Say no more Malibu; I will let you know as soon as possible. Cool; handle your business girl; I can have a buyer come pick it up A.S.A.P. and get it off my hands; if you guys can't. But since you're my people; you get first dibs at it. Alright; appreciate that Malibu. Yeah don't mention it! Come on yall; we have five minutes to be on the floor. Dylan stood up to warn them as she walked out of the dressing room.

Knock! Knock! Knock! Who is it! It's me Duck! Me who? Nina! Oh; hold on sis! He gets up from his kitchen table, slides the briefcase away from the edge, then go opens the door. Hey; did you get the cash? Yep; its right here; all 2 mil! Cool; come in; I'm about done with the briefcase. Did you want anything to drink; I have some beer in the fridge! What kind of beer? Red Stripe! Nah; I'll pass. Ok; suit yourself. What kind of briefcase are you using; combination or key? Combo for this job sis; AC already gave me the code earlier anyway. Cool; how much longer? I just have to reseal the lining; so we can fit the money in, set the combo and that's it. Well; how long is that going to take; I need to get to the agency! Ahhh; maybe 10-15 minutes! You can head to the Agency; I got it from here. Are you sure Duck? Yep! Alright; I will see you later then; I'm out of here! The money is on the counter. Ok sis; later!

Duck returns to the table to complete the task at hand. He held the hot glue gun steady; being extra careful as he spread it along the inside to reseal the suede lining of the briefcase. Ring! Ring! Ring! Dammit; who the hell is it now! Ring! Ring! Hello! Hey Duck; what's the status player? I'm putting the finishing touches on it now Coop! Great; don't forget the code; its 60 and 11pm! Got it bruh; I will be at your place in an hour! Alright; see you in a few Duck! Yep; see you later AC.

So what's the status Boss? He's finishing up now Manny; should be here in an hour. That's what's up; I'm going to run by the house for a minute before we do that drop off tonight; is there anything I need to do while I'm out? Yeah; call Fat Boy and meet up with him to discuss that Meth package. Consider it done; did you want me to call Derek too? Nah; I will take care of him. Ok; I'm heading out; see you later on Coop! Alright Manny; be safe around that Fat Motherfucker! No doubt bruh; always!

AC picks up the cordless phone then walks out on the balcony and dials a number. Ring! Ring! Ring! Yeah; who this! Its Coop fool; where your ass at Loon? Just parking the cadi in front of the Video store; is everything good with Duck? Yeah we're in play. That's what it is; so how did you want me to handle this here video joint? Run that shit as normal bruh; just put them hoes in check. Oh that goes without saying Boss man; you dig! I dig! Well go ahead and handle that Loon; Denna is headed out to the Ranch to straighten things out; so you're solo for now. It's all good AC; I got this. I'm sure you do man; peace out! Later bruh!

Loon puts the primed colored cadi in park, turned off the engine, stepped out the car and walked across the parking lot; checking for lot lizards. No crack-head whores were in sight. Loon smiled and thought to himself. They must have all gotten the message; since the last incident. As he walked; he saw the city bus pulled up in front of the store then opened its doors at the bus stop. Three young ladies stepped off; one white with short brunette hair, one light skinned with black micro braids and the other dark skinned with a pony tail hanging from under her UNLV ball cap. They all resembled college students wearing their Rebel sweats, as they approached the entrance to the Adult Video store. Hey Loon! Hey Chocolate! Diamond! Blue! How was your New Years? It's was cool; just another year; nothing special man!

Damn; why you sound so down Choc? I aint down Loon; I'm just sayin. Saying what? It's just another day; that's all. He looked back at the girls as he unlocked the heavy steel barred glass doors. Well; maybe today will make it all worth it; being a New Year. Shit; we'll have to see about that one Loon! Ha-Ha-Ha. The ladies laugh at Diamond's comment. Yall crazy; go ahead and get dressed while I open up. Ok man; we're going. Loon flipped the light switch; the dim fluorescent bulbs flickered over the narrow aisles of adult video tapes and novelties. The smell of mildew and stale cigarette smoke filled the air. A bright red glow emitted from the dark hallway; that led to the peep show booths. The only sound in the building came from the loud gust of wind; that blew through the air vent;

it felt like a warm wool blanket as it breezed across your skin.

Loon had just finished counting his drawer when a shiny dark hour glass shaped silhouette; appeared from the hallway. Hey Loon! Hey Choc; what's up? What do you think about my new outfit? I like it; it's sexy as hell. So come over here and let me dance for you, before we get busy. No Ma'am; I am definitely not; but you can come to me; behind the counter. Amidst her dark skin and caramel lips; Chocolate showed all 32 pearly whites as she responded with a bright smile. Ding! He pushed the cash register drawer shut, upon her approach. She grabbed a fist full of Loon's shirt and pulled him closer to her, away from the register. Slow down woman; are you sure you're ready for me? Chocolate looked in his eyes, smiled, than began kissing him. Loon; embracing the moment; reached down and slid her thongs to the side. During the heat of passion; he lifted her up then she wrapped her dark skinned, muscular legs, around his waist as he dropped his pants.

Slowly and lustfully she moaned; as Loon inserted himself inside her. He pushed up while gripping her ass; as she held his shoulders tight; enduring the sensual penetration. Minutes pass; drops of sweat fell as she rode and rode him. Ummm-Ummm-Ummmm. Damn Loon! Nah, don't give in yet Choc; I got some more strokes for your ass! Ummm-Ummm-Ummm! Yeah; this is what you wanted; right girl! Ummm-Ummm-Ummm! Oh yes! Yes! Ummm-Ummm-Ummm. Ding! Ding! The cash register drawer popped open as they bumped against it. Ummm-Ummm-Ummm!

Yeah; you like this dick; huh girl! Ummm-Hmmm. Excuse me! Excuse me sir! Oh shit! Choc get down; someone's in the store. No! Girl; move! Loon puts her down. Yes sir; how can I help you? Shit; you can start by letting me get some that you were getting. Ha-Ha-Ha! Sorry about that man; we thought the door was locked. Hey it's no problem; I was looking for your Heather Hunter flicks. Oh; there on the middle isle sir. Alright, thanks brother. Yeah; no problem! Hey Loon; we have to finish fucking before we get off! Oh yeah? Yeah, I want some more! Ok Choc; we'll talk about it; get to work! I'm going, I'm going; you need to zip your pants up! Oh; thanks! He looked down at his pants then zipped up. Ring-Ring-Ring. Hello; Adult Video; how can I help you?

Hey poppi! Hey Denna; what's up! Just checking on you babe; did you get everything ready for today? Oh yeah; I'm good! Where you at? I'm on the way to the Ranch to check on the girls. That's what's up; how long are you going to be out there? I don't know yet poppi; I'm calling AC once I get there, to see. Ok; just let me know when you find out baby; I'm cooking dinner tonight. Really! Yes Ma'am; I can cook! I know you can Loon; I'm just surprised that's all. Well; you're really going to be surprised tonight. Hmmm; I can't wait Mr.! It won't be long baby and I'm sure you're going to love it. Alright; I'm almost at the Ranch; I will talk with you tonight! Ok Denna; be safe!

The Sun was settling over the desert; dusk had sat in; sand clouds appeared behind the Limo as it entered the gravel parking lot of Angelica's Bunny Ranch. Several ladies sat outside on the porch smoking; watching the Limo pull up to the front. The driver parked; exited the vehicle and walked to Denna's door. Once opened; you could see her left foot touch the sandy parking lot. The gravel crunched under her feet as the sand formed a small cloud around her black Dolce boot. Just above the black door and tinted window; a tanned manicured hand appeared; wearing pink nail polish and a gold tennis bracelet. She pulled herself up from the Limo, using her left hand that was on the door. Black Dolce shades covered her eyes; long silky brown hair fell just over the shoulders of her pin striped; two piece pants suit that was accented by her pink silk blouse. Denna stepped away from the Limo and walked towards the porch, then stood there for a moment, in silence, soaking it all in.

The ladies on the porch stood to their feet and took notice. They could see themselves in the lenses of her black shades. Her pretty bronze skinned glistened just a little from perspiration, as she reached up to remove a strand of hair; from the pink lipstick that coated her lips. Well; Hello there ladies; I see we are having a smoke break! Yes we are; and who the fuck are you! Won't you girls put out your cancer sticks; come inside and I will tell you. The ladies now appalled, looked scared and confused. Denna with all her confident swagger; stepped up on the porch; opened the door and looked at the girls. After you ladies! They put out their cigarettes and came inside.

Alright girls; have a seat; you can sit at the bar; on the couch; I don't really care; just pay close attention; ok ladies! The girls sat down and looked at her; then at each other and shook their heads. Who does this bitch think she is? Excuse me! What's your name baby? Who me? Yeah you; the one with all the mouth! My name is Donna! Well Donna; I'm Denna and I'm your new Boss! Says who! Says AC; the new Boss of this business! I can see now that you are going to be a problem Donna. Look Denna; Dana, Dollie; whatever your name is; I'm the senior bitch out here on the Ranch and I call the shots. Is that right? Yes Ma'am it is! Denna unbuttoned her suit jacket then removed her shades. Donna is it? Yes it is! I apologize baby; I think we got off on the wrong foot. Damn right we did! Denna reached under her jacket and pulled out her Nine.

Oh shit; hold on Ma'am! Shut up ladies; this is between me and Miss Donna! Stand your ass up Donna; I said stand up Bitch! I'm sorry Denna; I'm sorry! No; no, no; don't apologize baby. You meant what you said and I did too! Pow! Ouch! Oh God! Ohhh you shot my foot! Oh God!

Now; I think we are on the same foot; how about you Donna! Yes! Yes! Yes Ma'am. Ok then; I'm the new Bitch in charge and what I say goes; got that girls! Yes Ma'am! Oh, you can call me Denna; I aint no old lady. Yes Denna! Good, that's more like it. Hey Donna! Yeeesss Denna! She answered in pain. You're fired; limp your crippled ass to the back and clear out your shit; my driver will drop you off at the bus station. Ok ladies; the rest of you; go freshen up and get ready for business; we got pussy to sell! The injured prostitute attempted to make her way to the back when two other ladies came to assist her. Hey; leave that hoe alone; she doesn't need any help! Take yall asses to the back and get ready for work! Ok Denna; we're going. Good; now kick rocks!

Donna hurry your cripple behind up; my driver is waiting! Yes Ma'am; I'm sorry! Denna just looked at the woman and shook her head as she limped to the back. Then she made her way over to the cashier's cage to use the phone. Ring! Ring! Ring! This is AC; who's speaking! Hey bro, it's me; Denna! Hey Sis; what's the word? Well everything is solid out this way. Cool; you didn't have any problems did you? Just a small one but it's handled. Alright; good shit.

So what are we going to do about staffing this joint bro? I have a bartender from the club coming to work out there and I'm going to call Monica and see if she wants the house mom gig. Yeah that's a good move poppi; Monica is good people! I just need you to hold it down until I can get them out there. Alright I got you covered bro; don't take all week though; ok! I'm on it today sis, I promise! I'm not worried AC; I know you got it; go take care of that; I'm going to find me something to eat; chat with you later! Ok; bye Denna!

Ring! Ring! Ring! What up; speak! Que Pasa; Fat boy! Who this! Manny! Oh what up yo! We need to meet; I'm pulling up to your detail shop now. Cool; I'm around back by the dumpster. Alright; be there in a minute. One could still feel the New Year's energy and excitement in the air as jovial patron's sat patiently under the street lights that lit up the detail shop parking lot. Manny parked his El Camino in front of the shop office; then made his way around back. Over in front of the green dumpster; rinsing out two 30 gallon black trash cans; stood a huge 6 foot plus white male. Baggy reebok sweats; hung from his big thighs with a matching hoodie that came down just above his protruding belly. The water from the hose; splashed off the cans and upon his white reebok sneakers. Hey Big Boy; what's up dude? Hey Manny; what's good yo! And it's Fat Boy! My bad Fat Boy; what's the difference? Big! Fat! Same shit; right! Nah; it aint yo! Anyway let's talk business; I'm on a tight schedule.

Fat Boy turned off the water and dropped the hose. Ok; we can talk over here. He walked over to a parked red pick-up with the tailgate down. Alright; what's the visit for Manny? He leaned forward; putting his stomach against the left side of the truck. Look; here's the deal my man; we have a new connect on some Meth; unlimited quantities; good quality candy; you comprende'! Yeah but what does that has to do with me; I don't have a market for it! See that's where we come in at! We who! AC and I; we're looking to aggrandize things my brother; it's a new Family in town! What Family; you and AC? Yeah but it's not only us, it's five others. Still; I don't know any of you guys; I'm not so sure about this Manny; what did the other crews have to say about it? First off Fat Boy; let me assure you; the seven of us have been together for at least ten years and it's all trust. We don't make any moves without discussing it in detail amongst the group before presenting it outside the Seven.

And to answer your question; no one knows about it yet; you are the first, because we believe it can move better in your territory. Really; and why is that Manny? The drug is fairly new and it's used by dancers mostly. Dancers; you mean strippers? Yep! No shit; really? Yes Sir. So that's why you're here; to get to the three Strip clubs in my territory. Now; you're thinking like a business man Fat boy. How do you know it's gonna move numbers? Brother; we have seen it move crazy numbers over at Dolls for that last 6 months. So; do you want in or not; the package will be ready for distribution in a week. Ok; what's my take? We can do; 45% on each package! Why not 50 or 55; I'm taking all the rest! True; but we're fronting you the product.

Well look; take your time and think about it; but I need an answer by tomorrow morning. Hold on; I'm in! Cool; I will call you with more details on the pick up later this week. Alright Manny; this shit better move yo! Don't worry Fat boy; you won't be sorry; I will call you later; I need to get back to the Towers. Fat boy looked at Manny then nodded as he walked away.

Knock! Knock! Come in; it's open! Duck; I've been waiting on you; what took you so long? Come on Coop; you know I had to make sure this thing was right bruh. Yeah; yeah; bring it over here; let me see it. They both walked over to the kitchen table. Duck sat the briefcase down and popped it open. Damn; are all those fresh bills? Hell yeah; that's what I said; Two Million dollars; all crisp bills. Alright; go ahead and set the combo. He closed the case, then Duck reached down to set the numeric, six digit; Combination. He turned the first dial to 6; the second to 0 and third to 2; on the first set of numbers. With his right thumb; Duck changed the first number, on the other second set of digits, to 3. Simultaneously; he set the last two numbers to 0. There it is Coop; all set my brother; 60 minutes and 11pm. 60-2300! Cool; I'm ready to get this shit over with! Hell yeah; me too; what time are they calling? Hopefully soon; it's 8 pm now! Didn't they say 24 hours! Yeah; I believe so Duck. Well; that should be around 10 or 11! I don't even remember bruh; I just hope they didn't hurt my girl!

I'm sure she's ok right now man; they want this damn 2 mill. Knock-Knock! It's open! Manny enters the condo. What's up soldiers; what's the word; are we ready to do this? Yeah Capo; Duck has the brief case ready; we're just waiting on the call. That's what's up; Duck are you riding with us? Of course! Nah; you better drive the Limo man; just in case we need another gun. Cool; say no more; done dada! Manny; turn on the radio or something; I'm going to fix me a drink; you guys want anything? Yeah; let me get one too! Me too Coop! Alright! "What's going on out there in Radio land; this is your night time jock; Shi C." "Happy New Year to all of you and I hope; all you guys made a good resolution; one you can keep!" "I know the gyms are loving it; because all the memberships are always at an all-time high around this time of year." "Anyway let's get into some good music" "This is one of my favorites; by Total."

"Uh, Give me all the chicken heads from Pasadena to Medina" "Bet Big get in between ya" "Then peek the prognosis, doses" " Blends and bends like Twizzlers." Here you go fellas; drink up! Thanks bruh! Yeah; no problem! So how did that meet go with Fat Boy; Manny? He's all in; a little hesitant at first but he came around. Good job Capo;

that will be some extra dough coming in by the week; a good bump! Thanks; it's what I do man. Hopefully; we can get the others to push it; after they've seen Fat ass make a profit. Yeah; that's the move right there Boss. All three gentlemen sat in the living room sipping on their drinks, music playing in the background; waiting patiently on the phone to ring. "Oh baby can't you see, what you do to me" "Our love was meant to be, you were meant for me." "Every time I see you, I get this feeling, oh yeah." Ring-Ring! Ring-Ring! Yo was that the phone ringing? I didn't hear anything Duck! I swore I heard the phone AC! "I can't wait for the day." Hey turn that down Manny! Ring-Ring! Ring-Ring!

Hello! You got my money nigga! Yeah I got it! That's what's up son; meet me on the top parking deck of Caesar's in a hour; come alone too nigga! Alright, then what? There will be a black Regal parked next to the elevators; go pop the trunk and you will find a radio; pick it up and call me when you get there! You're bitch will be close by; you get her after we get the 2 Mill. One hour nigga; don't be late or the girl dies. Click! Hello! Hello! Damn, he hung up. What he say Coop? Meet him on the top deck of Caesar's in a hour. Cool; let's make it happen. Hold on Manny; we have to be careful; he said to come alone. Dude; I'm driving; fuck that; you aint going alone. Duck's right Coop; we're going; we'll just drop you off and wait close by. I will bring the sniper rifle and post up; Manny you wait with the Limo, we'll catch up after he gets Brina.

That's a plan; we need to leave like right now then so we can scope out the area; we might get lucky and catch a peep at who we're dealing with. Let's do it; grab the briefcase and let's roll. We're right behind you AC! The guys stormed out of the condo; to the elevators and down to the lobby. Yo David! Hey Manny; what's up? Have the valet bring up the Towers Limo! Ok; I'm on it. Hey guys; I will meet you at the car; I need to get the Remington out of the trunk. Ok Duck; make it fast. AC held the door open for him to exit the Towers. Manny picked up a Chauffer's jacket from the coat rack and slid it on.

Come on Capo; here's the Limo! Ok; I'm coming! AC ran out to the driveway. Hold on Manny; don't forget this! Oh thanks David; need the hat huh! Yes Sir! He placed the hat on his head; jumped in the driver's seat then blew the horn. Beep! Beep! Duck bring your ass on! Come over here Manny! Duck shouted and waved for him to drive over. Coop sat in the back seat with the briefcase as Emanuel drove over to Dubai. Pop the trunk bruh; so I can put my rifle back there. AC rolled down the window. Hell nah; get in man; keep that with you; load and cock that motherfucker too! You got it Boss; let's roll.

Duck jumped in back with AC; then Manny drove a few blocks down to Caesar's. Alright; here's the play fellas! When we get to the parking garage; Manny stop on the level before we get to the top! Ok; got it! Duck; we are getting out by the staircase on the far end. Why are we getting out there AC? So you and I can go scout the top deck; bring your rifle. Cool; I got you. The night air was crisp amidst the red; green; blue and other assortment of neon lights that danced across the Las Vegas strip. Several statues in front of Caesars; reflected in the shiny black coat of the Limo as it entered the lot and drove over the gold brick driveway. Groups and groups of patrons gather at the valet booth; waiting for their cars as they headed back home from their New Year's celebration location.

Manny drove the Limo under the Casino overpass to enter the parking deck. Ok Capo; once you get in the garage; drive slow; so we can peep things out. I got you Coop. Duck; get your rifle ready. They entered the first level at a slow speed; looking carefully at every person and car as they drove by. Click! He pulled the bolt back; on the Remington. Alright; let's cap a motherfucker already. Ok Manny; I believe the next level is our stop; just park by the staircase; that's across the way; the opposite corner from the elevators. Hey Look! Look at what AC! That black regal that's driving up the ramp; I think that's the car. Slow down; park over here in front of these stairs. Emanuel stopped the vehicle; so AC and Duck could get out.

Stay here with the car Manny; we're going up the stairs to check things out. Alright; hurry up; we have 30 minutes before we have to make the drop. Ok Capo; we'll be right back. The two guys stepped out of the rear right door that was on the same side of the stairs. They ran up the steps; Duck with rifle in hand. There's the regal; right there AC; backing up. Yeah; I see it. I'm going over behind the cars; to get a closer look at the driver. Go ahead; I got your Six. Duck got in the prone position; down by the front passenger tire of a blue VW; that was parked by the stairs entrance; so he could see the target. AC walked in between the parked cars; staying low; being careful not to be seen. The regal backed into an empty space; adjacent to the elevators and staircase. The driver's door opens; an average size gentleman stepped out. Psst! Psst! Duck signaled to get AC's attention. Coop heard him and tried to get a closer look. Vroom! Vroom! Vroom! What the fuck! Coop said in a whisper. Vroom! A huge white truck; with large mud bogging tires; while passing; had blocked their view.

AC; now angry; hastily made his way back over to the staircase; signaling to Duck; to come on. Both of them made their way back down the stairs and to the Limo. Well, did you guys see anything? Man; hell nah; some red neck blocked the view; with his big ass truck. I saw a guy get out but couldn't see his face; did you get a glimpse of him AC? Just the back man; that's all I could see before the truck passed. Duck opened the Limo door to retrieve the briefcase. Here you go Boss; I will be in position armed and ready; just give me the signal; if you want me to lay that fool down! Boy; you're itching for a kill today; aren't you?

Shit; it's been too long since I killed me a fool Manny; I'm overdue bruh!

Alright; I'm ready fellas; it's that time; Manny keep this car running; Duck let's go! Time to get my Bitch back! Hold on Coop; roll the combination on that briefcase to set it! Oh; damn; can't forget that; I thought you did that already. Nah because we only have an hour after you open it, one time that's it! Ok cool! The guys walked up the steps to the top level; Duck returned to his position by the front tire of the VW; with a clear view of the regal. AC sat the briefcase down on the warm concrete and kneeled down beside it; to tie his white K-swiss while scoping out the area once more. He stood up; then bent over slightly to brush the dust off the right knee of his crisp Levi blue jeans. Standing erect; Coop's new white T-shirt hung just a few inches pass his leather belt. AC grabbed the bottom ends of the cocaine white sports jacket he had on and zipped it up to the center of his chest. With both hands; he pulled his all-white fitted, LA ball cap, down; just above his eyebrows; bent down; picked up the briefcase and walked towards the Regal.

This moment didn't seem real; the closer and closer he got to the car; his heart beat increased more and more. Now only a few steps away; it really hit him; every moment he spent with Sabrina had flashed through his mind. From that faithful day when they first met in the pizza joint, the night club, the Pepper Mill, Pharoh's death, the hot sex, Monk's death, the arguments and now this. Beep! Beep! Hey move out of the way crazy! Watch where you're walking! Oh shit; my bad Sir! Yeah; yeah; just move your ass and pay attention! AC stood aside to let the angry driver pass; before things escalated. He was now standing in front of the Regal. Coop took a deep breath; then walked to the trunk; then opened it to retrieve the radio.

Ummmm-Ummmm; hello! Yeah; you got my money nigga! Yeah; I got it! Cool; place it in the trunk; then walk back to the front of the car with both your hands in the air; over your head. Ok! Do it now nigga! What about Sabrina! Hold on! Come here bitch; say hey to your boyfriend! Daddy! Sabrina! That's enough; place the money in the trunk and do as I say; I will let her go after we get the money! Ok man; ok; I'm putting it in the trunk now and walking to the front. AC complies with the orders; a tall male wearing all black attire and a ski mask appears from the stairway entrance by the elevators. He walks to the trunk; opens it and looks inside the briefcase. Bam! He slams the trunk; places the briefcase on top of it and puts the radio to his mouth. Yeah; it's all here boss; send the girl out! The masked man; stood behind the car holding his 45 directly at AC. Just be calm nigga and stay there until you get your bitch; when she comes; turn the fuck around; keep walking and don't look back! Do you understand? Yeah; I got you! Good!

Ding! The elevator door opens; out walks Sabrina with a black scarf wrapped around her eyes and another masked man escorting her towards AC. Ok; stop right here bitch! Brina knees were shaking as she stood there nervous and pair toed, still wearing her black New Year's Eve dress and black stiletto heels. Red scars and blemishes; tattooed her wrist and ankles from where the kidnappers had her tied up. A few scratch marks were left on her neck; replacing the pearls that she wore; both ear lobes ripped at the holes; that recently kept the matching ear rings. Alright; take the scarf off that bitch! The kidnapper removed the blind fold and stood there beside his partner; watching

Sabrina as she walked towards AC. Oh Daddy! Daddy! Come here baby! Sabrina ran and jumped in Coops arms. Muah! Muah! She kissed him; over and over again. He grabbed her by the hand and started walking away from the Regal. The two masked men stood there watching until the couple reached the halfway point; then disappeared into the stairway entrance beside the elevators.

Coop grabbed Brina by the arm and started to run. Come on baby; hurry up; we need to get the fuck out of here! They ran to the stairway as Duck was standing up with his rifle. Duck! Hey Sabrina; are you ok baby? Yes! I'm so glad; yall came and got me! Manny was waiting patiently beside the idle Limo as the three of them exited the stairway. It's about time! Get in; let's get the hell out of here! Sabrina, Duck and AC, jumped in the Limo. What time is it Manny? It's 10:25 PM; Boss! Ok step on it; head straight to the Towers; we have 25 minutes! Manny raced down level by level; speeding through the parking deck in route to the Towers.

Chapter 2; New Alliances

The Limo pulled up in front of the Towers entrance. Manny jumped out of the driver's seat as AC, Sabrina and Duck exited the rear. Hey David; take care of this will you and put that Rifle in Duck's car. Yes Sir; no problem Manny! What time is it now Capo? 10:45 bruh! The four of them walked in the Towers and to the elevator. Did you get a chance to see who kidnapped you baby? No; they had me blind folded the whole time; they stole my pearls and everything daddy. Its fine now baby; you're alive and in one piece; that's all I care about. That other shit can be replaced. He embraced her as he leaned back against the elevator wall. Hey Coop! What up Manny! Push the button man; 44th floor nigga. Oh shit; my bad bruh! Yeah; you got other things on your mind. Ha-ha-ha. Duck what you laughing at!

I'm laughing at your ass; Boss! Man; whatever. Ding! The elevator door opens and they walk down to AC's condo. Coop hands Manny the keys. Open the door for me Capo! Ahhhh; home sweet home! Sabrina ran in; kicked off her shoes and walked towards the bedroom while pulling off her dress. See you guys later; I'm hitting the shower! Ok baby; close the room door behind you. Ok daddy! Duck turn the TV on. Alright; where's the remote? On the counter by the microwave! Oh; I see it! Cool, me and Manny are going to be on the balcony. What channel did you want it on? The 11 O'clock news bruh! Oh yeah! What time you got Manny? 10:59 man! Hey Duck; we got one minute; hurry up and get out here! I'm coming man; hold your damn horses! After turning the TV on; he joined the others outside. Down below; miles and miles of traffic; jammed the strip as they drove away from the Adult Playground; known as Sin City. Images of hot flames bounced off the car windows from the erupting volcano. Boom! Loud canons sounded off as the Pirate ships battled on the dark seas at Treasure Island while the MGM Lion stood guard over the devils playground.

The three guys hung over the rail; watching all the commotion below caused by the hung over locals and tourist. Boom! Boom! Boom! Skreeeeet! Skreeeeet! Beep! Beep! Yes! There it is; right on time! See; you guys can always count on Duck baby! Several cars instantly pressed on their brakes and blew on their horns whiled a vehicle exploded and burned at the entrance of Caesar's. Hold on fellas; wait a second there's one more coming. Boom! Yes! Now that's how you make a bomb my brother! Good damn job Duck! Thank you Coop! Hey amigo; you the man! Damn right I am Manny; that's my specialty baby. Police sirens sounded through-out the boulevard in route to the scene. Several fire trucks and ambulance; rushed to the burning vehicle as the foot patrol cops started to control the traffic.

All out chaos; had added to the already hectic; traffic situation on the strip. Look; there's the news truck; let's go see who Duck blew up! AC shouted as he ran inside to watch the news. "Hello and Happy New Year Las Vegas" "This is Katie Strong reporting your 11 O'Clock news" "Tonight at 11; footage from the concert on the strip during the New Year's celebration last night" "The New Police Chief, Chief Espinoza says it was one of the best New Year's parties in the last 6 years with less than 20 arrest" "Hold on! I have breaking News from our eye in the sky" "I'm going to pass it over to Lisa Daniels; live in the chopper right now" "Thanks Katie! We have a big mess on the strip right now" "A black hummer blew up as it was leaving Caesar's; just a few minutes ago." Black Hummer; who the fuck do we know with a black hummer? I remember seeing one not too long ago!

I don't know AC; how about you Manny? Nah; I can't recall! "I now have word that, three victims has died in the explosion; officers think it is crime related" "If you look; right behind me guys; you can see tons and tons of burning money floating above and around the vehicle" "Officers are saying that all three of the victims had New York State I'D's but they can't release names until next of kin has been contacted" "Back to you Katie" "Thanks Lisa!" New York! Isn't that nigga Steel from New York; Capo? Yep; damn sure is AC! Those crooked; sneaky ass motherfuckers! Hey; their some dead mofo's now Boss! Ha! Ha! Sure you right Duck! Sure you right!

Hey; you alright Boss? Yeah; why you ask that Capo? You're pacing back and forth bruh; is something wrong? I was thinking about something that Will told me a few months ago. What was that? He said that some of the dancers told him that Sabrina and Steel fucked around before. What do you mean; like fuck or she was his lady?

His lady! Damn; that's crazy my man. Yeah it is Capo! You think she was in on it AC? I don't know Duck but I'm about to find out. I'll be right back! Coop leaves the guys up front and walks into his bedroom. Sabrina! Yeah babe! Sabrina! I'm still in the shower daddy! He steps into the steaming bathroom and slides back the shower curtains. I have a question for you? Yeah; what is it daddy? I heard that you and Steel dated before. Yeah; but that was before I started dancing; I can't stand that punk now! Really; why don't you like him now? Because he's a damn punk; his boy Jesse tried to talk to me while I was at his place one day. I told him about it and he didn't do shit! Nothing? That punk said I should have given Jesse some ass! Well? Fuck you AC! What do you mean; well!

Keep talking Sabrina; I need to hear more than that! There's nothing else to be said daddy; I haven't said two words to that punk since. Ok; you better not be lying to me woman! I'm not baby! I swear; now can you please hand me a towel. Here! Thank you daddy; I love you. Yeah; yeah; I love you too. I'm going back up front with the guys. Ok daddy. So what did she say? She admitted to dating him; but I don't think she had anything to do with the kidnapping Manny. Hmmm; I don't know AC! Hey check it Coop; can I be frank? Yeah; go ahead Duck. You know; you my brother right; Death before Dishonor and all that! Yeah; spit it out already. Well, I don't know about Manny; but I'm going to keep an eye on your girl; I don't trust her. You can be mad or pissed off; I don't give damn; we swore to have each-others back and that's what I'm doing. Hey; he has a point AC. Damn; so you feel the same way Manny? Yep! Alright family; do what you have to; just keep that shit on the low.

Hey daddy; what are you guys talking about in here? I'm hungry; is there anything to eat? Yeah; there's some wings in the fridge. Great; I'm starving. Yo; we're out bruh; you guys need to catch up anyway. Alright Manny; Duck; I will holler at you guys later. No doubt; later bruh! Hey baby; get me a coke while you're over there. Ok daddy. AC walks outside and takes a seat on the balcony. Damn; these wings are good! Is this lemon pepper daddy? Yep; with some mild sauce! There good! Come over here and have a seat baby. Sabrina takes a seat in the patio chair. Are you ok Sabrina? Yeah; I'm good. You sure; I know last night was probably scary? Did you want to see a doctor? No man; I don't need a doctor! These are only bruises; they will heal soon enough. Did you at least eat something last night? Nope; nothing! He slides the other chair over beside her and takes a seat.

Hey; you know I care about you a lot; right Brina? Yes I do! I care about you too daddy! Muah. He kisses her on the forehead. We have some things we need to talk about baby; do you feel like talking? Sure! Ok listen; I need you to think real hard and take your time; this is very important. You're scaring me AC; what's wrong? Nothing is wrong; I just need some answers. What kind of answers? Is there any family members; of Bobby and Vinnies; that we have to worry about? She puts down the hot wings and leans back in the chair. Take your time baby. Sabrina runs her left hand through her silky, damp hair; looks over at Coop then points at him with her right finger. Yes; there is a cousin! Cousin Victor; Victor Delgato! Really; where is this Victor? If I'm not mistaken; he should be in Clark County. CCDC? Yeah; that one! Do you know what he's in for baby? Yeah; he got 12 months for larceny and marijuana possession. Thanks baby; is there anyone else?

Nah; that's the only family they have left. Cool; let me know if you think of anyone else. Sure daddy.

Ring-Ring! Ring-Ring! I'll be right back baby; let me get that. Hello! Yo Coop; is your girl alright bruh? Yeah; she's fine Will. Good; glad to hear that! What's poppin at the club? Your boy Dupree is up here; he says he needs a word with you; what time you coming? Tell him I will be there shortly; give him a bottle of Mo to sip on until I get there. Sure thing; see you in a few! Later! Hey Pree! Dupree turns away from the stage. What's up Will? He's on his way now; walk with me to the bar; I got something for you. Will waves him on as he passes by. Yo Red! Yes Will? Give my friend a bottle of Moet; will you? Sure no problem! Thanks Big man! It's nothing Pree; just enjoy yourself while you're waiting on AC. Damn right; think I aint!

"Alright; listen up gentlemen!" "Please remember these ladies works for tips and tips only; so pay the pussy bill!" "Oh yeah and don't forget to tip the waitresses and bartender's as well!" "I hope you have your ones ready, because coming to the stage; for your entertainment pleasure; is the one and only; Malibu!" "This is Dj Tru; and if you have any special request; I can play it for you!" "Just have the waitress deliver the message to the Dj booth!" "Right now; center stage; we have Malibu!" "Dancing to her favorite by Prince!" "I never meant to cause you any sorrow" "I never meant to cause you any pain" "I only wanted to one time see you laughing." Dylan and Barbie make their way over to the bar. Hey Red; what's going on babe? Same drama; different day Dylan! What are you having tonight? Absolut or Remy! Hit me with the Remy! One double shot of Remy; coming right up! What about you Barbie and why are you so damn quiet tonight? Because it's slow as molasses in this motherfucker! That's a good reason to get fucked up; I'd say! Did you want the usual or something different?

Girl; give me what she's having! Alright, two double shots of Remy on the way! "I only wanted to see you laughing in the purple rain" "Purple Rain, purple rain" Whew wooo! Work it bitch! Dylan; your ass is crazy! What; she working that thing up there Barbie; look at her! She must be high; that's the only time she dances good! Barbie you a fool! Here you go ladies; two double shots of Remy; straight up! Thanks Red! No problem ladies; no problem!

"Purple rain, purple rain." Oh Barbie; I need to tell your ass something! What is it Dylan? Well; remember I told you that I sold my old beamer. Yeah; last week right. Yeah; anyway; the lady gave me a check for Five thousand dollars for it. Ok; and! Girl be quiet and listen. I deposited the check in my account; over at the bank on boulder; by my place. Don't tell me; that motherfucker bounced! Girl; would you shut up and listen! Ok; ok my bad; go ahead; what happened?

Well I made the deposit before 2pm; so that it would post the same day. I forgot to take some cash out before I left the bank; I needed to go grocery shopping. So to make a long story short! Please hurry; because you're taking all day. Girl! Ok; I'll be quiet; go ahead! I get to Albertson's; over here by the club; get in the store and don't have any cash. Lucky for me; my bank has a branch across the street from the grocery store. So; I drive across the street; go in and withdraw $600. The money had posted by the time I gotten on this side. Damn; I thought it posted like after five or something! Me too! That was good though; right? Yeah it was but that's not what I had to tell you! Damn; spit it out then girl! Well how about; my bank called me the next day and tells me that the check was no good! I knew it; I knew it; that bitch gave you a bad check!

Yep; I was pissed; then I got to thinking! Thinking about what; busting her head to the white meat! Ha-ha! Yeah; that too; but this can be a come up! Girl; what the hell are you talking about? What if; when I went to the bank that day; I would have gotten all $5,000.00 out instead of just the $600. Then you would have had $5000 bitch; what's the point! Think about it Barbie; the check bounced; remember! Oh yeah; but wait a minute; if the check wasn't any good; then how did you get that $600? Now; do you see what I'm saying! They didn't know the check was bad until the next day! Bitch; you could have had $5,000 and been out of there like casper! Yep! Damn; that is a come up! Dylan; you got some brains in that head after all. Fuck you Barbie; are you down; or what? What the hell do you mean; down?

I'm saying; me and you can pull this thing off and make a few 100 thousand real fast! And how the fuck; are we supposed to do that! Don't you have a checking account? Yeah; but aint nothing in it! So; do you have a check book? Yep! Alright; tomorrow write me a check for $1,000.00 and deposited it in my account before 2pm. Why I have to write it; what are you going to be doing bitch? I'm going to be on the other side of town; waiting for you to call me; after you make the deposit. Then what; after I call you? I'm going to my bank and withdraw the money from my account. Girl; that shit sounds too easy. Hey Barbie; I'm telling you; this thing will work. Ok; what if it does? We will split the money after I get it; then we can do it again in a couple of days. Dylan; if we get away with this; we have to get more than $1,000 next time. I agree! Alright; say no more girlfriend! Tomorrow it's on! They both raise their glasses and make a toast. Clink! To getting this money!

Hey bitches; what's poppin! Hey Remy! Hey D! Aint shit going on; just slow as hell. What yall two doing up in here? We just came to get a few drinks; I didn't feel like working. You know how it is sometimes Dylan. Yes I do! So; are yall going to get that off Malibu? I need to test the product first Barbie; make sure that thing is legit; you dig. Oh I dig D; I dig! Where is she at anyway? On the stage; she has one song left. Oh damn; I didn't even see her Dylan! It's ok D; we know your ass is blind! Ha-Ha! Dylan; stop picking at my baby! Oh Remy; he knows I like to mess with them.

Yall; be easy; I'm going to see if I can get some dances from these little bit of customers. Come on Barbie; bring your nosey ass on. I'm coming; I'm coming!

Hey Remy; I'm going to speak to Will; can you order me a corona. Sure D; I got you baby. Derek walked across the somewhat packed club to the office. Knock-Knock! Yeah it's open! Hey Will! What's up D! Come in; have a seat bruh; what's going on with you player? Did yall speak with Fat boy about the Meth yet? Yeah Manny did; Coop's on the way over now; he knows the details. Big Will; what's up bruh! Oh shit; there he is now! What's up D! Dupree come in have a seat pimp! I was just telling D you were on the way. I'm here now dog; looks like we have some business to discuss. Who was here first Will? Dupree dog! Talk to me Pree; you got something for me? Man; I saw the news about that hummer blowing up! I know it was Steel's; that means his territory is open for business and I want it! Damn my nigga; you think you can handle all that real estate? No doubt pimp! I tell you what Pree; you can handle it for now; until I work out some details. Thanks dog! Pree; it's only temporary! Ok; I got you pimp! Alright; be easy player.

Derek my man; what's up with you! You ready to make some cake dog? Hell yeah bro! Will; you think this fool is ready to play with the big dogs? It's only one way to find out AC; let him sink or swim; that's what I say. D; you hear that bruh! Will you sink or swim? Bro; I swim like a shark! Ha-Ha-Ha. AC laughs as he places his hands on D's shoulders. Well this is the deal Derek. Fat boy has agreed to push it in his territory for two weeks. So; I need for you to get in your lab and start cooking your ass off brother. Ok; I'm on it! When did you want the first batch? This weekend; Saturday! Damn; that's in three days! Will that be a problem D; don't tell me you drowning already! No; No; I got it. Ok; what are you waiting on then; get to cooking brother and call me when it's ready. Alright; thanks AC! Yeah; it's no problem; just don't fuck it up! I won't man; I promise. Don't promise D; make it happen!

See you later bruh and tell your grandpa I said hello! Ok man; later! Later Will! Later D! Damn; I thought that fool was going to bust a nut, you made him was so happy. Ha-ha. He's hungry Will! How's business today? It's ok; we made $15,000.00 during dayshift. So how's Sabrina doing? She's a little banged up but other than that she's fine.

Good to hear; I see Duck pulled it off again; huh! Yeah; that boy can make some bombs! That's fucked up that it was Steel and Jesse that kidnapped her. I told you she used to date that nigga! Yeah; I asked her about that too. What did she say? She admitted it but said it didn't last long and it was a while ago. But it still seems kind of fishy to me Coop; don't you think? Yeah; Duck and Manny are going to keep an eye on her; make sure she's clean. Ok; I feel better now; I just don't trust her bruh. Hey; thanks for having my back man. Hey; Death before Dishonor AC; till the death brother!

Damn right; till death! Dap! Will and AC give each other a low five. I'm going to check on the staff Coop; make sure these cats getting money and not being lazy. Alright man; I need to make a call; be out there shortly. Ring-Ring! Hello! Hey baby; did you miss me? It took your ass long enough to call nigga! Damn Monica; I can't get no love girl? Yeah; I miss you hun. Next time; don't wait two months before you call me! I had to handle some things girl. Well did you handle them? Yep; everything is gravy now baby. Good; because I'm ready to leave my lame ass husband. Is that right! Stop playing AC! Can I pack my shit! Whoa girl; slow down; don't move so fast. Why not?

We need to do things right girl; so nobody suspects anything; understand? Yeah I guess! Listen; go put on one of those nice dresses I bought you and some of those heels I like; some of that perfume and come on over to Dolls off Industrial. Why am I going to a strip club? Just do like I say and stop asking so many damn questions! Alright; alright; I'll be there. Great; see you soon.

Knock-Knock! Yeah; it's open! Will enters the office with cell phone in hand. Hey bruh; Nina's on the phone! Alright; let me have it. What's up sis? Hey Coop; how's Brina? She's ok; nothing she won't get over. Good to hear that bro. How's business at the agency? It's kind of slow right now; our peak hours are usually 1am to 4am on Wednesday. I'm training Georgia on the phones right now though. Who is Georgia? One of the escorts; she's from Atlanta. Oh ok; how many girls do you have on call tonight? We should have 12 right now; but those two girls from Germany are coming in at 2am; so it will be 14. That's cool. Hey; Denna said not to forget about her! I didn't forget; I'm going out there tonight to handle that situation.

Ok that's what's up; tell Brina I asked about her and I will talk to you later; the other line is ringing. Ok Nina; later baby!

Here Georgia; answer this; just like I told you! Hello; thank you for calling Angel's; did you want a date tonight sir? Yes I do! Great; which lady did you want to see handsome? Is that Red head working? Uh, Uh, can you hold on sir? Yes Ma'am. Georgia pulls the phone away from her ear then covers it with her right hand. Nina; he's asking for me; what do I tell him? Ha-Ha. Don't panic girl; just get his information and see what time he wants to book you. Ok sir; sorry about that! It's ok baby. When did you want to book her? How about 3am tonight darling; I'm staying over at the Horse shoe. 3 is fine; what room are you in Sir and may I have your name also? I'm in 2389 and my name is Charles Williams; but you can call me Chuck! Alright Chuck; your date will be there at 3am and your total is $500; you can pay by credit card or cash.

I will be paying by cash darling! Great sir; enjoy your date and remember to have protection when the girl gets there. Thank you darling! That wasn't too bad Georgia; just remember to always stay calm; you don't want to make the client nervous. Ok; I think I got it now. Yeah; you will do fine; now get your things and head over to the Horse shoe to get that paper. Yes Ma'am; I'm on the way! Be safe and come back here when you're done. Alright Nina; see you in a bit; did you want me to pick up something on my way back? Nah; just that money! Ha-Ha-Ha. Ok; I'm gone!

Hello fellas, I'm Asia and this is my girl Malibu. What's your names? I'm Donnie and this is my brother Dave! Nice to meet you guys! Red can I have some Merlot baby? Sure Asia, did you want anything Malibu? Yeah the same thing baby! Donnie did you guys want some wine? Sure why not! Hey Red; make that four glasses babe! Got it Asia! Hey Malibu we should see if these guys want a table. Why girl, what's wrong with the bar? Because Will and AC are standing over in front of the office door; looking at everybody. You know AC's mean ass makes me nervous! Alright Asia; let's make sure these two has some money first before we ask them to move. Ok girl, thanks! Umm hmm! "Once again guys welcome to Dolls, coming to the stage we have the lovely China" "Let's hear it for her as she dance to one of my favorite tracks by Usher!"

"This is what you do" "This is what you do." AC's attention was on the front door; his eyes couldn't believe what was walking towards him. "You make me wanna leave the one I'm with" "Start a new relationship with you" "This is what you do." All he could do was shake his head in amazement as she got closer. The crowd parted as she glided across the room in her hot pink, six inch, closed toe, Louis V, stiletto heels. Monica's black DKNY dress, which was trimmed in hot pink, fell just above her calves, showing only a little of her toffee colored soft skin. Her layered; silky black hair; fell just below her cheek bone. He stood erect as she got closer to him. Muah! She puckered her pink; lipstick coated lips; lifted her toffee colored hands to her gorgeous face and blew him a soft kiss. Two steps later; they intertwined in an intimate embrace; then grabbed hands and headed into the office; away from the crowd. "Before anything came between us" "You were like my best friend" "The one I used to run to when me and my girl was having problems (that's right)."

Damn Mo; I miss you girl! I miss you too nigga! Yeah; you miss this dick too; don't you baby. Ahh; a little bit! That's all; just a little. Yep! Come here; sit on my lap; let me caress that juicy booty. He leans back in the office chair and roles it away from the desk; so she can sit on his lap. Ummmm; Hmmmm. I miss this right here girl! Do you have on any panties under that dress? You have to find out for yourself AC. Oh; you aint saying nothing! What you waiting on then? Coop slides his right hand up her inner thigh. Uh huh; that's why you're my bitch; you know just what I like; this kitty purring for some attention. Monica's pussy was smooth to the touch and moist too. He massaged it a little; parting the lips with two of his right fingers then stroking her insides slowly. Mo's pussy started popping as it got wetter and wetter. Yeah; you're ready now baby; stand up! What! Stand up girl! Umm! AC; what are you doing!

Shut up and stand there! But why the fuck do you have me standing on the desk AC? Uh God, Uh God, yes! Monica was now standing on the desk, facing Coop with her wet pussy in his face; his tongue inside her. She grabbed his head as he stroked counter clockwise, inside the vagina; cleaning the juices from her sugar walls. AC gripped Monica's ass with both hands so she couldn't get away from his tongue. You like this baby? Ummmm-Hmmmm. Don't stop! Slurp! Slurp! Slurp! He licked her clit; up and down; up and down; then up and down again. Slurp! Slurp! Slurp! Umm! This feels so good; I'm gone cum in your mouth! Slurp! Slurp! Oh yes! Oh yes! Oh yes! Ohhhhhhh; yes! Damn; damn! God I love you AC; you nasty motherfucker! Yeah I bet, that didn't even take long either; you was horny huh? Pop! Ouch! Why you hit me woman? Shut up AC.

I got something else for you too. What you got for me? What you wanted? I don't wanna fuck now; I already got my nut. Aint that a bitch! Ha-Ha. What; don't be mad AC. I aint mad; I wasn't even talking about giving you this dick. Yeah; whatever! Don't you wanna make some paper? Hell yeah; a bitch starving. Well; Denna needs someone to work out at the ranch. What ranch; the whore house? Yep! Man; I aint going to work in no whore house; selling this pussy; you done bumped your head nigga. Ha-Ha. Girl stop tripping! You tripping; coming at me like that. She needs a house mom; someone to keep a count of the dates and the cash. Oh; see I can do that! When did she want me to start? We can take the Limo and head out there now; if you want. I'm ready; let's do it!

Are you going to at least get me down from here then? Come on I got you, and you can use that mirror behind the door to fix yourself. What's wrong; do I look bad? No baby; but you might want to double check. Ugh! Monica sighs then walks over to the mirror. Boy; I'm straight; let's go. Ok; come on. They exit the office and enter the now busy club. What's up AC? Hey Dylan! Where's Megan? She's off tonight! Oh ok; who is this lady right here? This is Monica! Hi Monica; I'm Dylan; are you a dancer? Who me; child please! Why you say it like that! Because; I aint shaking my ass for no dollars; that's why! So you got a problem with dancers? Hey girl; do you; just don't look for me to join you; that's all! What; fuck you bitch! AC; you better get this stripper before I kick her in the damn throat!

Yeah; you wish; try it hoe! Alright; ladies calm down! Monica; go outside and wait for me by the Limo. That's right; kick rocks Monica! Dylan cut it out! Mo; keep walking! Man; why you got that ol uppity bitch in here anyway! Mind your business; go make some damn money before I fire your ass. Yo bruh; is everything alright over here? It's cool Will; damn Dylan just showing her red ass; as always. Listen; I'm about to head out to the ranch with

Monica; so Denna can show her what needs to be done. Alright Coop! Oh yeah; I almost forgot! Forgot what? Sabrina says there's one more Delgato we need to worry about! No shit; who is it? Apparently they have a cousin locked up in the county; call Hector and set up a meet; so we can handle that.

No problem; when did you want to meet with him? Whenever he has time; make it in the next week though. Say no more; it's a done deal. Cool; hold it down; I'll be back in the city; after me and Monica handle this hoe business. Later Coop!

AC makes his way out the front entrance where the Limo is waiting. Monica is leaning against the front passenger door talking to the driver; while he's smoking on a cigarette. Hey let's go; put out that damn cancer stick and start the damn Limo! Yes Sir Boss; where to? The Ranch man and make it fast! AC opens the door for Monica. Damn; you look sexy as fuck Monica! Yeah; you like this dress? Yep; one of my favorites; come here and let me kiss those sexy lips. They stand in front of the open door; tongue kissing each other. Hmm, those soft lips; makes me horny every time! Ha-Ha! I know; now come on and let's get in the Limo nigga.

AC! AC! AC! He stands up to see who was calling him. Bam! He slams the Limo door. Hey baby; what are you doing here? You should be home resting! Where are you going and who is that bitch that just got in the Limo? Oh that's Monica; I'm taking her to the ranch; Denna just hired her. Umm-hmm; don't get fucked up tonight AC! Girl; what are you talking about and why are you not at home resting? Don't play me Andy Cooper. I aint playing you; stop tripping. Come on; let's go inside! Sabrina and AC walk inside the club. Hey Megan! Hey Red! What the hell happen to your neck girl? It's nothing girl; got into a fight; that's all. What! Did AC do this! Red; don't even go there with that shit! Shut up AC; let her talk. No girl; it was some chica's trying to rob me for my jewelry. Damn; are you ok? I'm fine. Hey Red; make her a double Henn. Ok; coming up. Look baby; I need to get this girl out to the ranch; Denna has been waiting on me all day. Ok; daddy; I'll just hang out here for a bit. Cool; I will see you when I get home later. Ok daddy. Muah!

Damn nigga; that's your skinny Italian girlfriend? Mo; don't start! I'm just asking; daddy! Ha-Ha! She calls you Daddy! Hey driver! Yes sir! Get us out of here! Yes sir! Coop presses the divider window button to roll it up; so that they would have some privacy during the ride. Well; I have to give it to you AC. What's that Mo? You the man baby; you went from running that office we had on Charleston to being the Sin City Boss. Hey; I didn't do it by myself baby; my squad is deadly; we get shit done. I see nigga; I see! Did you want to hit this? Hit what? Mo reaches in her bra and pulls out a blunt. This! Hell yeah; light it up!

It's a slow night over at Angelica's Ranch out in the desert; Denna is sitting at the bar talking with her new bartender; a young man; standing 5' 11", black spiked hair, pale white skin and a thin goatee. So how long did you bartend over at Dolls? For like 5 months. That's it; five months? Yes Ma'am! Ma'am! Don't call me Ma'am; my name is Denna and what's your name anyway? Oh I'm sorry Denna; and my name is Joshua but you can call me Josh. Ok Josh; where did you bartend before Dolls? I worked over at Harrah's for 2 years before I came to Dolls.

Ok; that's more like it; I just wanted to make sure you knew what you were doing. You don't have to worry about me; this is my life and I enjoy doing it. Really! Yep! Alright; make me something! What did you want? Surprise me! Ok, I got something for you.

Josh places a rocks glass on the counter then added two cubes of ice. He picks up the shaker; adds some ice, a shot of Smirnoff, a dash of triple sec; puts the lid on and shakes it a few times. The bartender strains the contents over the ice in the rocks glass; then poured in some Blue Curacao and tops it with an Orange slice. Josh drops two stirrers in the filled glass and slides it to Denna. She stirs it up and takes a sip. Hmmmm; pretty good Mister! What's this? It's my version of a Kamikaze; some people call it a Blue Hawaiian. I like it! Thank you!

You're welcome. Did AC talk to you about what hours you will be working? No; he said that you would let me know all the details. Are you married Josh? Nope! Have a girlfriend? Nope! Damn; are you gay? Hell no! Ok; just asking. Why are you single then? I had a girl but she left me after I started Dolls. Oh yeah; I can see that happening. It's hard for a girl to deal with her man around so many women every day; especially when all of them are naked. Yeah; we argued about that all the time. Did you cheat on her Josh? Shit; I should have; I got accused of it every damn day. Yeah whatever; you cheated. Nah; I didn't but we called it quits because it was getting to be too much bullshit. She never trusted me and I was always honest; that was the hard part. I didn't even cheat on her. So that's why I'm single and doing my thing. Doing your thing huh? Yep! How about you; are you single? Nah; I have a friend; we are just now, starting to get serious. That's good; I think everyone should be with somebody; life is too short to live alone. I agree, but sometimes; a bitch need her space. Ha-ha. You're a trip Denna.

Bam! Josh; did you hear that? Yeah it sounded like a car door slamming. Good; finally some damn customers! The bell over the entrance door rung as the main door opened. Ding! Denna; what's up sis? Hey AC; it's about time poppi, where the hell have you been? It's been dead as a door knob out here boss. Probably because you don't have the billboard nor the open sign on! Oh shit; are you kidding me! Nope; the switch is behind the bar. Josh; turn it on please sir! Where is it AC? Right there by the other light switch; it says Open sign! Damn; ok I see it.

Denna; you remember Monica. Monica; remember Denna! Hey Monica; how have you been girl? I'm doing great; ready to get to work! That's what I'm talking about Chica! I think you two are going to get along fine. Hey she's about her business; I like that. Come over here girl; so I can show you how to do these books. Ok; let's do it. Hey Josh! What's up Boss? Let me get a Corona. Ok Sir; coming right up! Hey Denna! Yeah poppi; what is it? You can leave after you show Monica what to do; we are gonna stay here tonight. Are you sure Coop? Yeah; it's no problem; you need to check on Loon's ass anyway. That's what's up; but we need to talk before I go! Alright; come holler at me before you leave; I'll be at the bar! Ok poppi!

Josh! Yes Sir! Fix me a shot of vodka too! Coming right up Boss! Hey; make that a double! Yes Sir! This isn't hard at all Denna! I told you; it's a breeze Monica. One last thing though? Yeah; what's that Mo? How many days am I supposed to be working out here? Four days a week; every other week. Why every other week? Because; you and I will be alternating! Ok; that's cool Denna. Great; I'm going to speak with AC about some business then I'm leaving. Alright; thanks and be safe. You're welcome Monica.

Denna; makes her way across the dark lobby of the ranch. What did you want to speak with me about sis? Take a look around and tell me what you see AC? What; I see a whore house! Man; stop playing; I'm serious. I am too Denna! Just spit it out; tell me already! This place needs a make-over! What! You heard me! I knew it; I knew it wouldn't be long before you had to put your touch on things. So can I remodel this dump? What; the whole place? We're in this thing to make money; I aint trying to be closing down to remodel nothing! Bro; just give me the ok and I promise; I can get it all done without closing the doors. Ok sis; just make sure we're not losing money during your damn construction project! Thanks Coop! Muah! Love you bro; see you later; I'm going to check on Loon! Bye Monica; Josh! Bye Denna!

Hey Baby! What's up Mo? How are we getting home; both the Limos are gone. Oh; we're crashing in the Jacuzzi suite tonight; the Limo will be here tomorrow to pick us up. Nigga; you tripping! Why you say that Mo? I aint sleeping in no bed that those hoes been in! Girl; we're sleeping in the master quarters; it doesn't get used for business. Oh; ok! Come over here and sit down; have a drink with me. Ok; I'm coming.

Excuse me! Excuse me! Yeah man; what is it? Where can I find your girl on girl movies? The girl on girl tapes; are on isle 5 sir! Thanks man! No problem; is there anything else you need help with? No thank you, that's it! Loon steps down from behind the counter. Alright man; you sure! Yeah I'm good. Ok; let me know if you want the real thing; I have a few girls in the back that can put on a live girl on girl show for you! Oh really! Hell yes! Hey Loon! Hold on man; let me see what this girl wants; think about what I said; I will be right back! What's up Chocolate? The slide door is stuck in booth 5. Man; why yall hoes got to be tearing up shit. Ain't nobody tear up this raggedy ass building; yall need to fix it up anyway! Girl move your ass out of the way so I can look at this door and stop talking smack!

Loon makes his way over to the peep show room entrance to look at the door. He tries to slide the door to the left but it won't move. Damn; this motherfucker is stuck! I told you! Shut up Chocolate. Don't tell me to shut up boy! He steps away from the door and takes another look at it. Well; aint this a bitch! What! The damn lock is on Choc; that's what! Oh my bad; I didn't see it. Yeah whatever Choc; stop smoking that weed all the time and maybe you can stay focus. Whatever Loon! Ha-Ha. I'm just playing girl; you guys get ready; I'm trying to get this customer to buy a two girl peep show.

Loon! Loon! He hears someone calling him from up front. Loon! Oh hey Denna; what's up baby! I'm tired as hell! Well; you don't look like it baby. So how's business over here? Kind of slow baby; kind of slow! How did you like the Ranch? It's ok; but I'm remodeling it soon. No shit; did you ask Coop? Yep! Damn; you need to remodel this fucker too! You know what Loon; you're right! I'm serious Denna; think about it! There's nothing to think about; it's done; I'll let AC know. Cool; and you look sexy in that suit you have on by the way. Oh really; you like this old thing poppi? Hmmm-mmmmm. Come over here woman; where's my kiss? I haven't seen you in a day! Muah. That's all you get! What; just a peck on the cheek. Yep; I'm not starting nothing we can't finish; we're at the store; not a room. Ok; ok!

I'm going to speak to the girls; I'll be back shortly. Girl that nigga fucked the hell out of me! What nigga Chocolate? Loon girl! When did this happen? When I first got to work; while you guys was getting dressed! Yeah whatever Choc! I'm serious Candy! Well' all I know is; you better not let Boss lady Denna catch you! What damn business is it of hers? That's her boyfriend girl! Don't tell me you didn't know that! Who; Denna? Hey ladies; what about me? I know I just heard my name. Oh nothing boss lady; how are you doing? I'm good ladies; how's business? What business; we aint made no money yet? Be patient Chocolate; I'm sure business will pick up; it always does.

I hope so! I'm sure of it Candy! Hey boss; I was thinking about going all the way with this! What do you mean Choc! I'm talking being a straight ho! Forget all this damn dancing and peep show crap! Well; just let me know baby; I'm running the ranch now and my sister is running the escort agency. No shit! Yes Ma'am; we got you covered; just give me the word. Well; in that case; put me down too! Where did you guys want to work then; out at the ranch or escort here in the city? We have school; so escort would work better! Ok no problem; I will call me sister and let her know. Cool; thanks boss! You're welcome ladies; you guys have a good night; I'm taking it in; I need some rest. Ok Boss! Hey Denna! Yeah Choc! Since you're running the ranch; does that mean Loon will be running this place all the time? Yep; most of time he will be Choc! Oh ok! Why; is that going to be a problem with you guys or something? Oh no; we were just curious! Alright ladies; have good night! Bye Denna!

See I told you girl; you're gonna get fucked up; messing with Loon's ass. Candy be quiet; you just heard her say that she will be running the ranch from now on. So what does that have to do with anything Choc! She's gone be out in the damn desert every day; Loon is all mine! Whatever Bitch; you have a death wish. Buzz-Buzz. Hey someone is buzzing your window? About time some money comes up in this joint. Alright Candy; I'll chat with you in a few; let me go make this loot. Umm-hmm; you better think about what I said Choc. Whatever Candy; go do your make up or something.

Chapter 3; Currency

It's 9 Am on a Thursday morning; the traffic is at a slow crawl over on Sahara and S. Decatur Blvd. Dylan makes a right turn at the red light, then another quick right and enters the Albertson's parking lot. As she parks in front of the bank; she picks up her mobile to call Barbie. Ring-Ring! Hello! Hey Barbie where are you? I'm just pulling up to the bank over on Tropicana and Industrial. Cool; write the check for $1,000.00; go inside and write the information I gave you on a deposit slip and deposit it. Dylan; I'm nervous as a hell girl! Aint no need to be nervous; only you and I know what's going on; you understand. Yeah I guess so! Ok calm down; get yourself together; then go in there and make the deposit; call me after it's done. Ok; I will call you back in a few. Great; I will be waiting.

Barbie pulls out her check book and writes a check for $1,000.00 to deposit in Dylan's account. She grabs her purse; puts on her shades; exits the car and enters the bank. Good Morning Ma'am; how are you today? I'm fine officer thanks for asking. You're welcome Ma'am. She walks pass the guard and goes over to the island to complete the deposit slip then steps to the rear of the line. The closer she gets to the front; her hands began to tremble from the nervousness. Next in line please! Barbie approaches the teller. Good Morning Ma'am; what can I do for you today. Yes; I would like to make a deposit into my friends account. Ok we can do that; do you have her account number? Yes Ma'am; I have the check and deposit slip right here. Oh thank you; it will only take a second. Let's see what we have here; oh you have it all filled out. Yes I do. Great! Well; here you are Ma'am; you're all set! Is there anything else that I can do for you today? No Ma'am; that will be all. Ok have a great day Ma'am. Next in line please!

Barbie walked in a somewhat fast pace as she exited the bank and jumped back in her car. Nervously; she picked up her mobile to call Dylan. Ring-Ring! It's done! Ok; I'm going in now to make the withdrawal; I will call you after I get it. Ok Dylan! 9:25 Am; she exits her vehicle and enters the bank. There were hardly any customers inside; maybe three or four. Dylan picked up a withdraw slip and walked up to the available teller. Hello Ma'am; how can I help you today? I need to get some money out but I need a sec; I'm completing the withdraw slip now. Ok Ma'am; take your time. Here you go! Thank you! The teller looks at the slip and enters her info in the computer. How did you want this back Ma'am? All large bills or does it matter? All large is fine. Ok; one, two, three, four, five, six, seven, eight, nine, one thousand. The teller slid the money in an envelope and handed to Dylan. Thank you! You're welcome Ma'am; have a great day. You do the same!

Dylan put the envelope in her purse and headed for the exit. Oh; let me get that door for you Ma'am. Thank you Sir! You're welcome! She got in her car; pulled out the envelope; counted the money then called Barbie. Ring-Ring! Hello! I got it Bitch! No shit! Hell yeah! So; what now Dylan? Do you have any money in that account you wrote the check on? Hell no girl; maybe five dollars; why? Good, because if you had some; your bank would have taken it in a couple of days and put it towards that check. Oh no; that thing is always damn near empty; I hardly use it. Cool; I'm headed over to the Denny's across from the Stratosphere. Meet me there so we can have some breakfast and split this up. Alright; see you in a few Dylan.

Ring-Ring! AC; your cell phone is ringing! AC! Get up! Monica shoved him to wake him up. AC your phone! Ring-Ring! I don't care, let it ring; let it go to voicemail! What time is it anyway? It's 1 O'clock baby! What; aw shit; I have to go! Damn; I didn't mean to stay out here this long. Why not? Because Sabrina's at my place and I told her I was coming home last night. Yeah, yeah; she has your ass whipped nigga. Shut up Mo; hand me my pants! Get them yourself asshole! Why are you tripping girl? Thump! Ouch! Why you do that! Check your voicemail! You didn't have to throw the phone woman. After throwing the phone at him; Monica jumped out of bed still naked and walked over to the window.

Black satin sheets with red trim; covered the king size oval shaped bed with matching comforter and pillows. Mo slid the red curtains back just a little; so she could take a look outside. Well; the limo is already here waiting on your sorry ass. Look chic; the last I heard; you were the one married. If you're gonna be acting like this; every time I give you the dick; then I'm cutting your ass off. Whatever AC; you can't stay away from this right here boy and you know it. I can show your crazy ass; better than I can tell you; keep it up! Yeah ok; are you coming back tonight? I don't know yet; I will call you later on. You better call me to nigga! You need to call your husband; that's what you need to do. For what! So he won't be worried! Man; I left him a note last night. What kind of note Mo? I told him I wasn't happy and that I was leaving to follow my dreams. Ha-Ha. Stop lying girl; you aint do that shit. Yes I did!

Damn; you're a mess. He'll be fine; we don't have any kids together anyway. He has two from another woman. Are you sure that's what you want to do? One hundred percent sure! Ok; you know I got your back whatever you decide. Yep; that's why I did it! AC just stood there and looked at her; shaking his head while standing barefoot on the cold hardwood floor. He slipped on his pants, socks, shirt then walked over to the white, 8 drawer dresser to get his wallet, phone and Burberry shades. Coop sat down on the edge of the bed to put on is shoes then called his voicemail. "Hey AC; where are you daddy; I just woke up and you're still not home." Shit! What's wrong; was that your skinny Italian girlfriend? Shut up Mo. Monica walked over to the dresser; still naked, micro braids hanging to her back. She reached up to her head; then pulled the braids to the back and tied them up in a pony-tail.

Coop dials the Towers. Ring-Ring! Hello; thanks for calling the Towers; this is David; how can I help you? Hey David; it's AC! Hey Mr. Cooper; what's up? I need a favor man! What is it Sir? Call the Gucci store and have them deliver a few dresses and shoes to my place for Sabrina to choose from. Ok will do; anything else Sir? Yes; call Tiffani's and have them take a few pieces also; she needs some ear rings; a bracelet and a necklace to match her dress and shoes. Not a problem sir; I will get right on it! Oh; one more thing David! Yes Sir? Tell Sabrina to be ready in two hours and have my tux delivered to my place; it's in the cleaners downstairs. Alright Mr. Cooper; see you in a few! Thanks David! You're welcome Sir!

Damn; you're doing some big making up; aint you nigga? Mind your business Mo; I will call you later. She turned around; leaned back against the dresser; looked at him and smiled. Have a good time AC; and tell Sabrina I said hello. Ha-Ha. Girl you crazy! Muah. He kissed her on the forehead and left the room. Ring-Ring! Hello! Hey Monica; it's Josh. Hey Josh; what's up hun? We have two customers out here; they've already picked their dates; they're waiting to pay. Ok hun; I will be up there in a minute. Ok Mo.

Over on Rainbow blvd.; just a few blocks away from the Las Vegas strip; inside the gorgeous red and blue lit casino; patrons wait patiently in line to enter the Carnival buffet. What look like miles and miles of food; sat on display in the buffet stands along the brass and silver walls of the dining area. Asian; Cajun, Southern, Mexican, American, Brazilian and Italian cuisine sat on display for anyone to indulge in their heart desires. Hot seared beef, on the charbroiled grill, created a mouth-watering aroma, drawing you closer to the Chef; who prepared steaks by the order. Nina and Denna approached the register to pay for their meals; so they could enter. How are you ladies doing today; welcome to Carnival buffet. We're fine sir! That's good; the total is $15.00 each! I'll be paying for both Sir. Ok Ma'am; no problem! Nina pulls out two twenty dollar bills and pays the cashier.

Thank you ladies; $10 is your change; enjoy your meals. You're welcome and I'm sure we will; it smells delicious. Amidst the loud slot machines; patrons shouting for joy because of their winnings and the normal excitement of the casino. There in the Carnival buffet was the one place where there was solitude and peace of mind; among the chaos. Hey Sis; grab a table; I'm headed over to the Mexican section to get me a plate. Ok Nina; go ahead and bring me some shrimp taco's back. Alright; I got you sis; order me a coke. Denna found an empty table for two. Hello Ma'am; welcome to the Carnival buffet, what can I get you to drink? Hi; I'll have a coke and a sprite please. One Coke; one sprite coming right up! Thanks! You're welcome Ma'am.

Damn girl; you got a ton of food on that plate! Shit; I'm hungry! Where's my Taco's? Oh my bad Denna! I forgot sis! Yeah I see; your greedy ass! Excuse me Ma'am; here's your drinks! Thank you Sir. You're welcome. I'll be back sis; did you want something from the Brazilian bar? No thanks; I'm good. Ring-Ring! Damn; can a girl eat; without this damn phone ringing. Ring! Hello! Hey Nina! Hey bro what's up? I need you to make a run; where are you right now? At the Rio; having dinner with Denna. Ok, sorry to interrupt you guys. It's ok; what did you need AC? When you guys get done; can you head over to the Mansion and load three of those duffle bags up with money then dropped them off at my place. Ok; no problem; is there anything else? Oh; just give the bags to David; the concierge; he will be downstairs at Manny's old desk. Alright; got it! Thanks; talk to you guys later; enjoy your dinner. You're welcome; bye AC.

Ohhh; that looks good sis! Yeah I know chica; I asked you if you wanted some. Nah; I'll just try some of yours. Nina; you better not touch my plate! Ok, ok, I'm just kidding; dang chica. Yeah whatever; who were you talking to on the phone? Oh that was AC! What is he talking about? He wants us to go by the Mansion to pick up some money and drop it off at his place. Damn; how much money is over there? Sis; it's a damn safe; wait until you see it! That shit is crazy Denna! I, yi, yi, seriously! Yes! Damn; I wanted to go by that new casino but this sounds like it's going to be more interesting! What casino? The New York! Oh; that's right, it did open today. Yep. Oh well, duty calls, we'll catch it another day. Ummmm; this prime rib is delicious. It's melting in my mouth; how's your Mexican food sis? It's good.

Hey man, slow down, I want to check out this new casino we're passing. Yes Sir, no problem. The evening sets; and night falls over the neon city of light's bringing life to the casino's, gamblers, losers, pimps and prostitutes. The brand new Statue of Liberty stood proudly on the corner of Las Vegas Blvd. and Tropicana Ave.; facing the large gold lion just across the street. The Sears tower and its adjacent buildings reflected in the candy black paint of the limo and its tinted windows as it drove through the intersection. AC rolled down the back window to get a better look at the newest casino on the strip as they rode by. Hey driver; bust a u turn up here and take me over to industrial; I need to make a stop at the garage. Yes Sir; what garage is that Sir? It's about a mile up industrial on the right. It's the yellow and orange building or yellow and red; one of them damn colors! Ok sir; on the way.

Ring-Ring! Hello; thanks for calling the Towers; David speaking. Hey D; this is Coop; did you take care of that for me? Yes Sir; it's all taking care of. Great; now do me a favor and call up to my room. Tell Sabrina I said to get dress; I will be there in the next hour. Ok Sir; no problem.

Thanks. Hey man! Slow down; it's right there on your left. Oh; I'm sorry! Damn bruh; you telling me you didn't see that ugly yellow building! I'm sorry Mr. Cooper; my mind was somewhere else. Well get it together brother; your life depends on it. Yes Sir. Ruff! Ruff! Ruff! The loud vicious barks got louder and louder as they approached the gate. As the gate opened and the limo entered, the huge Rottweiler's ran along-side the car steady barking. Thor- Renegade! Sit! Hector shouted! The once vicious dogs; stopped barking and walked away from the car then sat by the fence.

Hector my brother; what's new man? What's up Boss man! Got some business for you bruh! Oh yeah; come over here with me so we can talk. Hector walked towards the rear of the garage and AC followed. Talk to me homie; what's business? I need to get rid of a future problem. What the are you talking about homes? I don't understand that future problem bs. Well; I need you to take out Victor. Who is that? He's the cousin of Vinny and Bobby! Damn; where is this fool at homes? That's the problem; he's in CCDC for another 60 days. Homes; that's no problem; that's easy! Oh yeah! Hell yeah; I got crazy soldiers in the lock up bro! Cool; that's why I fucks with you Hec! You know I got you homie. When did you need it done? ASAP my man!

Ok; give me a couple of days. You got it bruh; no problem. Oh; how much does this hit pay amigo? $30,000.00 Hec! Proper; I can work with that! The mark name is Victor Delgato. Got it homes! Alright; I need to get my ass home; I got a date with Sabrina. Call me after that job is done and I will make sure you get your 30 stacks. You'll be hearing from me Coop! Alright driver; let's go to the Towers. Yes Sir.

Ring-Ring! Hello! Hi; Mrs. Cooper! Yes! This is David at the front desk. Yes David; what is it? Mr. Cooper says that you should be getting dressed; he will be here within an hour. Ok thanks David; I was just looking at myself in the mirror with all this new stuff on. Do you like it Ma'am? Oh yes, I love it! Great; I'm sure that Mr. Cooper will be pleased to see you in it. Thanks David; have a good evening. You're welcome Ma'am and you do the same.

Away from the luxurious casinos, starred attractions and tourist traffic. Loon finds himself on the opposite end of the strip, at work; standing on a 6 foot tall aluminum ladder out in front of the adult store; just under the billboard. Carefully he placed a few letters on the top row of the sign. One N, an O, a W then H, I, R, I,N and G. Then he picked up a few more and placed them on the second. Two P's and two E's. He reached back down in the letter box and retrieved another set. One S, a H, an O and a W. Damn this is a lot of fucking work. Loon thought to himself as he placed the last letter on the billboard. Dammit; I'm still not done. He reached back in the letter box for some more letters. One D, an A, a N, C, an E, a R and a S. Alright; almost done! He reached back in the box for a few more letters for the third row. Two A's, a N, a D, an I, a C, two S, an E, one R and a H.

Ok, now that should do it! Loon closed up the box and climbed back down the ladder to take a look at his work. It read. "NOW HIRING, PEEP SHOW DANCERS, AND CASHIERS." Beep! Beep! A few cars passing by the store; blew their horns after reading the sign. Loon casually waved at them as they passed while he walked back in the building. Ring-Ring! Hello; LV Adult Store. Hey poppi! Hey Denna; what you up to baby? Just sitting her with Nina at the Carnival buffet; how are things over your way? Ok I guess; we need some more girls in this joint. Oh you just reminded me; hold a minute Loon. Yeah; no problem! Hey Sis! What is it Denna? I have two girls that attend UNLV; that wants to work for you, a few days a week. How do they look? They are nice looking girl's sis. What would you give them on a scale of 1-10? Maybe a 9! Ok; have them call me tomorrow. Ok cool! Hey Loon! Yeah I'm here!

I think we should put an ad out in the adult magazine or something. Well, I just posted a now hiring message on the billboard; hope that will help. Yeah, maybe it will pick up when we redecorate that old ass building. You got a point there Denna. What did AC say about it? I haven't asked him yet; I will when I see him later. Ok; go ahead and enjoy your dinner and tell sis; I said hi. Alright will do; later poppi. Hello Sir! Hello Ma'am; what can I do for you? I read on your billboard that you're hiring peep show dancers. Yes we are; do you have any experience? No; not really. That's fine; how old are you? I'm 22! Are you scared to get naked in front of strangers? Nope! Damn; you said that fast! I'm just saying; everyone has seen a naked woman before; right? You're right.

Well, give me a few minutes; I was just about to put these bells on the entrance door. Why are you putting bells on the door? Because I' m the only one working up front today and I need to hear when someone enters; if I'm not up front. Ok I get it. So; while I'm doing this; do me a favor and go down that hall right there behind you. Where? Right there with the peep show sign over the door, with the red light in the hallway. Why I am I going in there? You want the job don't you? Yes! What's your name by the way? Oh; I'm sorry; my name is Deshonda. Nice to meet you Deshonda; I'm Loon. Loon! What kind of name is that? Did your momma name you that? Ha-Ha. Of course not; my real name is Lionel but my friends call me Loon or Looney. Ok but why Looney? It's a long story; did you want the job or not? Yes I do! Well go down that hallway and go in booth number two. What am I going to do?

The number one thing Deshonda; it's the most important. What's the number one thing Loon? I need to see your body; I can't see a damn thing under that big ass blue bubble coat you have on and those blue jeans. Oh; my body is perfect? What's the number two thing? Can you even dance? Hell yeah! Is there anything else? Yes; one more thing. What is that? Do you have any freak in you? What do you mean by that? I mean; can you be seductive; you know; make a man want to nut in his pants; just by looking at you? I don't know; aint no guy ever told me he nutted in his pants; just cause he looked at me. Ha-ha. Oh you're a comedian. No; I'm serious! Well Deshonda; you are cute; nice caramel skin; big smile; big pretty eyes and pretty silky hair. Thank you Loon! You're welcome! We just need to see that body and most of all; see if your ass can entertain.

That's why you are going in the peep show room Deshonda; to entertain me. Oh! So go ahead and walk down the hallway and go in booth two. Ok! Take your clothes off when you get in there; I will be in after I put up these bells and start some music for you to dance to. Deshonda still with a mind full of doubt; slowly entered the dark hallway that was dimly lit by a red light. She unzipped her coat, took it off and placed it on a coat hanger that was nailed to the outside of the booths door. She lifted up her right leg to untie her shoe; put it down and did the same with the other. Deshonda stepped out of

95

her shoes, opened the door, pulled off her shirt then entered room number 2.

Ding! Ding! Loon stood there pushing the door open and closing it to check the bell. Yep; that will work. He makes his way back behind the counter to turn on the music. "Come inside, take off your coat" "I'll make you feel at home." Ding! Ding! Hello Sir; welcome to the adult store; is there anything I can help you find today? Yes there is? Ok; what is it Sir? I'm looking for the new Janet Jacme movie; did you guys get it in yet. No sir; all of our new movies are slated to be in this weekend. Aw man, dam. I'm sorry sir; would you like for me to hold one for you? Would you do that for me man? Yeah no problem, just write your name and number down on the back of this card for me and I will call you as soon as the shipment hits the door. Cool, thanks a lot man. No problem; it's my pleasure, is there anything else that I can help you find. Nope that's it; I'll see you this weekend. Alright, have a good evening Sir. You too man.

"I wanna sex you up" All night. Hey Deshonda! Yes! Are you ready? Yep! Loon opened the door to room number two and entered. Damn! What's wrong Loon; you never seen a naked girl before? Yeah but; damn you're fine as a hell! Wow; you were hiding a lot under those clothes. So do you think I have what it takes? Hell yes. So what now? Just relax and dance kind of slow and be sensual with it; make me want you. You mean like this. She swayed her hips slowly from left to right then rubbed her right pointer finger over her moist lips. Deshonda's perky c cup breast just sat there plump and round with pretty brown perky nipples. Her flat stomach moved sensually, as if it had a mind of its own while her six pack of muscles held her belly button captive.

"Let me take off all your clothes" "Disconnect the phone so nobody knows" "yeah." How am I doing Looney? Doing good girl, doing good! Am I making you want me? Yes you are. Deshonda moved closer to him, placing her left pointer finger on the tip of his nose. Do you want to nut in your pants? Nope! Awww, why? I don't know, you tell me? She continued to dance and placed both hands on her breast, massaging them slowly. "I wanna sex you up" "Making love until we drown" "I wanna sex you up." How about now? Nope but I'm hard. Really? Yep! Can I see it? See what? Your dick! That depends! Depends on what?

What are you gonna do with it? I'm going to make you nut? Well in that case, yes of course. Hmmm, let me see it. Loon unzipped his pants, pulled out his hard Johnson and sat there holding it in his hands. Here it is, handle your business. Oh yeah, I like that right there, nice big and hard. How much do you like it, I still aint nut yet.

Stroke it for me Loon, get it a little harder. He stroked it a little more just to pleasure her. There you go Deshonda; you got two minutes before this audition is over. She walked over to Loon, grabbed his dick and started stroking. What are you doing girl? I'm about to make you nut! Do me a favor and turn around Deshonda. For what? Just do it! She turned around with her back to him. Don't try nothing funny Loon. Tell me; what do you see Deshonda? I see a glass window, and a pole and a stage with red carpet is on the other side of it. Right! So what! You need to make me nut without touching me that's what! If you want to be a hoe, we have a whore house and an escort agency for that. If you want to touch your customers and make them nut, we have a strip club for that. But this right here is a peep show joint, the customers don't touch you and you can't touch them.

Do you understand where I'm coming from? Yes I do. Good, now what did you want to do? Be an escort, whore, stripper or peep show girl? Peep show girl! Ok, now make me cum without touching me. "I wanna sex you up" "Making love until we drown" "I wanna sex you up." Deshonda took a few steps back until she felt the cold Plexiglas window against her skin. Sensually she placed her right index finger into her mouth, sucking sexually and slowly while rubbing her pussy with her other hand. In and out, in and out, in and out she went, slowly, until her vagina lips began to glisten from her own penetration. Ummmm, oh yes, Ummm, you like this Loon? Yeah, you sexy as hell over there girl! You want this pussy, don't you boy? Don't you? Hell yeah. Oooh, I'm so fucking wet right now Loon.

Stroke that pussy girl, make it wet some more. Oh yeah, like this baby, like this. Deshonda took her finger and rubbed her clit back and forth, left to right, then up and down, several times until it begun to swell. Damn girl, that's a fat ass clit right there. Um; I wanna fuck you now, come over here! Noooooo, you can't touch; only look! Damn; ok! Are you ready to nut Loon? Hell yeah! She continued to rub her clit back and forth. Oh shit, oh shit, oh shit! Oh God, it feels so good! Damn girl, you're about to make me nut! Oh shit, ohhh here it comes Loon. Go ahead bring it girl; bring it! Squirt! Squirt! Squirt! God dammit; what the fuck! Oh yes; damn that felt good! Deshonda! Deshonda! Deshonda! Huuh! Girl you shot that shit all on my shirt! Ohh, I'm sorry Loon but it felt so good. Yeah I bet; you could have warned a nigga; let me know you were a Squirter!

Oh I'm sorry! Yeah whatever, now I have to change my damn shirt. So how did I do? Girl you got the damn job, with your freaky ass. Ha-ha. Thank you Looney! Yeah, you're welcome Shooter! Shooter? Yep Shooter, that's your stage name. Ok boss, when do I start? When did you want to? As soon as possible, a bitch is broke. You can start today but you need to go to the Sheriff's department to get your sheriff's card. Sheriff's card? Yep, you don't have any warrants do you? Nope, I'm clean. Ok, go down to Freemont Street and pick that up and be back here at 10pm. Ok thank you Looney! You're welcome Shooter, go ahead and get dress, I'm going back up front. Ok. Stop by the register on your way out, I'll give you the money for your sheriff's card. Alright, thank you.

Hey Dave is everything ready? Yes Sir; Manny and Sophie just arrived, they're upstairs with Sabrina as we speak. Thanks David, here's something for your services. Thank you Sir. You're welcome; we'll be back down in a hour at the most; have the driver switch to the stretch Navigator. Ok Mr. Cooper; got you covered. Smooth jazz melodies from the energetic Tower's lounge; echoed through the lobby as Cigar smoke filled the warm air. The elevator doors opened just as he approached and several patrons exited off into the lobby. The doors closed and he noticed himself as he looked in the gold mirrored doors while the elevator radio played as normal. AC tucked his shirt in his slacks, tightened his belt and fixed his jacket so he could at least look presentable in the clothes he wore the night before.

"Happy New Year Las Vegas, It's 1997 and tonight is the Grand Opening of the Motown Café at the all new, New York; New York Casino." "So get out your best suits and evening gowns for this one, I know it's going to be packed" "This is your mid-day Dj; Tone Luv signing out, have fun tonight and I will be here tomorrow, same time, same place." Ding! AC steps off the elevator, wipes his face and fixed his shirt one last time before entering his place.

There he is! Damn Boss man; we've been waiting on you, what took you so long? Hey Manny; I had to go by Hector's for minute. Ok that's what's up! Hey Sophie! Hi AC; how are you? I'm good sis, no complaints. Hey baby, come here, I'm sorry about last night, I had to stay at the ranch to make sure things were ok. It's ok; I'm just happy to see you. Muah! Daddy, your suit is on the bed, were going to have a few drinks while you're getting dressed. Ok baby; do we have any smoke? Yeah, there's a blunt rolled up for you on the dresser. Thanks baby! You're welcome daddy! You look nice in that dress by the way, where are the shoes? Oh, there in the room, by the bed. And it does look nice on daddy, I love it! Good, I'm glad you do Brina- Hey baby? Yes? This box that's on the bed by my suit; it's for you? What do you mean, what is it?

Open it and see! Ok, I'm coming! Sabrina pulled the front of her Royal blue satin dress up in the front; so she wouldn't step on it. Her silky black hair was tied up in a bun and pinned to the top of her head. Her light pink lip stick complimented her dress and baby blue eyes; while matching her finger and toe nails. Here you go baby, open it! She took the Tiffany's square black box from his hands then opened it. Oh my God! Thank you Daddy! Thank you! They are gorgeous! You're welcome, come here and let me put them on for you. Ok, ok! Coop picked up the Fringe necklace of cushion-cut that was marquise with round diamonds that he had laced in platinum, and placed it around her neck. Sabrina turned around and faced the mirror. Wow! This is fabulous! Hold on baby; turn back around so I can put on the ear rings too. Ok, ok! There you go, now give me your wrist! What! Is there a bracelet too? Yep! Ok put it on, put it on. Now, you're all set baby, looking like a million bucks!

Daddy, you are the best; I'm giving you the best damn blow job of your life tonight when we get home! Ha-ha! You might by licking the balls too baby! Uh! Shut up AC! I'm just saying! Ha-ha! I love you baby; let me take a shower so we can leave. I love you too daddy! Muah! Sabrina slipped on her heels, looked in the mirror once more then headed back up front with Manny and Sophie. Oh my God! Come over here girl and let me see! Wow, these are gorgeous! Thank you Sophia! Yeah, you look nice Sabrina. Thanks Manny. What's that man of yours doing; is he getting dressed? He's taking a shower now, it won't be long. Baby, why are you looking at me like that? I like her jewelry Manny. I figured you would. Oh really; then where's mine? I didn't have time to pick it up today. Whatever Emanuel; you're full of shit. Dammit Sophie; don't be mad darling. I'm not mad Manny; but you have to step your game up baby, you're the Capo. I know Darling! Then spend some of that money tight ass. Ha-ha. Ok Sophie, I can't have you mad at me all damn night. Manny picks up the cordless phone. Ring-Ring! Hello this is David. Hey Dave, it's Manny! What's up Boss? Is the jewelry store still open? Yes it is. Alright, I'm sending my wife down to pick out some things, tell them to put it on my card. Ok no problem; send her down. Thanks David. Ok Darling; you and Brina go downstairs to the jewelry store and pick you out something real nice. We will meet you guys at the Limo. Sophie stood up, looked at her husband and smiled then kissed him on the cheeks. Muah! She grabbed Sabrina by the hand; they both smiled at him and headed downstairs.

Emanuel walked over to the kitchen counter and poured himself another drink than sat on the couch to wait on Coop. Hey Capo; where are the girls? Man; your ass and that damn jewelry! Oh my bad Manny; did Sophie like them too? What do you think? Oh! They're downstairs at the jewelry store now. I don't know why you're tripping bruh; we can't take all this damn money with us. Spend it fool; enjoy life, I know I am. Yeah, yeah whatever! I'm serious Capo! I'll think about it AC. Hey did you speak with any of the fellas today? Yeah I spoke with Will and Duck. That's what's up, is everything on the up and up. Yep no problems! That's cool, I was thinking though. Thinking about what? We need a banker to wash this damn money; that's the only damn thing we didn't cover before we finished those fools off. Yeah; you're right about that, did you have any ideas?

I was thinking that we should open a car lot. Man; what the fuck are you talking about? A car lot! AC, who the hell do we know in the car business? Nobody legally, but Hector chops cars every day. That maybe so but Hector nor any of his soldiers are capable of running a car lot. I know that Capo, we can get Duck to run things and hire a sales team. That may work right there. See; I aint the Boss for nothing! What kind of cars are we going to sell? New, used, chopped, I don't give a damn, money is money Capo! How are we going to sell the chopped cars without catching any heat? Hector has some people inside the DMV to handle the plates and vin numbers. Alright, we may be able to make this thing work then Boss. What did Duck have to say about it? I didn't tell him yet; I wanted to run it by you first Manny. Well, I think it's a good idea. Great, we will work out all the kinks then have a sit down with him. Ok but that still won't cover all the money. Yeah, I need to call Diego and see if he can put me in touch with his bankers. Now that will work, I know that punta got bankers. Yep that's a no brainer, I'm ready Capo, we can head out.

Hello ladies; what can I do for you? Hi, my husband; Manny; sent me over to pick out something. Why of course; how are you Ma'am? I'm great Sir! Well come over here to the display case and let's see what we have for you. Did you want just a necklace or the entire set? If you have a necklace to match these diamond ear rings I'm wearing, that will be perfect. Ok, take a look around; see if anything catches your eye and I will put a few items together that I think may work, while you're doing that. Thank you Sir, come on Sabrina help me pick something out. The store was surrounded with mirrors and several counter style, glass jewelry display cases. Red plush commercial carpet covered all 3,000 square feet of this home to a ladies best friend. Soft white fluorescent light, bounced off the miles and miles of carats that were on display, creating spectrums of blue as the sparkles danced off the captivating diamonds.

Wow; look at this one Brina, I think I want it! Excuse me Sir; could you get me this one please? The salesman locked his case and headed over to the ladies. That one, right there! Oh yes; you have exquisite taste my lady! This is one of my favorites; it's our diamond swing necklace, this particular one is in platinum. Yes, let me try it! Not a problem Ma'am. Sophie leans over the glass counter so he could place it on her neck. What do you think Sabrina? It's lovely Sophie; I think you should get it. Really! Yep! It also comes with a bracelet and ear rings Ma'am; did you want to try those? No, I better not! What; yes she does! Come here girl! Sabrina took off Sophie's diamond ear rings then put the other ones on. Give me your wrist. She placed on the matching bracelet also. Now look in the mirror. Sophie turned around to take a glance. Oh my God, they are so lovely on. Yes I will take all of them. Ok no problem; let me ring them up for you, did you want me to put your other ear rings in a box. Yes, please.

Ok the necklace is $20,000, the ear rings are 17,000 and the bracelet is 15,000. Your total is... No need for that Sir, just charge it to my husband's account. Oh yes; I almost forgot that Mr. Emanuel was taking care of the bill! In that case, here's your ear rings, all wrapped up and your receipt. Thank you Sir. You're welcome Ma'am and you ladies enjoy your evening. We most definitely will and you do the same. Come on Sophie we have to meet the fellas at the limo.

David have you seen the ladies? They're still at the jewelry store Mr. Cooper. Thanks man! Here they come now Coop! Where Manny, I don't see them! Man, I swear sometimes you need glasses. Kiss my ass bruh, I can see. Oh, I see them now. Yeah, uh huh! Hey Manny, what do you think? I like it Sophie, I like it? How much was it? Never mind; don't answer that. You look good daddy; you need to wear suits more often. Thank you baby, you think so? Muah! Brina snuck in a kiss. Yep; they make you look powerful. Is that right! I just may do that baby, I just might. Let's go people, the limo is waiting. Manny stood there holding the door for the others to come out.

The driver opened the door to the stretch white Navigator and the couples stepped in to start their night on the town. A congestion of walking tourist, cars and locals jam the crosswalk at Flamingo blvd. and the strip intersection as the limo exits onto Las Vegas blvd. He merges into the left lane then makes a U-turn to head South down the strip to the NY, NY Casino that sat on the corner of Tropicana and the Las Vegas Blvd. Damn; it's quiet back here! Hey driver! Hey driver! What the fuck, is this fool deaf? Manny; what's that driver's name? Oh that's Mickey, we call him Mick! Hey Mick! Mick! Yes Sir! Turn some music on back here player! Sure, no problem! Girls, care for any champagne? We have a cold bottle of Dom right here. Yes Daddy! Sure AC, I'll have a glass. Capo; hand me some glasses will yah! Pop! Oh yeah, there's nothing like a nice bottle of bubbley to get the evening started. Here you are Sophie, Sabrina, Capo! Now I say we make a toast! Here's to a New Year and lots of dough! Cheers! "Tonight, tonight" "ohhhhhh...." Oh Mick, turn that up, that's my song! Yes Ma'am! Who is that Brina? It's Xscape daddy!

"So why don't you stay awhile" "I can't help it if you put me in a daze boy." Oh this is my part! Sabrina closes her eyes, holds AC by the hand and sings along. But you look so good to me, me. In your satin pjs! God damn, sing it baby! Tonight! Aw AC! What baby? You skipped a whole verse! Oops, my bad! Look we're here, time go anyway! Man yall two are nutz! Shut up Manny; they're just in love. I remember when you use to sing to me. See this Coop; first the jewelry, now she wants me to sing. Woman stop acting like that, you know I love you; my sexy Sophia. Muah! Ha-Ha! Don't laugh Sabrina; it's not funny. It's cute Manny. Ok folks, your destination, the New York, New York. Alright people; let's go enjoy some Motown sounds baby. Mick parks the Limo and exits to let his passengers out. The drop off zone is filled with limos and luxury cars, as patrons, dressed to a T; enter the Casino to enjoy a night on the town.

Mick opens the stretch Navigator door; Sabrina steps out first, Royal blue gown hiding her heels from view, jewelry sparkling under the neon lights, white rabbit fur draped across her shoulders. Sophie follows wearing her black Louis V evening gown, diamonds gleaming from afar, black Louis V heels and her sandy blonde hair; draped effortlessly over her chinchilla fur. Emanuel exited the navigator, tailored in his all black suit with a smoke gray shirt and black tie. The last to exit, AC, wore a black suit with gray pin stripes, black shirt, Stacey Adams and Royal blue tie. Sabrina grabbed Coop by the hand as Manny wrapped his arm around Sophie's waist and they walk inside.

Damn, baby your ass is blinging tonight! I know daddy, thank you again. Hey, anything for my baby. I see Sophie picked out some really nice pieces too. Yeah they look good on her; don't they? Yep; how much was it? About $55,000 to 65,000 for the set! Oh boy; Manny is going to be looking crazy in the face. Ha-ha! Are you serious daddy? Yep, that fool is stingy! It's not like he doesn't has it baby! Why is he like that? I have no idea but I'm sure you and Sophie are going to break him out of it soon. Ha-Ha! Why you say that? Because with all this new responsibility and money we are going to be real busy and doing some traveling as well; that means you and Sophie will be together a lot.

In that case you better warn him. Nah, he'll be alright, no worries. Damn, this place is packed Boss, which way is the café. There's the sign right there man, off to the right, down that walkway. As the couples made their way through the gamblers, waitresses and admirers they could hear sounds of The Supremes piping down the hallway. Oh yeah; now this is more like it. I hope the food is good daddy; I'm starving. I'm sure it is baby. I wonder if some of the original acts are going to be here tonight. Why wouldn't they be Manny? This is Vegas darling; home of improve, if we can't get the original, we will get damn near close. Ha-ha! Emanuel you are crazy.

Finally they reach the entrance, pictures of the greats line the walls, Diana, Marvin, Michael, The Temps and many more. Plush oriental patterned carpet covered the floor; black table clothes topped the front row tables with a bucket of champagne in the center. Several sky blue leather couches, u shaped the tables to create booths through-out the café as soft lights from the suspended chandeliers softened the atmosphere. Hello Sir; how are you guys tonight? Fine Ma'am! Great; welcome to The Motown Café; how many is with your party? Four Ma'am; we have reservations! Great; my name is Susan and you are? I'm AC; Mr. Cooper! Ok follow me Mr. Cooper; we have your seats ready. The café was filled to capacity, hardly an empty seat in the house. Here's your table, again welcome to Motown Café and please enjoy the show, your waiter will be over shortly. Thank you Susan! You're welcome! Manny pulled out a seat from the table for his wife as AC did the same for Sabrina. Good Evening ladies and Gentlemen; welcome to the sounds of Motown, I'm your host this evening. My friends call me; Mr. Bojangles but you can call me Bo! How's everybody doing Las Vegas? Good Bo! Ha-ha! That's what I like; a good crowd! Alright enough of me, let's bring on your first act. Ladies and Gents; introducing the Mighty Temps! The crowd claps as the gentlemen come out on stage and the music plays in the background.

The entire room becomes excited as they hear the drum lines, chords and piano leading up to the course. "It was the third of September" "That day I'll always remember, yes I will" "Cause that was the day; that my daddy died." Now this is good music right here baby. Yes it is daddy! What you know about Papa was a Rolling Stone; Sabrina? My father use to play this album sometimes. Oh really? Yes really; why is that hard to believe? It's not; I'm just surprised, that's all. Look at Sophie jamming over there! Gone girl! She looks at Sabrina and sings along. "Papa was a rolling stone, my son" "Where ever he laid his hat was his home" "And when he died, all he left us was alone."

"Hey Momma!" Hello folks, are you guys ready to order? Hold on a minute brother! Sabrina, are you ready? Yeah I'll have the T-Bone and Lobster. You heard the lady brother and I'll have the same. Ok how did you guys want your steaks? Mine medium well and hers well done. Ok that's two Steak and Lobster dinners, one medium well and the other well done? Yep, you got it! Ok and what will you guys be having Sir? I'll have the Chicken Fettuccine and the lady wants the Shrimp linguine. Alright; I have one chicken fettuccine and a shrimp linguine. That's correct! Did you guys want another bottle of champagne for your table?

Yeah brother, send out a bottle of Cristal please. No problem Sir; I will send the bottle right over. Thanks man.

Daddy! What's up baby? Thank you. You're welcome Brina, I'm sorry again about last night by the way. It's ok daddy. Well, you know with this new position, I won't always be home. Yeah I know. But you understand right? Of course I do. I'm not complaining; just don't forget that you have me at home waiting on you, ok. What does that supposed to mean? More money, more hoes, you know how the game goes AC.

Baby; you're always be my number one! I better be, or else. Come here, give me a kiss, you sexy Italian you. Muah! Man, cut that out over there; get a room! Manny shut up and watch the show. Aww he's just jealous, come here baby, you want a kiss too. Muah! Thank you darling. Ha-ha. Sophie laughs then looks over at AC and Sabrina and winks her eye. "Folks say papa never was much on thinking" "Spent most of his time chasing women and drinking." Are those the real Temps daddy? No baby; those cats pretty old now, I'm sure they can't move like that anymore. Well, they sure sound like them. Yeah, they are pretty good. "Momma I'm depending on you to tell me the truth" "Momma looked up with a tear in her eye and said, son."

Hey Capo, what's up bro? Let's take a walk! Hey ladies we're going to make a phone call, we'll be right back. Ok fellas. Manny and AC get up from the table and walk out into the hallway. What's the matter Coop, something wrong? I keep thinking about Steel, Jesse and Wes. What about them? Now that they are gone, what would be the best way to handle their territory? Don't you have Dupree running it now? Yeah but the jury is still out on that, we don't know if he can handle it or not? I just want to implement a plan B, just in case. I can understand that Boss. Did you have anyone in mind? That's the problem, everyone that I trust is already obligated, Duck was the only one left but we're gonna give him a car lot. Yeah I see the dilemma.

I thought about D, but he can't do it either. Why not? Because he's cooking the meth, that's a damn job by itself. Can you think of anyone Capo? No but I say we let Dupree handle it; he's the closest friend we got in this drug game anyway. Yeah you have a point there, he's due to pay up in a few days. We'll see how the package looks and take it from there. What if it's not good Boss? Then we will split the turf up four ways between him, Paco, Rose and Fat Boy. Alright that's the move right there, boy you're a sharp motherfucker! Hey; I couldn't be without you Capo, now let's go eat. The two give each other a hug and head back into the café. "Poppa was a Rolling stone."

Girls, come over to the bar! Remy, Dylan, Barbie, Asia, Malibu, ILona, Vicky and Gia are just starting their shifts at Dolls. Ok ladies get over here and line your asses up at the bar for your shift drinks! Alright Red, don't have a bitch fucked up before we get started! Dylan please, I know your ass is drunk already. Ha-ha. You don't know me Red! Red slams 8 eight glasses on the bar in front of the girls. Hey new booty, get your asses over here too, yeah you; ILona and Vicky! What are we drinking Red? Tequila Remy, what else! I was just asking bitch. Gia wake the fuck up with your high ass! I'm up Red and I aint high; yet! Ha-ha. Girl you a fool! Malibu; put down that damn lip stick and get ready. I'm ready Red, pour that shit already! Barbie and Asia, stop comparing your boob jobs and come on! Hey we love our boobies, you should get some! Barbie, Asia, don't make me fuck yall up tonight. I'm all natural D's baby, don't hate!

Alright, here we go; a double for you, you, you, you, you, you, you and you drunk! F you Red! I love you Dylan! Where's yours Red. Hold on; and one for me! Ok on the count of three! One, two, three! Ahhhhh! Whew, that was good, now go make some money bitches! Ha-ha! Thank you Red! Yeah no problem ladies! Excuse me bartender, excuse me! Yes sir, how can I help you? Can I have a Jack and Coke, make it a double. Yes Sir, one Jack and coke coming up. A double Ma'am! One double Sir! Here you are Sir, enjoy. Hey Red what's up baby? Hey Fat boy, what's going on man, are you having the usual? Yeah one bottle today and 1,000 ones. Ok baby I got you! Is AC in? Nah but Will is. That's cool, can you tell him I'm here. Sure hold on. Red walks over to the bar phone to call the office.

Hey Fat Boy is here to see you. Alright send him back. Okay. Hey man, you can go to the office; I will keep your money back here with me until you get back. Thanks Red, go ahead and take two stacks for yourself. Thanks fat boy! You're welcome, I'll be right back. Excuse me Ma'am! Excuse me! Yes Sir! Can I have another double please?

Sure; that was jack right? Yep! A double! Red pours the patron another double of jack and places it in front of him. Thank you momma; you're sexy as hell, you know that! Thank you. I'm serious; you look better than any of these damn whores in here. They are all whores, that's what they are. Whew, that's good. Can I have another double? Sure but this is the last one. Why is it the last one? Because you are getting too drunk and I will be responsible if anything happens to you from being intoxicated. Alright, alright last one then. Red pours one last drink. Thank you, sexy mama!

Fat boy; what's up big man, come in have a seat. Everything is good Will; I just came to make my drop for the week. Cool, how did you do? Man; I made an extra 18 stacks this week! No shit, 18 thousand? Yep! Is it because of the Meth? Hell yeah, those strip clubs on my side are gold mines! So did you want to keep the same volume or up it? I'm gone need to at least double that shit. Cool, we can make that happen; when you re-up this weekend the package will be doubled. Oh; that 18 I made; is my cut after yours. Damn; really! Yep, this is some serious cash. Here's yours. Will took the envelope from Fat boy and took a look inside. Sweet! Yeah, AC is going to like this! Yeah he's gonna love it! Did you need anything else Will? Nope we're good big man. Well; I'm going to sip on some of that champagne and trick on these hoes a bit, then I'm out. Alright boy, see you next time. Will opens the envelope and pulls the money out then sits it on the desk as Fat boy is walking out then starts counting. Damn; five, ten, fifteen, twenty, twenty five, thirty thousand dollars; from one drop! Oh yeah, the other crews definitely got to push meth too. AC is not going to believe this.

Hey momma, one more double! Nope; I told you that was your last one! Come on Red, one more! No Sir! Fuck you whore! Red ignored the drunk patron and moved down to the other end of the bar. Hey Red, can I have another glass; please baby. Sure Fat boy, here's your ones too! Thanks love. Girl look; its Fat boy! Come on Asia let's go. Hold on Malibu, damn! Where is he girl? Right there Asia, at the bar! Okay, ok I'm coming. What's up big boy; what you up to? Nothing, just sipping on some Cristal; did you guys want a glass? Sure why not? Hey Red, can you get them some glasses? Sure thing baby; here you go! Hey momma, one more jack please? Man, I already told you that you're done. Bam! He slams his empty glass on the bar top. Hey whore; give me a fucking drink! Ok that's it! Red picked up the bar phone to call Will. Yeah what is it Red. We have a drunk fool at the bar! Okay I'm coming.

You red headed whore; where's my damn Jack at. Hey; I'm talking to you whore! Yeah we'll see how long you're gonna be talking shit. What did you say whore! Give me my drink! Ouch! Hey! Hey! Get your hands off of me! Ouch! Shut up and get the out of my club; let's go! Hey let my pants go man! Ouch! You're hurting my nuts man! You should have thought about that before you started disrespecting my girls. Ouch! Thump! Will dropped the drunk patron on the hard sidewalk in front of Dolls. Stay your drunk ass out and don't come back; the next time you're going to jail buddy! Okay man; damn; but you didn't have to pick me up by my pants. Bye; get off my property now! Okay; I'm going, I'm going! The patron jumped in his car and pulled off the lot as Will went back inside.

Thank you Will! No problem Red. He didn't pay his tab either. Don't worry about it; I will take care of it. Alright, thanks again. Hey Will, can I talk to you? Sure Remy;

what's wrong? Some personal issues! Yeah meet me in the office. Alright, I have one dance to do and I will be in after that. Sure no problem. Ring-Ring! Hello, Will speaking. What's up bro! Hey Duck, what's going on player? Not much; just checking on you big man; how's the strip club? It's cool; I just had to drop a fool on his head. Damn; don't you have security for that? Yeah; but they needed to watch the floor, so I took care of it. Yo is that chic working? What chic man? The one I met at AC's a few months ago! Who Asia? Yeah I think that was her. Yeah she's here! Alright; I might stop by there to get some drinks and shoot a few games of pool. Cool bro; see you in a bit then. Will places his cell on the desk and takes a seat in the office. Knock-Knock! Come in, it's open. Hey Remy; come sit down baby.

So what's going on now; you said you wanted to talk about something. Not really! What do you mean; not really! My pussy got wet earlier when you kicked that dude out and I just wanted to give you some of this wet wet. Oh really? Yep. Hold on a minute; are you sure about that? Yes I am; why did you say that? Because we have business with your boyfriend; I don't need any bad blood around here. Hey; what he don't know; won't hurt him! I'm not telling; are you? Of course not! Remy lifted up her right leg, slid off her thong then pulled it off the other leg and placed it on the desk. Hold on baby, go lock the door first. Oh, ok! Will moved the club receipts and other papers off the desk. Damn; I am so wet right now. Come over here and let me see how wet. Remy walked around the desk to where Will was standing. He slid his hands down between her legs, massaged her pussy slowly, until he could hear the smacking sound from her moist vagina lips touching.

You like that Remy? Ooooh yeah; it feels so good big daddy. Ooooooh. How about now? Ummmm-Hmmmm. Finger this pussy! Ummmmm-Hmmmmm. Ooooh, stop playing with it and put it in. Is that what you want Remy? Fuck yeah! Fuck me! Will slid the desk drawer open and pulled a magnum from the office stash, opened it then slid it on. Turn around and face the door, bend that fat ass over. Remy bent over the desk, doggie style, her ass cheeks spread apart just a little as her pussy lips parted slightly. Across the small of her back was a tattoo that read, delicious. Who the hell is delicious Remy? This wet

wet; that you are about to stroke. Ok delicious; here comes Mr. Good bar! With one hand on each cheek; Will parted her ass just enough to force the pussy open for entry. Oh God! Oh God! Don't hurt me big daddy; don't hurt me! Shhhh! Don't cry now; you wanted it! Go slow big daddy, go slow, you're hitting my stomach! Ugh! Ugh! Ugh! Remy grabbed the edge of the desk and held on for dear life. Yeah; you like this, huh Remy? Yesssss, yessssss, oh you're fucking the shit out of me! Ummmm-Hmmmmm. In and out, in and out, in and out for several minutes they went. Pull my hair big daddy; pull my hair! Oh you're a freaky bitch; huh Remy! Yesssss, yes big daddy! Ugh! Ugh! Yeah pull it; tighter! Will reached down with his right hand and grabbed a hand full of hair then stroked her like he was riding a horse. Oh yes; tighter big daddy! Fuck me nigga! Fuckkk me!

Remy arched her back a little more and titled her ass up higher as Will penetrated deeper. Ugh! Ugh! Ugh! Oh God, I'm cummin big daddy, I'm cumin. Ooooohhh! Oooooh! Get it girl; get it! Ummmm-Hmmmm. Ummm-Hmmmm. Uggggghhhhhh! Yes! Yes! Knock-Knock! Shhhh, be quiet Remy, someone's at the door. Knock-Knock. Who is it?

Red! What's up Red? I need some more change at the bar. Ok I'm coming. Will pulls his dick from her soaking vagina, she stands up, kisses him on the cheek, walks over to the office restroom and brings him back a rag and paper towel. Thank you Remy, go clean up and wait about ten minutes before you come out. I'm going to take her some money. Ok Big Daddy.

Chapter 4, Stay Formless

Vroom! Vroom! Left lane, right lane, Denna moves in and out of traffic as she and Nina approach the Towers in her red BMW. Damn Nina; you wasn't bullshitting about that vault! I told you girl, it's unreal isn't it? Hell yeah. I wonder why none of the girls living there hasn't tried to rob it yet? Sis; them bitches don't want to die. That's our money; if they ever tried it, you and I will be the ones to lay their asses down. Ha-ha. You're right about that sis! Come on let's get these bags up to AC. She rolled the beamer to a smooth stop; just in front of the Towers entrance. Stay here with the money Nina; I'm going to get David. Okay, hurry your butt up. Denna parked the car, engine still running, got out then ran inside. Hey Dave! Hey what's up Denna? I have some bags to drop off for AC. Okay, where are they? In my car! Alright, I'll meet you out there; let me get a bell boy. Sure, I'll be waiting. Yo, where's David? He's coming Nina; why are you so anxious? I have a spa appointment in an hour. Girl please, it's not going to take that long. It better not! Okay Denna, can you open the trunk, the bell boy will load them on to this cart and take them up to Coop's.

David; I really recommend that you assist him with delivering the bags. Trust me; you don't want anything happening to them. Do you understand? Yes Ma'am! Good, now there are two in the trunk and two duffle bags in the back seat. The bell boy rolled the gold suitcase cart to the rear of the beamer and loaded the two bags from the trunk as David stacked the other two duffle bags on top of them. Okay we're all set ladies; I assure you that we will get them upstairs right away. Thank you David! Yeah, no problem! Come on sis let's go, I can't miss this appointment. I'm coming; I'm coming, hold your horses Nina. Vroom-Vroom! The ladies sped out of the entrance and on to the strip.

Come on Bell hop; let's get these bags up to the 44th floor before we get too busy. Yes Sir. David moved hastily towards the elevator as the bell boy followed. The two gentlemen stood there silent, staring at their reflections in the gold elevator doors as the radio played in the background. "Good Morning Las Vegas, this is your Daytime jock; Dj Tech; here's a new one form Dru Hill and let me tell you baby. It's burning up the charts!" "I got this feeling and I just can't turn it loose." "That somebody's been getting next to you." "I don't want to walk around knowin' I was your fool." "Cause being the man that I am, I just can't loose my, cool." Ding!

Alright let's go Bell boy, get the cart. Knock-Knock! Yeah; who is it? It's David Mr. Cooper! Come in D! Good morning Sir, I have some bags for you; Denna and Nina just dropped them off. Oh yeah, I've been waiting on those bags since yesterday. Just take them off the cart and sit them by the coffee table in the living room. No problem Sir. You heard the man bell hop, put them over there. Will they be anything else Mr. Cooper? No' that's it for now David, have a good day! Thanks; you do the same Mr. Cooper. Indeed I will, indeed I will. David! Yes sir? Leave the door unlock; I'm expecting company. Ok Mr. Cooper.

Good Morning Daddy; what's in all the bags? Dinero baby! Bills, ends, dividends! Ha-Ha! Damn; that looks like a lot of fucking money. Baby it's only a fraction, you can buy a whole lot of Louie bags with that cash huh? AC; you crazy! What you want for breakfast; I'm hungry as I don't know what! It doesn't matter baby, just make enough for

Manny and Duck; they're on the way over for a business meeting. Ok daddy, no problem.

I'm thinking about potatoes, scrambled eggs and bacon or sausage links? Sounds good! Shall I cook the links or bacon? Do both of them! Alright daddy! Hey baby, where's the bong? Look under the bathroom sink. What the hell is it doing under there? I had it the other night, took a few hits before I jumped in the shower. Oh ok! Turn the TV on when you come out of the bathroom daddy. Okay! Damn Sabrina, you left some chronic in the damn thing. You need to stick to the blunts girl; leave my bong alone. AC walked over to the television, bong in his right hand then pressed the on button with his left. "Good Morning Las Vegas, I'm Katie Strong." "Today we spoke with Chief of Police; Espinoza." "He's offering a reward for anyone that calls with information on the first murder of 1997." "This happened a few weeks ago when two patrons walked into a University area Liquor store and found the store clerk on the floor shot to death." "If anyone wants to come forward, please, call the Las Vegas police department." "In other news; the newly opened Stratosphere is filing for bankruptcy." "Sadly this stops the construction of the second tower." "The Stratosphere; an original addition to Bob's Vegas world is the tallest casino in Vegas." "On the other end of the strip, the Tropicana celebrates its 40th anniversary." "Ceasars and Desert Inn maybe facing new ownership, there's talks between Hilton Corp, ITT and Starwood." "We will have more on this story as it progresses."

The aroma of fresh pan seared potatoes, scrambled eggs, bacon and fried sausage links, filled the air. Knock-Knock. Who is it? The feds, open the fucking door! What the hell ever! Its open Manny; come in; you crazy fucker! Ha-Ha. What's up brother, hey Sabrina! Hey Manny! Duck is right behind me Coop, he stopped by the bar. For what; I got plenty of liquor up here. I don't know man, you know how Duck is. What about me! Hey Duck! Manny was just saying; you were on the way up. How you doing brother? I'm good Coop! Come on fellas, have a seat, my lady made us some breakfast, sit down. Yo, are you going somewhere Boss? Nah, why you asked me that Duck? Because, I see all those damn suitcases over by the coffee table! Oh; those are from the Mansion, Nina and Denna dropped them off earlier. So all of that is cash? Yep! Anymore question

Dubai? Go ahead man; don't be using my government name. Ha-ha. Come on, sit down and join us Duck.

Here you are guys, we have Oj and Milk? Which do you want? Just bring them both baby. Ok daddy. I'll get the food while you are doing that. No I got it Boss, sit down. Manny, don't be silly, you're my guest; I got it. Sabrina came back to the table with the drinks then took her seat. AC sat the plate of sausage and bacon on the table, along with the dish of potatoes and bowl of eggs. Alright people, dig in. These potatoes are good Brina; what did you put in them. Thanks Manny; I just simmered them in some olive oil with natures seasoning, sliced onions and cracked pepper.

Delicious; I have to have Sophie make me some. So Duck, we decided to open a car lot and put you at the helms. How do you feel about that? You know me AC; I'm down for whatever, just make sure I know what I'm doing. Look bro; you just have to keep an eye on the books and the staff; we're hiring professionals to work for you. That sounds like a plan Manny but I have to ask guys. Why the car sales business? You see that money over there Duck, it's all dirty and we need to make it clean so we can account for it and use it legally. That's cool but a car lot won't wash all the money we're taking in. You're right Duck but it can do some of it. I'm setting up a meet with Diego soon; he's introducing me to his bankers. Then there you go; problem solved; when are we going to open the lot? We're looking at some properties now, so maybe in a few weeks, maybe sooner. Ummm, Sabrina this is good baby, AC you got a winner here boss. Thanks Duck! Don't mention it Brina.

Hey Daddy; I'm going to visit Mom today, did you want me to pick up anything while I'm out? No I'm good baby; when are you leaving? Right after breakfast; I'm taking her to the Fashion Show Mall; we're picking up something for my Father's birthday. Oh yeah; it's the old man's birthday; pick him up a box of cigars for me. Sure I can do that. Ring-Ring! Damn these cell phones; I liked it better when we just had pagers. Ring-Ring! Hello! Is this AC? Yes it is; who is this? It's Rose! Hey Rose, what's going on? We need to speak! Sure; I'm free tonight. No Mr.; this is important; I was thinking like now. Well I'm at my place now; come by. Where do you live? In the Towers on Flamingo and the Strip! Okay I'll be there shortly. Where you going Sabrina?

I'm done AC, I have to go to Mom's; remember! Oh yeah! I will call you when I get to mom's AC. Ok baby, drive safe. Thanks for breakfast Sabrina! You're welcome guys!

So how did Fat Boy do with that meth? He dropped off a nice package the other day Duck. Oh really; how nice? Like 30 stacks nice. Shit; that aint bad Boss. Now we just have to get Rose, Paco and Dupree to push it too. I'm sure Pree will be down for it and Paco, but Rose, that maybe another story Manny. Well; we will find out soon, that was her that called me earlier; she's on the way over now. What if she doesn't want in on it Coop? Then we will do what needs to be down Duck. To be honest guys, I don't think she can push it to her customers on the strip, they're an haute crowd. You might have a point there AC, so why are you offering if you think that? It's good business Manny, she's a great earner and it's only right that she has the same opportunity as the others. Yeah but if she doesn't want in, what's the point! Loyalty Emanuel, loyalty! It goes a long way in this business. Well that's why you're the Boss bro, because I would have not even wasted my time telling her. What are you going to do with that cash over by the table? I'm gonna count it as soon as you guys leave then figure out what the fuck to do with it. Why, do you want to help Duck? Hell nah, you need to get a money counter machine, you're going to be all night doing that shit.

Knock-knock! Come in, it's open! White Gucci shades covered her eyes, honey blonde hair draped around Rose's round face, complementing her dark caramel skin tone. Her white fur coat hung to her waist, partly covering the satin red Prada dress that stop just above her calves. Rose's freshly manicured red colored nails, matched the red lipstick and Jimmy Choo shoes she wore. She entered the Condo, small leather white Prada purse in her right hand, Newport in the other. Gentlemen, how the hell are you! It smells good in here, did I miss breakfast? Hey Rose, how are you baby? I'm great AC, I like your condo; it's cozy with a nice view. Thank you Rose! You're welcome; remind me to give you my realtor's number, she's the best in Vegas. Why would I need your realtor's number? Look handsome; you're the Boss; this place was nice, when you were who you were back then. But now you make too much money to stay at the Towers. Some crazy broke fool is going to try and rob your ass eventually. Thanks for your concern Rose but I'm ok, plus I have the Mansion over in

Spanish Trails already, so stop hating on my shit. Sorry, I was just saying.

Yeah whatever woman, sit your ass down and let's talk business. Hey Rose. Hi Manny. Hi Duck. Alright so what was so important that it couldn't wait? The Casino Dealers Union President called me last night. What did he want? He says that he never received his payoff for this year. What payoff Rose? Damn, my bad AC, how could you have known! Spill it woman; known what? Well, Bobby always paid off the Union President at the beginning of the year so I could continue to operate on the strip. That's how I get the dealers to push my product, with no trouble from the cops. So how much is the payoff? $40 thousand! Alright, call this guy up and set up a meeting for tomorrow. What time? It doesn't matter Rose, if I can't meet him, I will send Manny. Consider it done. So how's business on the strip anyway Rose?

It's pretty damn good Manny, how do you like your new job as Capo? I love it, every day is an adventure. Speaking of the strip, we have a new product Rose that you might be interested in. What, not that meth shit. Yeah that meth shit. I'm not interested AC, that's for slums, whores and broke motherfuckers. My customers are none of those; I'll stick with the powder and occasional weed baby. Are you sure, the dancers use it to stay up for days at a time so they can make money non-stop? Yep; solid boss! Ok, just thought I would mention it, give you an option. Thanks but I'm fine AC, is there anything else, I need to go pick up my new Rolls Royce. Nope that's it Rose. Well gentlemen, it was nice chatting with you and I will call you with that time as soon as I get it AC. You fellas have a nice day. You too Rose; later!

Hey I'm about to take off too Coop; I need to meet Nina at the agency in a bit. Hold on Duck; can you drop me off at the detail shop to get my car? Sure man, no problem. Alright fellas; I will speak with you later, guess I better start counting this damn money. Manny and Duck, both give Coop a pound and head downstairs. Ring-Ring! Hello! Hey my friend, what's going on? Hey Diego, how are you my brother? Good my friend, I am good, so you need to see me? Yeah man, I need a banker; I have no idea where I am going to put all of this money. Relax my friend; I have some bankers for you. Great; when can I meet them? I have to travel to Rio tonight but I will be back in a few weeks, we can do when I get back. Cool, sounds like a plan, you will call me then? Yes, I call you the day before. Cool, have a good trip brother. Thanks my friend, see you soon.

AC places the phone on the counter and walks over to the coffee table then picks up one of the bags, unzips it, sits on the couch and started counting the cash. Each bundle was individually wrapped into stacks of five thousand dollars. Knock-Knock! Damn, yeah who is it? Ricky, I'm looking for Mr. Cooper! He stops counting, pauses and tries to catch the female voice. Who? Ricky; Amanda Ricky! He gets up and heads to the door. Yeah I'm Cooper; how can I help you? Hi Mr. Cooper, can I come in? Call me AC, where do I know you from? Don't you remember? No I don't, refresh my memory. Sure; I'm thirsty can I have a glass of water? AC looked at Amanda, trying to remember if he knew her. Ricky stood there 5'7" tall, wearing an all-black dress, white leather jacket, black knee high leather boots, and wire framed glasses. Her pale white skin was in need of a tan and her kinky brunette hair could have used a perm, under her arm she carried a large black leather purse. Sure come in, have a seat, I still don't remember you though!

Ricky walked over to the couch then took a seat, in front of the coffee table that held the large suitcase which was partially unzipped.

Here's your water Amanda. Thank you AC! Were we in the Army together or something? No we weren't Mr. Cooper. Then how do you know me? My name is Detective Amanda Ricky; Chief Espinoza transferred me here from New York. Well congratulations, why are you at my place? I was assigned to the murder case of Ashley, Jewel and Lisa. What does that have to do with me? Good question Sir! Well, are you gonna answer it or not? I was going through my evidence and found this VHS tape right here. So what? I think you want to know what's on this type Mr. Cooper! Oh really; what's on it Ricky? You and several of your friends covering up a murder! What the fuck are you talking about? I have footage of a black male breaking in your place and holding a gun to white females head, in the hall is two other females, tied and gagged. Soon after that you and your friends get off the elevator and... Well, you know the rest AC; don't you? Yeah I do, so what do you want? Clearly you're not locking me up, so you want something? I want to know who murdered those girls that day; over on Maryland parkway. All three of them are on this tape and you had an obvious relationship with one of them. So what; that don't mean I know who did it!

I think you do AC. Listen Detective Ricky, I know you're trying to do your job and all; but I can't help you. I think you can! How am I supposed to do that? You know people; ask around and see if anyone knows who killed those girls. What if I can't find out anything? Then the chief sees this tape and you all are going down. Damn, that's my only option? Yep! Man; you New York cops play it hard, don't you! It's my way or no way Mr. Cooper. AC slid up to the edge of the couch then turned to face Ricky with his left hand on the coffee table. I have a better idea Detective Ricky. Oh really, what's that? Zip! He unzips the suitcase then pulls out two bundles. Bam! He slams two bundles of money on the table. I think you need some friends in Sin City Detective, you being new and all. Are you trying to bribe me Mr. Cooper? No, no, no, never that. I take care of my friends. Oh really? Yes Ma'am!

You see the way I see it, you and I can be good friends, this right here is 10 thousand dollars and it can be all yours. You're out of line AC! Wait; hear me out! I will have my people ask around the city for info on that murder and let you know what we find out. In return, you sell me that tape in your hands; for this ten thousand dollars! Think about it Amanda, you're not planning on using it anyway. Detective Ricky took off her glasses then placed them on the table beside the cash. So you will help me with my case if I sell you this tape? Yes that's the deal. You got 48 hours Mr. Cooper; I want that info when I come back. Cool, stay right there Detective, let me get you a bag for that money! I don't need a bag, my purse is fine, here's your tape! I will see you in two days Mr.! Ricky stood up, grabbed the blood money, placed it in her large black leather bag and headed downstairs. Have a great day Detective! AC stood there holding the tape in his hand, with a smirk on his face as she walked out.

Sir, Ma'am, please put your personal items on the conveyer belt; remove your jackets, belts, shoes, and empty your pockets also; cell phones too! Alright Ma'am step forward, okay all clear. Sir, come forward please! Okay, all clear, you guys can take a seat over there to put your shoes and things back on. When you're done, go see the clerk and give her the name of the inmate that you are visiting today. Thank you Sir! You're welcome Ma'am. Okay, next in line please. Damn this is crazy; next time I'm leaving everything in the car! Chino, stop complaining and put your shoes on already. Hey Marcia; stop rushing me mija! Whatever punta! What's Benny's last name; so I can go sign in! Ortiz woman! Marcia stood up and slid on her black leather jacket, bent down to zip up her black biker boots, rubbed her fingers through her red haired Mohawk and walked over to the clerk's window.

Good Afternoon Ma'am and welcome to Clark County Detention, what's the name of the prisoner that you will be visiting today? Benny Ortiz Ma'am! Thanks, and are you the only visitor? No, my boyfriend is over there putting his shoes on. Okay sign your name right here on the visitors log and make sure he does the same. Ok no problem, can I take the clip board with me? Sure, just bring it back, we only have a few. She signed her name then took the clip board over to Chino to sign as well. Here man, sign this. Go ahead and sign it for me Marcia, I'm still trying to get this damn boot on! Ugh! Hurry up, you're so slow sometimes. Yeah, I don't hear you complaining when I'm eating that poonany slow. Ha-Ha. That's different baby. Yeah uh huh!

Blushing, she held her head down, signed his name then walked back over to the clerk. Here you are Ma'am. Thank you sugar! You're welcome; how long is the wait before we can see him? About ten minutes! Okay thanks.

Chino tightened the belt on his khaki's, slipped on his black skully and zipped up his black hoodie. So what did she say baby? Ten minutes! Oh, that's not bad; do you want a candy bar or something from the vending machine? Yeah get me a coke! That's it, no candy? No I'm fine. The waiting area was cold and dull with white commercial tile floors, lime green stone walls, orange, yellow and blue plastic chairs sat in formation facing the clerk's window. One small 20" TV sat mounted in the NE corner, just above the two vending machines.

Here's your soda, I got you some M&M's just in case you changed your mind. Thanks Chino! Yeah, no problem, come on, let's sit over here; I see two empty seats on the third row. Can I ask you a question baby? Sure, what is it Marcia? I want in on the contract hits, yall got with AC. What! You heard me; I want in on the action baby. I don't know Marcia, are you sure you're ready? Hell yes, I've been ready. Well, let me speak with Hector about it then.

I'm serious baby, don't bullshit me. I aint bullshitting you woman, I will ask him. Okay people listen up, I'm officer Dailey; I will be over your visitations today. When I call your inmates name, come over by me and form a line. David Ross, Kevin Henry, Joel Maddox and Benny Ortiz! Okay people, we are heading into room 45, there are four booths in this room; you will take a seat in the order that I called the names. Start from the far left booth and work your way back. For example! David Ross visitors, you will take the far left booth and so on. Do you guys have any questions? No questions! Good, follow me, you will have exactly one hour, at that time I will notify you that your visitation hour is over.

The officer opens the door to room 45. Alright people, enjoy your visit, if at any time you need my help, come and get me I will be right outside this door. The windows between you and the inmates are bullet proof and can-not be broken, so you need not fear. The visitors walked in the room, excited to see their loved ones. Benny; what's up cuz! Hey bro, what's poppin; who is the lady homes? Oh this is my old lady Marcia! Hey Marcia! Hi Benny! Hey, call me Beno! So I got that kite aye; why Hector green light that fool? That punta plugged in to some old money on the street and we controlling that shit now esse'. If he hits the outside, it's gonna be some tension because his family is gone home esse'! They aint coming back around here, he's the last of them. So big cuz got something for me? Yeah esse'! Que pasa? Trienta! Did you say; 30 American homes? Yeah punta; 30 thousand! Oh, that fool is done homes. Yeah cuz, I knew you were the man for the job. The kite say his name was Victor; right? Yep!

Alright, tell big homie that fool will get rolled up tonight. Cool, I will let him know cuz. Hey Chino, one more thing cuz. Que pasa? Put five on my books and take the rest to mama for me. No problem cuz, I got you. Click! Come on baby, let's go get some lunch then we can head back to the shop.

The night is young and Sin City is about to come to life. Huge pink neon letters illuminate the parking lot of Dolls as the billboard flashes tonight's specials and upcoming features. Dylan and Barbie just pulled in to the parking lot, driving their new cars, Dylan in her T top, black 300 ZX and Barbie with the bright cherry red, Mitsubishi 3000, both cars with the paper tags still on. Barbie parked her car, got out and walked over to sit in the car with Dylan so they could smoke a blunt before they headed in for work. Damn bitch, why you aint take the price tag off the back window girl? Oh; my bad Barbie! Take it off for me please! Girl you be tripping. I know man, it's this damn weed; I need to leave this smoke alone. Yeah right bitch, you will lose your mind if you can't get high! You might be right about that Barbie. How much money do you have left, I'm running low. Maybe 2500 Dylan, we need to hit some more banks soon. Yeah this damn car took all my money! Look at it this way, at least we paid cash and don't have any payments. I guess you're right Barbie but we have to open a few more bank accounts and hit some in Cali too, we don't have too many more options in Vegas.

Well, we got 180 thousand out their asses! Yeah but we need to open new bank accounts fast before our names goes to check systems and we can't open NO bank accounts! I agree with you there Dylan, I've been getting bank letters for the past few weeks about those bad checks. Yeah me too, so let's open two more accounts tomorrow, wait a few days and make a $20,000 run then head to L.A to set up. Sounds like a plan to me girl. Cool, give me your lighter, so I can light this chronic. Damn Dylan, that green is loud, where did you get that from? Dupree's ass, I went over to MLK last night. Oh his green is always top shelf, do you have some cd's in here? No, turn on the radio. "What's up Las Vegas, this is your boy Dj Shi C." "If you're just tuning in, we have some sad news in the world of hip hop." "About 1:30 this morning; March 9th of 1997, rapper Christopher Wallace aka Notorious B.I.G was shot down in a drive by in Los Angeles while in traffic on Wilshire Blvd." "He was pronounced dead on arrival." "Our prayers go out to his love ones and family." "So for the next few hours we will be honoring B.I.G by playing the hits, that he left us to remember him by." Damn Barbie! Did you hear that! That doesn't make any since for them fools to be killing each other like that, this world is crazy! That's why I keep to myself Dylan, aint no telling what be going through peoples head these days. Girl I hear you, that news done messed up my high, I don't even feel like working now.

Dylan we're going to work, we haven't been in a few weeks, so you know Will is going to be tripping. Yeah I know, I was just talking, come on let's go in, so we can hear his mouth and get it over with. The ladies exit the 300 and walk inside Club Dolls to start their shift. God damn, where you fools been all month? Hey Red! Come over here and give me a hug! Muah! I missed yall, where the hell yall been? Girl we got this other hustle that we're doing. What you talking about Dylan? I hope yall aint running no dope! No nothing like that Red. Well, I'm glad you two are back; you know Will is going to charge your asses for missing all those days right? Yeah I figured as much, is he in the office? Yeah he's in there Barbie! Okay, we better go get this over. Alright ladies, hurry up, first round is on me! Later Red!

Do you think he's going to be real mad Dylan? Girl I wouldn't care if he was; what can he say as long as we pay the fine. Knock-Knock! Come in! Hey Will! Well look what the cat drug in. Come in ladies, have a seat! Hey Will, can we work? Sure you guys can work, after you pay your fine. How much is it? Let's see Dylan! Will looks down at his calendar. You two haven't been to work in three weeks, I was just about to have your lockers cleaned out tomorrow. We're sorry Will; we had to take care of some business out of town. Just give me $200 a piece and you guys can go back to work, next time you plan on being away that long, let me know. Ok no problem and thanks! Yeah don't mention it, just give the $200 to the house mom and get to work! Thank you! Muah. The girls jumped out of their seats, kissed Will on the cheek and ran out of the office.

Ring-Ring-Ring! Hello Dolls! Hey Will! What's up Boss? I'm about to go with Diego to Cali, hold shit down until I get back, I couldn't get in contact with Manny, he and Sophie at the damn mall or something. Ok Coop; got you bruh. AC hung up the phone, grabbed his suit jacket, watch, wallet and 357 then locked his door behind him and walked to the elevator. Ding! Hello there young man, I'm going up, are you? Yes I am Ms. Harvey, how have you been Ma'am? I've been good, you're looking sharp; do you have a hot date? Oh no, just going to take care of some business. Good, glad you are still busy, you know what I always say! Yes Ma'am, busy is always good! That's right! I'm headed to the 56th floor to meet Mrs. Ross, her husband passed a few days ago. Oh I'm sorry to hear that, please give her my condolences. Sure, I would be happy to. Ding! Well this is my stop, see you around Mr. Cooper. Okay Ms. Harvey, take care. Fourteen floors later, AC had reached the roof top. Down below, the neon lights danced across the night sky as traffic lights crawled down the strip in both directions. Strong winds whipped across his face at two second intervals, accompanied by a loud hovering noise. The pilot spotted Cooper on the far left corner of the roof, standing in front of the exit and waved him over to the chopper. AC saw him signal and ran towards the helicopter while ducking to stay below its propeller's. Both gentlemen started yelling at the top of their voices so they could hear one another over the loud propellers. Hey are you AC? Yes I am! Cool, hop on and buckle up, Diego is waiting for us! Where is he? In California! How long is it going to take us? Only an hour at the most! Ok! Why, are you scared of flying AC? Nah, I was just curious. Oh hold on, we're on our way!

The pilot proceeded to lift the chopper off the Towers roof top, hovered away from the building then flew over the strip in route to California. The long narrow row of neon lights faded slowly into the darkness, the further they got away from Sin City. Ahead was total darkness over the dry desert with a speckle of white lights here and there. As minutes turned to 30, then to an hour, the bright lights from the City of Angels sat upon them like the second coming. Here we are AC, Los Angeles! Wow, this is a nice view; I'm usually in a plane, everything is so surreal from the chopper. Yeah you can't beat this. The chopper hovered over Sunset blvd. then headed towards Wilshire to land on top of Diego's condominium. Down below they could see him, holding a bottle of champagne in his right hand, glass in the other. Diego's light blue three piece suite and long black hair, flapped in the wind as the chopper landed. The loud propellers slowed down and the wind came to a stop as Coop stepped out of the helicopter.

Hey my friend, how was your flight? It was good Diego, thanks for seeing me brother. Hey no problem, come have a drink, the bankers are on the way. Sure! AC took the glass that Diego handed him and followed the drug lord inside. How you say? This is my get away pad! Look at the view, you like? Yeah man, it's straight; I love the chopper deck though. Oh yeah, who drives when you can take a chopper. Ha-ha! That's what's up, now I will drink to that. So come sit down, let's talk business. The get-away pad over looked L.A from 90 stories up, its walls were glass from every angle, floors hardwood, inside pool, four master bed rooms, six baths, restaurant style kitchen, helicopter pad and a Brazilian live in made named Maria. Come, come sit down. AC stood there for a second taking it all in, admiring Diego's taste. You're not big on furniture I see! My friend, I like open space, that kitchen table and chairs are for guess. All I need in this room is this white sectional, my coffee table and big screen TV. That is it, no more, oh and beds for my bedrooms.

Well it looks good though brother. Thank you my friend, sit down; sit down. So tell me, you have problem with too much money? Yeah I need to wash it, so I can use it how I want. I'm sure you understand. Of course, of course! I use three bankers because of this problem, one in Rio, one in Dominican Republic and one here in U.S. Which one you want? All of them brother, all of them! Good, all of them will be here shortly, so don't worry. Thanks Diego, I really appreciate this. No problem, no problem my friend. Are you leaving once we finish business? What do you mean? Are you going back to Vegas or are you staying here tonight, in L.A? Brother I aint going no-where tonight, Vegas will be there tomorrow. Good; let me get you some company my friend. Maria! Maria! Yes Diego! Come in here darling. Maria walked in the room wearing a thick white rob over her Brazilian brown skin, no shoes and hair still wet from her shower. Yes Diego! Call your friend Selena and have her come over tonight to accompany my friend AC. Okay Diego, when did you want her to come over? Tell her two hours, we have a business meeting first then we play after! Okay Diego, is there anything else? Yes, get some champagne, coke and weed ready for our party too. Alright; will do Diego!

Ding-Ding! Maria, get the door baby! Ding! That should be the bankers AC. Cool, let's get to business. Gentlemen, how are you tonight, come in have a seat! Three guys, all dressed in blue suits, white shirts, matching blue ties and black shoes entered the room. All three were of Latin decent. AC these are my bankers, you can trust them, they are like family, I personally sent all of them to school and I know their families from home. So this is no funny business, you can trust them. How are you Mr. AC, my name is Guillermo and I represent the Dominican Republic Bank. Hello Sir; I'm Donatello and I represent the Bank of Rio. Hi AC; I'm Michael and I work here in the U.S with several banks and investment firms. Nice to meet all of you gentlemen! Go ahead my friend, tell them what you want, I'm going to help Maria get dressed. Ok brother, thanks again. No problem.

Gentlemen, I'm sure Diego has made you aware of my situation; I have a ton of money that I need to wash and put into legal business ventures. Can I speak sir? Sure Michael; go ahead. Do you know what type of businesses you want to invest in? I have some ideas but I'm open to suggestions. Well in that case can I bring some information for you to review when I come to Vegas Sir? Yes of course, I wouldn't have it any other way. I want to know all of my options. Great; I will take care of that for you. Thanks Michael. Sir! Yes Donatello? How often did you want to make deposits in Rio? At least twice a week Donatello! Is that possible? Yes Sir it is, however many times you like. Great! Sir! Yes Guillermo? Will you be visiting the Dominican Republic to make your deposits or should I make arrangements in Vegas. I will be visiting but not to make deposits, you can handle all of that in Vegas. Ok, thank you Sir. You're welcome! So gentlemen, can we make this happen? Yes Sir, it's no problem. Great; when can we get started? Tomorrow if you want Sir! AC stands up, the three bankers follow suit. Gentlemen, I do believe we have a deal; I will have my Capo Manny, get in touch with you to set things up. Thank you sir, glad we could help.

No; thank you fellas! They all shake hands and the bankers exit the get-away pad as Diego comes to check on Coop. Hey my friend! Everything ok! Yep, we're in business Diego, thanks again. No problem my friend, no problem! Turn on the TV get comfortable, there's some weed and coke on the counter, help yourself my friend. Thanks brother, do you have any more champagne? Sure, look in the cabinet by the fridge, get two glasses, Selena will be here shortly. We'll come join you in a second. Maria's putting on her dress! Okay Diego, take your time bruh, I'm good. AC takes a seat on the couch, pulls out a blunt, guts it, sprinkled in some chronic, rolled it up, licked it a few times, ran the lighter over it, lit it then got up off the couch and walked to the window. A huge feeling of accomplishment came over his body as he stood there over-looking the city of Los Angeles from the glass house that towered above the buildings. He took a long pull off the spliff, inhaled, held it for a few seconds, exhaled, held his nuts with his left hand, panned another view of the city from right to left then took another pull off the blunt.

Chapter 5, Calculated Steps

"Alright inmates; chow time!" Buzz! 12 noon, the mod doors come unlock and the inmates exit there modules for lunch at the Clark County Detention Center. Blue commercial carpet covered the first floor of the 6,000 square foot area, white stoned walls incased the quarters from the floor to the ceiling of the second tier. Heavy blue steel doors with one 3"x 12" window, separated the inmates 6'x 6' room from the outside bay, which they were only allowed to enter twice a day.

There are 50 modules upstairs and 50 below, two men in each. All 200 men rushed to the serving area to eat chow and politic. Benny walked out of his downstairs mod then joined his other brown brothers in line. Dark blue scrub tops and bottoms, orange socks and brown sandals, not by choice but was every inmate's attire. Yo homes, what they got up there today? Same shit we had last Wednesday Beno; baked potato, boiled egg and a lump of hamburger. Man I don't want that crap, meet me at the table with the fellas Angel. I'm going to get some soup out of my room.

Alright Beno! The bay tables begin to fill up as the convicts got their trays; stainless steel rectangle shaped, 4'x4' tops with cement benches on all four sides covered the center part of the mod floor.

White boys populated the middle portion; the brothers had the back and Latina's who held the majority maintained the front. Hey homes, what kind of soup is that you sipping on? Its clam chowder bro, I can't eat that jail house food today; my stomach is already messed up. I aint took a dump in days. That's crazy aye; you backed up. Ha-Ha. Angel shut the fuck up. I'm just saying aye! What's up Yogi, why you so quiet bro? What's poppin Beno; my girl is tripping yo, got a lot on my mind esse'. Bro you got 4 years after you leave county, you can't do that stretch worried about no bitch. Yeah I know esse' but what the fuck am I gonna do? Bro let her do her thing, as long as she's there for you when you need her. You'll be alright. I guess so Beno.

Yogi, it's nothing you can do but stress out, you locked up fool, let it go. Angel, where is Sandavol's ass at? Taking a dump aye. Man that fool is always shitting. Yeah; not like you aye! Ha-Ha. Alright enough of the jokes homes, I'm gone bust your head open, keep it up. Damn, calm down Beno, I was just kidding aye, damn. Yeah whatever homes, you play too much. Beno my man, what's up! Hey Sandavol, I'm good homes, have a seat, I have something we need to discuss. All four gentlemen leaned over their trays to speak quietly amongst the group. Okay, listen up, my people came to see me the other day and they need a favor from us. What kind of favor aye? We need to roll this wop up. What wop Beno? That fool name Victor, he processed in a few weeks ago, he's a short timer. Here on some bullshit; he has like 30 days left in the wake up.

So are we rolling that punta up or PC that ass? Yogi what did I say; roll up fool, he got the green light! Is he connected or what, what's his angle. He's a Delgato, Sandavol; the last of the family. My people are running the streets now and if he gets out he will cause problems, all the Delgato soldiers will follow his lead. What's in it for us aye? I will put $500 on your books and guarantee you a spot in the family when you walk out of CCDC. You guys cool with that? I'm down esse'! Cool, how about you Yogi? I'm in! Angel what's up? Let's do it aye! Alright it has to be done today! Beno how the fuck! The guard is right there homes! Calm down Yogi. Benny reached under the table and pulled something from his sock. Here Angel, take this to the guard when I tell you to. Ok just let me know when. Which one is Victor bro? That short stocky punta, with the slicked back hair. So how and when are we going to do this?

It's simple Yogi, just pay close attention. Do you guys have your shanks? Of course! Cool, chow time is almost over, we'll hit him when everyone is heading back to their mods; his is only four doors down from mine. What about his celly Beno? I got that covered Sandavol. Oh yeah, how are you going to do that? Let's just say the guard owes me a favor; get your shanks ready. Angel; take that chronic to the guard and tell him Delagato. Tell him what about Delagato? Nothing homes, just do as I say. Okay, you want me to go now? Hold up for a minute- Beno looks up at the clock; over the guard's booth. Alright Angel, go give it to him and come right back over here. Yogi and Sandavol; get ready to murc that punta on my mark, we move in when Angel gets back and the guard makes his move.

Excuse me officer! What is it Convict? This is from Benny; he says to tell you Delgato. Alright; I got it; keep it moving esse'. Angel headed back over to the table with the others as the guard called in to the C.O from his radio. "Hey Cap; we got a shake down in mod 58; that's inmates Victor Delgato and Michael Damon." "Roger that officer; proceed with the search; back up is on the way." The inmates stacked their trays and prepared to head back to their cells. The guards rushed in, dressed in full riot gear. The confused inmates then became rowdy as the guards proceeded to search Victor's mod. Yo man, why you fucking with my house? Stand down Delgato or we will lay your ass down. Do you understand convict!

Yes officer! Good; now back the fuck up! Two officers search the cell, throwing mattresses, pillows and their personal belongings on the floor and in the door way. God damn this is foul brother, why are they in our cell Vic! What you got in there man? Michael shut your trap, aint nothing in there you don't already know about. Inmates gather in the bay watching the guards rip Delgato's room apart. Alright Yogi, go hit the left kidney; Sandavol you get the right, Angel shank the neck, I got the head. Come on esse', go!

Victor stood in the crowd of inmates watching his room go to pieces, as his celly tried to pick up the items the guards threw in the bay. Yogi slipped through the crowd and walked up hastily behind him, shank in his right hand. Ugh! Ugh! Oh! Two jabs to the left kidney. Sandavol ran through the crowd and attacked. Ugh! Ugh! Oh Fuck! Two jabs to the right kidney. Victor wrapped both arms around his waist, slouched over holding his sides. Angel cut through the rowdy convicts and stood in front of Delgato. Ugh! One jab to the throat! Ugh-

Victor tried to scream but his voice just gurgled, blood covered his blue shirt and squirted from his neck. Bam! Beno stood over Victor, then smacked him in the back of the head one good time with a lunch tray. Then as his body fell face first, Beno bent over him and whispered. "La Raza!" Delgato's, bloody, now lifeless body; fell to the ground while the inmates scattered away from the scene as if nothing happened. The guards left his room and found themselves standing in a bloody murder scene. Victor lay dead in his own blood on the red soaked carpet. Buzz! Buzz! Sirens sound as the guards made the prisoners go to their rooms and locked the module down. Alright ladies, we're on 24 hour lockdown! The C.O yelled out while standing over the body in the center of the bay floor. Officer; get a medic in here and notify the Sheriff of a 187 at CCDC. Got it C.O, calling it in now!

"Vegas Metro; come in please." "This is Metro, go ahead CCDC." "We have a 187 over here and need Detectives and medics on the scene." "Roger that CCDC, in route." "Thanks Metro; Over and out."

One guard moved in to check Victor's pulse. Yeah, he's gone man! That's a shame; he only had 30 days to go before his release. C.O somebody had other plans for that convict, that's the only reason he didn't make it. Alright officers back to your stations, we will take care of this, aint much we can do now anyway he's dead. Call in for the Coroner, there's nothing for the meds. Roger that sir!

Beep! Beep! Lunch traffic jammed the strip in front of the Towers as cars filtered in the parking lot for a weekend of partying and gambling at the Towers casino. Up on the 44th floor, Sabrina and AC are just waking up. Ahhhh! Damn I slept good, wake up baby! No daddy, I'm not ready to get up, let's lay here all day. Brina, you know I can't do that; I got business needs to handle. Come on AC, one more hour, you know you want to. Oh you're gonna play dirty like that, why you got to rub on my dick. This is my snake daddy; I can do what I want. Oh yeah? Yep! Handle your business then baby. You're hard as a brick too; just how I like it. That's that early morning hard on girl, go ahead and put them lips on it. Slurp! Slurp! Yeah, go slow baby, go slow. Slurp..... Slurp.... Slurp..... Ummmm-Hmmmm. I like that right there, suck it girl. Who dick is this baby? Who dick is this! It's my dick daddy! Say it again girl! It's my dick! Give me that wet pussy, climb your ass up here, so I can fuck it!

Sabrina lifted her head, slid her hands up AC's torso then straddled him while inserting his cock in her throbbing wet pussy. Damn, you're soaking wet baby. Smack... Smack... Smack.... Her vagina lips sounded off every time they hit Coop's nuts. Sabrina arched her back, placed her right hand on his chest, left one massaging her breast and continued to ride, stroking back and forth. Pop! Pop! Yeah daddy, smack my ass again! Pop! Oh shit, smack it! Pop! God damn daddy, you feel so good! You like this black love baby, don't you! Hell yes! Smack my ass daddy, smack it!

Pop! Pop! Ummmm! Whose dick is this baby? My dick daddy, my dick! Yeah baby, give me this pussy, you sexy bitch! Take it daddy, take it! Pop! Pop! Ring-Ring! What the hell, this damn phone! Ring-Ring! Don't answer it daddy. I have to baby, you know that. Ring-Ring! Hello! Hey Nigga! What's up?

God damn, fuck me daddy! Fuck me! I'm cuming, I'm cuming. Ummm-hmmm, cum baby, cum! What you doing Coop, fucking that skinny white girlfriend of yours? Whatttt- do you want Mo? I need to see you? I'm busy, can't you hear that! Not now, later tonight! Alright- I have a meeting with the fellas, we can meet after that. I'll call you when we're done! Oh yes, oh yes, yesss! Damn, that was a good nut daddy! Who is that on the phone? Oh, I'm sorry, was I too loud daddy? Nobody baby, you good! What do you mean nobody, fuck you AC! Hey calm down, I will see you tonight; we can discuss our business then. Yeah whatever, bye nigga! Click!

Meanwhile out on the Ranch. Hey Josh, how's everything? Hi Denna, I'm good, just stocking up! What are you doing out here? Monica's off tonight, I'll be here with you until tomorrow. Oh that's cool, did you want a drink?

Sure, make it an Apple Martini. Coming right up Boss! Thank you bartender, how many girls do we have on shift? We have a full house; none of the ladies took off this week. Great, more money for the house then! Here's your Appletini! Thanks Josh! Ding! The bell rung over the door as the first customer of the evening entered. Well howdy Haus, you must be new, I haven't seen you serving drinks before. Oh yes Sir; I'm Josh, nice to meet you. Howdy Josh; where's the other feller! I don't know Sir, we're under new ownership and I just started, so I never met him. Ok, howdy Ma'am; how are you? I'm fine Sir and yourself? Happier than a pig in mud with a slop bucket! Ha-ha! What! Oh; it's just a joke Ma'am, glad you found it funny. By the way; yall can call me Ronnie.

Nice to meet you Ronnie; I'm Denna. Hello Denna, are you one of the pretty ladies working tonight? Oh no; I'm the new Manager, we still have the same ladies with the exception of one. Well that's good to hear Ma'am because I want my two little ladies I had last time. Who was that Ronnie? That'll be Trish; my chocolate bunny and Gloria, my little peanut butter cup. Josh; page the ladies for this fine gentleman and get him a draft on the house. Yes

Ma'am, I'm on it. Josh walks over to the intercom to page the ladies. "Gloria and Trish to the front please; you have a date." What are you drinking Ronnie? I'll have a Bud Haus! Hey Ronnie! Sugar plums; come over here and give poppa a kiss! Muah! We missed you cowboy, where you been for so long? I had to go to Texas for a bit; my little peanut butter cup. Did you miss me? Hell yeah cowboy! Don't you stay away so long next time poppa! I promise I won't chocolate drop. Hey Josh, three double shots of Jose' for me and the ladies! Coming right up!

Bam! Your three shots Sir! Thanks Josh! Ladies come on, let's drink up! Both ladies stood beside him, Trish to the left, Gloria on the right. Ok Cowboy, on the count of three! Alright peanut butter cup, count it off. One! Two! Three! Ahhh! Whew! That was good, how much do I owe you haus? $30 Sir! Ronnie reached for his over-stuffed wallet, sat it on the bar and slipped two 20 dollar bills from his stash. Trish stood there looking at all of the money protruding from Ron's billfold, then without thinking she reached up and pulled a few bills from the stack as his head was turned. Bap! What the fuck do you think you're doing girlie! Denna turned to see what the noise was. Hey!

What the hell is going on over there! I'm sorry Ronnie! Bap! How dare you steal from me! Click! Click! Ronnie stood still as the cold metal touched his right temple. Listen up Cowboy, I know you're pissed because she took your money but I can't allow you to be hitting on my girls. Trish give him his money back then take your ass to the back, you too Gloria. Ok Denna! Hurry up, put the money in his front pocket Trish and get the hell on.

Alright Cowboy, do we have a problem here or do I need to pull this trigger? We're good missy, I'm gonna be on my way. Good answer, I'm sorry about this and I will take care of Trish, don't you worry! Now I'm removing the gun, so you can go about your day, no hard feelings; it was just business. You don't have to apologize Denna, I would have done the same thing, yall have a nice day you hear! Ronnie tilted the front of his cowboy hat with his right hand then exited the whore house. God dammit Josh, why didn't you pull out on that fool when he hit that girl? Pull out with what boss? What do you mean with what; where's your gun? I don't have one! Awww shit, this can't be happening. Do you own one at least? No Ma'am!

Ughhh- I suggest you get one young man, you never know when you might need it. Fix me a damn shot of that Jose'! Yes Ma'am! Disgusted she took a seat at the bar and pulled her cell phone from her purse. Ring-Ring! Que pasa! Hey Hector! Who is this? Your cousin esse'! Who? Denna! Oh hey cuz, what's up? I need two soldiers out here at the Ranch. When you need them? As soon as you can send them, we have a trailer they can stay in. Oh, you need them to be on point like that? Hell yeah; I just had to check this old cowboy a few minutes ago. Okay, I will send two soldiers your way; take care of my people Denna. I will let AC know to add them on the payroll; we got you cuz. Alright, later Denna; stay safe out there! Thanks Hector!

Ring-Ring! Hello! Hey AC! Hey Denna, how's business at the ranch? It's cool; I just had to pull out on this cowboy. What! Why? He slapped one of the girls. God dammit, did Josh help you? No, that fool doesn't even own a gun! You're kidding right! Nope, it's ok though, I called Hector and he's going to post two of his soldiers out here for us. Alright, that's what's up, be sure and tell him I will take care of him. I did! Cool, everything ok now though? Yeah I'm good; just wanted to touch bases with you and let you know about that bullshit. Thanks for calling sis. Yeah it's no problem; what you up to? I'm headed over to Sam's Town to meet the guys; we're pulling in the lot now. Ok get back to business; tell those fools I said what's up. Sure will sis, talk to you later.

Hey Mick! Yes Sir! Just drop me off at the front entrance, don't park, go pick me up two bottles of Hennessy and some Alize' for later tonight. Okay boss, no problem! I'll be here for about two or three hours, I will call your cell when I'm ready. Ok, can I make a stop at the Deli and grab a bite after I get the liquor. Sure, that's fine! Just be close to here when I'm ready to go. Oh of course Mr. Cooper. Later Mick! AC steps out of the limo and enters the loud, Smokey and crowded Casino. Hey Boss, the boys are upstairs waiting. What's up Manny, how long have you guys been here? Not long, maybe 15 minutes. I booked the presidential suite on the 5th floor so we could have some privacy. That's cool, how's Sophie and your kid? They're fine bro, I'll tell them you asked about them.

Alright let's go handle this business; we have a lot to discuss. Did you order a bottle of Martel? Yeah I got two and the shrimp and lobster should be up within the hour.

Good, I'm starving, I ate some pancakes this morning but I guess I burnt it off already. Whose running the Adult store? Loony hired a few new people; he has it taken care of. Great, that's what I like to hear. Did you speak with the sisters today? Yeah Denna called me not too long ago. Is everything good at the ranch? For the most part, she had an incident but she handled it. Manny and AC finally reached the elevators after walking through the casino of locals and visiting senior citizens. Ding! Damn it's Smokey in this place; what floor is it Capo? 5th! AC pressed the 5th floor button. I heard Fat Boy is kicking ass with that meth! Yeah most of it comes from the strippers over on his side; they hit that crystal and be up for days. Ding! Take a left Coop! But you know they like that, I bet they can work four straight shifts without sleeping; getting that money. I couldn't do it Manny; my black ass needs to sleep. I know right. Oh, it's just over here AC, two doors down. What's up fellas! AC, where the hell you been brother; somewhere laying up? What up Loon; your crazy ass and hell yeah I was. See; I knew it! Ha-ha! Will what's up? Just chilling boss man, you know how I do. How you doing Duck? I'm good Coop, just hungry as fuck! Red commercial carpet covered the suite, gold curtains hung at the windows, two cream leather sofas, a love seat and chair surrounded the white marble oval top coffee table. Knock-knock! That must be the food. Let him in Manny; hurry your ass up! Shut up Loon, your greedy ass! Damn right, a nigga is ready to grub boy. Hello Sir, I have 5 lobster tails and two trays of shrimp. Thanks man, just roll the cart over there by the coffee table.

There you are sir! Thanks; here you go pal. Thank you kind Sir, Thank you! Damn Manny; what you give that boy, he acted like he wanted to kiss your feet. I gave him a fifty Loon! No wonder! Will walked over to the cart and picked up the plates and handed each of the guys one. Yall can get your own food, that's far as I go. He placed a lobster on his plate and a pile of shrimp. The others got up and followed suit. Hey Manny, bless that bottle player and pass that thing around. Emanuel picked up the Martel, tapped the bottom twice then opened it, poured himself a drink and passed the bottle to AC.

Let's get to business my brothers! Loon, what's the status over at the Adult store? We need to make a few changes AC. Like what kind of changes Loon? First we need to renovate the inside, update the product, new carpet, some new shelves and redo the peep show booths. The parking lot is good to go; we just need to paint the building. If we take care of those things; I'm sure business will increase as well as the amount of dancers on staff. All of that sounds plausible; I heard you hired a few new staff members already. Yeah, only a few, but we will pull in a better quality of applicants and more I believe; after the changes. Okay bruh; make it happen, you got a $100,000.00 budget. That should be more than enough. Hell yeah, I can make that joint look like a casino with that budget. Cool, handle your business and keep me posted with your progress.

Will how are things at Dolls playboy? Everything is straight for the most part Boss. Are you sure, no ideas? Since you asked; I think we should bring in some featured acts! What do you mean? Like some hot porn stars! Hey we have to be careful with that shit Will; don't need any extra heat from the pigs. Nah, the porn stars can do a soft stage show then set up a table and promote some of their movies after. That's a good idea; have them sell some autographed copies to the customers. I like that idea Will, what does something like that cost? I'm not sure, but I can call a few agents and get some numbers. Yeah do that bruh. How is the staff doing? I love the staff; we don't need any improvements there. Oh yeah that reminds me! What's that AC! Sam and Smiley will be down in a week or so with some new ladies. That's cool; are the new girls working at the club or the agency? I don't know yet Will; it depends on who needs them at that time. Ok cool. So how's Red handling running the dayshift? A piece of cake AC, she says to tell you thanks by the way. Yeah, be sure to tell her she's welcome. Another thing I want to add is; I'm going over to Thailand with Sam and Smiley when they leave this time. Why are you doing that Coop? I'm going to hand pick some girls Manny; Sam and Smiley are good people but I want a different flavor of girls to add with our current staff. That's what's up, I can dig that. Anything else Will? No we're cool; I'll contact those agents and get some figures.

Well Loon and Will, I decided to open a car lot as a front to wash some of this cold cash we're pulling in. Since you guys have the club and store, I'm gonna let Duck run the car lot. Manny and I have discussed it in detail already and found a building a few days ago. Congratulations Duck! Thanks fellas! Dubai, Manny will meet you and Hector over at the lot after we get the licensing and contracts done; I will be in Thailand by that time. Thanks Coop but why is Hector meeting us at my car lot? Because he has someone inside the DMV to handle the tags, titles and registration for the chopped cars we'll be selling. Oh that's some gangster shit right there Boss! You know how we do it baby, fuck the law!

That's just the extra cash end; we will also be selling legit clean cars too. I've already got the contracts set up with the car manufactures to deliver the shipments soon as the license are signed. Damn; I'll drink to that! AC you're the man my nigga! It's a team thing Loon, I can't do it without the crew baby! What kind of cars will we be selling Coop? Only luxury cars Will, top of the line baby! So we're gonna have access to Benz's, BMW's, Jags; Bentley's the whole nine? Yes Sir; Rolls Royce and Maserati's too! Duck you need a new wardrobe playboy! Ha-Ha! Whatever Loon! You know I love you boy; but we're going shopping tomorrow! Yeah whatever! I aint bullshitting Duck, be ready.

I know Denna and Nina are not here but I spoke with both of them and things are on the up at the agency and

Denna's going to renovate the ranch. She just hired some of her cousin Hector's soldier as security out at the ranch. I think you all should follow suit with that except for Dolls. Why not dolls Coop; we really don't know those guards they were there from before. It's your call Will, fire them if you want, I can care less just do it fast. Alright, I will call Hector tonight and make it happen. Ring-Ring! Hold on fellas; let me get this. Ring-Ring! Hello! What's up homes? Hey Hector we were just talking about your ass, what's up bruh? That problem is solved, rolled his ass up the other day. The streets belong to you homes! Thanks my man; I appreciate that; expect a few calls for some more soldiers. We got some more cash for you player. Hey homes, it's all love baby. Damn right Hec! Alright; get back to business Boss and tell those fools I said what's up homes! For sure!

That was Hector, he said what's up! Is there anything else you guys wanted to discuss while we're all here? Yeah what's the move with the Meth, are we distributing it to all the territories? Nah; Fat boy is the only one pushing it right now Will. Rose doesn't want any parts of it and Dupree didn't give me an answer yet? Dupree is about his paper; I'm sure he's in boss. We'll see about that Duck, he's going to let us know when he drops off his tax. Trust me AC, he's in. How's Derek doing with production? He has it under control Manny; for now anyways. I know his girl Remy has some good ass pussy though! Will you hoe; you fucked that man's girl? AC I couldn't help it, the bitch came in my office wet and horny, was I supposed to turn it down. I mean she was practically begging for it. Big Will; you got to have more control than that brother, her dude makes a lot of cash for us. That bitch pussy aint worth half the dough he makes us! Alright, she's off limits, I won't hit it no more Coop. Good, you damn whore.

Listen up, Victor is done for, Hector took care of his ass, now there is no one in the way of us getting this paper. We need to keep the bodies at a minimum; so we can get this loot without any roadblocks, yall dig. We got it! What about the cops, you know they're going to be snooping around. Damn; I'm glad you brought that up Manny! There is a new Detective in town from New York; her name is Detective Amanda Ricky. Chief Espinoza recruited her; this bitch came by my place the other night after you guys left. What the hell did she want? Duck get this; she was investigating Ashley, Lisa and Jewel's murders. Man that case is cold as a Witch's tit! Did she have anything? Manny, she had the security tape from the Towers, the one they took when they investigated the break in. Oh shit! Oh shit is right Will; she has all of us on that motherfucker! Doing what? Shooting Monk, wrapping his ass in sheets and dumping him! God damn AC; we're done! Calm down fellas; I took care of it. Don't tell me you shot the bitch Coop! Nah; I did one better Duck! What was that! It just so happened she didn't want us, but was more interested in finding Ashley's killers.

Sitting there in amazement, eyes stretched wide open, all of them slid to the edge of their seats to hear what happened next. So I made a deal with her, I opened my suit case and offered the bitch $10,000.00 for the tape. She hesitated for a bit but took the money, gave me the tape and told me to find out who killed the girls. She tried to play hard and said she will be back in 48 hours for some answers. So that dumb ass took the money! Yep; not dumb, hungry Capo! She knows I'm not giving her no fucking names; she wants to be on the payroll. Is she? Is she what Manny? On the payroll? Hell yeah, that's all we needed, a dirty cop. Ha-Ha-Ha! The fellas all laugh at the story then sipped on their Martel. Sin City, it's all ours baby! AC stands up, looks at the guys, holds up his glass then shouts. You can say that again Loony; it is all ours baby!

Ok fellas we're done; I have to meet Monica, she's crying because I haven't spent enough time with her. You guys take it easy and I will speak with you later. Later Coop! Ring-Ring! Hello! Hey Mo! What's up Nigga, don't call with no bad news. Girl, stop tripping, where are you? I'm at the Flamingo having a drink. Stay there; I'm on the way now. Ok baby; hurry! See you in a few Mo! Ring-Ring! Hello this is Mick. Mick; meet me out front, I'm on the way down now. Yes Sir. AC makes his way onto the elevator and head five floors down to the casino. Ding! As he exits the smoke hits him in the face, noise rings his ear drums and patrons clatter the aisles as he walks towards the exit. The black limo is parked in front of the entrance, his driver standing there in front of the back door awaiting his approach. Mick how was dinner? It was good Sir, where are we off to? The Flamingo and make it snappy, there's someone waiting on me. Yes Sir, right away Sir.

AC sat in the back seat, quiet, looking through the tinted passenger window as they pulled off the Sam's Town lot and on to Boulder Highway. The past years events ran through his mind as he pondered on how he arrived to be where he was now. A pocket full of money, more woman than he could handle but his heart still empty. A smirk came upon his face when he thought about his ex-wife, kids and the good times they all shared. Then just as quickly as it turned to a smile it went to a frown then back to being the cold hearted monster that he now was. How far do we have to go Mick? Not long Sir, we're on Flamingo now! Hurry it up; I told you that someone was waiting on me. Vroom! He sped up the limo, zoomed in and out of traffic, running a few yellow lights and maybe some red too. Pulling up now Sir! Thank you; no need to open the door for me, take it in! I will call you tomorrow; I'm going to be here all night. Okay Sir, good night Sir! Good night Mick! He stepped away from the Limo, stood outside the Flamingo entrance, reached for his cell and called Mo. Ring-Ring! Hello! I'm here! Hey baby, come up stairs, I'm in suite 1205. Ok, on the way up.

The hot pink lights from the Flamingo's emblem, mirrored in the black paint of the Limo as Mick pulled away and Coop walked inside. Twelve floors later, he found himself knocking on temptations door; as he closed his eyes and thought to himself. This rekindled relationship with Monica could in no way be good for him. Hey baby, you made it, come in. Hey Mo! What's wrong baby; is everything ok? Yeah, I'm good; do you have some chronic? Of course, there's a blunt on the end table, I just rolled it for you. Thanks, can I have a glass of cognac too. Sure; I'll get it for you, make yourself comfortable. Thank you Mo; you look nice! Thanks baby! When I put it on, I was debating if I should have put on some panties or not? Can you tell by looking? Turn around and let me see. Mo stops in her tracks then slowly turns for him. Her height grew six inches because of the royal blue stiletto heels that matched the royal blue silk dress that fell just above her knees. Mo's smooth toffee tone skin; looked flawless under the soft white lights as her muscle toned thighs perfectly supported her juicy round bottom. The soft silk dress bounced lightly off her butt as she turned and posed for AC. No I can't but you look good as hell in it though baby!

Thank you; Big Boss man! Ha-Ha-Ha. You crazy girl! Did you want ice baby? Inhaling off the blunt, he answered while blowing out the smoke. Yeah, a little… Did you talk to your husband? You mean my ex-husband. Yeah whatever, did you? I did, he's still upset but he'll be ok, I'm moving on. I got big plans and he can't help me get there. Oh really, is that right? Yes Sir! Turn on the rest of the lights so I can see the room, this is my first time in the Flamingo. Damn what size is that bed? It's a California king! It looks bigger that, I have a California King and it looks way bigger than mine. Well that's what the girl at the front desk told me. Why do you have the curtains closed? Because, I look at the strip enough; and I don't feel like seeing it right now. Well excuse me woman; here you want to hit this? Nah you go ahead; here's your drink. Thank you Mo. Umm-Hmm.

Coop takes a pull off the chronic; then a sip of cognac then leans back on the couch. Can I ask you something AC? What is it? Do you love Sabrina? Yeah I guess I do; why you ask? Do you love her more than me? What are getting at Mo? Just answer the question nigga! Girl you know I love you; Hell, I always had feelings for you, even before I met her. But do you love her more than me? As of right now I would have to say yes. That's fucked up AC! Why you say that; I think it's fair; we haven't been seeing much of each other until recently. So you can't be upset, she's been there, plus you were married! I aint married now! Give it some time Mo; it will all work itself out in the end. Ok AC; I here you; you better not start tripping either. Girl nobodies tripping, I always will have love for your crazy ass; come over here and hit his blunt so we can try out the big bed. Ha-ha. Boy you silly.

While you're laughing; you can start with some of that marvelous head of yours. You owe me one anyway. Give me that blunt nigga, your horny ass. What; I'm serious, you know you owe me. Monica slung her hair to the side, looked at him then took a pull off the blunt. Yeah, um-hm. AC unzipped his pants and pulled out his dick. Look; he misses you anyway; kiss him and let him know you missed him too. You make me sick, here; hold this. He took the blunt from her, took a toke and watched as Mo went done to do work. Exhaling he speaks. Yeah..., you're the best girl; I love your mouth on my cock.

Hmmmmm. Hmmmmm. Hmmmm. Slurp! Slurp! Slurp! Oh shit baby, keep on. Hmmmmm. Hmmmm. Hmmmm. Hell yeah girl, hum on that motherfucker, blow it like a horn. Hmmmm. Hmmmm. Hmmm. Slurp! Slurp! Mo lifts up and looks at him. I'm ready to do it AC, let's get in the bed. Okay, just a little more head and we can do it. Hmmmm. Hmmmm. Hmmmmm. Slurp! Slurp! She lifts up again. That's it nigga, come on let's go fuck! They rise up from the couch; he pulls her silk dress up over her head and tosses it on the floor. Mo pulls down Coop's pants, he steps out of them and they head over to the bed. Facing each other; their lips lock into a French kiss as their bodies touched, her hard nipples to his chest, his hard Johnson to her stomach. AC rubbed his hand through her hair as she rubbed hers down his back. The tension for love making was in the air, two warm bodies sharing celestial magic was upon them, a long ways from just fucking. Their pupils connected; looking deep into each-others souls, blinded to the physical attraction of one another's bodies. Two energies had merged and begun to inter twine under the covers of the comforters on this huge sized bed.

Still kissing, Mo lay on her back, legs open, AC on top, legs rested in between hers as their hearts beat in unison. Mo reached down, grabbed his black love then inserted it in her Godly womb. AC placed his hands in hers, inter locking their fingers as he started to slowly stroke. Um-hmm, this is what you missed; huh girl? Yeah baby; this pussy misses you. Ugh! Ugh! Ooooh this pussy miss you boy, oh you're so good. Um-hmm, give me this wet pussy girl. It's yours baby, it's yours. I know it girl, I know it. Tell me you love me Coop! Um-Hmm! Tell me you love me! I love you girl, I love you. Ugh! Ugh! Fuck your pussy baby, fuck it. Oh God, you're so good, fuck this pussy. Minutes turned to hours and hours turned to sweat as Monica's body finally surrendered. Um- hmm, why you're trembling girl? You're ready to cum on this dick? You ready? Ugh-huh! Don't stop AC, don't stop! Um-hmm, give it to me, cum for daddy baby, cum for daddy! Ugh! Ugh! Ugh! Ugggghhhhh! Ummmmmm........

Chapter 6, Divine Decree

Hey Deacon; unlock the back and give me that duffle bag. Hold on youngster; let me crack my back first. Man; I'm leaving your old ass at the church next time. You're holding me up! Watch your mouth Dupree, that's no way to talk to your elders. You got that right Moses; get that bag and come on; we need to make this drop and get back to business. Yeah; yeah, I'm coming! Don't catch a heart attack when you see these naked girls in here either! They better watch out; I got that OG love for em! Ha-Ha! Deac you crazy pimp; come on man; Will's waiting. "Gentlemen, please tip my dancers, the wait staff and the bartender." "Welcome to lunch rush at Dolls, on the menu today we have delicious fried chicken, macaroni and cheese, mashed potatoes and green beans." "Enjoy your lunch guys; coming to the stage we have the lovely Malibu." "This is Dj Tru baby! Let's get this party started!"

Hey Red; what's up momma? Hey Dupree; how are you baby? Who is that you got with you? I'm good Red, this is my man Deacon; he's helping me out today. Hello Deacon!

Hello young lady; nice to meet you. Is Will here Red? Yeah; he's in the office. Alright, thanks; we're going to drop this bag off. Can you have a bottle of Moet and two thousand ones for us, when we come out? Sure, that's not like you to stay and have a drink with us, you're usually in and out. Hey baby, business is more than good and I want to show old Deac here a good time. Great hun, I will have that waiting for you when you guys come out. Thanks Sexy! You're welcome Dupree.

Hungry patrons filter in Dolls, every second on the minute, in groups of two, threes, fours and five. Business men, Casino dealers, Hustlers, Factory workers and everyday Joes crash the bar for free lunch and some premium eye candy. Knock-Knock! Who is it? Dupree pimp! Hey, come in player! Will stands to his feet as the door opens; his hands placed flat upon the desk, palms down, slightly bent over, head up; looking straight ahead. Damn man, what's in the bag? Shit; this here, it's your cut playboy! Man stop fucking around; how much is it? I aint bullshitting you Big Will, we made all of this last week. Well, actually more than this but you understand! So how much is in the gym bag Pree? 60 stacks Will; it could have been more but I ran out of product Friday night, well early Saturday morning. Damn, why didn't you call to see if someone could of front you something? Playboy I wasn't even thinking, we were busy counting our take for the week.

Dupree walks over to the desk, unzips the bag and dumps the cash on top. Good job Pree! Thanks Will! You guys should really think about letting me keep Steel's old territory; I can make a whole lot more than this. That sounds good and I admit you did your thing last week, but do you have the man power to handle it? Hell yeah playboy; just give me the nod and I can increase to however many men I want. Hold on, let me call Coop! Sure! Oh Will my bad man, you remember Deacon from my spot? Oh yeah old timer from the door, what's up brother? How you doing young man? I'm good Deacon, have a seat, let me get AC on the phone here. Ring-Ring! Ring-Ring! Dupree takes a seat in front of the desk. Ring-Ring! Hello! Yo Coop, what up bruh? Hey Will, what's going on man, something wrong? No, hold on; Dupree is in the office, I'm putting you on speaker phone. Ok; go ahead! Alright all set! Hey AC! What's up Dupree; how's business?

Did you have any problems moving product on Steel's old territory? Hell nah, we pulled in 60 stacks for you last week playboy, Will has it piled up on the desk right now. 60 stacks huh!

Yep! AC! Yeah Will? What do you think about letting Dupree keep Steel's turf? Pree; do you have the manpower? I have more than enough men; like I told Will; all I need is the nod. Alright; go ahead and handle your business! Thanks AC! Yeah no problem, don't fuck it up or I'm going to be the one coming after you- not Hector! Yo, it's all good playboy, you can count on me, see you same time, same place, next week. Oh Pree; one more thing! What's up AC? I have a fresh supply of Meth that's high quality; prices are %20 lower than what you're getting it for now. Shit; say no more sign me up, have it in my re-up this time. Cool, I'll make the call; have a good day brother. You do the same Coop; Will; see you later pimp! Alright Pree, Deac, be easy! Yo Will, you still there? Yeah Boss, I'm here. Are they gone yet? Yep! Alright, I will see you at the BBQ later; I have to pick up Sam and Smiley from the airport first. We're coming by the Mansion after. That's what's up; later AC.

A lengthy line of patrons stand along-side the wall, awaiting their turn to pile their plates full of free lunch as Dupree and Deacon bypass them on the way to the bar. "Alright fellas, eat that chicken, wash your hands and get ready for some heated adult entertainment, for the next four songs, all dances are two for one." "So find your favorite dancer and tell her to get naked!" "I'm gonna slow it down for you with a new hit from En Vogue!" Hey Dupree, here's your bottle on ice and two thousand ones, are you guys staying at the bar or going to a table? We're good right here Red! Ok, enjoy fellas! Thanks Red; take a hundred for yourself. Aw, thanks hun! You're welcome playgirl! Deac, find you a girl OG!

Hold on man; don't rush me, lemme see what's in here first. Damn playboy; haven't you been looking already. Yeah; but I aint done! Okay; whatever; we don't have all day to be tricking off with these bitches, so get to it old man. Deacon looked over at Dupree, winked his right eye then waved a girl over as the music played in the background. He admired her as she approached. "What's it gonna be, cuz I can't pretend" "Don't you wanna be, more than friends" "Hold me tight and don't let go." Hey

189

poppa, what's your name? They call me Deacon baby; what's your name? Gia, poppa! You wanna give me a dance Gia? Sure, can I do it off of this song, it's my favorite. Sure, go ahead baby! She untied her thong, dropped it on the floor then slipped her top off over her head; stepped between Deacon's legs and started dancing as the song played.

"I often tell myself, that we can be more than just friends" "I know you think that if we move to soon, it would all end." So is this your first time in here poppa? Yes it is. What brings you in today; did you come for the free lunch? No, I came over with my friend Dupree, on some business. Oh ok! Gia rubbed her caramel colored thighs across poppa's penis until it became erect, then leaned in closer to smother his face in her silicon D cups. You like that poppa? God yes; can I take you home with me! Ha-Ha! How much money you got? However much I need baby! Ha-Ha! You're a bad old man. No; I'm a horny old man. Shhhh. She placed her right index finger over his lips and gray mustache to silence him. This song is almost over, shall I keep going. Um-Hmm!

Dupree; what's up nigga; where have you been; I called your ass yesterday! Hey Remy; I've been busy getting that cheddar playgirl! What's up with you? I was looking for some of that good chronic last night. I came by the church and they said I just missed you. You still need it? Hells yeah! I got a dub sack on me. He reaches in his pocket then hands her the weed. Thanks; here you go! Nah, keep your money; it's on me. Consider it an apology for missing your call last night. Cool, that's what's up! Did you want a dance? Sure; go ahead and take that shit off, let me see what you working with. Oh snap; you got a fat cat down there Remy. I likes that! Oh, you do? Yep! Pree reaches on the bar and picks up three stacks of ones, pops the bands and started throwing them on the floor by her feet as if he were dealing cards.

Hey Dupree; what's been up Baby? What up Malibu, Asia; aint nothing but getting that paper. Why don't yall get naked and join the party; that's my man Deacon that Gia is dancing for; make sure you show him some love too! The girls hastily stepped out of their thongs and started dancing in between the group, rotating places with Remy and Gia. Deacon; take some of this money and tip the girls man. Thanks Dupree; you're alright, no matter what your mother says about you! Ha-Ha! Kiss my ass Deac!

Ok keep the wheel straight and tap the gas, watch the bumper when you roll off the ramp. It's 4pm, 60 degrees and not a cloud in the sky; 5 huge car carrier trucks sit curbside on the corner of Sahara and Rainbow Boulevard while passer's by, slow down to watch the dozens of brand new Mercedes Benz, BMW's, Lexus's, Jaguar's and Range Rovers constantly pull into the enormous corner car lot. Manny and Duck stood at the entrance directing the drivers, telling them which rows to park what cars while the construction crew painted the outside of the Automobile office and showroom building. Yo! Yo! Park the Benz's on the first row, closer to Sahara! Manny; tell that fool to park that Benz on the first row with the other ones! Damn, he can't see that's where the rest of them are! I got you Duck, stop stressing brother. Hey my man, park on the first row on the Sahara end with the other Benz's. The driver looked at Manny and nodded then went to park the car.

Vroom! Vroom! Drivers drove the silver; black, gray and white Jaguar's on to the lot, one after the other; stopping in front of Duck as they entered. Yo; park those to the left; facing Rainbow! Yes Sir! Vroom! Vroom! The Jags filtered in, one car after the other, filling up the first row that faced Rainbow Blvd. Hey Manny! Yeah bro! Have them park the Lexus's behind the Benz's and park the BMW's on the left behind the Jags. Alright, no problem! What about the Rovers? Have them park those in front of the building facing the entrance. Cool! Thanks Manny; I'm going inside; Hector is on the way to pick up these pictures for my custom orders. What damn pictures Duck? Oh; I have pictures of some cars for his crew to look at so they can jack them. Like what kind of cars man? Bentley's, Rolls Royce, Porsche and a Maserati. Damn boy; you going all out; aint you! This is supposed to be a front to wash money, not a real dealership!

Manny; let me run my business; I don't tell you how to be Capo; do I? Okay, ok, calm down brother; do your thing. Thank you; tell Hector I'm in the office when he gets here. Yeah; um-hmm! Emanuel stands at the gate and continues to direct the drivers to the right locations when two Ducati 1500's pull up. Beep! Beep! Hey Amigo; what's up! What's up Hector! How you doing Chino? We're good Manny;

where's Duck? He's waiting in the office. Ok, thanks homes; the lot looks good too! Thanks! Hector and Chino, pull the visor's back down on their helmets then rode up to the building. Yo Duck! Hector's voice bounced off the walls of the empty building as he entered and shouted.

I'm in here Hector! Duck shouts from the office where he sat on a table looking at several pictures. Chino and Hec entered the empty room that was occupied by Duck, his pictures and one black card table. What's up homes; this shit is looking good; you have a lot of nice cars out there! Thanks Hector but I'm counting on you to get me these custom ones right here. He looked down at the table and pointed at the photos. Chino walked over and picked up one of the pictures, Hector follows. These are nice Duck, but we can't jack them here in Vegas.

It doesn't matter to me where you get them from, as long as you can fill the orders. My grand opening is in a few weeks and I want to have those cars here in my showroom when the doors open. Can you make that happen? Homes; I can make anything happen, we will get the cars from California; I know the perfect area. Cool; just make sure I can sell them! Duck; that should be the least of your worries, all the V.I.N numbers and serial numbers will be changed at the shop. I have some people inside the DMV to take care of the titles and registrations. The only thing you need to worry about is selling them amigo. My friend; that's what I wanted to hear! What's up Duck; you guys got that business handled already? Yeah we're wrapping it up now Manny! That's what's up; I will get at you fools later, I need to go make these cash pick-ups. Alright Capo; later! Later Manny! He gives Duck, Hector and Chino a fist bump then heads off to pick up the take from the Ranch, The Agency; The Adult Store and Dolls.

Ring-Ring! Ring-Ring! Hello! Hey Bitch, where you at? I'm pulling up to the bank now Dylan; did you make the deposit? Yeah; I got up late, so I just wrote the check for $12,000; we don't have time to do the other deposit. I hear that, my head is killing me. We partied too damn hard last night girl! Barbie you were off the damn chain girlfriend; so I know your head has to be throbbing. You had about 20 tequila shots! Damn, did I? Yep! Okay, I'm about to park and go get the money; I will call you when I leave the bank. Alright girl; I'll be waiting; remember to write the slip for $12,000! Oh ok! Barbie exits the car, slams the door, straightens her long green dress; slings her hair to the side and puts on her Dolce shades then walks inside the bank.

The security guard standing at the entrance greeted her as she entered; by tilting his head while observing her actions. Next in line please! Hello Ma'am; what can I do for you today? Hi, I need to take some money out of my account; can I have a withdraw slip? Sure; here you are Ma'am. Barbie took the slip, filled it out and placed it back on the counter. Okay Miss; give me a minute and I will have you on your way. Thank you so much! You're welcome! Excuse me Ma'am; I can't release the funds right now. What! You can't release the funds! No; not right now, I can't. Why not! Because it's over $10,000 and anytime the amounts over 10 we have to report it to the IRS before we can release it. Well aint this a Bitch! When can I get my money, how long do you need? You should be able to get it tomorrow Ma'am. This is some bull! Are you serious! Excuse me Miss, can you hold your voice down. Dude; get your toy cop ass out of my way! Fuck yall!

Barbie hastily storms out of the bank, jumps in the car and pulls off the lot. This is some straight bull! Ring-Ring!

Hello! Hey girl, did you get it? Hell nah! Why not! The lady said because it was over $10,000, the IRS requires the bank to hold funds for a day and report it to them. Oh shit; that aint good girl, get your ass over here now. I know; we're going to fucking jail aint we! Calm down Barbie; just hurry up and get to my place so we can plan this thing out. Ok girl, I'm on my way. Barbie started her car and drove slowly off the lot, nervous and scared. Scenes of her in jail passed through her mind, she was in deep and knew the end was near.

Beep! Beep! Hey watch where you're going lady! Still dazed she almost T-boned a car that had just pulled onto the lot. Tears filled the corner of her eyes at the thought of prison. Her name was on the checks and she couldn't lie about it. If the cops wanted her they had them both red handed. Barbie reached in her purse and pulled out her small purple valve of cocaine, snorted it then headed straight over to Dylan's to come up with a plan to avoid going to jail. Scared, high and nervous she continued to drive through the busy Vegas traffic trying to make it her partner in crimes location. Was this the end all be all, everything was in a daze as she disappeared into traffic.

"Lasssss Vegas! Its Easter weekend baby, 75 degrees out and you're jamming with the Mid-day Captain, The G man!" "Fire those grills up; turn up those radio's and just enjoy yourself baby!" "The Old School concert is tomorrow night and I have two tickets to give away to the 5th caller." "When you hear any song by Rick James, pick up that phone and call the Captain, for your chance to win!" "Now let's get into to some music baby..." "Boy you'll never find another love as good as this" "So you better represent, cuz my love is the shhhh" "The bomb baby, bomb baby." Nina who is that girl? Who are you talking about Denna? On the radio? Oh, that's Something For the People! I like that joint, it's jamming!

The warm Vegas sun; beamed off the chlorine filled, blue pool water in the backyard of the mansion in Spanish Trails as Nina, Denna, Sophia, Sabrina and Monica sat pool side sipping on Martini's, while Loon and Duck attended to the grill. You girls need to take off those Sun dresses and get in the pool with us! Will you crazy; it aint summer yet boy! Come on Denna, you know you want to sis! Nope, you and Manny can have it! I'm fine right here, soaking in the sun and sipping my drink. Baby, come take a dip with your husband! No, I'll pass Manny!

You guys suck! Sabrina, Nina, Monica, what about you guys, you getting in? No Will! I'll get in, it's been a while since I swim anyway. That's what's up Monica, come on and have some fun. She stands up, places her drink on the concrete by her chair then slides her yellow sun dress off her shoulders, steps out of it and walks towards the pool. Damn girl, you got back don't you! Shut up Will! Monica's soft brown skin; glistened under the Vegas sun as the sky blue; two piece she wore; exposed her six pack and voluptuous bottom. She tied her shoulder length; sandy blonde, micro braids to the back then jumped in. Hey Loon, did you speak with AC? Yeah, he's picking up Sam and Smiley from the airport, there coming over after. That's what's up, are they bringing some more girls in? As far as I know Duck. Cool! How's the car lot coming along? It's going smooth so far, just waiting on Hector to complete this special order I put in. What kind of order are you talking about Duck?

Oh just some top of the line whips. Like what bruh, be specific. Rolls Royce, Porsche, a couple of Bentley's that's it! Hope yall fools know what you're doing with them hot cars, one screw up and the Feds will be in our shit bruh. Stop worrying Loon; it's all covered, from tags to titles to the V.IN. Okay, I hear you my nigga; flip those steaks there about to stick. How's the Video store going? It's getting better, got a few new chicks and AC approved the remodeling, after I get that done, sky is the limit. Hey baby! Yes Loon! How do you want your steak? Medium well poppi! Man I don't believe you two are still together. Why you say that Duck? Bruh; Denna is crazy as bat shit and your ass is a hoe! What's gone happen when she catches you cheating! I aint getting caught! See that's what I'm talking about dummy! You gone die, don't get caught! Duck shut up and flip that other steak; I got me! Worry about you, I don't see you with a woman anyway!

Dude I'm staying single; so I can sleep with many women as I want. Yeah whatever; you mean your five fingers. Bap! Damn nigga, why you smack me in my head! I didn't; it was my five fingers. Ha-Ha! You aint funny! Hey everybody; the food is almost done, just waiting on these chicken wings than we can eat! I'm making sure Duck don't burn them! Ha-Ha! Loon laughs as he takes the steaks over to the table. Bam-bam! Did you hear that Nina? Yep; it sounded like car doors. It might be AC; Mick was supposed to bring him over after they left the airport. Oh ok! AC, Sam, Smiley and two Asian girls exit the limo and walk up to the front door of the Mansion. Alright girls; when you get inside you can go wash up and get comfortable, find an empty room to put your things in then you can come out back and meet everyone if you want. It's up to you, you can stay in the house if that's what you want to do, me and the guys will be outback. Ok Sir; thank you Sir! Yeah, you're welcome. Smiley, Sam; come on, let's go out back and get some BBQ!

Lead the way my friend! The girls journeyed up the elegant stairway to the second floor as AC and his visitors made their way to the back door. God dammit; who invited her! What's wrong my friend? Nothing Sam, just talking to myself; come on let me introduce you to my family. They exited the back door and stood at the top of the back deck, looking down pool side. Monica, Will and Manny swim in spurts while conversing amongst themselves. The others had begun to gather around the two outdoor tables to enjoy the BBQ. Hey Daddy; come on down. You're just in time. AC waved at Sabrina to signal that he was coming; as he gazed through his Burberry shades at the situation he was about to encounter. Mo stepped out of the pool, no towel dripping wet, skin gleaming; body banging. Coop, Smiley and Sam made their way down the steps to pool side.

Hi everybody, this is Smiley and Sam, our partners from Croatia, they recruit our overseas talent. Hey Sam! Hey Smiley! Everyone shouted! Well AC; you guys are just in time; the food is done and it's time to dig in. Who cooked it Loon? Me of course! Umm-umm! Oh and Duck helped a little! The plates and forks are on the table and drinks are in the cooler; some beer and sodas. Monica watched everyone take a place at the tables while she dried off. One table was full and the other only had one seat left and that was between Coop and Manny. Sabrina sat to Coops left and Sophie to the right of Manny. Mo sat in the vacant seat, piled some food on her plate and ate quietly while the others talked. Damn; I forgot about Mick! Where is he Coop, did he leave already? No Manny, he's waiting up front. I'll go get him, so he can eat some of this BBQ. Just call him Capo! Alright, where's the mobile? Right here!

Thanks! Ring-Ring! Hello! Hey Mick; this is Manny, lock up the limo and come in the back and fix yourself a plate.

Nah, I'm ok! Man; bring your ass back here, that's an order! Okay, ok I'm coming. He's coming. Lean over here daddy, you have some sauce on your lip. Ok got it! Thanks baby! Mo continued to eat her food with her right hand as she slid the other under the table then between Coop's legs, rubbing and caressing until it became erect. She unzipped his pants then pulled out his Johnson and started to stroke it slowly while he and the others conversed while they ate. Excuse me guys I need to go the bathroom, I will be right back! He moves her hand, puts his dick back in his pants, backs away from the table and gets up. Hey Mick; go fix yourself a plate, you can use my seat. I'm done anyway. Thanks Boss! No problem my man! We need to get you some suits; you can't be driving us around in that black hat and dusty black suit every day.

I'm fine Mr. Cooper! Non sense; Manny make sure you take care of Mick; get him a few suits and new mobile phone too. Our driver should represent us not look like a Chauffer! No problem AC; I'm on it. Great; I'll be back in a minute! Thanks guys, the food was delicious! You're welcome sis! Denna, pour me another drink please! I'm not drunk enough yet! Nina; don't over-do it! Girl I know my limit; now pour my drink. What you think Mick, is it good? Yeah it's ok! Ok! Man; I slaved over that hot grill to cook that shit and you're talking about ok! I'm sorry man; I was just answering your question. Calm down Mick; I'm just fucking with you man. Yeah don't pay Loon any attention; he's off his rocker. Why do you think we call him Looney! Don't make me bust you up Duck! What; I'm only telling the man the truth. The ladies leave the table and return pool side, sipping on another round of drinks as Manny, Loon, Duck, Will and Mick chill at the tables.

Ring-Ring! Whose phone is that sis? I don't know Nina; it's not mine! Ring-Ring! Oh it's Monica's! Monica your phone is ringing honey! Okay, thanks Denna! Ring-Ring! Hello! Hey what are you doing here? Who invited you? My boss lady invited me! You need to behave yourself; you can't be doing that craziness while Sabrina is here. I know; I'm sorry, I won't do it again. I promise that I will behave from now on. I aint fucking around Mo! I said I'm cool nigga; damn! Don't make me cause a scene out here in front of your skinny girlfriend. Monica; I'm about to have your ass escorted out, keep playing. I'm cool AC, damn! You promise! Yes baby; I promise. Good; I will make it up to you later! Um-hmm; you better, are you coming back outside? Yeah in a minute! AC places his phone on the kitchen counter, walks back to the front of the house and makes his way over to the Julius Caesar statue. He pulls down the arm, the secret door opens and he enters.

The elevator comes to a stop then he exits off into the vault. Stacks and stacks of money filled the shelves and center of the vault floor. He couldn't believe his eyes, Nina had told him about it but this was the first time he had seen it for himself. He hastily left the vault and went back up-stairs, picked up his cell and called his Capo. Ring-Ring! Ring! Hello! It's me! What's up Coop? After the BBQ; I'm leaving for Thailand with Sam and Smiley, when I get back I want to see a state of the art heavy duty Safe door; downstairs on this vault. This damn thing is wide open; we can get robbed anytime! Can you handle that Capo! Sure no problem; I got you…. Click!

Ring-Ring! Hello, thank you for calling Las Vegas Metro; how can I help you? This is Detective Casey, put the chief on please. Ok, please hold. Espinoza speaking! Hey chief this is Casey, you got a minute; I have some questions about this jailhouse murder case that me and Briggs caught. Sure, I'll be in the office; how far are you? Outside now Sir! Ok, come in! We're on the way chief! Casey and Briggs parked the black Crown Victoria in front of the precinct, closed the doors and walked inside; Briggs with three case files under her right arm. Uniformed officers constantly walked back and forth in the precinct assisting victims and criminals to their destinations while the telephones seem to ring non-stop.

Knock-Knock! Come in its open! Hey Chief! Casey, Briggs what you got? Well that case we took over at Clark County DC the other day; sparked some interest and we believe it's connected with two cases we worked late last year. Ok Casey, slow down, you're saying the DOA at the jailhouse is connected to two of your old cases. Yes Chief. Alright explain! The deceased at the jailhouse name was Victor Delagato, the two gentlemen murdered in the bank robbery past Christmas were the Delgato brothers. The case we caught at the video store late last year where that old guy was murdered was owned by the Delagato's. Let me get this straight Briggs, you're saying Vinny and Bobby

Delgato owned the video store, they were killed in a bank robbery after the video store murder last year; now we have another dead Delgato? Yes Chief! Well, are they related to the jailhouse body? We checked on it chief and they were first cousins, he was doing a year for larceny, his release date would have been in a week now.

Good work Detectives, head over to public records and find out what other properties the Delgato's owned and who owns it now, if there is any. Some-one had motive to see these guy's dead and if that's the case; that bank robbery was a front for a hit or worse. Jump on this thing quick detectives, I don't think we have much time, something doesn't smell right! Alright Chief, we'll let you know what we find out. Thanks; get out of here and take care of that, I need to make a call, I have a hunch. Ring-Ring! Hello Detective Ricky speaking! Hey Ricky, it's Chief! Hey Chief what's up? How did that interview with Mr. Cooper go? Oh it was cold, he didn't know anything. Are you sure about that Detective? Yes Chief! We just got some new evidence in on a few cold cases, pay him another visit and ask him if he knows anyone named Delagato and let me know his reaction. Did you say

Delgato Chief? Yes Delgato! Okay, I will get right on it Sir! Thanks; let me know what happens as soon as you're done questioning him! Roger that Chief.

Chapter 7, All things Considered

Beep-Beep-Beep! Damn Denna; it's a mess out here, when are they going to be finished paving the lot. This damn steam roller is blocking the customers from leaving. They shouldn't be much longer Monica; the inside is lovely; don't you like it? Yeah I do; I'm just ready for them to be finished. Calm your nerves girlfriend; we're not losing any money. Pussy is selling better than ever! You're right about that sister! These guys are coming in by the dozen. Exactly; so don't worry about them finishing the lot; we just need to make sure the girls are on their jobs.

I guess you're right Denna. I'm going inside to enjoy my new office. Okay Mo; I'm going over here to pay the contractor; hopefully everything will be done once they leave today. Two construction workers are in front of the ranch picking up debris while the other continues to pave the parking area. Excuse me Sir! Yes Ma'am? Here's your check, you guys did a great job! Thank you Ma'am; I'm happy you like it. He's finishing the lot now; we're going to leave a few cones blocking that last part; so it can dry. Ok;

how long will I need to leave the cones up? Just until tomorrow Ma'am. Great; thanks again! You're welcome Ms.

Well I'm going inside so you guys can finish up. Denna walked back up the new brick steps and into the newly renovated ranch. Four huge picture windows, emitted with pink neon lights displayed the girls inside at the bar and waiting area as you looked in from the outside. The walls inside held several lit poster frames that featured the ladies on duty with their names in lights. Josh washed down the new glass counter top as Denna entered the bar area. Hey Josh; can I get a Corona Sir? Sure Boss, coming right up! Hot pink carpet, covered the waiting area floors wall to wall with white leather couches through-out; complemented by platinum bar stools at the glass bar. One Corona! Thanks Josh! No problem Denna! So how do you like the place? It looks really good; clean, sleek and sexy! Sleek and Sexy; I like that Josh!

Oh yeah; I forgot to mention; we have security now! Really, where are they? Next door at the mobile home for now; they just got in. I told them to take some time to put there things away. They are armed and will be here 24 7.

Cool; I feel much better now! Yeah; did you get a gun yet? Yes Ma'am; I have it right here! Let me see it! That's a nice 45; can you shoot it Josh? Hell yeah; it's my Father's; he used to let me shoot all the time. Ok; keep it with you always. You don't have to tell me twice boss. Great; well you guys take it easy; I'm headed back to the city; see you tomorrow. Alright, bye Denna! Later Josh! Mo; hold it down baby I'm out! Ok; talk to you later!

Ding! Ding! Hello Ma'am, welcome to Angelica's! Hi! What can I get you? A screwdriver is fine! Okay, one screwdriver coming right up! Josh pulled a clean glass from the rack, added a few cubes in the shaker, a shot of vodka and OJ, shook it up then strained it in the glass. Here you are Ma'am, one screwdriver! Thanks buddy! You're welcome. Say, do you have any Latina girls working tonight? Yes, we have a few! Great, can I see them? Sure, take a walk around the corner there, all the girls are in the lounge area. Thanks man! Yeah; no problem! The lady patron; dressed in Levi jeans, Durango boots, green and black plaid shirt and cowboy hat grabbed her drink and headed to the lounge area.

The plush hot pink carpet formed to her feet as she walked towards the ladies, whom were conversing among themselves and other patrons. Gloria was bent over the arm of the couch chatting with another girl when the cowgirl approached. Smack! Ouch! What the fuck! Calm down missy, come here a minute. You could have asked nicely, you didn't have to smack my ass! That's how you mark your territory where I'm from missy. Your territory huh? Yep, that's what I said. You must have a lot of money if you want this honey. Money is no problem; let's say we go to one of those rooms yall got in the back. Oh really; you think you can handle this Puerto Rican ass? Damn skippy! Well, I charge double for girls? Like I said, money is no problem. Ok; I need a thousand to pay the house mom and we can go to my room.

The cowgirl's pale white cheeks turned red as she reached for her billfold. She pulled out ten crisp one hundred dollar bills then handed them to Gloria. Thank you, I will be right back. Well, come on I'm ready, don't just stand there cowgirl! What's your name anyway? Melissa! Nice to meet you Melissa; I'm Gloria! She grabbed the cowgirl by the hand and led her to the back. So

Melissa; did you want to get fucked tonight or you just wanted me to lick that tight pussy of yours? I'm the only one doing the sticking missy. Oh really! Yes really. Okay, this is my room, come in and get comfortable.

Gloria dimmed the lights and turned up her sounds of nature cd, with sounds of waterfalls running in the background. Well take your clothes off Melissa, come and get this pussy. As Gloria lay there on the bed watching her date get undress, her eyes stretched wide when she seen what Melissa brought to the party. And what do you think you're going to do with that? I'm gone fuck that Puerto Rican pussy! Oh hell nah! Calm down Gloria; don't run baby. Bitch that thing is like 11 inches long! Yep; and you're getting all one thousand dollars-worth. God damn; lord help me! I call him black Moses. Oh no, whew, let me catch my breath first Melissa. You better put on some of that K Y jelly too; this thing doesn't cum Missy. One hour of straight stroking!

Jesus; help me! Gloria massaged the k Y on her nervous vagina, preparing it for what was to come as Melissa stood at the foot of the bed, stroking black Moses and adjusted the straps around her waist, assuring it was strapped on tight. Oh I can't look! Get on all fours then Missy! Yeah like that; toot that ass up for me. Ummmm! Uh huh; feels good doesn't it? Ummmm! Hold on a minute! Gloria grabbed the tube of K Y and rubbed some on Black Moses. Whew, God damn; ok come on. Ummmm, Ummmm, Ummmm. Melissa reached down and pulled Gloria's hair while she punished the cock. Ugggggh! Ummm! Ummm! My stomach! Ummm! Ummm! Oh lord! Ummmm! Ummm! My stomach! Shut up and take this cock, we got 40 minutes left! Ugggh! Ugggh! 40! Let me suck it! Hell no! Ummmm! Ummmm!

Back that ass up girl, back it up! Oh my stomach! Uggh! Uggh! Lord, help me! Ummm! Ummm! Please let me suck it! Smack! Ugh! Bitch; why you hit me! Stop asking to suck it and take this dick! Ok, ok! Uggggh! Ugggh! Ummm! Ummm! Oh God, my stomach! 30 minutes left girl, don't give up now! Uggh! Uggh! Shit; put it in my ass! Ok, you asked for it Missy! Whew.... Uggggh! God damn! Take it out! Take it out! I can't take it! Smack! Shut up and stop crying! Uggggggh! Uggggh! Lord, help me! Ugggh! Uggh! Please Melissa, please! Put it back in the pussy! You're killing me. Ugggh! Ugggh! Hang in there Gloria, 15 minutes left! Ummmm! Ummmm! Ugggh! Ugggh! Ummmmm! Yes! Yes! I'm cumming! Ummm! Ummm! Thank you God! Whew..... Gloria's pussy now plump, red and swollen was indeed done for the night. Melissa pulled out Black Moses, slapped Gloria across the ass with it then laid across the bed beside her. Ahhhh.... Another one bites the dust! Smack! You ok Gloria? Um-Umm.

How you doing Sir; getting the full wash today? Yeah; hook me up player, clean the inside real good and add some of that new car scent too son! Alright; you can leave your car here Sir and wait over by the vending machines inside. Damn; it's hot in Vegas; feels like 100 degrees out this bitch! Hope yall got the AC on inside! Yeah; it's like 90 degrees today but it's cooler inside with the AC. Good; is your boss in? I need to holler at him! Sure; just ask the receptionist when you go inside. Thanks man; clean my Lexus good now! I will make sure it's squared away Sir, did you want wax too? Sure go ahead! The customer got out of the car, standing 6'4", bald head, 275 pounds, blue jeans; Timberland boots and white tee. A huge tattoo defaced his right forearm with four letters that read CRASH. Hello Sir, welcome to Clean Whips, you can just have a seat in the lobby while you wait for your car. Thanks lil mamma; but I need to speak with your Boss; is he in? Sure, hold on a minute.

Ring-Ring! Yeah what's up! Fat Boy, there's a guy here to see you! Thanks baby; send him back. Okay! Sir; just walk down this hallway and it's the last office on the left. Thanks lil mamma! You're welcome! Crash exited the lobby and entered the hallway in route to Fat Boy's office. Hey my man; are you the boss? Yeah; what can I do for you? Crash came in the office, turned around and closed the door behind him then reached in the front of his pants. Yo what the fuck! Check it white boy, just shut the fuck up and listen. I said! Sit your fat ass down; don't make me put one of these 45 slugs in it! I'm looking for AC; the word on the street; he's running things now. That buster knocked off my cousin Steel and his boy Jesse. I'm here from the rotten apple to handle business. This aint got shit to do with you white boy! Just deliver the message; tell AC I'm in town and I'm coming for his ass. You got that!

I got it! Good; let that nigga know I'm here and he better get his guns ready! Pow! Oh shit motherfucker! That's your warning!; stay your fat ass right here until I leave! If I see you come out this office; I'm spraying your employees white boy. Got it? Yeah man; yeah. Crash walks hastily down the hall and through the lobby then outside to his car. Get your ass out of the way; give me my shit! Hey; hold on man; what you doing! You need to pay! Click-Click! Ok, ok take it! The employee backed down while at gun point as Crash jumped in his gold Lexus and pulled off the lot.

Oh my God! Fat Boy; are you alright? Yeah; I'm good baby, get back to work. Ring-Ring! Hello! Yo Manny, we got a problem! What's the problem Fat Boy? This motherfucker just left my shop looking for AC. Slowdown my man; who are you talking about? Some NY punk named Crash; says he's Steel's cousin and he's gunning for Coop. How does this fool look? About 6'4", bald head black fucker, with a tattoo on his right arm with CRASH on it. Ok thanks for the message bro; we got it from here. If you see that fool again; call me! Alright Manny; if I don't cap his ass first! Hey; do what you need to do bro. But I'm gone put my crew on it. That's what it is; later Capo!

"This goes out to all the women in the world" "Especially her you know it." Yo Derek; come here for a minute! Remy can wait; she needs to work anyway. Man, that girl aint trying to work she wanna do that crazy ass dance. What dance? The one that goes with this song; she seen the video last night. Have a seat then and let her dance! That girl is a trip Will; what's going on though? Hold on D, hey baby come here; get me a Hennessy; D you want something? Vodka on the rocks is fine. You get that baby? Yes Will; I got it! "I put my hand upon your hip" "When I dip you dip we dip" "You put your hand upon my hip." Um-hm, this is the song, freak nasty or something; yep. What's the problem D; your girl is just having fun; doing the dip. Aint no problem Will, did you want to talk to me about something? Yeah; I wanted to let you know that everyone is happy with the product; here's a bonus for you. Will reached inside his suit jacket pocket, pulled out a gold envelope then slid it Derek.

Damn; thanks Big Will! Don't mention it; you earned it brother. Ha-Ha! Oh shit; are you seeing this! Ha-Ha! Yeah who is that Will? That's ILona and Vicky; them ho's can-not dance! Here you go boss; one Henn and a Vodka on the rocks. Thanks baby! Um-hmm. I'll be right back Derek; don't go anywhere; let me handle this real quick. Hey girls;

get off of the stage and follow me to my office. Who us? Yes you two! Come on; get down, come on. The other girls stopped for a second to see what was going on as the girls followed Will to the office. Ok girls; have a seat; right here in front the desk is fine. Look; both of you are gorgeous but neither one of you can dance a lick. Yes we dance! No you can't.

I think it's best you work with Nina full time; I can't use you girls here anymore. Why not here! Because you can't dance Vicky and she can't either. Go escort, that doesn't take much skill anyway. What, you no like us? I like you fine ILona but you can't make any money here. Go get dressed and I will have Mick drop you guys off at Nina's. Ok thank you; we'll go get dressed. Thank you girls; you'll do much better as an Escort; trust me.

I'm going to finish my drink; come over to my table when you're dressed and I will walk you guys to the Limo. Ok thank you. No problem ladies. So; what happened Will? I'm sending them over to Nina; ASAP. Man you're crazy; those chicks are sexy. Yeah but they can't dance, the motherfucking customers was laughing at them! You didn't see that D? Nah, I didn't. Well, it's handled now, where were we? The envelope! Oh yeah, did you count it? Yep, damn sure did, thanks again! You're welcome player; here's your girl; she can smell money can't she? Ha-ha! You aint never lied about that shit! Hey baby; what you got in the envelope? Nothing! Stop lying Derek; let me see! Remy chill; go dance or something. Alright; don't ask for no ass, when we get home either. Remy don't act like that! Nah; I aint acting! Will takes a sip of his Henn and watches Derek and Remy go back and forth. It's 10 stacks baby, that's all.

Damn; where's my half? Ha-Ha! Aint that a bitch, you better give her, her half D! Will mind your business; my man knows what time it is. Derek pulled a few bills from the envelope then handed them over to Remy. Muah! Thank you baby; I'm gone ride yo white ass real good when we get home. Yeah, you better! I got you white chocolate, I got you. Ha-Ha! You two are hilarious; I'm going to finish up this paperwork. Take it easy D; see you next time you come through brother. Alright, be easy and thanks again. No, thank you D, keep that product coming!

Ok we're ready Will! Oh shit; I forgot about you two! Come on follow me. Will heads outside to the limo as

Vicky and ILona followed. Hey Mick! Yeah what's up! Take these two lovely ladies over to Angel's please. No problem! Here you are ladies, right this way, have a seat and make yourselves comfortable. Thanks Mick! You're welcome, just doing my job.

Ring-Ring! Hello! Hey Sis! Who is this? It's Will, Nina! I can barely hear you; the music is too loud. Hold on a sec, I'm almost in the office. Hello, can you hear me now? Yeah, what's up Will? I just sent those two German models over to you; put them on full time, I can't use them over here. Why not; they're some nice looking chica's. That may be true but they can't dance a lick! Ha-ha! Poppi you're crazy, ok I got you covered. They can go on this job with us tonight. Alright thanks a lot sis. You're welcome; see you later bro.

Hey Georgia, you don't have to book the last two girls; we have two on the way over that can join us. Ok Nina; are you going tonight too! Yep; these are some special clients that booked this gig; I can't afford to have anything go wrong. So whose answering the phones tonight while we're out? Me girl, we'll just forward the calls to my mobile. Oh ok, I never thought of that. That's why I'm the boss and you're my assistant. Hey order us a pizza and some wings from Sunset; I'm starving! Ok, what kind of pizza Nina? Canadian bacon and pineapple is fine. Knock-Knock! Come in! Hello Nina! Hey girls, come in and have a seat, what's the problem at the club? Will says we can't dance! Yeah; he called me. Don't worry about it; you will make 4 times as much working here in half the time.

Go to the restroom and freshen up, get your make-up and hair right. If you need anything, I have almost everything in that closet behind you. Alright thanks, where's the restroom? Down the hall to your right! How long before that pizza gets here Georgia? Like ten more minutes. Those girls are cute, where are they from? Germany, we have two more at the house from Asia. Cool, when are they starting? Probably next week, they have to get there sheriffs cards first. Are they working with us? Not sure yet; I will have to see what they can do. Cool. Tonight will be your first big party won't it Georgia? Yes, my first. Well, just enjoy yourself, mingle with the guys and have some drinks, everything will work out fine.

That doesn't sound hard. There's nothing hard about it; well actually there will be but.... Ha-Ha! Our girls will be

222

the only ladies at the party and the clients have already paid for all of you, so just do your thing. Wow! It's like 10 girls tonight right? Almost, only 9! Are you working Nina? Yeah, making sure you guys are on the job and collecting this paper. That's about the extent of me working. Knock-Knock! Who is it? Sunset pizza! Come in! How much do we owe you? That will be $25 Ma'am. Here's 30 keep the change. Thank you Ma'am! You're welcome; you can put the food on the desk.

Oh yeah; I'm sorry; I was excited about the tip. Ha-Ha! I see. Thanks again. Yep; have a good evening young man. So, how do we look now Nina? Come over here and let me look at you two. Hair is good, make up is good. Lift your dresses! Excuse me! I said lift your dresses; both of you. I don't understand. Nina stood up, faced both girls, bent down and lifted their dresses. ILona; that's a nice shaved pussy! Vicky, what in the hell are you thinking; go in the restroom and shave that bush! Wow; you have to be kidding me; when was the last time you shaved? Never mind, don't answer that! ILona take her in the bathroom and make sure she does it right. I want it to look like yours when she's done. Ok, come on Vicky.

Damn that girl had a forest, did you see that Georgia? Nope, I was eating my wings! Give me some of those. Thanks! The other girls should be meeting us downstairs by the limo in an hour. No one called in, did they Georgia? Nope; everyone is supposed to be here. Great; it's going to be a good night. Ring-Ring! Hello, thank you for calling Angel's Escorts; would you like to book a date? No; can I speak to Nina? May I ask whose calling? Her sister! Sure hold on please! Nina, it's your sister. Hey Girl, what's going on? I'm off tonight was about to head over to the Pepper Mill; you wanna join me? Aw, I wish but we have a big party tonight and I have to be there to make sure theses chica's are working.

Well maybe next time sis; go make that money, I will call you tomorrow. Ok, bye sis; thanks for asking! Come on Vicky, come on. The German girls return to the office. Is she straight ILona; lift it up. Now that's what I like to see Vicky; nice and neat. Are you girls hungry, have some pizza before we leave. Thank you Nina! You're welcome; there are some wings over here too, if you want some. So how many guys are you expecting to be at the party? I have no idea Georgia; it's some kind of private event at this mansion out in Summerlin. Summerlin, what's that Nina? Just another ritzy neighborhood on the out skirts of town. Oh ok! Well ladies; it's time; let's get downstairs to the limo.

Georgia; you guys gather your belongings and meet me at the limo. Lock up the office too. Oh; I almost forgot to forward the calls! Nina ran over to the desk, picked up the phone then entered the code to transfer the business calls to her mobile. Alright all set; see you ladies at the car, I'm going to make sure the other ladies are accounted for. Ok Boss, we're going to clean up this mess then head down.

Hello Ma'am; I pulled the navigator out for tonight, how many girls will be joining us? 10 including me, three are upstairs and the other six should be out here already. I saw two cars pull in a few minutes ago with some ladies in it. There they are walking up now! Yeah that's them! Hey ladies! What's up Nina! Time to go make this money; are you guys ready? Yes Ma'am, let's do it! Great that's what I like to hear, just take a seat in the limo, we're waiting on Georgia and the two new girls come down. The six ladies all dressed in evening attire, took their seats in the limo as Nina stood out by the sidewalk waiting for the others.

It's about time; what were you guys doing? Vicky's greedy ass was eating the rest of the pizza? Are you kidding; come on and let's go. We were ready to leave ten minutes ago; go ahead and get in. Georgia, ILona and Vicky entered the limo as Nina followed. Where are we headed Ma'am? Oh I'm sorry man; take us to Summerlin; the address is on the back of this business card. Thank you; Summerlin here we come. You ladies buckle up and there's some fresh Champagne in the cooler, I just stocked up less than an hour ago. Cool, now get your ass behind the wheel and let's go.

Yes Ma'am, right away! As the limo pulled off the lot and made a left onto Sahara blvd, the scene changed from office houses and buildings to large parking lots which surrounded the Las Vegas Convention center and up above you could see miles and miles of water theme park rides at Wet and Wild, just above the Sahara Casino. The driver cruised across Las Vegas Blvd., passing the corner of souvenir shops then over the Sahara bridge that crossed over the Crazy Horse Too. Neon, Casino lights faded in the distance the further away they got from the strip and traveled towards the spaghetti bowl interstates.

On this side of town, things became normal, lights were white; casino's turned to four slot machines in any gas station on any corner and businesses closed at 5pm. Houses, Condo's and Apartments alike all consisted of one of three colors; beige, tan or rust with brick tiled roofs and rock or gravel lawns, some with grass to order; that landscapers actually laid like carpet and just added water. As they got closer to their destination, lawns were lit with solar yard lamps that outlined flower beds and drive ways as tall mansions lined either side of the street, with large arc windows capturing beautiful chandeliers that offered a peek inside of how the wealthy lived. A dozen other limousines filled the half-moon cobble stone drive away as men of distinction gathered in several small groups along the walk way dressed in Black tie and tuxedo suits.

Alright girls, looks like we have arrived at our destination; did you want me to wait here Nina or come back for you? No you better find a park close by just in case. Yes Ma'am; as you wish. Ok ladies, be on your best behavior and remember everything has already been paid for, so no negotiating just mingle and go with the flow, I will find you when it's time to leave. One question Nina? Yes what is it

Georgia? Who are these guys? Well, I didn't want to tell you all earlier, because you would have gotten nervous. Well spit it out boss, we're here now. This is our cities tax dollars at work. In this house you will be mingling, and God knows whatever else with Nevada's elected officials. Senators, Judges, DA's, Police, Casino owners, Union officials and so on! This my ladies, is how we keep the billion dollar sex trade going in Nevada; these gentlemen sign the bills and pass the laws to make that happen. Needless to say, be on your best behavior and do me proud!

Well I'll be damn; let's go secure our future then! Ha-Ha! You said that right Georgia! Let's go ladies, go do your thing, I will be seeing you around. Evening Madam; welcome! Why thank you judge! You're welcome Ms. Nina; I was taught to always open the door for a lady. Well you mean ladies; don't you, your honor? Why yes Nina! Ladies this is the judge, no last name needed and you will address him as such for the rest of night. Yes Ma'am! Hello judge! Ladies, do join the party! Judge stood there holding the door open with Nina by his side as the other nine beauties exited the Limo to do their part in assuring that the Nevada sex trade was indeed to be a continued success.

Why thank you judge, you know every time I see you that hair of yours gets whiter and whiter. Well, I credit that to a wife of 30 years and two kids in Law School. The stress can be intolerable at times, I must say. Judge; a wise man once told me that some man aren't meant to be happy; they're meant to be Great! And that is so my lady, that is so! Come; join the judge for a cocktail! Why; I don't mind if I do your honor! Right this way then, Ms. Nina. The huge mansion door stood ajar as they entered. A sleek marble stairway just off to the left, lead up to the second level of this 2 storied 20 Master Bedroom and bath palace. Seven of the ladies had found their partners for the night and slipped away to a place where the four walls would never tell the actions of the evening. Nina and the judge approached a gentleman and two ladies as they entered the mansion.

Why Chief; how come you're still out here in the foyer with these two beautiful ladies? Well judge; I was waiting on you. I didn't want to keep them both to myself; you would have been without a companion but as I see now, you're in beautiful company as well. Indeed I am Chief but Nina here, is just over seeing this evenings events. Hello Nina; how are you this fine night. I'm fine Chief and yourself? I am having a wonderful time, where did you say you were from; I can sense a Latin accent? I didn't say! Oh Ms. Nina; you will have to excuse Chief Espinoza here; he's a newly elected member here, he doesn't know any better. He's always on the job even when he's off the clock. It's no problem your honor, allow me to introduce the ladies. This gorgeous specimen on your right is ILona and the other gem is Vicky. They both hail from Germany; and have only been with us a short while.

Hello Ladies! Hi Sir! ILona is it? Yes sir! Would you care to join me in my quarters my lady? Yes I would like that. Great; than right this way! Later Ms. Nina, we shall speak again soon! Yes of course, later your honor! Well Vicky that leaves me and you; let's get a drink and get to know each other a little better. Okay Chief; I'm ready when you are! I'm ready now; what's your favorite drink? Vodka Sir! Why I should have known that; you Germans love your vodka! Oh; it was a pleasure to meet you Nina; have a good evening. Same here Chief, you do the same!

Nina; now all alone found herself walking the halls of the marvelous estate as the help continued to man their post by the bar and desert table. Moans, groans and screams echoed off the walls as eight of the 20 master bedrooms, captured unforgiving memories of lust, whips, sex toys and multiple orgasm's. She ventured up the stairwell, staying only a few steps behind the chief and Vicky as they entered the ninth dwelling of lust. As the door closed she passed by listening to the sounds of her girls at work. Oh yes Mama; I've been a bad boy! Hit me! Whip! Oh yeah, hit me again Mama! Whip! Whip! Nina ventured down a little further. You like that daddy; does it taste good to you? Yes baby; it taste like candy! Oh yeah; what kind of candy daddy? Cotton candy baby! Damn right daddy; eat this pink cotton candy! Ummm. I like it baby; I like it!

Oh shit poppa; you're eating the fuck out my ass poppa! Lick that asshole some more poppa! Oh hell yeah! Lick my ass poppa! Slurp! Slurp! Lick it poppa, God damn! Slurp! Slurp! Oh hell yeah. Nina smiled and continued to walk, every step she took assured her of the crews ongoing success in the sex trade. Uh huh, suck this dick bitch! Yeah, suck it you skinny German bitch. Slurp! Slurp! Open your eyes young lady and look up at me! Do you like my cock in your mouth girly? Yes judge! I can't hear you young lady! I said, do you like my cock down your throat? Yes your Honor! That's right, keep sucking girly! Slurp! Slurp! Nina paused as she heard the judge scream at ILona as if she couldn't believe her ears then continued to walk down the stairwell away from the busy girls and their customers. Nina got to the bottom and continued outside then reached in her purse, pulled out a blunt, then stood in the driveway among the limo's and luxury cars.

Damn Loon, what's that smell? Good afternoon to you too Choc; and that's the new carpet that you smell. Oh snap! It looks good! Why are all the shelves empty though? Because you guys are about to help me put the movies back up before we open. The bell over the door rings as someone entered. What's up guys? Hey Shooter! It smells funny in here! Wow; is this new carpet? Yep; you can put your bags down right here by the counter for now. Why; what's wrong with the locker room? Nothing, I just need you guys to help me put the movies back on the shelves before we open. Ding! It looks different in here, are we closing? Hey Candy and no we're not closing! Come in and help us put these movies up.

Dude, that's not in my job description. Girl; shut up and come help us! Hey don't make me drop kick your ass Chocolate! Child whatever; come on, so we can get this stuff done. Yall lucky, I got love for yall! Alright ladies; at the beginning of each row is a box, the movies have letters on the side, just match the letter to the shelf. Cool; that's easy! It is Shooter; the faster you guys finish the faster we can open. Okay, ok, are you going to help us Loon, or just watch? Yes Candy, but I'll be in the dressing room; throwing away some boxes. What boxes? Oh I didn't tell you; we re-done the dressing room, peep show booths and the hallway. Thank you Jesus; what about the bathrooms? Yes Chocolate, them too!

Well hurry up Loon; clean up those boxes so we can get in there! After these movies are back on the shelves Shooter, then you guys can come back. I'll be done in a few minutes. Okay Loon; we're on it! Thank you Choc; I'll be back in a few. Girl, I am so happy. Why Candy? Because those bathrooms had a smell to them; I hated using that thing! Didn't you smell it Shooter? Yep, that's why I always lit a cigarette when I used it. Ha-Ha! You bitches crazy; come on and let's fill these last two rows, so we can get to work. What the hell is this? What Candy? This movie right here! "Girls who like Horse's!" What, stop lying! I aint lying Choc, look!

Let me see! God damn; she got that Horse cock in her ass! Ugh! Put that thing on the shelf; who would want to see that mess! Somebody does Choc, or else it wouldn't be in here. Yeah, they're sick whoever they are! Let's just finish! Damn bitch; look at this one! What now Shooter? Can we just finish! Calm your ass down Chocolate; it aint that serious! Who the fuck do you think you're talking to new booty? My name aint new booty; it's Shooter! Fuck you shooter! Bap! Bap! Bitch; throw another box and I will kill your ass! You're lucky that shit didn't hit me- Bap! Ouch you bitch, I'm gone kill you! Bap! God dammit! Get her Choc! Get her! Stop running ho; I'm gone whip your ass!

Hey! What the hell are you fools doing in here! Stop playing around! I'm not playing Loon, that crazy ho; threw some movies at me. Who, Shooter? Yeah that ho! I was just playing with her Loon. Man, yall take your asses to the

234

back and get ready for work! I'm gone get you back Shooter; don't slip! I'm sorry Choc; I was only playing with you. Don't apologize now; it's too late! Yall two ho's are crazy! Aw shut up Candy; you were cheering her on! Get her Choc! Get her! I heard you bitch! Yeah just like I thought; no comment! Don't be scared of her Candy, you don't have to take her shit. I'm going to get dressed, I'm not even getting in you guys mess.

Ding! Ding! Good afternoon Sir; welcome to Adult Video and Peep show! Hey man, man; I,I,I,I, wanted to get, get a peep show before, before I go back to, to, to work. Do you, you have any new girls, girls. Yeah, I have a new one name shooter; you will love her my man. Ok, ok, let me, me see her, her then. Alright hold on, let me see if she's ready! Ok, ok! Loon walks up behind the counter and goes to the intercom box. Hey Shooter, you got a show! How long do you need? Five minutes Loon, send him back, booth 3! Ok baby! Sir, you can go ahead to booth 3, just slide the money in the slot when you're ready. Ok, ok, thank you, you Sir! You're welcome man, enjoy the show!

As Shooter enters the peep show booth entrance the money appears in the slot. Dressed only in, knee high red stiletto boots, her birthday suit and a red satin robe she pressed the button to raise the blind then selected number two on her cd player that linked to the booths sound system. Hello handsome how are you today? I am fine, fine. Great; just have a seat and let me turn you on baby, don't talk, just watch. It's your lucky day too, you get to watch me perform to Brian Mcknight; he makes me so horny! "I can hear her heart beat for a thousand miles" "and the heavens open up every time she smiles" Umm-hmmm, you like this handsome? Slowly she danced, moving like a belly dancer, mesmerizing her customer as Brian's vocals serenaded her away to another world. Her hands became his, caressing her breast and massaging her clit. "She gives me love, love, love, love, crazy love" "She gives me love, love, love, love, crazy love."

Fantasy became reality as the red carpet touched her backside. Shooter's right hand, caressed her wet pussy as the middle finger went inside slowly but steady, getting moist with every small stroke. Her left hand pinched an erected nipple as her back arched off the floor. In and out, in and out, one finger then two, in and out, in and out, two fingers became three. To the customer Shooter appeared all alone but that didn't seem to matter to him, his Johnson was on the bone. Her ass slid across the red carpet as she arched higher and more intense; biting down on her bottom lip as it disappeared under the top, her pussy muscles contracted. In and out, in and out, two fingers then three! In and- out, in and- out! Ummmm! Skreet! Her juices hit the window as her body jerked. Oh shiiitttt, shiiittttt! That, that was, was sweet, sweet! You, you, wet the, the- window pane.

Chapter 8, Crime Inc.

The sun has gone in for today but temperatures still roar between 110-118 degrees; sweat glistens on the legs, arms and backs of the tourist and locals as they venture up and down the boulevard of Pattaya Beach in Thailand. Gorgeous Asian girls, resembling brown and light skinned African American women seemed to populate the area more than most. Well my friend, welcome to Pattaya Beach, where the girls are plenty and the parties last all day! I hear you Sam; but I wouldn't have believed it, if I didn't see it with my own eyes. Now tell me; why haven't you recruited any of these sisters to come work for me in Vegas. My friend; they may look black but they are Thai! Bullshit Smiley; that girl and that one are black. Look at them! No, no AC, watch this! Hey! Hey! Smiley waved the two gorgeous peanut butter tanned ladies over. Now; ask them anything you want AC!

Hello sexy, what's your name? He-He-He! Why is she laughing? She don't understand you AC; she's Thai not black my friend. She damn sure looks like a sister to me.

You Chocolate Man! Ah huh! See she can speak English. Yes I am chocolate man, you chocolate woman! No, my poppa soldier! Your poppa was a soldier? Um-hum! War time! Well I'll be damn; all these damn girls over here looking like sisters got black daddies. See my friend, that's why we never bring them to Vegas. Why the fuck not Sam? Because they look like black American girls! Man you're crazy, these girls can make us a ton of cash back home. You two clowns just sit back and follow my lead; I'm picking my own girls this trip. I should have come out here a few months ago and did this. These girls are exotic, and exotic is always good.

You King, chocolate man king! Yes I am a king baby, come on let's go party. AC wrapped one arm around each of the ladies waist and escorted them down the sidewalk as the music from several clubs and store front bars, echoed in the streets. The date on his left arm wore a two piece bright yellow bikini and the other a baby blue two piece. AC walked as if he was in heaven as the three entered a long narrow dark hallway just off of the boulevard. Red flashing lights bounced off the cement walls while female silhouettes crowded the entrance way. Arms with busy fingers; grabbed at his body and clothing as they got closer to the music and smoke filled area. Lighters, flashlights and glow necklace's, spiraled in the dark complementing the beat. Hey guys; you two better grab some dates, these two are mine! Don't worry my friend; we have dates, just wait, you will see. Come, Come this way, we have reservations on the next floor.

Hey Sam! Hey Smiley, over here! Look my friend, see our dates! Where? Over there in the VIP, waving! Oh; nice ones boys. See, you not only King! We're kings too. Ha-ha! Smiley you're a damn fool, come on let's get fucked up. Hello girls, this is my friend from America; AC! Hey AC! I'm Kulap and this is Kamlai! Hello ladies, you speak pretty good English. Yes, we went to NYU! Oh ok, so you both live here in Thailand now? No, just visiting; we're both attorney's in Manhattan now. That's great ladies; what are you guys drinking over here? Oh we have a bottle of Mekong! Mekong! What the hell is that? It's Thai liquor my friend. Liquor huh; pour me a cup, let me try it.

Does it have some kick to it Smiley? It is ok! Alright, if this drink aint poppin, I'm gone need some Hennessy or something. Oh, I'm sorry Kulap and Kamlai; these are my friends, um-um. Dammit, I didn't get you girl's names? Don't worry about it AC, they don't speak English that well anyway. Yeah you're right Sam; fuck it! Here you go; drink your Mekong. Thanks Smiley, this better be good. Coop grabs the glass, took a deep breath then turned it up. Umm-Umm! Damn that was strong; is that rum? Nah, it's whisky my friend! Alright pour me another shot Sam! So you like? Oh yeah, let's do it, pour it up. Here you go my friend, be careful! Chill out Smiley, I got this, I can handle my liquor. Ok, ok AC.

Coop continues to take shot after shot of the Mekong liquor then the music got louder and his head begun to throb just a little. Hey Smiley, I want these two ladies to come work for me in Vegas. Get your girlfriend to speak Thai to them and ask them. No problem, I will take care of it. Thanks bro, damn it's getting hot in this mother! Yeah, you're sweating my friend, you ok? I'm good, I need another drink. AC poured one more shot of Mekong, turned it up then sat down on the couch. The music kept getting louder and louder, his two dates stood in front of him dancing while their gorgeous bodies glistened under the strobe lights. Thump-Thump! Thump-Thump!

Coop closed his eyes, tilted his head back then placed his hands over his sweating face. Thump-Thump! Thump-Thump! The room temperature raised 50 more degrees as the sweat turned to water flowing down his face and on to his shirt. My friend, my friend you ok! Too much Mekong huh! Ugggghhhh! Ugggghhhh! AC crunched over while holding his stomach as he spilled his guts on the oak wood club floor. Uggghh-Uggghh! Here you go my friend, wipe your face, are you ok? I'm good Sam, pour me another shot. No, no, we are about to leave, you had enough for one night.

Come on girls, we're going to finish this party at the hotel. Sam, that's the best idea you've had all day. Let's take the Party to the hotel; we got plenty of Hennessy there and some vodka too. I am done with that Mekong brother! My friend, you know want any more Mekong? Hell no Smiley, keep that stuff away from me. Come on girls! AC, Sam, Smiley and the ladies make their way through the crowded night club and back to the alley. Which way Sam? Make left AC.

"(You lied to me) all those times I said that I love you" "(You lied to me) yes, I tried, yes, I tried" "(You lied to me) even though you know I'd die for you" "(You lied to me) yes, I cried, yes, I cried."

"Once again gentlemen, remember my girls work for tips and tips only!" "So please pay the pussy bill, we have the lovely Gia on stage right now for your entertainment pleasure, getting sexy off of Mark Morrison's Return of the Mack" "This is Dj Tru, playing the hottest jams all night long, right here at Club Dolls!"

Hey Red, did you see Dylan and Barbie come in? No Will; I haven't! I'm about to fire them two knuckle heads, they can't seem to stay consistent any longer. One week they work two days, another week they work four days. Hell sometimes they skip the whole fucking week; I'm done! Just hear them out Will, maybe there's a reason. Well if they happen to come in anytime soon, send them to my office before they sign in! Ok Will; I'll let them know. Thanks Red! Hey Will, hey Will! A soft voice yelled out to him as he walked by the stage. Hey Will! Hey Remy, what's up baby? I know why they haven't been coming to work! Who; Dylan and Barbie? Yep! Why not, are they working at the Palomino? Nope, they got a new hustle, hustling banks. What you mean? They're getting money from

243

different banks by writing checks. Remy, you sound crazy girl, go get some dances or something, your ass is drunk. Ok, don't say I didn't warn you, when the FEDs run up in here.

Go make some money woman and get away from me with that non-sense. Okay, ok, I'm gone Boss! Malibu! Malibu! Huh? Put your damn leg down from that man's shoulders; get a VIP room for that! Oh, I'm sorry Will! Yeah, don't make me tell you again or I'm charging your ass. Damn; what's his problem baby? That's my Boss, he's in a bad mood today, don't mind him, he's tripping. Yo Tru, play some Tupac Nigga! Tru you heard me! "I heard you Remy, come pay a nigga!" Man I got you! "Ok fellas that was Ms. Gia, she's stepping down to work the floor and VIP area, be sure to get a dance or private from her; you won't regret it!" "Coming to the stage next we have that pretty gangster we call Remy" "Get your money ready to tip her as she starts her first set with Run the Streets."

"You can run the streetz with your thugs" "I'll be waiting for you" "Until you get through" "I'll be waiting."

Hey Red, what's up bitch! Same ol, same ol girl, where yall been; Will's been asking about yall. Handling some business, what's he been saying? Is he mad? Yeah Dylan; he's tripping because yall been in and out and not keeping a schedule. Damn, does he want to see us? Barbie, that's a dumb question, of course he does! Now go ahead and take yall late asses in the office. Alright Red, we're about to go now, I hope he doesn't fire us! I hope he don't either Barbie. Girl; come on and let's get this over with, we'll be back Red, can you watch our bags? Sure Dylan, I got you.

Knock-Knock! Come in! Well damn; look who the it is! Hey Will! Come in girls, have a seat! Man, we're so sorry; we had a lot going on for the past few weeks. Oh really, what this time? Man we might be in big trouble! What kind of trouble Dylan? First let me explain so you will understand the whole story. Alright; I'm all ears Dylan, continue! Ok a few months ago I sold my old beamer. This lady gave me a check for it for like five g's I think it was. Anyway I deposited the check into my bank account then took a few hundred dollars out. Well a few days after I get a call from my bank stating that the check wasn't good. What do you mean it wasn't good Dylan, didn't you deposit it and took money out from the check. Yep, that's the same thing I said to myself, I was confused so I asked my bank about it.

Hold on; let me make sure I'm hearing you right. You deposited the check, took money out from the check and now the check is no good. Yep! So what happened next? My account went negative for the 200 dollars I took out a few days ago! Damn that's fucked up, how long did it take for the bank to find out that the check wasn't good? Like three days! Damn; you should have taken all of the money out in that case. I'm sorry to hear that that happened to you Dylan; do you need a loan or something? No man; me and Barbie have been writing checks for a few stacks and depositing them at different banks and taking the money out from another bank across town. We got plenty of cash, that's why we haven't been coming to work Will. So what's this about you guys being in trouble? I wrote a check for 15 thousand the other day and Barbie went to take out the money and they wouldn't give it to us! No shit Dylan; it was over ten thousand dollars; anything over that amount has to be reported to the Government! Yeah; we know that now. Barbie why are you sitting there so quiet, Dylan is doing all of the talking! She's already told you everything; I just don't want to go to jail! What can we do; are they coming after us? Eventually they will be; because you fools used your real names and both your bank accounts. So it's only a matter of time now girls.

Damn, that's fucked up! Isn't there something you can do to help us Will? Why should I help you guys Dylan, this isn't my problem! Man, we can't go to jail man; please help us. How much money have you guys taken so far? Somewhere around $195 thousand! That's a lot of cash Barbie! I know but it was so easy to get. Really; how easy was it ladies? We just wrote a check out to each other and deposited the checks in to each-others accounts, then went to different banks to get it out. It was that easy Will, the only time we had any problems was when I went to get that 15 thousand the other day and they held it. Well if it's that easy; I might have a solution girls but it has to stay between us and AC. Man I don't care, I won't tell a soul! Me either!

Alright here's the plan, I'm going to speak with AC when he comes back about getting into this hustle with you girls but we're going to do it our way. First thing I want you guys to do is pay those accounts off, get your names in the clear. Will pulls open the bottom drawer of the desk and pulls out a few stacks of money. You said you took 195 thousand right? Yep! Ok take this 200 thousand, pay the banks off, get your accounts positive then bring me the receipts back!

I don't have to remind you to not fuck around with my money; right Dylan! Oh hell no; you don't have to worry about that Will. Cool; I just wanted to make sure that we understood each other. We understand! Glad you do Barbie, now listen up. After you guys take care of that, we're going to meet with some people and get you guys some fake ID's, social security cards and all that. Why do we need that? Because Barbie; you two are now in business with me and AC, consider us your partners! You didn't think that I was just giving you two 200 stacks for nothing; did you Dylan?

I didn't know what to think Will. Well, here's the move baby. You two are gonna use those ID's to open new bank accounts and I'm going to recruit a few more girls to help us out. Once you guys repay my 200 stacks plus another 75 for interest; you can leave the operation or stay on, that's your choice; we're taking this thing to Cali, Arizona and Utah it's plenty of money to be made! Well God damn Will, that's gangster right there! I'm down like four flat tires, let's get this paper daddy! What about you Barbie; are you in? Hell yeah bitch, let's ride! Ladies, just remember to come get this money before you go home tonight then pay off that debt in the morning. Bring me back the receipts and we'll discuss our game plan when AC comes back. Thank you so much Will! Yeah, no problem, now go shake some ass! Ha-Ha! Whatever! Come on Barbie; let's go get dressed girl!

Beep! Beep! Beep! Hector and his convoy of Stolen Luxury Vehicles; blow their horns to clear the turning right lane as they traveled up Sahara to Rainbow Boulevard then turned into the lot of Las Vegas Luxury Auto. The warm desert winds blow the white tarp, Grand Opening sign back and forth as it hung high above the lot's entrance. It's only 9 A.M; two hours before his Grand Opening as Duck stands out front directing the convoy of 4 cars in through the office Bay doors. Hector my man; good damn job bro! Park it at the end facing the street. So what you think homes? Did we get some hot ones or what? Hell yeah, this damn Bentley is cleaned as a whistle boy! Yeah, I had them detailed and everything homes. This black paint looks like glass, you did a good job Hector. I told you not to worry amigo! I'm gonna park so they can pull in the Aston Martin and the Rolls!

Alright go ahead; I'll direct them as they come up. Chino; what's up brother? Hey esse', this Aston is fast my friend; where you want it? Just park it over beside the Bentley; facing the opposite way though! You got it esse'! Vroom-Vroom! Hey Marcia; they got you driving the Rolls huh? Yep, it's so pretty; I love silver; so I kind of took it before they had a chance. Ha-ha! Well; be careful parking it, just pull beside that Red Aston and park facing the street. Ok Duck; gotcha baby! Vroom-Vroom! Oooooh wee! Pull that clean white motherfucker up here; let me look inside! Damn bruh, this Maserati is tighter than a virgin's pussy; how does it ride? It's smooth homes, like gliding in the air. Damn, I might keep this one for myself; go ahead and park it beside Marcia; facing the opposite direction. Ok my friend, no problem! Vroom! Vroom!

So what time are you opening the doors Duck? At 11 Hector; my staff is on the way now! I appreciate this my man; these are some clean cars; they should sell pretty fast. Hey it's no problem homes; let me know when you're ready for another order; we have to go. I got a ton of work to do at the shop. Alright Hector; thanks again! Hey punta's; let's go! Chino looks at him then shouts back. We're coming esse', we're coming! Marcia, Chino and the other driver head to the bay entrance to accompany Hector; then they jumped in the white Suburban that had been waiting on them out front.

Now this is what I call a show room! Hello; excuse me! Yes; how can I help you Ma'am? I'm looking for Dubai; I'm from the temp agency. I am supposed to start working today. Oh yeah; start what? Receptionist Sir! Oh that's right! Well; I'm Dubai and you are? Jackie Sir! Nice to meet you Jackie; follow me; let me show you where you will be working! Jackie's heels echoed through-out the bay area, every time they touched the white marble floor as she continued to follow Duck. Here you go young lady; your desk, your phone and your chair; any questions for me? Yes, what time do we open and when do we close? Today we open at 11 A.M and close at 8 P.M. Thank you Mr. Dubai! You're welcome Jackie; there's some coffee and doughnuts in the break room if you want any. Ok thank you so much.

You're welcome, and so that we are clear. Your job as the receptionist will be to answer phones, assist me, my sales team and our customers. Can you handle that? Yes Sir; most definitely. Oh, one more thing Jackie; the break room will also be your responsibility, keep it cleaned and stocked up with coffee, snacks, cups, napkins, etc. Make a list of anything that you'll need and I will give you the cash for it! Ok Sir; is there any specific kind of coffee or snacks? Hell baby; I don't really care, as long as my staff and customers are happy; just figure it out as you go. Yes Sir; I can do that! Good, now get to work; our sales team will be here shortly; be sure to introduce yourself. Okay and yes Sir. Jackie took a seat at her new desk and prepared for the long day that was ahead.

Derek come on baby; you're gonna make me late for work! Hold on Remy; let me wrap this last one up! Okay; hurry, I'll be in the car. Ok baby; it won't take long. Ring-Ring! Ring-Ring! Dammit; can I finish this damn package without somebody interrupting. Ring-Ring! Hello! Yo D! Yeah, who is this? This is Will! Hey what's poppin big man?

I need a favor! Yea what is it? Paco just bought a new Lexus Truck from Duck and I need you to drop it off! Drop it off where? I was about to bring Remy to work. He's over at the Swap Meet in North town. Okay I can do that! Cool, take Remy with you. Go to Duck's lot, pick up the truck, have her follow you to the Swap Meet then you can bring her to work after. Cool; that sounds like a plan; see you in a bit bro. Hold on D; one more thing. What's up? You got anything ready? Yep just finished like 4 orders. Sweet; take three of those to Paco, just stash them by the spare tire in his new truck.

That Lexus truck has the floor that lifts up, know what I mean? Yeah I got you. Ok my man, good looking out; I got you when you get to the club. Ok bet! Damn; it's about time baby, what took you so long? Will just called! Shit; I told you I was gone be late; come on let's go! No calm down woman; he wants me to make a run; he said bring you in after. What kind of run? We need to go over to Duck's lot and pick up this new Lexus truck for Paco. Paco! Yep! Where is he at; in North town still? Yeah at the Swap meet! Ok; let's go do it then baby. He wants three bricks too! Who? Paco girl! Shit; what you waiting on then, start this car up and let's roll. Ha-Ha! Remy you nuts! I know but you love me honey; don't you? Of course I do! I wonder if Paco got any of those new Gucci bags in; he's always hooking Red's ass up with something new!

We'll ask him when we get there; see what's good! Really D! Yep; anything for you girl! Muah! That's why I love your white ass! Hey after I drop you off at work; I need to get back in the kitchen and cook some more product; I wasn't expecting to drop these today. I need to be ready for the Re-up when AC calls. That's fine; handle your business hun; just don't be late picking me up! I won't; I promise! Um-hmm; I heard that one before. Slow down honey; the car lot is up here on the right; you need to get over in the right turning lane before you pass it. Damn; these are some hot rides out here! Oh my God Dennis; look! What baby! Right there in the show room; that White Maserati! I got to have it; oh lord! I need it in my life! Girl calm your crazy butt down, we need to sell a whole lot more bricks to get that one! Derek; it's not as much as you think hun; Duck will probably give you a deal anyway. Yeah maybe next time, but we got business to handle now. Get in the driver's seat; I'm going to get this truck.

Hello Sir, welcome to Las Vegas Luxury Auto; how can I help you? I need to speak to Duck! Excuse me; who did you ask to speak to again? Duck woman! Duck! There must be some kind of mistake Sir! Is the owner in Ma'am? Yes Sir he is! Can I speak with him please? Sure; one moment! Mr. Dubai; there's a gentlemen here to see you! Ask his name Jackie! Excuse me Sir, what's your name? Derek Ma'am! He says Derek Sir. Send him back. Okay Sir; you can go in now. Thank you Ma'am! Derek my man; what's up, how's business? It's great Duck; how's the car business going? Couldn't be better brother; couldn't be better! Come on follow me around back, the truck is back there. Jackie; I'm going out back for a minute; if anyone calls; take a message and tell them to call back in 15 minutes. Ok Sir!

So Derek; did you see anything on the lot that you liked? I saw a few! Brother, you can get anyone you want; which one did you like most? Remy saw that Maserati and lost her damn mind. Yeah, I did too when I first seen it! I tell you what; bring me 60 stacks and it's yours. Man; quit bullshitting! Does it look like I'm playing D! Nope! Brother you're family; we take care of our own, plus I only paid a little for it; so I will be making a great profit. Here's the Lexus right here; it rides smooth and has a quick take off, so don't get a ticket on the way to the swap meet. It's clean as hell too! Yep; Paco went crazy when he heard I had some over here; that fool called me 3 A.M this morning. Damn, no shit! That boy got issues; tell Remy to pull around here so you can put that package under the floor. Ring-Ring! Hello! Baby; pull around back! Ok honey; I'm coming!

That Maserati would look good on you though brother! Yeah; hold it for me; I'm gone surprise Remy; get it for her birthday! See that's what I'm talking about my man; spend some of this money we're out here making. We can't take it with us! Hey Duck! Hey Remy; how are you doing today? I'm good man; where yall want this? Just put them right there by the spare tire; lay them side ways around it. Cool; that should do it; you can close it now D. Alright I have to get back to work, you guys drive safe and I will holler at you folks later! Ok; bye Duck! So did you ask him honey? Ask him what Remy? About the car! Oh yeah; he already sold it! Aw man; that sucks; guess it wasn't meant to be. Yep, guess not! Come on get in the car and follow me to North town, let's get this job done. Alright; let's roll white boy!

15 minutes, a few neighborhood changes and North Las Vegas cop cars later. Derek pulls in to the parking lot of the swap meet located on the side of town that was so notorious for its crime; that the city implemented their own police force. Ok baby; stay here with the cars; I'm going in the office to get Paco. Why are you going in the office; he has a store inside right? Why would you go in the office looking for him? Remy; Paco owns the building; he leases the spaces out for stores. That's why I'm going in the office; so stick to what you do and let me handle this! Damn; my bad honey; I didn't know. Yep just wait here; I'll be right back. Hello Sir; welcome to North Las Vegas Swap Meet; are you interested in renting a space. No Ma'am; I have an appointment with Paco. Ok; what is your name Sir? Derek! Hold one moment! Ring-Ring! Hello! Yes; there is a gentlemen name Derek here to see you. Alright; tell him to meet me in front of the building; I'm coming out

now. Sir; he asked that you meet him out in front of the building he's on the way outside now.

Sure and thanks a lot! You're welcome Sir; have a nice day! D exited out onto the parking lot and waited for any sign of him. Amigo! Over here amigo! What's up my friend, where is it! Hey Paco; it's right over here man. They approached the silver Lexus truck as it sat there clean, waxed and all shiny. Did it drive good amigo? Oh yeah, smooth as water. Derek; I hear that you're the man now with the magic potion. Is that true? I do my best! No my friend; the streets say your product is the best product; did you bring my three horses? Yeah; there in the back! Good; if it's as good as everyone says, I will need four, same time next week. Ok; just let AC, Manny or Will know and I will have it ready. No, No, No Amigo; I am talking to you right now. What's da matter; you got no balls for yourself; huh? I have balls but I also have a business arrangement with AC; and I aint fucking crossing AC! I love my life and don't plan on dying anytime soon Paco, how about you? I love my life too amigo; but I got balls my friend! Big ones too! Look man; if you want more, go through the right channels and you will have it. Other than that, be careful out here;

you keep carrying on this way and you will be dead soon. Don't be a dumb ass and cross AC; meanwhile, enjoy your new ride and that product! I'm out; I got shit to do; see you around Paco! Derek opens the passenger door of Remy's car and jumps inside. Later amigo; think about what I said! You only live once my friend, only once.

This fool has a death wish! What's wrong hun? Nothing Remy, just drive baby; let's get you to work!

As the warm night falls over sin city, the large bright orange guitar; standing on display; illuminates the corner of Paradise road and East Harmon as Rose and Manny exits her yellow hummer parked in front of the valet. Hello folks; welcome to the Hard Rock; are you checking in or just visiting us this evening? Just visiting! Ok Ma'am, here's your ticket; please hold on to that and present it when you're ready to leave. Thank you! So Manny; how are things since you made a career change? Things are great Rose; couldn't be better! I must admit, your boss has a knack for business. I never made this much money under Vinny and Bobbie's rule. I'm glad that you're happy Rose; what time is this guy meeting us? In about 15 minutes! The two of them stand inside the entrance; gazing over the floor as patrons gamble, drink, celebrate and weep. Come on Rose; let's go to Mr. Lucky's and wait for him. I want one of those good sandwiches anyway. Yeah I can use one too!

Hold on; let me make sure everything is on point. Rose walked over to the glass case that a held some items from the artist; formally known as. You look good Rose! I know that honey but I have to see how I look one more time before this meeting. Manny folded his arms and watched as she adjusted her blue, body fitted dress and twirled her white pearls to sit perfectly upon her chest. Rose stepped back a few feet to check the appearance of her white Louis opened toe heels then adjusted her white pearl bracelet to fit a little tighter. Rose! Bring your ass on; I'm hungry! Ok, ok, I'm ready; let's go!

Woman; you are too much! Why because I like to look good Manny? No because you're slow! But I'm never slow with that cash; am I daddy? Ha-Ha! You got me there; that's always on time. Hello; welcome to Mr. Lucky's; you may sit wherever you like! Thank you young lady! You're welcome Ma'am. Did you bring the money with you? Of course Rose; by the way, is there anything I should know about this union president? No; he doesn't talk much; just introduce yourself; better yet; I'll introduce you. Just hand him the envelope then he will be on his way. Sounds good to me; is he going to call you when he gets here? Yeah he will. Hello folks; welcome to Mr. Lucky's; are you guys ready to order or did you need more time? I'm ready baby! Ok Sir; what are you having? Let me get the Reuben with some fries! Alright; and for you Ma'am? Roast Beef with fries! I have one Reuben and a Roast Beef with fries, anything to drink?

Yeah; can I have a root beer? Yes you can Sir! Ma'am? Water and lemon is fine baby! Ok I will be back with your orders shortly. Thank you baby! Ring-Ring! This is him now Manny! Ring-Ring! Hello! Hey Rose; I'm walking in the door. Ok; we're at Mr. Lucky's! Thanks; see you in a bit. How long has this guy been Union Pres? About 7 years now; he's in too deep; aint no turning back for this poor soul. That money has him trapped! Hey Pres; over here! Hello Rose! Sir! How are you guys doing? Pres a tall 6'4" slim gentleman; wore a couture black suit with a white shirt and black skinny tie. His complexion was in need of much Sun and his head could have used a hair piece to cover his obvious balding spot that he raked a few strands of hair over. Beady blue eyes, pierced through his large square framed glasses as stubble traces of hair occupied his five o'clock shadow. Have a seat Pres, we just ordered some sandwiches; did you want one? No; I'm fine! Well this is Manny; he's one of the guys that you will be dealing with from now on. If you have any problems he can solve them; all prior arrangements are as they were; I keep my same dealers and casino's and move the same product as always. Sounds good to me Rose! Manny reaches in his jacket pocket and pulls out the white envelope that held the 40 stacks.

Nice to meet you Pres; are you sure you don't want anything? Thanks for asking but I'm fine; I need to be leaving soon, I have another meeting to attend. Manny placed the envelope on his lap, unwrapped his silverware, took the white cloth napkin and placed it over the money then slid it across the table to Pres. Rose it's always a pleasure and it was nice to meet you Sir. You guys enjoy your sandwiches, I have to be going. Pres stood up, grab the napkin, slid out the envelope then left the table. Damn that dude was quirky! He's harmless Manny; don't get yourself all worked up. Ok folks! Who had the Roast Beef and fries? Right here young lady. Here you go! Thank you! Reuben and fries for you Sir! Thanks baby! One water with lemon for the lady and a root beer for the gentleman. Is there anything else that I can get you guys? Nope we're good baby! Okay enjoy your meals and let me know if you need anything.

Chapter 9, Prodigious Summer

"Ladies and Gentlemen; this is your pilot speaking, please fasten your seat belts and bring your seats to the upright position." "Today's temperature in Las Vegas is 102 degrees; we will be landing momentarily; we ask that you remain seated until the plane comes to a complete stop." "If you're visiting, enjoy your stay and win lots of money!" "If Vegas is home for you; we would like to say welcome back and welcome home." "The current time is 4:30 P.M!"

Thank you for flying with us Sir; enjoy your stay! You're welcome Ma'am; have a good evening, I enjoyed the flight! Ring-Ring! Hello! Mick; where are you brother; I just landed. I'm waiting outside of concourse C; Mr. Cooper. Great; see you in a bit!

Hello Sir; how was your trip? It was great Mick; had a good time; anything interesting happen while I was gone? No Sir; all is normal in Sin City! Cool; take me to the Towers; I need to wash up and get out of these clothes. Yes Sir; right away! Damn I was only gone for a few days;

when did they put that Tyson billboard up? It just went up yesterday Sir; the fight is on June 28th! Oh that is right; isn't he's fighting Holyfield? Yep! This should be a good one; isn't it a rematch? I believe so Mr. Cooper! Will you be attending the fight Sir? Hell yes; all of us went last time, when he beat Seldom down! Oh that was a crazy fight Sir; it didn't last two minutes! Yeah it was Mick; I wouldn't have believed it; if I didn't see it with my own eyes. I don't think this one is going to end that fast though! I agree with you on that Mick; Holyfield is a true fighter.

Okay Sir; we're here; did you want me to get your bags? No man; I got it; thanks; here's something for your troubles. Thank you Mr. Cooper! You're welcome man. AC exits the Limo, stretches then heads inside the Towers. Hey AC, you're just in time! Why you say that David! There's a woman waiting for you in the lobby. What woman? She said her name was Ricky! Awww shit; can a nigga get home first before going through this drama! Where is she man? Sitting by my desk Sir! Thanks Dave! Detective Ricky; how nice of you to drop by! What can I do for you? Hello Ac; how was your trip? What trip would that be Amanda? The one you just came from; I've been calling you for weeks and days on end! Why haven't you returned any of my calls? I'm a busy man Detective; come with me; we can talk at my place. I'm beat; need a shower and a cold beer.

I hope you haven't been waiting long! Not long at all, AC! Did you find out anything on those murders? You know I asked around and no one seems to have seen anything Detective! I have some associates of mine looking into it; to see what they can dig up. Oh really? Yes really; I'm a man of my word Amanda! I sure hope so Mr. Cooper! What did you mean by that Detective? I just would hate to find out that you were lying to me AC. Coop stood in the elevator door waiting for Amanda to enter. Are you coming Detective? Yes; I had to make sure I had my radio but I'm ready Mr. Cooper. So where did you go? I just went to visit some friends for a few days. Don't you ever visit friends Amanda? Not lately I haven't, these cold cases are kicking my butt. Ding! This is our stop Detective. I was wondering if I could talk to your associates. Hold that thought; let me open this door! Here we go; come in detective have a seat. Now here's the deal Amanda; word on the street is that it was some kind of robbery that went bad. That's all anyone is saying. Now who committed that crime; I have no idea!

Coop places his bags by the door then walks in the kitchen to get a beer. Care for a cold one detective? No I'm fine! Are you sure? Yes I'm sure! Ok; I'll be right back; I have to get something from y room; you can turn the TV on if you want. Thanks but I'm good! My; aren't you in a bad mood today! Here; this should cheer you up! What's this! What does it look like detective? Money! Exactly; it's the same amount as before. Don't expect any special favors for this AC! What favors Detective Ricky; I'm just making sure your stay in Vegas is pleasant. Yeah whatever; do you know of any Delgato's? No; can't say that I do; why you ask? Chief Espinoza has this crazy notion that they are connected to some cold cases. Oh; I never heard of them. Did you guys ever find out who those guys were that got burned up in that hummer outside of Caesar's early this year? Yeah; it was some guys from New York; Chief said one went by Steel; ones name was Jesse and I forget the other guy name. Damn; that's fucked up! Why; did you know them AC? No but I heard of them on the street, maybe seen them out a few times in the city.

Well; I have to be going Mr. Cooper; let me know if your associates come up with any more information on those murders. I sure will detective; have a good evening and don't spend all of that money in one place now! What money are you referring to Sir; I don't see any money! Oh; I stand corrected Amanda; have a good evening! You do the same Mr. Cooper and call me if you hear anything! I will! AC locked his door, slipped off his shoes, took a seat on the couch and sipped on his beer. In his mind he knew Detective Ricky was going to be a problem if he didn't figure out something soon. He placed his feet on the coffee table, leaned back and looked up at the ceiling contemplating on what to do about Amanda.

Hello Ma'am; welcome to Las Vegas Luxury Auto; I'm Dubai. Is there any particular car that sparks your interest? Hi Dubai; I'm Karen; I want to test drive that new E class! Which one Ma'am; the E 420 or the E 320? The 420; black! Wow, a lady that knows what she wants! Yes I am; can I take it for a spin? Sure; hold on; I will get the keys. Thank you so much; I'll be right here waiting on you Dubai! Karen stood patiently by the row of Mercedes; gazing over the lot like a kid in a candy store. Her long satin black hair blew across the bottom of her face as her big orange straw hat protected it from the beaming heat. Karen's wedge heel sandals propped her 5'5" frame up just a few more inches; displaying her tone legs and muscular calves just below the matching orange sun dress she wore. Her shiny lip gloss, sparkled in the sun while her brown skinned gleamed from a soft layer of coco butter.

Okay gorgeous; we are all set, let's take this black one on the end here. Great, it's so pretty! Yeah isn't it! Duck opened the driver's side door to let Karen get under the wheel. Now, how does that feel? I like it, it feels comfortable! Good; now let's take her for a spin! He runs around to the passenger side as she reached across the seat and opened the door. Thank you Karen! You're welcome, now give me the keys! Ha-Ha! Why of course; here you are. Thank you!

Alright Karen; let's go up Sahara, down the strip then over to Sunset; we can park over at the landing site then you can tell me what you think. That's a long way Dubai; are you sure you won't get in any trouble? Who me trouble, nah baby; this is my car lot! Oh; is it. Karen smiled then titled her head in his direction. Yes Ma'am. Well ok then boss man; let's be going. I like this cream interior; how's the sound system? It's pretty good, turn it on. "What's up Las Vegas; this is your mid-day homie; DJ Tech" "Get your outfits ready and stack your money; Tyson and Holyfield will be going at it on June 28th." "I don't know about yall but my money is on Mike!" "The city will be crazy with celebs and after parties as only Vegas can do it; the players playground!" Damn, that's going to be a good fight right there! I don't care one way or the other myself. Why not Karen? I'm not a fan of boxing that's all. Why not? It just never sparked my interest. Do you watch any kind of sports? Yep, basketball and soccer! Cool! Oh my bad Karen, slow down and get in your left lane, we're taking this left on Sunset.

About two miles down on the left, there will be a parking area in front of the landing strip; just pull in there. Okay I can do that. So what do you think so far? I love it! Well do you want to buy it today? I do but I have to find a bank to finance me. I'm sure we can make that happened Karen. You sure sound really confident Dubai. I mean; it's what I do. How's your credit? It's ok! Why isn't your man here with you anyway? Because I don't have one! Wow, I'm surprised! Why are you? A nice gorgeous lady like yourself shouldn't have a problem getting a date. That's the problem Dubai, I don't want a date. I want a man. Pull in right here on the left Karen.

I'm sure you can have one if you want Miss. I wish it were that easy sir but it's not. So what kind of down payment do I need to come up with? How much can you come up with Karen? Hmm, whew it's hot out, can I turn up the AC. Sure, go ahead. Karen placed the car in park as they sat there in front of the landing strip, watching the planes land and take off. She removed the large orange straw hat from her head, shook her hair down, opened her legs just a little and slid up to the edge of her seat, back arched, head resting on the cream leather seat, right hand on her inner thigh. So what about you Dubai? What about me? Are you single as well? Yes I am! And why is that? Because I love pussy and can't seem to stay with one woman!

Well maybe that's because you haven't found the right one! I wish I find her, this single shit is for the birds. Speaking of pussies, mine is so hot right now, you don't mind if I let her get some cold air, do you? Ugh-sure, go ahead! She pulled her linen sun dress all the way up to her

271

waist, exposing bare ass and pussy. Damn Karen, you always walk around free Willie. Ha-Ha! Free Willie? Yep, everything hanging out, just free, that's what I call it! Yes I do, if that's what you call it. Umm, she's throbbing now, you want to touch it? Uh... Give me your hand! Duck surrendered his left hand to Karen as she slowly guided it down towards her vagina.

Umm, you're so wet. Yeah, you're making me wet boss man, you and this E 420. Is that right, we turn you on? Fuck yeah; I love a man with power and a sexy motherfucking car too. I want you more and more every time I think about it! Think about what Karen? Me riding you over there in that passenger seat! Shit; don't think about it, bring your pretty ass over here.

Ummm-Ummmm. Rub my clit some more, get it juicy so you can just slide in me baby. Dubai gently inserted his two middle fingers inside Karen's soaking wet hot box, in and out, with just a few seconds after each stroke. Pull your cock out baby, I'm want it in me! He unzipped his pants with his right hand letting his erection take command. Hell yeah, I like that, do you have a condom? Oh hold on. Duck pulled a condom from his back pocket, slid it on then guided Karen over to him. The AC still on high, blew strong gust of wind across their warm bodies as she straddled Duck while facing the front window. Um-hmm, Um-hmm, Um-hmm, take this pussy! Um-hmm, Um-hmm, Fuck this wet pussy!

This some good pussy girl! Um-hmm, good pussy! You like this good pussy! Don't you like this good pussy! Hell yeah, I like this pussy! Um-Hmm, Um-hmm, Um-hmm! Damn, ride it girl, your fine ass! Um-Hmm, Um-Hmm, Um-Hmm! Knock-Knock! Oh shit! Knock-Knock! Sir! Sir; Roll down the window please! What in God's name do you guys think you are doing? Ma'am, get up and get in the driver's seat and let me see your ID's. Come on move it! Sir, do you know this woman? Yes I do officer! What's her name Sir? Karen! Karen what; do you know her last name? No I don't sir! Ma'am; ID please! Here you are officer! Thank you! Ok Karen, do you know this gentleman? Yes Sir! What's his name Karen? Dubai sir! Sir; your ID please! Ok people, I could have given you guys a ticket for prostitution or public nudity but I ran the plates and see that this is a dealers vehicle. Dubai, are you the dealer? Yes Officer! Is this your girlfriend? Yes it is officer, she just came to visit me on my lunch break and…. Yeah, yeah, put your dick in your pants and take this car back to the lot. Get a room next time! Sure no problem officer, we're so sorry!

Yeah, yeah don't mention it! Have a nice day! Oh my God Dubai! That was close! Ha-Ha! Close aint the word, I almost pissed myself when that office knocked on the window. Me too Dubai! Ummm it was good though, wasn't it? Oh yeah, you got some good pussy woman, we have to do this again. How about later tonight Dubai, you can pick me up from my place! Sure why not, it's a date! Now let's get back to my lot!

Traffic is almost at a stand-still on the strip as the stretch Navigator comes to a complete stop. Hey Mick; let us out here my man! Come on Sabrina; hurry up; we're holding up traffic. I'm coming AC, hold your horses! Loon put that glass down and come on! Denna, don't rush me woman! Beep-Beep! Come on Loon! I'm coming, I'm coming! They can wait; it's not like traffic is moving on the strip anyway. Boy why are you such an asshole sometimes? Hey; I'm your asshole though baby. Yeah, whatever Loon! Hey you guys ready to have some fun?

Coop, fun is my middle name player; let's go win these girls some stuffed animals and shit! Larger than life size white statues of lions, tigers and Clowns towered over the entrance way to the Circus-Circus, Casino.

I don't know about you Sabrina; but I can do without the shit! Ha-Ha! Me too Denna! Aww, yall know what I mean? I know you fools need to hurry up; it's hotter than hell out here! Well go inside daddy; we're right behind you. AC, Sabrina, Denna and Loon enter the big circus tent casino. So what are we doing first daddy? Let's try the skeet ball baby. Ok I'll meet you back over there. I'm going to get some tokens. Hey Loon, take the girls to the skeet ball game bruh! Alright, get me about 100 in tokens. Just 100? Yep, that's all I need man!

So baby you wanna go to the fight? Of course I'm going; that was a crazy question Loon. I remember how pissed you were last time we went, that's why I asked. Oh that was over too fast; I sure hope it doesn't end like that this time. I think this one is going to be a better match up, Holyfield can hold his own. I sure hope you're right Loon, all that 45 second bull aint cool. What are you wearing this time Denna? I don't Know Brina, we should go shopping.

Yeah we should, when do you want to go? I'll let you know tomorrow, I have to see if sis wants to go. Alright girl; just call me when you find out! Ok people, let's play some skeet ball! Here you go Loon, 100 tokens. Thanks Boss!

Hello ladies and gents, welcome to Circus-Circus, skeet ball challenge! Are you guys ready to play? Yep, let me get 7 balls. Ok Sir, here's your seven balls, roll when you're ready! 25 gets you a key chain, 40 gets you a mug, 60 gets you a hat, 80 gets you this small lizard and 100 gets you this huge Panda! Daddy, I want that Panda! Come on AC; roll that 100 player! Coop steps back, takes his stand then rolls his first ball. Oh-oh-oh-oh! 60! Here you are Sir, your lovely clown hat! Man; get that out of my face! Come on daddy, you can do it! AC takes another stand, pauses then releases his second ball. Oh-oh-oh-oh-oh! 40! Dammit! Here's your mug Sir! Sit it down man! Come on AC, let's do it bruh! Come on poppi! Come on daddy! Coop steps back once more, gathers himself the rolls his third ball. Oh-oh-oh-oh! 100! Yeah! Just like that; give me my damn Panda! Here you are Sir, congratulations! Thanks, here you go Sabrina. Yes; I knew you could do it!

Come on Loon, let's see what you got! Man; this won't take long, watch this! Loon walks over to the game, prepares himself; then rolls his first ball. Oh-oh-oh-oh! 100! Now that's how you do it brother! First time! Here you are Sir! Thanks bruh! Here you go Denna! Thank you baby! Ring-Ring! Ring-Ring! Daddy; your mobile is ringing. Ring-Ring! Hello! Hey nigga, what you doing? What up Mo; I'm just kicking it over at Circus-Circus, everything cool at the Ranch? Yeah, I was just thinking about you that's all. Oh really; what exactly were thinking about? How you put it on me that night at the Flamingo. Oh that night was crazy, but I'm gone have to call you later though. Why, you got your skinny girlfriend with you? Don't start Mo; you know what it is. Yeah, yeah whatever nigga! Click!

Hey Boss; you alright? I'm good Loon what's up? You look pissed! I'm cool, that was Mo's jealous ass. Man, you're a whore. Loon I know your ass aint talking! AC; you need to slow down on the pussy bruh. Loon shut up! Hey ladies, what you guys want to do next? Let's go shoot some hoops daddy. Brina; can you shoot girl? Yeah girl, I played some in High school. Ok that's what's up, let's go shoot then, first one to 15 points win. I have to see this

Coop; your girl says she can shoot! I got $100 on Denna! I'll take that bet Loon. Sweet, you might as well pay up now bruh; Denna aint losing. Don't speak too soon Looney boy. My girl might bust that ass! Well we're about to see.

You two knuckle heads need to shut up, me and Brina are just having fun, it doesn't matter who wins. Are you ready Brina? Yep! Daddy; put some tokens in the machine will yah? Oh my bad baby, here you go! Loon; load it up baby! I got you sexy, hold on. Alright girls, all set, start at the buzzer. First one to 15 shots win. 5,4,3,2,1,Go! Denna pulls up then releases her first shot. Swish! Brina follows. Swish! Denna misses the next and the next. Brina hits the next three. Denna hits her next two shots. Sabrina hits one then the other rims off. Denna hits her next two. Ok, what's that AC? Ummm-5 to 5! Sabrina hits her next two then misses two. Denna hits four in a row. Sabrina follows up with three in a row. Denna misses her next two. Sabrina hits another three in a row. Come on Sabrina, you can do it baby! Denna hits two in a row then misses one. Sabrina shoots a brick! Denna bust two more! Sabrina shoots a set shoot from three steps back. Swish! Denna shoots one off the glass. Swish! Sabrina takes two steps forward, picks up a ball then releases it with a high arch. Swish! Yeah baby! Yeah! Pay up Loon! Pay up! Aww man, come on Denna, what happened baby? Loon shut up and pay then man, no one told your ass to bet anyway! Here's your money Coop! Nah keep it, you can buy us lunch, I'm hungry anyway let's go to the buffet. Yeah I am too, alright let's go then.

Damn baby, I had no idea that you could shoot hoop! I can do a little something. Well you just won us some lunch, I'm gone have to take you out to Sunset and shoot a few games. Man, don't be getting happy because your girl lucked up, she aint good enough to get on the court. Loon haven't you learned your lesson already, shut your pie hole! Ha-Ha! That's right Loon, listen to your girlfriend! Whatever AC, that shit ain't funny.

"Good afternoon Las Vegas; tonight is the night of the big event!" "Iron Mike takes on Evander "Real Deal" Holyfield" "it's gonna be a hard hitting rumble tonight at the MGM baby!" "Ladies pull out best dresses; Guys get out those three piece suits, the whole world will be watching." "And if you're in town for the fight!" "Welcome to Sin city baby!" Daddy; get up, what do you want for breakfast? I don't care baby; whatever you feel like cooking. I don't feel like cooking anything! Then call room service baby. What time is it anyway? Almost four o'clock daddy!

Damn, hand me the phone please. Here! Ring-Ring! Thanks for calling the Towers, this is David, how may I help you? Yo Dave, it's AC! Hey Mr. Cooper what can I do for you? Call our guy at the MGM and have him reserve the first two rows on the south side of the ring. No problem Sir, I will take care of that right away! Is there anything else? Yes, send the tailor up to fit me for a tux and my lady a dress. Ok Sir, I'm on it! Thanks David! You're welcome Mr. Cooper! So is everyone going to the fight tonight daddy? Yep! Damn, how many people is that? The entire crew baby, I don't know how many, do me a favor and write everyone's names down, I have to take a piss. Alright daddy, I will be in the kitchen. Ok Brina.

Ring-Ring! Towers; how may I help you? Hey David, it's Sabrina! Hello Ma'am, is everything ok? Oh yes, I just wanted to order some waffles and bacon. Sure no problem, will Mr. Cooper be having anything? Yeah the same! Ok, two orders of waffles and bacon, I will have the waiter bring it up shortly. Thanks David, you're an angel! You're welcome Ma'am! Hey how many names you get baby? Oh I just started writing daddy; I ordered us some waffles and bacon. Cool that will work.

Let's see we have Loon and Denna, Manny and Sophia, Duck plus one, Nina and Will! That's eight people; oh 10 including us. What about Derek and Remy baby? Oh yeah, I forgot about them two! So 12 is the total number. Ok now call all of them and tell them to meet us downstairs in the lobby at 7:30 tonight, we're taking the stretch Navi from here. Alright I have to pee, where's the cordless? I'll call them while I'm in the bathroom. It's on the couch baby. Knock-Knock! Who is it? Room service! Damn that was fast! It's open; come in! Hello Sir, where did you want your breakfast? Just place it on the table man and take that 10 dollar bill with you. Ok and thank you Sir! Yeah, you're welcome.

The warm sun rays beamed through the balcony doors and shined off the sterling silver tops that covered their food. The tourist population tripled overnight, traffic had gotten terrible and taxis and limos multiplied by the thousands. Visitors looked like ants down below walking up and down the strip as AC watched from above. Ok daddy, I called everyone and who is Karen? I don't know baby; who is Karen? That's whose Duck bringing. Then you'll have to ask him who she is baby, I never met her, I'm just glad he's bringing a date. Why you say that daddy? Duck just always seems to have a problem keeping a girl; that's all. Well; maybe this time it will be different daddy. That remains to be seen, come eat baby, our food is getting cold. Ok I'm coming; did you want something to drink? Yeah; a glass of milk please!

Turn the TV on daddy; it's too quiet in here. Alright, hurry with that milk, I'm about to choke off this waffle woman. I'm coming, I'm coming. "It's another hot one today folks, be careful out there and drinks lots of water." "The city is busy tonight with thousands and thousands of fight fans." "Everyone is excited about Tyson and Holyfield two; it should be a hell of a show." "Tyson is seeking revenge after losing to Holyfield back in November of last year." "I don't know about you guys but I'm putting my money on the Las Vegas resident himself; go get him Mike!" "This is Katie Strong reporting for your evening news; we'll be back after this commercial break."

Knock-Knock! Umm that was good; I'm glad you ordered that baby, it hit the spot! Knock-Knock! Who is it? It's your tailor Sir! Oh hold on; I'm coming. Baby; go put a shirt on over those perky breast of yours! Hand me one daddy! Hold on man I'm coming! Here take mine! Thank you! Well put it on, so I can let the guy in already! Oops, I'm sorry, ok you can let him in now. Hey brother; thanks for coming; I just need to get fitted for a tux, I'm sure I've added a few pounds since the last time I wore one. Sure it's not a problem Mr. Cooper; just stand right here so I can get your measurements then I will be on my way. Cool, have at it! Stretch your arms out for me; please Sir. Thanks, it will only take a second, good; now stand still so I can get your height, great; now your waist. Good sir, now all I need to do is your chest then the lady can come over. Say man; what's was my waist? 38 Sir! Damn; I went up two inches! It's this good loving and home cooking daddy! Yeah, what home cooking?

My home cooking! Sabrina; save it, your ass don't cook that much. Yes I do daddy! Umm-hmm; come over here and get measured baby so he can go pick up our clothes for tonight. You can just stand here Ma'am; that will be fine. Ok and don't tell me the numbers I don't want to know. As you wish Ma'am! Ok I got your waist now I just need to get your height then I will be done. So whose driving the limo tonight AC? Mick baby; who else? That guy must be your favorite driver, he's always chauffeuring you around; you don't even ride your bikes or drive the Rover anymore. Why should I, when I have a driver! I'm just saying, maybe you should take the Harley out sometimes, we haven't gone for a ride any this summer.

Maybe you're right baby; we should go for a ride later next week. Please daddy; it will be so much fun! Alright just remind me. Ok folks, I'm all done, what color tux did you want Mr. Cooper? Keep it traditional man, black with bow tie and cummerbund. What color tie and cummerbund sir? Let's do a baby blue this time. Great choice sir and what color gown for you my lady? Baby blue as well Sir! Alright, I will have them sent up immediately and I hope you two have a marvelous time at the fight tonight. Thank you brother! Anytime Mr. Cooper anytime, later now!

Aww daddy; he was nice! He's supposed to be Brina, that's his job. Not everyone is nice AC and you know it!

Yeah whatever, I'm going to wash up, we only have an hour or so before we have to meet the crew downstairs. Alright daddy, I'm about to smoke me a blunt while you wash you up. That's what's up, roll me one while you're at it. I got you daddy, you didn't even have to ask. That's why you're my girl Sabrina; always know what her man likes. I'll be back in a few! Ok daddy, wash up real good too, it's been a minute since I gave you some of this awesome head. Oh yeah; I'm over-due for some of that action.

Yes you are! Sabrina relaxed on the couch while smoking and flipping through the channels. Damn; aint shit on this TV! "Are you or one of your family members having problems staying away from the slot machines?" "Do you spend your hard earned pay checks at the craps table?" "Are you constantly arguing with your spouse because they gambled away the rent money?" "If you answered yes to any of these questions, then you need to give us a call today!" "Call 1-800-702-7777, Gamblers Anonymous; we can help!" Sabrina removed AC's shirt then laid back on the couch, topless, as the warm sun rays beamed across her breast. She put the blunt to her moist lips then inhaled slowly, held it for a sec then exhaled it just as slow.

3,4,5 then 6 tokes later; she found herself leaned back on the couch, looking up at the ceiling. Hey daddy, daddy? Yeah baby what is it? Where did you get this weed? From Dupree; why? This smoke got me fucked up; I can't move. Oh; that shit is from Alaska, it's that Matanuska Thunder Fuck! Mata what! Ha-ha. You'll be ok baby, come take your shower, just don't smoke no more, you're good for the rest of the night; trust me! Alright, alright I'm coming. Daddy! Yes Sabrina! I can't feel my heart beat and the room is spinning. Baby you're just a little paranoid, I promise you will feel much better after your shower. Coop still wet from his shower walked up front to get Sabrina. Come on I got you! AC grabbed her by the waist then walked her to the bathroom, took off her panties then escorted her in the shower. There you go baby, let that cold water run over your face then wash up, we don't have long. Okay daddy; thank you; I love you so much. I love you too baby, now go ahead and wash up. I'll be up front; our clothes should be up anytime now.

AC now wearing only his thick white cotton robe, took a seat on the couch then lit the blunt Brina rolled for him. Ummmm, oh yeah! Good shit! Damn, don't anything ever be on TV! Coop picked up the remote, took a pull off the Matanuska, held it in for a bit, then exhaled it through his nose then flipped through the channels. Knock-Knock! Who is it! It's David Mr. Cooper, I have your clothes! Oh come in Dave! Hey Sir, where did you want them? Hang them over the closet door David! Ok no problem, enjoy the fight Sir! Thanks and I will David, oh tell Mick to get the Navi ready we're taking it to the fight tonight. Yes Sir, see you in a bit!

Sabrina! Sabrina! Yesssss daddy! You ok in there? Yeah I'm good! Good, your dress is here! I'm about to get dressed, so hurry, the crew will be here soon! Okay, I'm finishing up now, be there in a few seconds. Ahhh, I feel so much better! Ooooow you look good Daddy! I've never seen you in baby blue before. Thank you baby, you need to hurry. It won't take me long, boy I needed that shower! Don't ever let me smoke anymore of that Matanuska shit! Ha-Ha! You said you were a smoker baby, I guess not huh! Chronic is the strongest it gets for me, none of that exotic crap you've been smoking lately. How do I look? You look good baby, are you putting on the diamonds or the pearls? I don't know, what do you think? Since it's baby blue go with the diamonds you wore to the Motown Café, the pearls won't do anything for that dress.

Look at you Mr.; you're a fashion designer now? Nah girl, I just know what looks good; that's all. This is good smoke though baby, you sure you don't want any more? Stop playing AC; get that crap away from me. Ring-Ring! Put your shoes on Brina so we can go. Ring-Ring! I am, get the phone already. Ring-Ring! Hello! Coop; bring your ass down stairs nigga! Loon; hold your damn horses we'll be down in a minute. Yo; Duck got a bad bitch bruh! It's about time with his tricking ass, he needs a girl so he can stop wasting his money on ho's. AC you're a nut, see yall in a bit. Alright Loon! Who was that daddy?

Looney! Are they here yet? Yep, downstairs waiting on us, no I meant you. Come on slow poke. Ok I'm ready, how do I look? Great, come on woman. AC holds the door open as Sabrina walks out then he follows behind. I hope this fight isn't like the last one; we didn't even get to finish our beers. Yeah that was a joke! This one is going to be a whole lot better, Holyfield already whipped Mike's ass in November; remember. Nope I don't! Ding! Hi guys; up or down? Down! I'm headed down also. Cool, come on baby get on the elevator. A short chubby white gentleman, dressed in an all-white fleece sweat suit, wearing dress shoes and a black toupee stood in the corner staring at Sabrina and AC through his brown tinted, squared, gold framed shades as if they couldn't see his eyes. Hey perv, what the fuck are you looking at?

Whoa, watch it pal, I can look where the hell I want! Not at me you can't! Hey pal; do we have a problem here! It will be if you don't turn your fat ass around. Look buddy, I don't want any drama; I'm just going downstairs to grab a beer and a bite to eat. I don't give a fuck what you're going to do; look at me again and your fat ass will be catching a ride in an ambulance. Daddy calm down, it's not that serious. Yes the hell it is, that fool was making me uncomfortable. Ding! Yeah you better get your ass off; damn pervert! Daddy, no more weed for you, that Matanuska got you tripping.

I ain't tripping Sabrina, I know what I saw. Hey; there he is! What's up Crime Boss! What up Capo! What up Loon! You and Manny are nuts! Why you say that Coop! Why in the hell are yall wearing white suits and red ties? AC; stop hating bruh, you just mad that you didn't wear white!

Yeah whatever Loon; where's Duck and the others? Oh; in the store getting some liquor. For what; there's plenty drinks in the Limo! They're taking it in the fight! What! You got to be kidding right, all this damn money we got and them fools sneaking alcohol into a boxing match. Those are some cheap motherfuckers! Bruh, I don't give a damn how much money I got. I aint paying $8 for no damn beer like we did last time, that was crazy, then Tyson's ass knocked the nigga out before we could even finish drinking them on top of that! So kiss my ass bruh, call me cheap.

You can buy that damn $8 beer. How you doing Sabrina? I'm doing great Loon, thanks for asking. Yo Coop, you got any-more of that purple weed? I have a blunt left Loon; Sabrina tried to smoke some earlier and couldn't hang. Brina that ain't for rookies baby; did it have you twisted? Like a mother, I aint ever smoking that again as long as I live. Yeah that's a good idea! Manny are you good over there, you're not saying much. I'm just relaxing AC; I didn't get much sleep last night. Damn Sophie was going hard like a teenager. Damn Capo, you tired, your wife wore that ass out. Yep but her ass is still full of energy. I don't understand, she must be on something. Why she got to be on something Manny; your old ass just aint got no stamina. Coop kiss me ass! Ha-Ha! I'm just saying!

The white stretch Navigator did a slow roll in front of the Towers entrance then came to a stop; Mick exited the vehicle then walked around front to wait on the passengers. Manny did you get that vault taking care of? Yeah, the safe guy put a steel door on it and installed some cameras too. Good job Capo, now I feel much better. How was Thailand; I haven't had a chance to ask you about it. It was sweet man, boy they got some fine ass woman over there too. I saw a lot of black and Thai mixed girls. Well; did you find any to come over and work for us? Of course; I got two bad ones; Sam and Smiley are taking care of all their papers this week. They should be down by the end of the summer. That's going to be good for the club AC! Yep, some international flavor. Hey AC, Sabrina! Hi Sophie! How are you doing sis? I am great bro, it's good to see you. How have you been Sabrina? Loving life Sophie, I can't complain. That's wonderful; I love this baby blue on you two. Thank you, AC picked the colors. What is this material Sophie? Oh it's cashmere. Wow it is so pretty; what color is this? It's wine. Oh my God I love it, so long and soft. I got to have one of these gowns! Don't worry I'll take you over to my designers shop whenever you're ready. Really! Sure, it's no problem.

Thank you so, much! What's up people; I see everyone is looking nice. Hey Nina, hey Will! The group shouted as the two approached. Loon where is my sister dude? She left the store before we did. She went to check her make-up. Hello everyone! Hi Duck! I like you guys to meet my friend Karen! Hi Karen! Karen this is AC, his lady Sabrina, that's Manny and his wife Sophie, this is Loon and that's Nina and Will. Nice to meet you all! Nice to meet you as well Karen! Hey yall look at this guy! Who Manny? Derek, look he and Remy are walking in now. Damn, Remy looks totally different with clothes on! Thump! Ouch woman! AC, stop it, that wasn't nice. What, I was only complimenting the girl Sabrina. Yeah whatever! Hey Remy, you're looking marvelous! Thanks Brina! Hey D! Denna approaches the crew. Hey yall what's up! It's about time sis, it took you long enough in there. What were you doing girl? Nina; don't start, hey everybody! Hi Denna! Nice dress Remy! Thanks Denna! That's a DK right? Yeah. I like it; I tried a red one on the other day. They didn't have that purple one though, where did you get it? Over at the Caesar's shops! Oh ok, we were at the Fashion show mall.

Alright people let's mount up, Mick's waiting! With the exception of Manny and Loon the other fellas kept it simple with traditional black tux, bow tie and cummerbund. Derek, Will and Duck wore red cummerbunds and ties while Nina and Denna wore red matching gowns. By now the day had long turned to night as the running boards along-side the white stretched Navi lit up from light blue bulbs. Neon lights lit up the strip and the hot desert sky as traffic crawled down to the MGM while smarter fight fans walked unrushed to the arena from their nearby hotels. The towering bright emerald green MGM billboard, stood over the strip like a keeper of the city as Iron Mikes mean mug welcomed locals and guest to another sold out Don King event.

Holy smokes, it's more people here than for the other fight; look at how many folks are walking to the MGM. This is crazy! They said it was sold out two days ago Duck. Damn I didn't know that AC, how much was our tickets this time? Like $1500, for our section. We need to get us a prize fighter and get him to fight Mike's ass. Boy you're crazy, stop dreaming. Manny aint nobody dreaming, think about it! I did; that's why I said you were crazy! Ha-Ha! Aw man, all yall can kiss my ass. We should have walked like those folks, this limo is barely moving. It might be barely moving Derek but we have air condition them fools don't. You got a point there AC! But we'll just get out at the light on Tropicana and the blvd. that way we won't have to wait in that line at the valet entrance. Sounds like a plan to me Boss.

Hey Nina, tap on the glass and tell Mick to let us out at the next light. Alright hold a sec! Tap-Tap! Yes Ma'am? Hey we're going to get out at the next light so you won't have to wait in that drop off line. Oh it's no problem, I can wait. No; we don't wanna wait! Ok Ma'am, I will stop at the next light of Trop and the blvd.! Thanks Mick! Hey ladies don't forget to put those fifth's in your purse. I'm not putting anything in my purse. Come on Denna, stop playing baby. I'm not playing, if I won't something to drink, you're just going to pay for it. Girl, do you know how much a drink is in this place? Yep but you got it, so stop tripping.

Ok people, this is your stop! Thanks Mick! Open the door Duck, before the light turns green! I got it Manny, hold on a minute. The crew hastily exited the limo and took the cross walk over to the MGM. Hey guys; just in case we get separated; we have the first two rows on the south side of the ring. Alright Coop, see you inside player, I'm hitting the bar before I come in! Anyone coming with? Yeah Loon, hold up! Come on D, we only have 30 minutes! Hey Remy, I'll catch you inside baby. Ok hun, see you in a bit.

Inside; the arena was filled to capacity, Vegas had The Real Deal Holyfield as a 21 to 1 favorite over Iron Mike. Both fighters however; were in for a 30 million dollar payday, 30 mil each 60 total. Not many times in Tyson's career has a fighter come along who didn't fear him and one who actually beat him. The noise decibel was pretty high from everyone excitement and conversing before the fight as the hip hop tracks played over the speakers. The early fights on the fight card had ended and it was only minutes until the main event. "Ladies and gentlemen we ask that you take your seats; we will all rise in five minutes for the singing of the national anthem then get ready for the main event!"

Alright people me and D, are five shots in! Did we miss anything? Nah Loon, you guys are just in time, sit down.

I'm sitting, I'm sitting. "Beer, Popcorn, Peanuts! Beer, Popcorn, Peanuts!" "Anyone care for Beer, Popcorn or Peanuts!" Hey daddy, can I have some popcorn? Sure baby! Hey my man, over here! Yes Sir! What would you like beer, popcorn or peanuts? Popcorn for my girl and give me one of those beers. Hey guys; yall want anything? Yeah Coop! What? Forget it guys, I'll just get everyone a beer. My man; make that 12 beers all together and one popcorn. Ok Sir, here you go, we have the new plastic bottles no more cups. Great; give me twelve of them. Cool, here you are! He passes the beers to AC and he passes them on. Alright that's 12 beers and one popcorn; your total is $101.00 Sir! Damn, $101? Yes Sir. Here is $120 lil man, keep the change! Thank you Sir! Ha-Ha! Loon; don't start!

I told you Boss; didn't I! $100 for a 12 pack is ludicrous. Well, you didn't have to pay for it, so don't worry about it. "Ladies and gentlemen, please stand for the national anthem." ""Oh say can you see, by the dawns early light" "What so proudly we hail'd at the twilight's last gleaming?"........

"Ladies and Gentlemen; welcome to tonight's main event; Holyfield Tyson II, The sound and the fury." "This bout is for the WBA Heavyweight title and is scheduled for 12 rounds" "In the visiting corner in his signature black trunks, hailing from Catskills; New York, we have the former two time champion with 45 wins, 2 losses and 39 wins by way of knock out." "Let's hear it for Iron Mike Tyson!" Tyson! Tyson! Tyson! "In the opposite corner wearing white and purple we have the WBA Heavyweight champion of the world, with a record of 33 wins, 3 losses and 24 wins by way of knock out." "Hailing from Atlanta, GA!" "Let's hear it for the Heavyweight champion; Evander "The Real Deal Holyfield!" Yay! Yay! Yay!

Ok fellas let's have a clean fight, no hitting below the belt, and I will be calling any and all files! Touch gloves and let's fight! Ding! Ding! Yo I got $100 on Mike; anybody want some of this action? I'll take you up on that Will, I got 100 on Evander! Alright Loon, anybody else want in? I'm in Will! Ok D, you can get some too! Anybody else; ok going once, going twice! Fellas get ready to pay up! No Will your ass is about to be out of $200! Loon stop wishing brother, watch the fight. Ok; don't say I didn't warn you bruh!

Come on Mike, thump his ass, I got money on the line over here!

Round 1. A minute into the round no fighter seems to be gaining any ground, Holyfield lands a few jabs to Mikes head, steps back and dodges a charge by Mike then counters with a hook. The fighters hit the ropes and tie up, Mike's keeping close trying to avoid Holyfield's long reach. Tyson swings with a right hook, then follows with a strong straight left that seems to touch Evander just a little. The fighters tie up in the center of the ring; tussle then the ref separates them. Holyfield takes a few swings, one to the body then lands a hook to Mikes jaw. Ding! Ding!

Man this is a bullshit fight, nobodies doing anything, them fools keep wrapping each other up! Calm down Loon, it's just warming up brother; Tyson is just sizing that boy up. Will; Mike can't do nothing with him, that's why he keeps holding him! You're not looking at the same fight my man. Holyfield aint doing shit! Whatever Will, whatever! Just be ready to pay up! Ding! Ding!

Round 2. Nina and Denna stand to their feet to cheer Tyson on. Come on Mike, you can do it baby! Come on

Mike! The fighters meet in the center of the ring; Tyson charges in and takes a hard right, to the body of Holyfield, then a left to the head but Holyfield seems to be unfazed. The two work their way over to the ropes and wrap up again, Tyson jumps up signals the ref after a head butt to his right eye by Holyfield. Blood starts to run from the 3 inch gash now over Mike's right eye. The ref breaks them up and gives Tyson's corner time to tend to the cut. The fighters continue, Mike swings cautiously but Evander ties him up again. Mike furiously signals to the ref to watch for the head butts. But to no avail, the fighters continue to swing on each other with no success. Ding! Ding!

Man I could have stayed home and watched this damn fight on TV tomorrow. This shit is boring. It's only the third round daddy, it will get better. I hope so Sabrina, I'm ready to go already.

Round 3. Ding! Ding! Mike charges Evander with a vengeance looking like the Tyson of old. He swings right and connects. Evander wraps him up, chest to chest, head to head; Mike moves in closer; up close to his opponent's right ear. Tyson's mouth piece falls out then all of a sudden Evander starts jumping up and down as Mikes spits something bloody on the mat.

In a rage Holyfield is pointing at his right ear, it was bleeding and a chunk of it was gone. Oh shit! What the fuck, he bit that man's ear off! Will; pay up homie, your boy done lost his mind! Hold on Loon it aint over yet; the ref is letting the fight continue. Evander's corner rinsed his ear with water, cleaned it as best they could and sent him back in to battle the villain. Tyson had the fury of a lion in his eyes as he charged Holyfield, he took his signature jab and grazed Evander just a little. Holyfield held Tyson once more then wrapped him up. Mike not having it, went in for the kill again and bit Holyfield's left ear this time. As the round ended; furiously he complained to the ref as the tension in the ring escalated and the fighters retreated to their corners. Ding! Ding!

"Hold on ladies and Gentlemen, I believe the ref is calling the fight!" "Please stay in your seats as we figure this thing out, what an insane scene of events that have taken place here tonight." "To the viewers at home watching and to the fans here with us tonight that paid so much for their tickets, I know this is not what you expected to see." Will give me money bruh! Oh I'll take mine too Will! Man; forget both of yall, here take your $100. This is crazy, that nigga bit the man's ear off, damn Mike! You believe this crap Manny? I'm still amazed AC! Wow, these fools are going crazy in here now! Look the cops are stomping some fools out over there!

"Ladies and gentleman the fight has been called!" "And still, The WBA Heavyweight Champion of the world by way of disqualification." "Evander "The Real Deal" Holyfield!" Man this is nuts, I need a drink! Hey guys; Sabrina and I will meet you at the bar. Alright Coop; we'll be there in a minute, let me finish this $8 beer! Ok Manny, see you guys in a bit! Come on Brina; let's go. We could have stayed home baby and kick it. It's ok daddy; I still had fun. Oh yeah? Um-hmm! AC now pissed, grabbed Sabrina by the hand and escorted her down the aisle away from the rowdy arena.

"Hello fellas, welcome to Dolls" "Please don't forget about our Saturday night drink specials!" "$2 Domestic drafts all night long baby!" "This is Dj Tru; come holler at your boy for any song request." "Right now we got Ms. Asia coming to the stage!" Hey lady! Hello Sir, how can I help you? I'm looking for this fool named AC. I heard I can find him around here! It depends on whose asking. I see him around here sometimes! Oh is that right? Yep! What's your name pretty lady? Red; what's yours? Crash baby! Hi Crash, what are you drinking? I'll take a double shot of Crown and one of those drafts you got on special. Ok, a double crown and one draft coming right up. How come you're not on the other side of the bar? Nah, that's not my thing, I can't handle too many people touching me. Oh, I understand that! Here's your drinks honey! Thanks lady.

I need to find this AC cat though, we have some unfinished business. Well' I don't have his number, just hang out for a while he usually pops in around this time. Ok, thanks Red, I'm going to have a seat and enjoy the stage show. Ok Crash, you're welcome. Red now curious walked over to the bar phone to notify Will of their visitor. Ring-Ring! Yeah what is it Red? There's a guy out here looking for Boss, says they have some unfinished business. Oh really, is it someone we know? I don't think so; he has a New York accent and a tattoo on his forearm. Did you get has name? Yeah, he said they call him Crash. Thanks baby, where is he? Sitting by the stage! Ok thanks, we will handle it. Will turned the security monitor around so he could see Crash then called Manny.

Ring-Ring! Hello! Hey Capo! What's up Big Will? What did Fat Boy say that guy name was that paid him a visit; looking for Coop? He said Crash or something like that. Ok that's what I thought. Why what's up? Playboy is here at the club right now, looking for AC. Ok hold that fool, we're on the way. Say no more bruh, see you in a bit! Ring-Ring! Hello, the bar! Red, send the security guard to the office, the one at the end of the bar! Ok got you. Hey Man! Will wants you in the office. Ok thanks Red! Knock-Knock! Come in! Hey Boss, you wanted me? Yeah, see that guy sitting at the stage. Right here man, with the beer in his hand. Yeah I see him. Go get him and take him to the kitchen. Don't ask him shit, just take that fool back there. Ok I'm on it!

Ring-Ring! Hello kitchen! Hey Sil, it's Will! What you need Will? Unlock the walk in freezer, we have a visitor. Alright; doing it now Boss. Excuse me Sir, I need you to come with me! What for man, get your hands off me! Chop! The security guard; chopped Crash across neck quickly to put him to sleep then dragged him into the kitchen. Will and

303

Sil are sitting there on the stainless steel cutting table when the guard brings the New Yorker in. Sil put that chair in the walk in. Hey bruh take him in the walk in and sit him in that chair, I'll be in, in a sec. Ok boss.

Will picked up the duck-tape from under the counter then entered the walk in with the others. Here Sil, tape his feet to the chair, I'll get his hands and mouth. Thanks bruh; you can go back on the floor; tell AC and Manny we're in the Kitchen when they get here. Ok boss, got you. Hey Sil, when we get done with this guy, you need to give me your meat order for next week. I have to call it in Monday morning. Sure no problem!

Hey Red where is this fool at? Will took him in the kitchen AC! Thanks Red; come on Manny. "Gentleman once again; don't forget to take advantage of our $2 draft specials!" What's up Sil, how you been old man? I've been good AC. That's great; did you enjoy your vacation? Oh yeah and thank you again for the tickets, me and my wife really needed that. You're welcome old timer.

Manny take the tape off this punks mouth. Damn, look at him; sleeping like a baby, fucking tape aint even phase this nigga! Damn, it's cold in here; this isn't gonna take long. Sil go get your tools ready. Ok Boss, I'm on it! What kind of questions was this guy asking about? He told Fat boy that he was Jesse and Steels people. What; are you serious; doesn't he knows those chumps are dead? Yep, that's why he's here; to smoke you! Man wake that fool up! Pop! Pop! Manny slapped Crash across the face twice. What the fuck! Untie me motherfuckers! Hold on player, calm down. I heard you have been looking all over town for me. Are you AC! Guilty as charged. Yeah nigga, you smoked my people and I come to bust your ass! Bruh, in case you haven't noticed. You're not in the position to be making any kind of threats. Nigga I aint scared to die; kill me now if you gone kill me son.

Son; I aint your son! You New Yorkers kill me with that son shit. What's stopping me from putting a cap right-there in the center of your head; right now. Not a damn thing; if you gone do it; do it and get it over with. But I don't think you man enough to face me one on one, because I will bust your black ass AC. So let me get this straight; you know you're a dead man either way this thing plays out but you want to fight me one on one to prove a point. Yep, you damn right. I tell you what SON! I'll fight you one on one, if you win; you get to leave here alive. If I win it's curtains. Let's do it nigga, untie me. Untie him Manny. Will; slide all of that meat to the back; let me put a combat whipping on this fool real quick.

You get 10 minutes city boy; let's do this. Crash; 6' plus muscle tone statue assumed the defensive stands and faced off with the Sin City Boss. Manny and Will stayed back out of the away standing in front of the freezer door. Woomp! Crash swung at Coops head and missed. Kapow! AC jumped in the air and came down on Crashes left knee with his right foot. Crash fell to the ground. Kapow! Coop went across his opponent's face with a right hook. Get up New York; you can do better than that. Crash stood up limping and bleeding from his right eye. Woomp! Ugh! Crash swung a right hook to the body. AC bent over. Thump! Crash elbowed him in the top of the head. Kapow! The Sin City Boss caught Crash on the chin with an upper cut as he came to his feet from the body blow. Kapow! AC kicked Crash in his other knee. Crash fell to the floor on both knees; mouth and right eye bleeding. Kapow! AC came across his face with a strong left hook then his opponent slouched over in pain. Fuck you AC! What; did you say something New York. Coop slowly walked over to Crash then stood behind him while he was kneeling down in pain, wrapped his left hand around his opponents head, right on his chin, then pulled. Snap! Crash fell to the floor, busted knees, bloody mouth, wounded eye and broken neck. Sil get in here! Yes Sir! Handle this garbage will you! Yes Sir! Manny, Will, I'm hungry let's go get something to eat!

Chapter 10, Sky High

800 feet above Vegas, on a bright sunny day, the energy flows as Manny and Sophie wait to be seated at The Top of The World Revolving Restaurant. Hello Sir, your table is ready now; please follow me. Hey honey; this is really high, I'm not sure I want to sit by the window. Come on Sophie, stop being a chicken. I say we get on the roller coaster when we leave here. Are you crazy Emanuel? I will do no such thing. Ha-Ha! I'm only kidding babe. Sir; Madam this is your table, your waiter will be with you shortly. Thank you so much. You're welcome, enjoy your meal. Damn, you really can see everything up here; I wonder how scared the construction crew was when they were building this thing. I don't know but it couldn't have been me Manny, this is insane.

Hello Sir, Ma'am! I'm Nathan and I will be your server this afternoon. Hi Nathan, how are you? I am fine Ma'am; thanks for asking. Have you guys decided on something to drink yet? You know what Nathan; we'll have a bottle of your best Red Wine. Great Sir; we have a 1997 Opus One;

Proprietary Red Wine. Where is that from Nathan? Napa Valley Sir! What kind of Grape Nathan? It's a Bordeaux Ma'am. That will do fine then Nathan. Ok; I'll be right back with your wine and to get your orders. Thanks young man. You're welcome Ma'am. So what are you eating today honey? I am ordering the lobster and sirloin baby. Umm, that sounds good; I think I'll try the T-Bone and grilled shrimp.

Ok guys; here's your Opus Red. Nathan begins to pour Sophie a glass of wine. Just tell me when to stop Ma'am. Half way is fine Nathan! Alright, here you are Ma'am and Sir; half a glass for you as well? Yeah that will be fine. Here you are; have you guys decided on your main course yet? Yes, the lady will have a T-Bone medium well and the grilled shrimp. I will have the Lobster and Sirloin, make mine medium well also. For you Ma'am; I have the grilled shrimp with a medium well T-Bone and for the gentleman; I have the Lobster and medium well sirloin. That's it Nathan, you got it buddy. Well you two, enjoy your wine, I will be back with some complimentary appetizers after I place your orders. Did you say complimentary? Yes Sir; whenever someone orders the Opus they get comp appetizers. We'll isn't that something, thanks Nathan. You're welcome Sir; I'll be back shortly.

Hey Sophie; I got something for you. What you got for me hun? Here take a look and tell me what you think. Manny placed a silver rectangle size box on the table in front of her. Well, open it baby! Oh my God it's gorgeous! When did you have this done honey? I had the jeweler make it a few weeks ago; he had to cut the diamonds to spell your name, so it took a while. Muah! Muah! Wow this is gorgeous; I've never seen a diamond bracelet with the diamonds cut to spell my name. Awww, thank you honey! You're welcome baby; I thought you might like that. Are you kidding, I can't wait to show it off; I freaking love it!

Ok guys these are our signature crab cakes; they're delicious! I can't get enough of them; they should hold you for a few minutes until your main course is ready. Thank you Nathan! You're welcome Ma'am. Here; try it Manny. Umm; there good babe, try one before I eat them all. Alright; don't be greedy Emanuel. Nope just hungry, that's all. So how is junior doing in school? I've been so busy with this Capo thing I haven't had a chance to spend time with him like I used to. He's doing pretty good; we need to start helping him plan for college. He's going to be a senior next year. Yeah I know, damn the time has flown by! Yes it has, you're getting old honey. Ha-Ha! I'm not by myself either. Who me? Manny I stop counting 10 years ago! Oh wow; so you're still 25? Yep exactly, look at you, so smart. Woman, you are crazy. Alright, it's time for the favorite part folks! I have a T-Bone for the lady with grilled shrimp and Sirloin with Lobster for you Sir. Umm, it smells delicious! If you guys need anything else let me know, your condiments are right here by your napkins, steak sauce, salt and pepper etc. Thank you Nathan! You're welcome folks, enjoy your meals.

Sabrina help me clean this closet out in the guest room, I only have a few blankets left to move. Where am I going to put them? Put them in the bathroom closet, I need to add these three shelves and this bolt lock. Why; what are you doing? You'll see in a few minutes, come back after you put up those blankets. Ok daddy, whatever you say. AC drills the screws in the three additional shelves he added to the guest closet, removed the door knob and installed a deadbolt lock. Ok daddy ;what's next? Look under the bed and get those four suit cases. Sabrina got on her knees, looked under the bed then pushed the suit cases out on the other side. What's in those cases AC? Come look baby. Holy shit! Why do you have all of this money in the damn house, someone is going to rob us!

Sabrina calm down, nobody is going to rob us, nobody knows but me and you anyway. I don't understand why you have it here in the first place. It's garbage money baby. What do you mean garbage money? It's only ones, five's and ten dollar bills. Boy that ain't no garbage money, it's real money! Yeah but we only bank 20's and up. So I'm making this closet a safe for this garbage money. I have two keys, one for me and one for you. Now help me stack it in the closet on these shelves. AC; sometimes I have my doubts about your ass. What you mean woman? You're border lined crazy, that's what! Oh yeah, I could have told you that. Ha-ha! Daddy you're a trip! How much is this anyway? Like a quarter mil. $250,000.00 AC, how long are we supposed to keep it there? Baby you don't get it, do you? Apparently not AC, please explain. This is our play money, anytime you need cash, you don't even have to ask, just get it out of this closet. Spend this shit, that's why it's here. Get rid of it however you want! I have tons and tons of money coming in from like 8 different places and it aint stopping no time soon. Baby; I'm the motherfucking Boss, do you understand what that means?

Oh daddy; I understand very clearly and even more so now. I saw some shoes I wanted, a few dresses, a couple of bags, some watches. Hell daddy, I might get me one of those 1500 Ninja's like you. Go ahead baby; get whatever the hell you want. You're the Queen B girl, you can have it all! AC I'm so wet right now; I can fuck the shit out your black ass. Ha-ha! Money got you dripping huh? Hell yes! Well, hold that thought; we have to put this money up before the crew gets here; we have a meeting with our banker. Alright, alright, I'll start on this other bag. Damn daddy; would you have imagined us in this position a year ago when I met you? Baby, there's no way I would have even thought about something like this. It's like a dream, a gangster's paradise! Yeah I agree with you there daddy! A gangster's paradise!

Knock-Knock! That must be Michael the banker, finish putting this up, I need to go sit down with him before everyone gets here. Knock-Knock! Go handle your business daddy, I got this. Thank you baby! Knock-Knock! Hold on; I'm coming, I'm coming! Knock-Knock! Who is it? Michael! Hey Mike, what's going on man, I was just doing some cleaning, have a seat on the couch, the rest of the crew will be here shortly. Did you want some bottled water or coke or something? Water is fine Sir. Alright, make yourself comfortable; I'll be right back. Ok thanks.

Here you go Mike! So what you got for me? I have your balance sheets from all three banks and I brought the reports on the last two quarters of the stock market like you asked. Good, did you have a chance to research those computer companies like I asked? I did! What did you find out? Well I came across several computer stocks that may be good investments. They're saying computers are supposed to be the wave of the future. Yeah that's what I'm hearing too. So which companies gained the most ground in the last two quarters? Hold a second; let me get out my spread sheets. Ok Sir; according to my research; Compaq, HP, Dell, Gateway and Apple are the best companies to invest in at this time! What the hell is Apple? It's a new computer company Sir, some of my friends in San Francisco says to keep an eye on them. How come

Mike? They say the CEO is a go getter and has been making waves in the industry. Alright; if you say so Michael!

Knock-Knock! AC; open up! It's open guys; come in! Here's the crew now Mike! Manny, Loon, Will, Duck, Nina and Denna enter the condo. Guys this is Michael the banker I told you about. What's up Mike! Hello everyone nice to meet you! Guys have a seat, we don't have long; we have to get back to our places of business soon. Well, I asked all of you to come here today because I asked Mike to find some companies for us to invest in. We are making a ton of dough and I think it would be smart to invest in some public companies to secure our financial future. That sounds good AC but what kind of stocks are we talking about? Nina; I suggested computer stocks; the technology sector; every company that we know of is gearing up to use several computer systems in their future business modules. I think it's a great investment.

It sounds good to me bruh, what companies and how many companies are we talking? Good question Loon; I'll let Mike answer that. Well guys, like I was telling AC earlier, after some extensive research. I found several companies that fit our investment profile. There's Compaq, HP, Dell, Gateway and Apple. I heard of most of them but who the hell is Apple? Manny, excuse me; it is Manny right? Yes Sir! Apple is a fairly new company in northern California that I have some very good insight on; I think they fit our portfolio perfectly. Man look, as long as AC trust you; we trust you. How much are we investing in these companies anyway? I'll let Mr. Cooper answer that one Sir? Will; I'm putting up 1.5 million for each of you, so we all will be investing 500 thousand dollar into each company. Does everyone agree with that?

Count me in Coop! Me too Boss! Man all of us are in, that's a smart move AC, I can dig it! Thanks Duck! Well Mike, go ahead and start the process. Guys, Mike has some investment forms for you to complete so you can get credit for your stocks. Once you get done with that you can get back to business; I will call you all later to check on things. Thanks Mr. Cooper; everyone the forms are on the table, just fill in the blanks and I can handle the rest. The crew; gather around the kitchen table to fill out the paper work then head back out to run their businesses. Yo Duck; how's the car lot coming brother? I love it AC, I'm a natural at it! Good shit boy; I have to check out one of those Benz's you got. That's what it is; I'm ah hit you later bro, let me get back to this lot! Later guys! Alright Coop, later!

Ruff-Ruff! Ruff-Ruff! Ruff-Ruff! Hey homes; what the hell are you doing! Get these serial numbers off these Bentley's! Duck is expecting them first thing tomorrow! Put that weed down and get to work esse'! I swear; sometimes I wanna fuck you up Chino! Damn Hector; can a brother take a break around this place! Hell no fool, take a break when all the work is done. I need to get this paperwork over to my girl at the DMV today! So hurry your ass up; take those numbers off and put the new ones on! Get Carlos to help you! He can't! Why the hell not? He's setting up for the dog fight! Damn; I forgot about that; what time is it set? In two hours esse'! How many pits we got fighting? Three I think! Alright, take care of these numbers; I got a few calls to make.

Ring-Ring! Hello! Yo Manny, what's good! Whose this? It's Hector! Hec; what's going on bro? Yo I'm putting on a dog fight in a few hours here behind the shop. Put the word out, if you know anybody that's trying to get in on the action. I can do that bro; I might come through and see what's poppin! Alright Manny, I appreciate it homie! No doubt Hector; later! Hector exits the back door of his garage then walks over to speak with Carlos while he's putting the finishing touches on the ring. Los; how's it coming? I'm wrapping things up now Hec. How many fights do we have scheduled? At least six so far; I'm keeping the entry line open until 3o minutes before the first fight.

Cool, how many people are you expecting? About 50 or so! That's a good number; I reached out to Manny; he's gonna put the word out too. That's what's up, I'm about to feed the dogs before I forget. Go ahead and handle your business Carlos; I need to go check on Chino anyway. Hey Esse'! Yeah Hector, what is it? How long before you finish with this Bentley? I just removed the serial number from the door panel, Poncho is gone put the new one on while I take the V.I.N plate out of the window dash. Cool, be careful not to mix those things up esse'. Those fuckers look just as real as the ones that come on the cars. I don't know how they keep making those decals look so real in Mexico! I noticed that a few weeks ago when we chopped that

Maserati; luckily Marcia wrote the real serial numbers down while we were doing inventory. Ruff! Ruff! Ruff!

Vroom! Vroom! Who is that coming up on that bike? Ruff! Ruff! Oh that's Marcia, I asked her to come help me finish up the Bentley's before she starts working the door for the fight later. Ok, that's what's up homes. How much are we charging to get in? $100 at the gate for spectators and $200 if you got a dog in the fight! Sweet! Hey fellas; what's going on? Hey Marcia, it's all good, what's up with you? Just another hot ass day in Sin City Hector, that's about it. Hey babe; what you need me to do? Hey Marcia, I just need you to start taking the serial numbers off that white Bentley in the last bay; I'm about done with this one. Cool; who are we selling them to? Oh these are for Duck! Damn, did he sell those other cars already? Yep, he only has the Maserati left in the bay area and that's already sold too.

We're headed back to LA tomorrow night to snatch another Rolls and a Porsche. We might get a Maserati if we have time too. Alright cool, I guess I will get started. Thanks for helping out Marcia; I appreciate it baby. It's no problem Chino; you know I got your back. Ruff! Ruff!

Damn Rotts, who are they barking at now? Ruff! Ruff! Yo Chino, go tell Carlos to get up here. Fat Boy is out here with a dog! Ruff! Ruff! What up homes, stay in your truck for a minute; let me lock these Rotts up. Alright Hector.

Hey Los, Hector needs you up front! Ok, I'm coming esse'! Yo homes what's up? Fat Boy got a pit he wants to enter in the fight. Oh ok! Hey homes; get your dog and follow me. You're good Fat Boy; the Rotts are in the pin. Alright Hec! Come on boy! Come on! Fat boy opens the back door of his white Tahoe and lets his grey eyed, tiger striped pit out. Ruff! Ruff! Calm down boy, come on. He grabs the dog by the leash and follows Carlos. Ruff! Ruff! Ruff! The pit and the Rotts go haywire when they see each other. Ruff! Ruff! Hey shut up! Hector yells at the Rotts.

Ok homes, you can just chill over by that bench, there's some shade over there and some water for the dogs; it's gone be $200 to enter the contest. The fight starts in an hour, I will let you know your match up; 15 minutes before the fight. Ok yo; you said two right? Yep! Ruff! Ruff! Sit boy; sit! Here you go yo, 200! Thanks homes. Ruff! Ruff! Come on boy, let's go rest and get you some water. Ruff! Ruff!

Hey Hector; you putting your pit in the fights? Nah, he's at the house, I aint about to drive to Green Valley to get him. So this Bentley is finished? Yep; the other one will be too, as soon as Marcia put on that new V.I.N plate. Ruff! Ruff! Damn, it must be getting close to fight time; it's like four cars coming through the gate. Yeah Hec, it's like 45 minutes before. Ruff! Ruff! Hey Marcia, you done yet baby? Yep all finished Chino. Cool, help me cover these cars up, it's almost fight time. We don't need these punta's looking at our shit. You guys handle that, I'll go handle these people out front, just whistle when you're ready to let them in back. Alright Hector!

Come on Marcia, hurry, let's get these covers on. Chino pulled two blue car covers from the shelf. He and Marcia placed one over the white Bentley first then headed over to put the other over the blue one. Cool, all set, go set up by the back door baby and get ready to collect the money. It's $100 for spectators and $200 for everyone that has a dog in the fight. Ok I'm on it! Thanks Marcia! You're welcome Chino, now go tell Hector we're ready. Oh shit, that's right I forgot! He whistled twice to signal Hector. Ok people; head through the bay doors and you will see a lady sitting at the back door. Pay her, then you can enter the fight area. A group of 5 spectators and 3 guys with pits walked through the bay door then over to Marcia. Ruff! Ruff! Hector unlocked the entrance gates as the cars continued to pour in one after the other. Every thug in the city had seemed to find their way over to his chop shop for the dog fights.

The gates now locked; bay doors down and the back of the building filled to capacity with spectators and dog fighters. Money and adrenalin consumed the atmosphere for what would prove to be a prosperous and eventful gangster's fight night. Ruff! Ruff! Carlos stands on top of the picnic bench, just beside the ring then shouts. Alright motherfuckers; place your bets! Ruff! Ruff! Fighting out of the red corner, hailing from North Las Vegas! Ruff! Ruff! We have the red nose Pit Bull that goes by the almighty Bone crusher! Ruff! Ruff! And his opponent, no stranger to the square circle; hailing from Henderson! Ruff! Ruff! We have the gray eyed; tiger striped Pit Bull; who goes by 187! Ruff! Ruff! Motherfuckers are you ready! I said are- you ready! Ruff! Ruff! Fighters at the sound of the gun; release your pits! Ruff! Ruff! Pow! The red dust from the desert sand, created small clouds in the square circle as the two ferocious pits clashed nose to nose, bumping the four foot tall wooden pallet walls that contained them to the area. Come on Bone crusher! Get em baby! Get em! A spectator yelled! The pits bumped the wall, rolling in the sand as one another's jaws interlocked into the others thin skin. 187 rolled on top, his killer grip now around bone Crushers neck. Crusher fought and fought but couldn't get up! The power and force behind 187's powerful jaws and muscle toned legs; kept him pinned until his body caved in. Pow! That's it motherfuckers! And your winner of the very first battle! The Gray eyed, tiger striped assassin; 187!

Hey daddy; what do you have planned for later on? Nothing in particular; why you ask Sabrina? My aunt asked me to take my little cousins trick or treating. Did you want to come with me? Who me, go trick or treating! Girl you buggin! No, I mean ride with us, I'm taking them through the neighborhood in the car. No I'll pass on that one baby, you go ahead. Well, can I use the Rover; it has more room than my car. Sure go ahead baby; I don't care if you use it. Thanks daddy; I'm about to leave then it's almost six and I want to start around seven. Ok baby, just call me when you're done; I'll be around somewhere. Ok daddy! Muah! See you later! Alright baby, be careful and bring me some snickers back! Yeah whatever, I thought you didn't want to go! I don't but I want some snickers; just sneak some out of your little cousin's bag. Ha-Ha. Bye daddy, you silly! Ha-Ha. Bye baby.

Ring-Ring! Hello! Hey nigga! What's up Mo! Ain't shit, what you doing? Not a damn thing, sitting here holding my nuts and watching TV. I want to see you today baby. What time you want to do that Mo? Soon; we can hook up now since you're not busy. Where are you right now? About to walk in Caesars! Alright; I will meet you in front of the water fountain in 30 minutes, I'm gone walk over. Ok AC, don't be playing either! Mo; nobodies playing; see you in a bit.

AC still in his boxers; got up from the couch and went in his room to put on one of his sweat suits. He grabbed his navy blue Nike fleece from the closet and all white air force ones. Slipped everything on then headed for the door. Then he stopped. Hmmm, should I. He thought to himself. What the hell. AC went to his coat closet and got his all white LV leather back pack, went to the guest room, unlocked the closet, took out 5 bundles of cash then placed the five g's in his Louis bag and headed over to Caesar's to meet Monica. AC ran across the busy intersection of Flamingo and Las Vegas Boulevard, then across the sharp green lawn of Caesar's just under the iron horse that stood on the corner. He ran onto the brick sidewalk and entered the Gorgeous Casino. Roman soldiers greeted him as he passed the foyer and ventured down the gold and milky marble hallway that led to the shops. Angels and Unicorns danced above on the light blue ceiling's that resembled the heavenly sky. Julius himself began to speak from the fountain ahead that rotated in the center of the mall as spectators watched in awe.

It's about time, I thought you weren't coming. You panic too much Mo. So, what you getting out of here? I don't know, I just felt like shopping, spending some money today. Well let's go buy some something then! Hold up; you treating or something nigga? I mean, the way you said it! I got five stacks to spend on you. AC; don't start those games man. Mo! What? Here; unzip it! Why! Girl; unzip the damn bag! Zip! Oh my God! Boy why are you carrying around all this cash? It's gone be empty when we leave here, so it doesn't matter. Now let's go shopping!

How much is in there? I told you five stacks. Hmm, I can get a few things with that; come on Mr., follow me! Lead the way baby! Where's your girlfriend, I don't need her to be walking up on a sister while she's spending her man's money. She's busy with her cousin's, trick or treating! Oh how sweet, why you ain't go? Mo, stop tripping, what store are we going to? Oooh, right here; Gucci! I saw a bag and some shoes I wanted. Then come on woman!

Hello folks, welcome to Gucci; how can I help you? Hello Ma'am; I want those shoes and that matching purse that you have on display in the window. Ok, will there be anything else Ma'am? No Ma'am, that's it! Oh; I need the shoes in a size 9. Ok have a seat and I shall return with your items. Thank you. You're welcome Ma'am, it's my pleasure. She's so nice; isn't she Coop. Yeah, only because you're about to spend $1800 bucks. Well; we're hitting two more stores after this and that shall kill that 5 stacks. Shit; it didn't take you long huh? Man; I've been window shopping so long, I know where everything I want is at!

Here you are Ma'am, a size 9 and your matching Gucci bag. Did you want to try that on? No I'm fine thanks, you can ring it up now; he will be paying for it. Ok right this way Sir. Your total will be $1897.98. Will that be cash or credit Sir? Cash Ma'am! Coop removed the white Louis bag from his shoulders, unzipped it and pulled out two bundles. Here you go Ma'am, keep the change. Oh my; how much is this? It's two thousand dollars, like I said; keep the change. Well- I don't know what to say Sir! Um, thank you, here's your receipt. You're welcome Ma'am.

Ha-Ha! Come on AC, let's go, your crazy ass. Where to next Mo? The Louis store; there's this red bag I want! Ok lead the way baby; oh, how's everything out at the ranch? It's cool, I had no idea men would drive way out in the desert to buy pussy! It just goes to show you Mo, that there is a lot of power in pussy. You can say that shit again. You're making a killing though nigga, aint you? I do alright! Boy please; this is Monica you're talking to. I know how you operate; AC doesn't waste time on anything unless he's getting paid. If you knew the answer, why you asked? Because I was curious but I did the math! You're stacking from the whore house, agency, club, video store, dope boys and now the car lot. And that's just what I know about, but I- know you.

So I wouldn't doubt it if you got some other business plans in motion, but I ain't mad at you. I got your back and you know that, just don't let that girlfriend of yours mess your focus up. Who Sabrina, she's harmless! Yeah ok, don't forget about what you just said. What was that? That pussy was powerful. Yeah whatever Mo! I'm serious, don't get caught up nigga. Come on, here's the store right there.

Hi welcome to Louis, is there anything particular I can help you guys with? Yes Sir, I want that red signature bag you have; right there behind the counter. Ok, did you want to look at it Ma'am. Nope, box it, bag it, whatever you do and he's paying for it! Well ok Ma'am, give me just a second and I will box that up for you. Thank you Sir! Oh it's my pleasure. AC don't be tipping nobody else either; your crazy ass. Why not? Because it's cutting into my spending money, this is a retail store not a restaurant; they don't work for tips nigga. Aright, your total is $1257.75! AC unzips the bag, places a bundle on the counter then peels $258 from another stack. Here you go Sir; nice doing business with you. Why thank you guys for shopping with us, do have a wonderful evening.

Come on woman, you got like $1844 left or something like that! Good I can spend that on these blue Jimmy Choos I saw the other day. It's about three stores down, come on. Lead the way Monica, make it quick too, I'm getting hungry. Ok but I need to try these on; this will be my first pair of Jimmy Choos. Alright but we're going to Wolfgang's after this store. Cool, that's a bet. Hello Sir, Ma'am, welcome to Jimmy Choo, what can we do for you this evening? Yes, I would like to try that blue shoe on in a size 9. Which blue shoe Ma'am? Oh, I'm sorry the one that the mannequin is wearing. Sure I will be back in a moment. So what do you think AC? It's cute but I have to see it on. Here you are Ma'am, a size 9. Monica places her left hand on Coop's back, slides her foot from her left shoe then slipped on the blue Jimmy. Oh yeah; this feels nice on. How does it look on, AC? I like it, it's you! Great I'll take it, you can box it up Ma'am! The gentleman will be paying for it. Ok right this way Sir; I will get your total for you then box these up for the lady. Thank you Ma'am! Looks like your total is $1689.47 sir! Coop places a full bundle on the counter top, then peels off $690 form the roll of cash he had in his pocket. There you go, keep the change. Thanks guys have a nice day and thanks for shopping with us.

Nigga you crazy, keep the change! It was only 50 cents, I think. Ha-ha! You're a nut, thanks for the shopping spree though. You're welcome, it was fun, now I am about to starve, let's go eat already!

Hi Ma'am welcome to the Towers, My name is Melanie and I'm the Property Agent. I'm sorry; I didn't get your name! Oh you can call me Nina. Nice to meet you Nina; on your voicemail message you inquired about purchasing a Condo here; is that correct? Yes it is. Ok I made some copies of our floor plans; here you go, you can look them over while we're talking. We have two Condos available at this time. One is a 3 bedroom, 2 bath and it's on the 33rd floor, overlooking the East side of the City. The other is our Presidential Loft, it's 4,000 square feet with a Jacuzzi, one and a half baths and it overlooks the strip from the 46th floor. Does either one of those fit what you are looking for? Yes; the presidential sounds more like me.

Great; if you would follow me, we can take the elevator up then you could check it out for yourself. That would be fantastic! So is this your first time visiting us here at the Towers? Oh no; my brother lives here, well, my best friend he's like a brother! Oh ok, and who is your brother, if you don't mind me asking? Oh Mr. Cooper; we call him AC! Oh really he's a great tenant, been here for a while now. Wow, well welcome home, I'm sure you're going to love the presidential. Just press the 46th floor that's where we're headed. Ok got it. How soon will you be ready to move if you like it? As soon as possible! Ok and will your bank be financing the condo for you? What's the list price on it Melanie, I only checked the price for the other one. The Presidential loft is listed at $389,000.00 but you can make an offer at that price if you like. Well, let me see how it looks first then I'll let you know something. Ok, well we're almost there two more floors. Ding! And here we are, just go to your right Nina, it's two doors down, number 4678.

Ok the crew just painted three days ago and the carpet and tile are new, so there's kind of a new smell in the place. Oh that's fine, let's see it! Melanie placed the key in the lock, turned it and in they went. Wow! This is so awesome, and this view is amazing! I can wake up to this every morning and go to sleep to it every night! Oh my God, I'll take it! I'm going to pay cash, how much of the list price can you take off, if I pay cash. Well- um, let me call my boss and see! Go ahead take your time, Oh I love this marble tile, what is it a rusty brown, and this Jacuzzi is huge, where did you find this material for the counter tops? Is it marble too?

Melanie; I love this place! My sister Denna; is going to be sick when she sees it! The rust colored, marble tile; covered the entire right side of the loft while the other 2,000 square feet on the left complimented it with pecan colored hard wood floors. A long panoramic window with a sliding door in the middle covered the entire back wall, which faced the strip. Soft crème paint covered the walls and the stainless steel, appliances in the kitchen complimented the stainless steel light fixtures that hung from the ceiling through-out the loft.

Ok Nina, I spoke with my boss and she said that I can deduct $50,000.00 if you are paying cash and willing to buy today. What; I am not leaving this place; I'm calling the furniture store right now to deliver me all new things! Here baby; I'm writing you a check right now! Where's my purse? It's over on the counter Ma'am. Damn, I'm so excited I'm forgetting shit! Oops! My bad Melanie, I didn't mean to curse. It's ok Ma'am, I do understand! Nina pulled out here bank book. Can I borrow your pen Melanie? Sure, here you are! Who do I write this thing out to baby? Oh; The Towers Corporation Ma'am. Alright, let's see, $339,000.00 and no cents to The Towers Corporation!

Here you go Melanie! Thanks Nina, here's your paperwork; fill it out and you can call me when you're done then I will come pick it up. These are your keys and welcome to The Towers! Thank you girl, I'm so excited, let me call this furniture store! Alright, I'm going to leave you to your business, just call me when you're done with those documents. Ok girl, I will, thanks again! You're Welcome Nina!

Ring-Ring! Hello, Bradford Furniture! Hello how are you Ma'am? I am good and yourself? I'm doing great! Listen; I need a favor, my name is Nina and I have purchased all of my furniture from you in the past. Oh hi Nina, it's Dana, I remember you! Oh hey Dana, girl I just purchased a Condo at The Towers. Congratulations Girl! Thank you! Did you need help moving your things? Oh no, I need all new things, my old furniture can't do nothing for this loft honey. Did you want me to send a rep over with a catalog? Yes Ma'am, could you please! Sure, I have a few of them available now, when did you want to see one? Now baby; as soon as possible!

Sure it's not a problem; what's your Condo number? Oh it's on the 46th floor and it's number 4678. Alright, Nina! I'm sending someone over as we speak. Thanks Dana, you're an angel! You're welcome and congratulations again. Thank you baby!

Ring-Ring! Hey Sis; what's up? I did it girl! Did what Nina? I just bought a condo at The Towers! What, over where AC is? Yep! Go ahead bitch, do your thing! Call the girls and get them together for a house warming, you guys have to see the place! When did you want to do that, you need to move in first! Tomorrow is fine; I'm waiting for the sales rep from Bradford's to come over, he's showing me the catalog so I can get some furniture delivered tonight. Why are you getting new stuff sis? My old stuff can't do anything for this place, it is gorgeous; you have to come see it. Ok, I'm going to pick up a bottle of champagne and head over, what floor are you on? 46th, number 4678! Alright; see you in a bit!

Chapter 11, Treacherous Winter

Ok Will; explain this thing to me again! Dylan and Barbie came up on a way to rob banks by using checks. Man that sounds crazy, how in the hell are you gonna rob a bank with a check? I was confused at first too; until Dylan broke it down. Then break it down brother. Ok here's how it works. Dylan would write a check to Barbie for a few thousand and deposit it in Barbie's account. Barbie would be waiting on the other side of town at another branch. Dylan would call Barbie after she made the deposit and Barbie would go in the bank and take out the money. So what's the point; aint nothing illegal about that! Hold on Coop, that's not all.

There never was any money in the account. So how did Barbie get the money if it wasn't there? The banks have to honor the checks when you first deposit it and it takes like two days before they find out that the checks are no good. Well I'll be damn; who did you say came up with this scam? Dylan man!

AC stood up from the office chair and walked around to the front of the desk where Will was. This thing could work Big man, what's your plan? Well, Dylan and Barbie had built up a $200,000.00 bad check debt on their accounts. Damn Will, they skimmed that much of money? Hell yeah bruh! I paid the debt then called our boy over in West Las Vegas to make 8 fake I.D's! Why you do that? Because; they're gonna open new accounts under fake names here, in Cali, Utah and Arizona. Ok; I can dig that! I assembled a team of 8 girls to work the banks for the next two weeks. 2 here, 2 in Cali, 2 in Arizona and 2 in Utah!

I sure hope we can trust those bitches? Of course Coop, they all work for us anyway; we can trust them. So when are we putting this thing in motion? I told them to meet us here at the club at 12 today. That's in 30 minutes Will; we better go unlock the front door, it's almost time to open anyway. You get the door; I'll grab the stock for the bar. Just tell the girls to wait in the office when they get here. Alright boss! Knock-Knock! Will; open the door boy! Hold up Red, I'm coming! Hey baby; how you doing?

I'm good, where's AC, I see the Limo out front! He's in the back getting your stock. Oh cool, I'll go get the money for my cash register. Is the office open? Yep, the money is on the desk. Ok thanks. Red! What's going on partner? Hey AC; I am great baby! Thanks for getting that stock! You're welcome! Hey Will, hit the lights bruh! I got it! The pink lights lit up the steps to the stage, Dj booth and ceiling as the pink felted pool tables glowed under the black lights. What's up everybody! Hey Remy! Red can I get a double shot of Henn baby? Sure girl, you want it now? Nah; I'll wait until after I'm dressed. Ok; I got you girl.

Damn Dylan, where in the hell; you and all them bitches going! Hey Red, we have a meeting with AC. Oh he just went to the office. What's up Gloria and Trish, you girls don't even come speak to a sister anymore since yall started working out at that Ranch! What's up with that shit? Red; that is too far to be driving girl! I miss you though pookie! Ahhh, whatever Gloria, you're full of it. You too Trish! Stop acting like that Red; you know we love you girl. Well damn; I sure can't tell, not even a phone call from either one of you ho's! Girl you need to calm down; it aint that serious; we will talk to you after this meeting. Come on Trish, leave Red's crazy ass be!

What's poppin Red head! Hey Malibu, same ol shit baby. What's up Asia? About to go in this meeting; can you fix me a glass of Merlot? Sure and who are these two girls? Oh this is Shooter and Chocolate, two college students that work over at Loon's peep show joint. Oh that's what's up! Hey ladies, I'm Red nice to meet you! Nice to meet you too Red. Asia here's your wine baby. Thanks girl; come on yall; let's go to this meeting. All eight ladies made their way to the office where Will was standing outside of the door. Hey Dylan; I spoke with AC about everything and he's with it. Asia, Malibu, Gloria and the rest of you guys; we will fill you in on the job in a minute. Go ahead in and find a seat, make yourselves comfortable.

Hello girls! Hey AC! We don't have much time before we open; so I'm going to make this fast! So; listen up and pay close attention girls. Will and I have decided to capitalize on a scheme that Dylan and Barbie came up on by accident. We have put together a plan that will make each one of you, 15 grand a week. What; I'm in! Ha-Ha! We know Malibu; that's why I chose you as one of the eight. Each of you ladies that are in this office right now; has what I call that street mentality. No fear; get it by any means necessary attitude. Make no mistake that what I am about to share with you is illegal but we took the necessary precautions to protect you; and our interest. So if either one of you want out; now is the time to leave.

Will and Coop, gazed over the room slowly as they watched the 8 ladies. So you guys are in then? Hell yeah, I know I can use an extra 15 stacks a week. That's what I like to hear Chocolate; do the rest of you feel the same way? Yes! Great let's get to business then! Will hand me those I.D's off the desk! Ok girls; these are your new I.D cards and Social Security numbers! Why do we need those AC? We don't want anyone to use their real names Shooter. This way if something happens; your identity is safe. Oh ok, that's cool right there! Now I want you all to take these I'D's and go open up a checking account at every bank in Vegas. What! You mean all the banks! No Asia I mean the different named ones, like Key, Wells, The Credit Union, etc. Oh, ok I get it.

Now after you guys open your accounts, make sure you get a book of temporary checks so you can use them to deposit money. Today is Friday, so when you all leave here, go directly to a bank. Monday morning at 8 A.M;

meet Will and I hear for your orders. You guys will be working in pairs and in different cities. Dylan and Barbie you're headed to L.A.; Chocolate and Shooter; you have Phoenix; Malibu and Asia; Utah! And Gloria, you and Trish are staying here to work Vegas. Each of you ladies will make an $8,000 deposit and withdraw every business day. That's Monday through Friday. One girl deposits the money in the others account; then the other takes it from her own account. Out of the eight stacks, you keep three and bring us back the five. At the end of every-day we should make 10 stacks and you three gees each. For you girls that's 15 thousand a week and 50 thou a week for us!

If you did not understand what I just said let me know, because if you fuck this up, your stinking asses belong to me! Do you girls understand? Yes Sir! Great; now get out of here and hit up those banks, get those accounts started. And don't forget everyone back here at 8 O'clock Monday morning. Ok AC and Will; see yall Monday! Bye ladies! So what do you think bruh, can they pull it off? Will those chicks can do this shit with their eyes closes bruh. 15 stacks a week for any stripper is a lot of cake. When you look at it that way Boss, who wouldn't do it huh?

All I know Big Will; is we're going to make an extra $400,000 in two weeks! Now that's some gangster business right there Coop! All day player, all day! Say, how long are you gone keep them on the road? Just those two weeks then have them come in so we can see how things went. Yeah that will work but how are we going to get our cut while they are on the road? Shit, we gone have some of our henchmen pick that up and bring it back to Sin City. What Henchmen AC? Hector Will! Hector! Oh ok!

Hey Red! Hey D, what's up man, why are you in here so early? I came to surprise Remy, it's her birthday tomorrow. No shit, really! What did you get her? I can't tell you Red, it's a surprise! Come on man, you can tell me. Nope! Can you page her for me though! Sure I guess. Red walked over to the bar phone and sent a page to the dressing room. "Remy to the front, you have a visitor!" Damn, can a bitch get dressed first; who the hell is it. Remy got up from her chair then walked to the dressing room door to see who it was. Oh hey hun, hold on I'm coming! She yelled.

She aint even dressed yet D! That's good Red; I need to take her outside for a minute anyway. Boy what you got up your sleeve; something smells fishy! Hey hun, what's up; something wrong? No babe, I got you some cupcakes from Albertson's for your Birthday. Come help me get them out of the car. Ok hun, come on! Red I'll be back! You didn't have to buy me any cupcakes Derek. I couldn't resist Remy; I know how much you like those red velvet ones, so I had to go get them. They made their way over to the club exit. Oh hold on baby; let me unlock the door. I don't see the car Derek, where did you park? Hold on; I'll hit the panic button to find it, I forgot where I parked. Beep! Beep! Beep!

Oh my God! Shut the Front door! Honey; I know you motherfucking didn't! Why is that car beeping? That's yours baby! What! The Maserati! That's the white one with the red leather interior! From Duck's lot! You said he sold it already! He did; to me! Oh my God; thank you D! I love your white ass boy! Remy ran to the car and jumped inside. Beep! Beep! The panic button was still active. Baby press the remote button! Oh I'm losing it hun, I'm sorry! Churp! Churp! This is the best birthday present ever! Can I start it up? Yeah baby; go ahead, start it, it's yours. Vroom! Vroom! Vroom! D; get in and let's take it for a spin! Don't you have to get ready for work Remy? Man, please, I'll pay that late fee! Let's take this joker for a ride! Vroom! Vroom! Vroom! Errrrt! Remy peeled out of the Dolls parking lot onto the highway, zooming in and out of traffic until the tail lights on her white Maserati disappeared in the distance and the engine's roar dissipated.

"Hang on the Missile toe; I'm going to get to know you better!" "This Christmas" "Happy Thanksgiving Las Vegas, this is your Love Captain; Dj Shi C!" "Wishing you all a Happy Holiday, don't eat too much turkey today people." "You got to have room for that desert." "I would also like to welcome all of you that are visiting us for the Holiday's here in Vegas." Manny I still can't believe you're not deep frying a turkey this year man. Coop; it aint that serious brother, relax, Loon and Denna deep fried it! They should be here any minute. Man Loon can't cook, I bet he burnt it.

You need to be worrying about Sabrina and Monica in the kitchen together. Aww; worried for what? My women don't cause drama Capo. That's because Sabrina doesn't know about her, that's why. And that's how it's gone stay too; Manny! Hey don't look at me; I don't have those kind of problems. What's gone happen when she does find out Coop? Capo I'm not having this conversation right now, throw me a beer out of that cooler and why is it so damn cold this garage man? Because the door is open brother! You should get one of those outside heaters like they have at those restaurants.

Dude you crazy, for what? What's up fellas, where's the turkey Manny? Loon is bringing it Will! What; don't tell me he cooked it. Yep! Damn, I know I should have stopped by In and Out on the way over here. Ha-ha! I'm just playing Manny! What's going on Coop. Cold and hungry, other than that, just chilling big man! Manny; where's junior? He's down the street at Tony's! Ding-Dong! Ding-Dong! Sophie; get the door babe! Ding-Dong! Alright honey! Happy Thanksgiving Sophie! Thank you guys! Umm, that turkey smells good; here, let me put it in the kitchen. I got it Sophie; did you want it on the table? Yeah that will be fine Loon.

You look nice Denna! Thanks Sophie! You're welcome sugar. Well, who is this young lady Duck? Oh my bad Sophie, this is my friend Karen. Karen this is Sophia; Manny's wife! Hello Sophie, you have a nice home. Thank you Karen, come in and make yourself comfortable. Loon and Duck the guys are in the garage. Cool, where's junior?

Oh he's down the street at his friends Tony's house. Ok it smells good in here; I can't wait to tackle that mac and cheese. Well everything will be ready in 45 minutes, oh could one of you tell Manny to bring some drinks from the garage when you guys come in for dinner. Sure Sophie, I'll tell him. Thanks Loon! Duck, come on man, let's go burn one! What you got Loon? I have one blunt left of that Matanuska. Come on; I'm down bruh. Karen I'll be in the garage with the guys if you need me. Duck go on; she's fine with us! Alright Nina; don't be telling no family secret's either. Don't worry brother; your little secret is safe with me. Nina; don't start! I'm only kidding Duck! Karen did you want a glass of wine baby? Sure; I'll have one.

Fellas! What's good! What up Duck; Loon where's that turkey? It's in the kitchen. Did you burn it man? Kiss my ass Coop! It's nice, brown, tender and juicy! I hear you man, we'll see soon. What you fools doing in here anyway. Not much Duck, just bullshitting, talking and sipping on some beers; waiting on dinner. I got some smoke; did you two want to hit it? Yep; light it up Loon; I can use a good high right now. I bet you can Coop; you got your ol lady and your girlfriend in the kitchen, you're a cold cat boy. Duck, I got this player, watch and you may learn something about being a bona fide player. Yeah ok, we hear you Boss. Ha-ha! Looks like you getting serious with this Karen, Duck. Is she the one? She might be Manny; so far so good. No drama; you dig! That's the money talking boy; it always makes things look easy. You think so AC? I know so Duck; go broke and see how smooth things go. It's always about the loot bruh, please believe that. Loon takes a long toke off the blunt. Inhales; hold it, then releases. Yep- he aint lying Duck, cash is king bruh. Here you go, hit this purple and ease your mind. Fresh candied yams, greens, mac and cheese, ham, fried turkey and sweet potato pies scented up the entire house. Alright guys; the food is ready; come eat!

Damn; pass that blunt Duck; let me hit before we go eat. Here you go AC, I'll see yall inside. Hold up Duck, we're coming player, slow your roll; let the ladies fix our plates first. You're moving too fast. Ha-ha! That's because he's not used to having a woman Manny. Yeah you right Loon, we need to train our boy, just be patient and follow our lead bruh. Hit that smoke one more time then we can take it in. AC takes one last pull, then passes the Matanuska to Duck. He takes two pulls, looks at the blunt, takes another pull then puts the roach in the ash-trey. Alright I'm ready! You sure! Yep, I'm good AC. Ok then let's go grub fellas! The crew gathered around the table for another Thanksgiving together, blessed the food then went on to eat. See Duck, the plates are all ready set. We didn't have to do a thing. I see that Manny. This is what happens when you play your part as a man and you got a good woman on your side. Well, I can get use to this. I know you can Dubai, it's the life brother. Now enjoy that plate that your girl fixed for you.

Yo Josh, this is some bull. It should be busier than this tonight! I agree with you Denna, something is not right. Ding! Hello Sir; welcome to Angelica's. Hey what's going on! I'm great Sir, what can I get you to drink? A cold draft would be fine young man. Ok, one cold draft coming up. I see you folks got some competition out here tonight. Excuse me, what do you mean by that Sir? I was just across the street Ma'am, at that RV, parked just across from here. Its three California blondes over yonder; churning out the business, they're some lookers too! They don't have any beer; so I came over to get me a cold one, whiles I wait my turn. Hold on a minute; did you say it's some whores across the street blocking my business. I believe that's what I said Ma'am.

Well aint that some disrespectful bullshit! Josh I will be right back; I need to go teach those bitches a lesson. You be safe Ma'am, there's a tall fellar in the driver's seat collecting cash at the door there. Thanks for the warning Sir but he's the one that needs to be safe. Josh; call the security shed and tell one of those guys to meet me outside. Ok Denna. Angry and frustrated; she stands up, checks her-self in the wall mirrors then head outside where the guard is waiting on her. Is there a problem Denna? It won't be for long; just watch my back and make sure no one runs up on us while I handle this business. Ok Denna; I got you covered.

Knock-Knock! Denna pounds on the door of the RV while the guard stands out front watching. Knock-Knock! Hold on a minute, it will be 10 minutes before the next girl is free. Knock-Knock! God Dammit, I said hold on! Knock-Knock! The door swings open and a tall, slim, black man with Shirley temple curls, peach suit, yellow shoes and yellow framed glasses, starts shouting at the top of his voice. What the hell is your problem bitch, why are you knocking on my place of business like you aint got no sense! Look; you cartoon character pimpin motherfucker! You got five minutes to move this trailer out of my city or else! Or else what bitch! What did you say? I said- or else what bi--- Pow! The tall skinny pimp and his bright peach suit, yellow shoes and glasses fell down the steps and onto the red Mojave, desert dirt. Ah! Oh my god! One of the girls shouted after running up front and seeing her pimp lay dead in the dirt; blood running from the side of his head and over his cracked yellow glasses.

Hey blonde bitch, you got ten minutes to pick that dead fucker up and drive this piece of shit trailer out of my town or all three of you are next! Yes Ma'am! She jumped out of the RV then dragged the dead pimp up the three steps and onto the RV's floor then started the vehicle. Vroom! Vroom! The whore started the RV as the tricks pulled up their pants and jumped off the moving vehicle as it left town. Vroom! Vroom! Desert sand and rocks clashed against the underbody of the RV; leaving a cloud of dust behind. Come on man our business here is finished! Yes

Ma'am; you showed them huh? Damn right! How dare they come out here and disrespect my business. Thanks for having my back man. You're welcome Denna but you had it covered anyway. Well, that's cause for a Corona. Denna walked up the steps to the ranch then went inside. Well; what happened Denna? I took care of it Josh; they won't be around here again; ever! Sir, would you like to go over to our lounge area and meet the ladies? I was just about to do that Ma'am! You're a spunky little something aint you? I just don't like anyone disrespecting me; that's all Mister. Well from the looks of things, you can handle yourself pretty good. I try my best Sir. Um-hm, well on that note; I'll be over yonder with yah ladies. Ok Mr., enjoy yourself!

Hello Sir, how much to ride bus? What did you say lady? I said; how much for me and my friend to ride bus? It depends! Where are you headed, this bus is going north; down to Freemont street. Where do you guys want to go? Yes, yes, we want to go to Freemont Street. Okay, it will be $2 each, just slide the money in this slot here Ma'am. Oh ok, thank you Sir! Umm-hm, you're welcome; just take a seat so we can get going. Here you go, two dollars! Vicky come on; stop standing there and come sit down. I'm coming ILona; gosh! The huge city bus cruised down the strip with ease as the sun begun to set. The red and blue lights of the Stardust reflected off the bus window panes as the German ladies admired the sights. Look Vickey, up there; it's the Stratosphere! Yeah I see it; that's really high! You ladies know there's a roller coaster up there too! No way! Yes Ma'am, if you look close enough you could see it going around the building. Wow that's amazing. Yes it is Ma'am! Say; where are you two girls from anyways? Germany Sir! Oh really! Are you guys just visiting or what? No we just moved here for our jobs. What kind of work you girls do? We-.Ugh! Ugh! ILona why are you kicking me!

Well; this is your stop ladies! The Freemont Street Experience; enjoy yourselves and be careful. Ok Sir thank you! Vicky come on; let's go! ILona and Vicky dressed in their CK1 denims, 6 inch heels and fitted tops, hair swinging, walked off the bus and onto the sidewalk. Overhead a large movie screen covered the entire distance of the Freemont street casino sidewalk, from the 4 Queens to O'riley's. Wow, that is so pretty, do you see it Vicky? ILona I am right here, of course I see it. The two of them stood there for ten minutes admiring the Freemont Experience; overhead show of jets, entertainers and announcements that flew across the large screen overhead.

Vicky! My neck is hurting, come on; let's go check out the 4 Queens. What! I said let's go over here. Oh ok. I want to play the slot machines. Yeah me too ILona, but we need some change; don't we? I'm sure they have some in here. The sound of slots chiming, patrons screaming and Wayne Newton singing over the speakers, welcomed them in to the smoke filled casino. Over there Vicky, that window! What about it? That's where we get change!

Hello Ma'am; can I have change for this $100? Sure Miss, how did you want it? Did you want chips or coins? Uh, quarters Ma'am. Sure; one minute please. Here you go Miss, $100 in quarters. Thank you! You're welcome Miss. Next in line please! ILona why did you get all those quarters? So I can play the slot machines silly! Not me; I want to play the penny slots, I can play more times! Next in line please! Vicky; go ahead! Oh I'm sorry Ma'am! How can I help you Miss? Can I have $50 in pennies please? One minute Miss! Vicky you are silly! Why; because I got pennies? Yep! Here you are Miss, good luck! Thank you Ma'am!

Alright Vicky; let's go win some money! Yay; let's go! America is ok ILona, what do you think? I like it, no snow! Ha-Ha! Right; no snow! Excuse me ladies! Excuse me ladies! Yes Sir, what is it? Me and my friend here are in town for the weekend and we are looking for a place to party. Do you nice ladies know where we can go party? This is Vegas, you can party anywhere you want! Oh really, I'm sorry I didn't get your name. It is Vicky! Hi Vicky, I'm Scott and this is my buddy Matt. Hi Matt and nice to meet you Scott. This is my best friend ILona. ILona huh, where are you guys from? We are from Germany! Oh that's great; do you guys live here now or just visiting? Oh no we came here for work! What kind of work Vicky? Uh, how you say in America, um working girl. Did you say working Girl? Vicky; be quiet! No, no it's ok Vicky I have friends that are working girls. Are you and ILona working now?

No, we are just out having some fun. Well, how about coming to have some fun with me and Scott. That's ok; come on Vicky let's go. Hold on ILona, we can pay you. How much you pay Sir? We can pay $1000 Vicky. How about you Matt, can you pay $1000 too? Sure, it's no problem. Ok fellas, 1 minute, I need to talk with ILona. Come on Lona, it's $1000 one time. No Vicky, Nina said only work through the agency. She never find out Lona! Come on; please. Ugh! Just once and we go back to the house after. Ok! Thank you ILona! Ok guys, do you have room? Yes we do Vicky! Great, can you pay now and we walk with you to room. Sure here you go, that's my thousand. Thanks Scott! Here is my thousand ILona! Thanks Matt! Ok guys, let's go party! Click! Click! Hey hold on! Ladies you are under arrest for prostitution! Hey! Stop! We do nothing wrong! Vicky; prostitution is illegal in the city of Las Vegas. But we thought it's legal Scott! That is why we move here! Nope, not in the city, only in the county! Let's go ladies, the police station is only two blocks down, we don't have far to walk. No! No!

The patrons went about their business as Matt and Scott escorted the ladies outside and down to the precinct. Calm down ILona, you are only making things worse. Here ladies, have a seat on this bench while we process you. Where are your I'D's? In my purse! Thanks Vicky! Where is yours ILona? In my pocket! Thanks! Do you ladies need to call someone? Yes, yes please! Ok, hold on a minute; I can let one of you make a phone call. ILona call Nina and tell her! Shut up Vicky! Alright; whose making the call? Me Sir! Ok stand up ILona and come over to the counter. Hold on a sec; let me take these cuffs off. You got two minutes, make your call. Ring-Ring! Hello; thank you for calling Angels escorts, would you like to book a date? Georgia! Who is this? ILona! Hey girl, what's up; are you guys having fun? No, no, we are at the jail! What! The jail! Hold on a minute! Nina this is ILona; she says they are in jail! What the fuck, give me that phone. Hello! Nina; please help! Girl; how in the hell did you two get locked up. We were in casino and two guys asked us to go party for $1000. We took money and they say prostitution is illegal. I do not understand. Bitch it is, that's why I told you to only date through the agency, we screen our customers.

I am sorry Nina, come get us please. I'm not coming to get you two. Why not Nina! ILona, calm down baby, bitches get locked up every hour for prostitution in Vegas. They're just going to give you guys a ticket and let you go. Oh ok, I am sorry Nina! Don't apologize girl, just listen next time. Bring yall asses to the office when you get out; so I can take care of those tickets. Ok Nina, thank you! Yeah, you're welcome; see you guys later. ILona what she say? She say we get out soon and come back to office. Ok Ma'am; back over here to the bench. It will take an hour to write these citations. Yes Sir. You girls made the same mistake that a lot of the girls do when they come here. Prostitution is illegal in the city of Las Vegas. If you want to be a prostitute, go out to the desert and work at one of those ranches. Yes Sir. Don't let us catch you again, the next time you will be spending a week in jail with us. Now just wait there and I will be back after I finish this paperwork. Yes Sir, no problem.

Next in line please! Hi Sir, did you find everything ok? Oh yeah; the fat girl porn is always easy to find! Will that be all for you? No, let me get a box of those vagina pops? Ok, anything else for you? Nah; that will do it! Ok Sir, your total is $33.97. Here you go brother; you can take it out of this 50! Sure, and $16.03 is your total. Thanks man! You're welcome; next in line please! Hey Loon, what's up fool? Hey Carlos, what you doing here boy? Come to get this new Heather Hunter joint homie! Oh, she's giving up the business in that flick player! What; is it good? Man that chick taking it in the ass and everything. I'm talking all her holes got plugged.

Damn, that's what's up; I wouldn't mind hitting that sexy red motherfucker. Stand in line Carlos, you and about 100 thousand other fools. Is that going to be all for you bruh? Yeah, that's it. Hey, yall coming by the Ritz for the Christmas party? Nah, we're having a company Christmas party, I think AC is doing it at the Drink this year. Oh that's what's up, how much I owe you homie? Oh $17.89 bruh! Here's a 20, keep the change; buy you some lunch or something! Ha-ha! Fuck you Carlos! Later homie; hold it down! Next in line please! Yeah do you have some of those midget flicks? No Ma'am we don't! Why not? I don't know Ma'am, we just don't! Well can you get some, me and my husband like to watch them. I'll see what I can do Ma'am; check with me next week. Is there anything else I can do for you Ma'am? Excuse me Ma'am, I'll be right back! Loon, closed the register, walked around the counter and over to a customer in the middle of the isle wearing a long tan trench coat. Hey fool! Hey fool! Open that damn coat! What; man kiss my ass, get away from me! Open the coat man, this is my last time asking?

I ain't opening shit! Click-Click! Say what! Ok Sir, just calm down and put the gun away. That's what I thought nigga, now open that damn coat, now! Ok man, ok! God damn, aint this a bitch! Man; put my movies on the floor and get your thieving ass out of here! Ok Sir, I'm putting them down. You aint moving fast enough mister! Drop all of them and get the hell on! Pow! Oh shit; I'm going, don't shoot me Sir! Please don't shoot me! Next time it's going to be in your ass and not the ceiling! I'm going, I'm going; come on baby! This nigga is crazy! What! You mean to tell me, you're with him! Pow! Oh shit come on baby! That's right get your midget movie watching asses out of here! Crazy ass people, done made me shoot two holes in my new ceiling. Damn it, if it aint one thing it's another!

The balcony door's ajar over at AC's as the cool winter breeze blow in through the white satin curtains that covered the opening. The two curtains rippled and danced as the clear night sky sparkled from the stars above while a rainbow of lights danced off the glass casino buildings down below. Daddy it's a nice calm night out, I'm going on the balcony. Sabrina, it's cold out there, don't freeze your pussy off wearing just that T-shirt! I'll be fine; this shirt is like a gown anyway. Alright, I hear you woman. Are you coming out daddy? Yeah; after I finish shaving. Cool, did you want a glass of wine? Sure, I'll take one.

The wind blew her long shirt; tight against her model framed body, her hard nipples pierced through the T-shirt while she held the bottom part down with her free hand. Damn it's chilly out here girl! It's not that bad AC, come on out. Alright, I'm sitting down though; fuck that wind blowing in my face. Coop walked out on the balcony then sat down in the patio chair that was against the wall, attempting to dodge the wind. Sabrina placed both bare feet up on the rail, holding on tight with her left hand while holding her glass of wine in her right. Baby I know your pussy is cold; it's all out in the open. Look at it, it's turning red! AC stop playing, no it isn't. Coop slid his chair over behind Sabrina so that he could get a closer look. Yes it is Sabrina. Yeah whatever, it feels fine to me. Coop reached up and places his hands on Sabrina's hips. What are you doing daddy? Taking a closer look baby, hold still!

He slid his hands down to her butt cheeks, spreading them apart so that her vagina would expose itself a little more. Ummm, daddy, what are you doing? Shhhh, be quiet baby. Coop leaned in closer so that his lips were now upon hers. Slowly he licked around the outside, then to her clit then inside her sugar walls. Ummmm, daddy! Slurp. Slurp. You like that baby? Um-hmm! The glass of wine tilted left than right then..... Oh shit AC, I dropped my wine! Slurp! Slurp! Slurp! Ummm, oh shit! Sabrina gripped the rail a little tighter, now using both hands. Coop sucked on Sabrina's clit while rotating his tongue counter wise around the little man in her boat. Ummm, daddy!

His nose bumped the crack of her ass, just above her butt hole, every time he tongue fucked her. Umm, eat that pussy daddy! Slurp! Slurp! Slurp! AC stuck his tongue in deep as it would go then licked her senseless until she fell back on his face. Oh my God! Umm! Umm! Umm! Slurp! Slurp! Slurp! Umm! Umm! Umm! Slurp! Slurp! Slurp! Shit you feel good daddy! Umm! Umm! Damn it! Uhhhhh! Uhhhh! Uhhhh! Uhhhhhhhhhhhhhh.

Chapter 12, Season Greetings

Alright Sam, Smiley we're here; AC should be inside. Thanks Mick but hold tight; don't leave yet, I don't know where Coop wants us to take these new girls. Ok Sam, I'll be waiting. Come on ladies this is Club Dolls; it's where you will be working. Smiley and the two black and Thai mixed girls followed Sam out of the Limo. You ladies remember AC right? Yes, from bar in Pattaya. Yeah that's him Mali! Well he's inside waiting on us. Oh I like, he's the chocolate man! Yes Dao, that's him, come on he's waiting. Hello fellas! Hi Red, is AC in? Yeah babe, he's in the office. Ok; he's expecting us! Alright Smiley; go ahead back.

Sam and Smiley made their way to the office as the new girls followed. Mali and Dao were similar in size and facial features, peanut butter colored skin and jet black hair that was cut in a bob style that hung to their cheek bones. They both stood only 5' tall, with perky c cups and thin sexy lips with pretty gray eyes. Knock-knock! It's open! Hey my friend! Sam, Smiley, what's up, how was your flight? It was good like always. Chocolate man! Hey ladies, welcome to

America, or should I say Vegas! Come over here and give me a hug. Dao and Mali ran over to the desk to hug Coop. Wow, you too look great, are you guys tired? Yes and eat too! Ha-Ha! You're hungry! Yes! Ok, we'll take care of that! By the way, this is my partner Will. Will, this is... Damn my bad, ladies what's your names? Me Mali , her Dao! Hello ladies! Hi! They will be working for you big man, here at the club. Will stood there looking at the ladies while nodding his approval. I can dig that!

Hey Sam; did Mick leave? Nah, I told him to hold on. Cool, take the girls to get something to eat then head over to the mansion and relax. There should be a few empty rooms; have the girls pick one out. Ok Coop; we'll go handle that now. Alright girls go with Sam and Smiley, I will see you later. Ok chocolate man! Ha-ha! You can call me AC! No, we like chocolate man for you. Sure whatever you like! Ring-Ring! Will, get that will you! Ring-Ring! Hello! Hey Will; Dylan and the girls are here to see you two. Cool, send them back. Who was that? Red! What she want? She said Dylan and the girls are here. Did you tell her to send them back? Yeah they're coming. Knock-Knock! Come in! Hey Will, AC! What's up ladies?

Man we should have been doing this a few months ago; it's easy money! Oh you think so Gloria? Hell yeah AC, it was like taking candy from a baby. What did you think Trish? I'm with my partner! It was like taking candy from a baby. That maybe so ladies but this is still illegal, so don't ever get too comfortable. We hear you Coop, it was just easier than we expected. How so Asia? Dude all we did was write a check then deposited it, then waited for the other to take the money out. Too easy! I'm glad that you all thought it was easy. How was your trip Dylan? It wasn't any different from hitting the banks here AC, I did see some banks over there that we can hit though. What you mean Dylan? It was like two banks that they have in their city that we don't over here. Oh ok, we can add them later than. Did you girls have any problem meeting up with our connect for the drops? It was ok; I just think you should use someone cleaner. What do you mean by that Chocolate?

I don't know about the other crews, but our connect looked like a gangster. I think the connect should be cleaner looking, so they don't appear suspicious. Yeah I do too AC! So you agree Barbie? Yeah; because I was kind of nervous when I gave him the money! Even though I knew you sent him; it felt like we might get jacked! Will; what do you have to say about this? I understand their concern but at the same time you don't want no soft ass picking up $200,000 a week either. We need someone that's going to protect our interest and they must have that no nonsense attitude about them. For me, our guys fit the bill perfectly.

Yeah I agree with you Will! Ok ladies, it's December; Christmas is around the counter and everyone has some kind of Holiday stuff to do. So take the rest of the month off and enjoy that 30 thousand yall made. Let's meet back here on the first weekend of next year for our next run. If you don't have your tickets for the Christmas party; be sure to stop by the bar and get one from Red. Where is the party at this year Coop? It's going to be at The Drink; Dylan! Oh hell yeah, I'm about to go shopping bitch, you coming? Nah you go ahead girl, I have some other business to handle. Alright then Barbie, holler at me later. Ok I will, bye girl! All eight girls moved hastily out of the office and on to their next destinations, eager to enjoy their earnings from the prior two weeks. Will, my man, this is going to be a great Christmas! I agree Coop! I agree! So what are you getting Sabrina for Christmas? I don't know Will; I have a few things I'm thinking about. You don't have long Coop. Man I know! You'll figure it out though. Yeah, I'm sure. You've done a good job with the club though Will. Thanks AC; I appreciate that. You're pretty good at this Crime Boss thing too though. Man I try my best, you guys make it easy. We all are just playing are parts man like we've always done way back to our Army days. When you look at it that way Will; who can stop us? Nobody Coop, no fucking body! My brother; let's hit the bar, we're gone drink to that! I can dig it; lead the way Coop!

Ring-Ring! Hello; thank you for calling Las Vegas Luxury Auto! How may I help you? Yes Ma'am, I just wanted to know what time you all closed tonight. My wife gets off at 7:30 P.M and I wanted to bring her buy to look at a new car. We close at 9:30 Sir. Thank you Ma'am, I appreciate it. You're welcome Sir, no problem. Ring-Ring! Yes Mr. Dubai! Jackie could you come to my office please; I have something for you. Ok Sir, be there in a second. Jackie got up from her desk and headed over to Duck's office, her heels made a loud clogging noise as she walked across the marble tile floors.

Yes Sir; Mr. Dubai! Here you go Jackie, this is for you. Merry Christmas! He hands her a red envelop. Thank you Sir! You're welcome! Hi Jackie! Hi Karen, how are you? I'm fine, thanks for asking. She stood there impatiently as she opened the red envelop. Oh my; thank you so much! Merry Christmas Jackie! She stood there grinning from ear to ear with five $100 bills in her left hand two tickets in the other. Thank you again; Mr. Dubai! Are these tickets to a party? Yes to our annual Company Christmas Party, there good for you and one guest. Wow! This is great, ok I'm going back to my desk now, thank you so much. You're welcome!

Aww Duck, that was so sweet! It's nothing Karen, just taking care of my employees. Oh really, so did you give all your employees $500; even the sales people. Hell no; they only got $100. Well that's still good. It better be! Ha-ha! Duck you are crazy! So I've been told! What's this Christmas Party about? Oh; me and the crew have a party every year with all of the company employees. What company? Karen between all of us, we have like 10 different businesses but they are all ran by AC. He's the CEO, The Boss, The HNIC! Together we call them the companies and he's at the top! Damn Duck, how long have you guys been in business? Long enough to make a difference baby, long enough! Well am I invited to this party? Of course Karen, you know you're my baby.

Alright, I was just making sure Mr.! Are you going to eat your sandwich, I have to go out on the lot soon. Of course, where is it? Oh snap, I never gave it to you? No you didn't Duck! You got a girl sitting here starving. I'm sorry baby; I must have left it in the break room fridge. I will be right back. Umm-hmm. Karen reached in her purse and took out a small mirror, looked in it, fixed her hair then replaced it. Here you go baby, it was in the fridge. Thanks Duck. What kind of sub is it? It's an Italian Meatball from Mikes; over off Sahara. Ummm, it smells good too! What do you have? The same as you baby! Customer after customer pulled on to the lot while Duck and Karen enjoyed their lunch. The dozen sales people became too few and the customers became impatient as the phones continued to ring for what seems like forever. Ring-Ring! Hello, thanks for calling Las Vegas Luxury Auto, please hold! Ring-Ring! Hello, thanks for calling Las Vegas Luxury Auto, please hold! Ring-Ring! Hello, thanks for calling Las Vegas Luxury

Auto, please hold! Jackie stood up and screamed to the top of her lungs. Mr. Dubai! Karen; I'm sorry baby, I have to go help, it's getting crazy out there! Alright, thanks for lunch, go to work, I will chat with you later. Thanks, bye baby! Muah! Ring-Ring! Hello, thanks for calling Las Vegas Luxury Auto, please hold!

Jackie, I'm going on the lot to help out; if anyone calls; take a message! Yes Sir, take a message. Ring-Ring! Hello, thanks for calling Las Vegas Luxury Auto, please hold! Ring-Ring! Hello, thanks for calling Las Vegas Luxury Auto, please hold! Ring-Ring! Yes; Mr. Dubai is not available at this time; would you like to leave a message? No Ma'am. Ok Thank you. Ring-Ring! Hello, thanks for calling Las Vegas Luxury Auto, please hold! Ring-Ring! Hello, thanks for calling Las Vegas Luxury Auto, please hold!

Ok people; have your tickets out when you get to the door. This is an exclusive Christmas Party tonight at The Drink. If you don't have a ticket or if you're not on my VIP list, you might as well go party somewhere else. I'm Big Rick and no one; I mean no one enters without seeing me first! Rick stood out front of The Drink night club, dressed in his all black Tux with clip board in hand laying down the law. Normal patrons got frustrated and turned away because they couldn't enter. The sign at the corner made of a big drink, with an umbrella in it, lit up the parking lot entrance as the Limo's and VIP guest entered. Loud music from the outside speakers played in the background while the cars and Limo's approached the valet booth. "Flipmode, Busta Bus, Nine-Seven, Hot Shit, Check it out" Vroom! Vroom! The Valet opens the door to the black limo as it stopped in front of him. Hello ladies welcome to the party; have your tickets out so Big Rick can check them at the door. "Hit you with no delayin so what you sayin yo" "Silly with my nine milly what the dealy yo!" Oh girl that's my jam, Busta Bus! Come on yall, let's go crash this Christmas party, I'm about to get my money worth out of this dress! That is; a hot ass dress though Dylan; Red looks good on you! Thanks Barbie! I almost got that cat suit like you but your ass is fatter than mine, you rocking that mother! I don't know girl; I almost didn't get it! Why not; it's hot! Because I wanted the blue one but they didn't have my size. Girl that black is better I think. Well thanks Dylan! You're welcome baby, where is Asia and Malibu? Still in the Limo hitting the rest of that blunt! Malibu; bring your butt on here girl, put that blunt out. Oh I'm done; Asia's taking the last pull off it now.

Asia, we will be inside you're too damn slow. What Malibu, I think not. Don't make me karate kick yall three bitches tonight! Girl please; I'll cut that foot off! Ha-Ha! Dylan you're crazy, I'm ready though, damn I'm high; that was some good chronic. Come on girls; let's go crash this party! Lead the way Dylan, we're right behind you. Asia and Malibu straightened their black dresses then followed Dylan and Barbie inside.

Vroom! Vroom! Vroom! A white Maserati cruised up to the Valet booth and parked then the Valet opened the driver side door. Remy stepped out dressed in red leather boots and matching dress. Derek walked around the front of the car, wearing blue jeans, white Air forces, white button up and Red Suede Blazer and white ball cap. Welcome to The Drink folks, please have your tickets ready when you get to the door. Come on Remy, I got the tickets in my pocket. Ok honey I'm ready. Two Limo's pulled up to the Valet, one behind the other, while a third car; a yellow Hummer, parked behind them. Three Valet's, ran to assist the passengers in each of the vehicles.

Hello people; time to get your party on! Rose is in the building! Valet; make sure you park my Hummer up front darling, with the VIP's. Yes Ma'am, not a problem! Thank you handsome! Hold on darling, how do I look? Rose stood there posing her perfect figure and slanging her hair while zipping up her mink three quarter jacket that covered her black Prada dress that was complimented by her black Prada boots. You look good Ma'am! Thank you Darling! Muah! I'll see you after the party!

Welcome to the party ladies, you all look great in your black dresses. Thank you Valet guy! Chocolate; you're crazy! Why you call him Valet guy? Because that's what he is Shooter, a Valet guy! Ha-ha! It's ok Ma'am, I don't mind. See Shooter! Hey Chocolate do you have the tickets? No; I thought you had them Gloria. No I don't! Calm down ladies I have them! Whew, thanks Trish you're a life saver; let's go take some shots! Enjoy the party girls! Thanks Valet guy! Ha-ha! Chocolate you're a mess. What Shooter? Nothing; come on.

Hello folks welcome to The Drink! Hey how are you? I am good Ma'am. Are you two sisters? No, why you ask? Because you don't see two red heads at the same time unless their kin. Well the answer is no! I'm Red and that's Gerogia! But her hair is red too Ma'am! Yeah but I'm the oldest; so you can call her by her name. Red what are you tripping about girl? Nothing Monica, just schooling this Valet! Come on Josh, what are you doing in there? Hold on Mo, I need to fix my tie. Come out, I'll do it for you. Thanks Mo! You're welcome; you look nice in this black suit Josh. Thank you again Monica. Umm-hm. You guys ready? Yeah Red! Ok, let's make our grand entrance then. Monica, Red and Georgia's green dresses blew in the wind as they walked down the red carpet behind Josh.

A pearly white stretch navigator entered the lot and rolled up slowly to the Valet booth. The door swung open before the valet could get to it. Loon, Manny, Big Will and Duck stepped out, all dressed in black suits, red shirts, black ties and shoes. Nina, Denna, Sophia and Karen followed, all wearing Red dresses, red heels and white fur coats. Hey Sis, did you speak to Coop? Yeah Loon, He's on the way! Ok cool, thanks Nina! Well; it's chilly out here, let's go in and greet our guest. I agree Will, lead the way brother! No Capo; after you!

As the scene became busier on the outside, Big Rick was on alert for the constant flow of invited guest who was now walking up to enter. The brown brick building was lit up on all four corners while photographers lined the Red carpet to snap pictures of the underground lords of crime and their associates. Vroom! Vroom! Vroom! A silver convertible Porsche pulled up to the front, parked by the curb then the driver exited the vehicle and walked up to the red carpet. Excuse me Sir! You can't park there! My friend, I park where I want! You Understand! No Sir! We need to move it! My friend, if you move my car, I will kill you. Do you want to die my friend? No Sir, but.. My friend what is your name? Jason Sir! Jason, I am Diego, maybe you heard of me, no? Oh yes Sir! Good, so now you understand? Yes Sir. So you leave my car where it is; now I go inside and have a few drinks and chat with my friends and enjoy the party. Ok Sir, have a great time.

The Valet stood at the booth watching, as a white impala led a convoy of cars onto the lot, one white Tahoe, followed by a silver Lexus truck and a black Range Rover. Hey Amigo; park my car and don't scratch punta! Hector and Chino exited the impala then after some words with the valet headed inside while Fat Boy squeezed out the Tahoe. Yo I aint staying all night so don't be parking my truck way in the back! Yes Sir, no problem Sir. Alright, you got me then yo? Yes Sir. Paco jumped out of his Lexus as Dupree walked by, both guys leaving their keys in the ignition. Hey Pree wait up Amigo! What up Paco; how's it hanging playboy? Everything is good Dupree, life is good! Shit I have to agree with you there player, let's go pop some of these bottles.

Hey Mick, slow down a little before you pull on the lot, I need a few minutes. Ok AC, no problem. What's wrong Daddy? Nothing baby, I need to give you your Christmas present. AC you could have waited until tomorrow. I like to open my gifts on Christmas morning, not Christmas Eve. I know that Sabrina but I want you to have this one now. Ok daddy, just this one. Coop got up off the Limo seat, kneeled down on the floor and pulled a small box from the wine cabinet. Sabrina! Oh my God what are you doing AC! Sabrina! Daddy! Baby, calm down and let me talk. Ok I'm sorry, go ahead! Sabrina; will you marry me? Oh My God! Yes Daddy! Yes! Sabrina dived from the seat and into Coops arms as the limo pulled up to the Valet.

Oh this is so beautiful daddy, is this platinum? Yes baby! How many Karats? 21 Sabrina, only the best for my baby! Oh I'm going to be Mrs. Cooper; I like the sound of that. Come on let's go tell everyone the news daddy! Good Evening Mr. Cooper, welcome to The Drink, your partners are upstairs on the VIP Balcony, you may enter through the side entrance. It's right where those steps are going up along-side the building. Thanks bruh, come on Mrs. Cooper, let's go celebrate!

AC; dressed in his all black suit, black shirt and red tie, grabbed his bride to be by the hand and escorted her up the stairs, being careful not to damage her black cashmere dress and red leather jacket. The doorman opened the door slowly as they approached. Hello Sir, your party has been waiting on you. Chronic smoke clouded the doorway as the loud music danced with the red and green lights that bounced off the walls. "What's up party people, this is your boy; Dj Skillz!" "Merry Christmas Eve!" "I wanna give a shout out to my boy AC for throwing this slamming ass party!" " I see you up there in the VIP player!" "Alright yall; I'm gone keep this thing rocking with some that Junior Mafia!" "Niggaz grab your dick if you love Hip Hop"

"Bitches Rub your titties if you love Big Poppa!" Coop what's up fool! Merry Christmas Loon, what's going bruh! Popping bottles, what took you two so long? We've been here for 45 minutes already. I'll tell you later! What! I said I'll tell you later! Alright that's what's up.

The crew gathered in the VIP balcony that overlooked the dance floor from two stories up. Denna, Nina, Sophie and Karen waited at the private VIP bar for their drinks while the guys stood over the black steel rail looking down at the crowd of people below. "Now who smoke more blunts than a little bit" "What are you a idiot" What's up girls? Hey Brina, Merry Christmas girl! Thanks Nina, same to you baby! Oh My God, Sabrina what is that on your finger? Sophie; he proposed to me! What! When? On the way here! Let me see that thing Brina! Wow! Isn't it pretty Denna! Hell yes! Congratulations Girl! Thank you Karen! So have you guys discussed a date yet? Sophie I haven't even thought about it, I'm just so excited!

Ladies, here's your drinks! Thank you Sir! The girls now with drinks in hand and just as excited for Sabrina as she was for herself, hurried over to congratulate Coop. "I blow up spots like little sisters" "G'wan grit ya teeth, g'wan bite ya nails to the cuticles." Damn Capo; look how far we came in a year! Hey, we put in the work Boss, when you put in work like we did; you get paid. That's the name of the game huh Manny; crime pays, fuck what they say! Damn right! Yo Will, this place is packed fool, there's twice the amount of people here compared to last year. That's because we know how to get money; we let all of our people eat bruh. And when everybody eats, everybody is happy, right Coop! I couldn't have said it any better myself Duck! Hey where is Hector? He's down there somewhere smoking Manny; I told him to come up.

Well; congratulations AC! What for Nina? Poppi; are you serious! For this thing! Sabrina; show the guys your rock! Wow! Coop what's that? It's a ring Loon, you aint blind. Damn brother; you're about to tie the knot huh? Yes I am Capo, is something wrong with that? Nah my man; that's a good move as long as you're happy! Everybody I propose a toast! The crew held their glasses up while Loon announced the toast. To The Sin City Boss; AC, and Sabrina, The 1st lady! Here's to getting money, cracking skulls and living life to the fullest! Cling! Their glasses clash as they shout the crew motto. Death before dishonor! Hey

Brina, you're blood in now sister, we rock with you til the death. Thanks Denna! You're welcome girl, now let's party punta's! "Niggaz grab your dick if you love hip-hop" "Bitches Rub your titties if you love Big Poppa!"

Loon, what's taking you so long baby? I'm coming Denna; I had to put on my long johns! Well hurry up, we only have like 4 hours of day light left. I made you some coffee; it's over the fire place. Denna stood by the window, gazing at the beautiful snowcapped; Lake Tahoe Mountain tops. The fire place crackled and popped from the burning logs that kept the log cabin warm and cozy. One old fashioned; wood stove sat in the corner by the single door fridge and kitchen sink. A cinnamon, brown bear rug was pinned down by an eighty year old, oak coffee table that sat in front of the black leather sofa and love seat that was in the center of the living room. Yeah, this is more like baby, nice and warm! Poppi, you look like a fat kid that can't walk. How many long johns you put on under that snow suit? Just one baby! Looks more like three! Loon walked over to the fire place, picked up his thermos of coffee and headed over to Denna. You ready to ride these snow mobiles baby? Yep, let's do it fat boy! Ha-Ha! Whatever, I bet this fat boy will have you eating snowflakes. We'll see about that Looney. Hold on Denna, don't you think we should put the fire out. Yep that's a good idea. Loon picked up the muzzle then covered the flames. All set, now let's go ride!

Denna in her red snow suit, Loon in blue, exited the cabin and headed outside to the parked snow mobiles. Thousands and thousands of snowcapped trees surrounded the cabin on every side except for the drive way. Vroom! Vroom! Come on Loon, start that bad boy poppi! Hold on; give me a second. It's all those damn clothes you got on! Ha-Ha! Nah, I got it. Vroom! Vroom! Yeah Poppi, that's it; let's ride! Vroom! Vroom! Denna took off down the snow filled drive way; Loon followed close behind. About a mile later, the trees faded away as everything turned completely white. No more drive way or snowcapped trees, only white mountains, miles and miles of snow, Skiers, Snow boarders and Snow mobiles. Lake Tahoe at Christmas time was one of Denna's most favorite places to be! Come on Loon, keep up poppi! Vroom! Vroom! Snow flurries flew up from the rear of the snow mobiles, as they glided over the pure white snow alongside one another.

Loon pulled ahead of her then she pulled in front of him. Vroom! Vroom! Back and forth they went for the next few miles, blowing snow on one another's ski mask and goggles as they enjoyed the winter wonderland. Loon pointed ahead to the Ski Lodge where everyone boarded the ski lift. Nina gave a thumbs up then took off behind him. Vroom! Vroom! A half a mile up the hill the two pulled in to the ski mobile parking space right outside the cabin. Whew, now that's what I call an adrenalin rush poppi! Hell yeah baby; that was the shit!

I'm hungry poppi, let's go inside and get something. Alright what you want? The Lamb stew; I have been dreaming about that thing for two nights. Really! Yes really, you must have never had it! No Denna, never tried it! You have to eat some of mine! Ok I will taste a little bit. They knock the snow from their boots and walk inside the Ski Lodge. Hello Sir; do we have to wait to be seated? No Ma'am, just sit anywhere you like. Thank you! Where do you want to sit Loon? Over by the window is fine baby. Wooden tables and chairs sat alongside the wall and down the center of the restaurant seating area. Puddles of water from melted snow; stained the wood finished floors and dripped off snow suits and ski mask as they hung on the rack by the entrance.

Hello people, I will be your waitress today. Can I start you guys with some coffee or coco? Yeah honey, some coco for me! Ok Ma'am; and for you Sir? I'll have the same! Two coco's coming right up! So; how does your sister like her new place? Man, she is crazy about it; you have to see it! I know; I haven't had a chance to go by there yet. She's having the New Year's Eve party there this year, it should be nice. Is it big enough? Poppi it is huge, a little bigger than AC's place. Damn, that's what's up. Does that mean you are moving out of your one bedroom too? I don't know Loon, I kind of like my place. Why you ask? I was just curious that's all; I'm thinking about moving too. Oh really, what's stopping you?

I want a bigger place, like a ranch house or something. That sounds nice poppi! Why a ranch house? I'm just not all that crazy about steps and elevators; one floor is fine with me. Well, have you started looking yet? No, I wanted to talk with you first. How come poppi? I got to thinking, since we're together now, maybe we should move in with each other. Oh, you want to shack up? Excuse me; here's your coco. Do you guys know what you want to order yet? Yes Ma'am, I'm having the Lamb stew! And for you Sir? I'll have the grilled cheese and baked potato!

I have one Lamb stew, a grilled cheese and baked potato! Yep that's it! What did you want with your potato Sir? Just butter, sour cream and bacon bits! Alright, it should only take a few minutes. Thank you honey! You're welcome Ma'am! Now, what were you saying poppi? I said we should move in together! Why should I move in with your crazy ass Loon? Because you're my woman, that's why! Loon, I don't think you're ready for that. I'm ready, why you say that? I say that because if I catch you looking at a bitch or even trying to talk to one; I will kill your ass. You do know that right?

Yeah I know. If you think that we can live together with no drama and you can keep your dick in your pants; I will give it a try. Really! Sure, as long as you understand what I just said. I understand! Ok Loon; I suggest you think about it for a while before you decide. I know we just started fooling around but I know your whoring ass. We've been friends for years before this, so you can't fool me. I've thought about it Denna and I'm ready. You sure poppi?

Yep! Well, let me know when you go house hunting, I would like to go with you. Cool, now that's what the fuck I'm talking about! Loon, don't start acting up; you were doing pretty good, calm down poppi. Loon placed both his hands on the table and looked at Denna with a smile. I'm calm baby. Alright people here's your food; Lamb stew for the lady and Grilled cheese with one bake for you Sir; butter, sour cream and bacon bits on the side. Thanks for visiting The Lake Tahoe Ski Lodge guys; enjoy your meals! Thank you! You're Welcome; enjoy!

So Sabrina and Coop are tying the knot, I still can't believe that shit. Why not Loon? I have a funny feeling about that girl; I still think she had something to do with her own kidnapping. Poppi that's spilled milk, leave it alone, just be happy for them. I guess so baby, but it will always be on my mind. How's that Lamb stew? It's great, here, try some! Umm, it is good. I told you! You should make some of that for the New Year's Eve party. Who me? Yeah you woman! I don't know if I could make it this good poppi. I think you can Denna. I don't know Loon; I'll have to think about that one. Well, I think it's a good idea. Maybe I will cook it for us, I'm sure Nina is going to have the party catered anyway. We need to hurry poppi, it's going to be dark soon. The snowmobiles have head lights; don't they! Loon, don't make me kick you in the knee! He looked up at Denna and smiled. Girl you're a trip. Um-hmm, eat your sandwich.

Knock-Knock! Knock-Knock! Who is it? It's the caterer Ma'am! Ok hold on a minute! Denna; can you get the door for me Sis; I'm still getting ready! Yeah; I got it already! How are you Ma'am, where did you want the food set up? You can use the kitchen table; that will work fine. Ok and how about the bar; it's on wheels; so it can go where ever you like. Cool, roll it over there on the left, just in front of the panoramic window. Thanks, we'll be done setting up in 30 minutes. What time are you expecting your guest to arrive? In another hour or so, you guys have plenty time to set up. Yeah that's plenty. Will you be bartending? No Ma'am, I will be serving the food, that gentleman with the bar is the bartender. Great, I'll leave you guys be, don't mind me.

46 stories up, the crisp night sky created an amazing back drop through the panoramic window that covered the entire back wall which also featured a balcony on the

opposite side. Red, green, yellow, blue and purple neon lights danced over the skyline and glowed through the panoramic; lighting up Nina's cream colored walls. Oh great just in time, the food is here. How many people did you invite Nina? Maybe 15 or 16, just the family and a couple of the ladies from Dolls! Is cuz coming? Yeah he and Chino! Did you invite Monica? No I didn't Denna, I thought you did. Well, I told her to come anyway, she'll probably be here. That's fine, I like Mo, she's gangster. You are definitely right about that girl!

Knock-knock! Who is it? Sophie! Come in, it's open! Hey Girl! Hey Nina, Denna, wow it looks great in here, look at that view! Hey ladies, Happy New Year! Hey Manny! I know; I fell in love with it the first time I seen it Sophie. I think that's the main reason I bought the place. That's a huge balcony; does it go the entire length of the window? Yeah it does, come on take a look bro. Manny and Nina walked outside on the long balcony admiring the view as the strip began to fill with people down below. Ring-Ring! Hello! Hey baby, I'm in the lobby, do you guys need anything from the store. No, we got everything Loon, thanks for calling poppi. Ok I'm on the way up; is anyone there yet? Yeah, Sophie and Manny! Ok, see you in a sec!

Hey Loon! Hey Loon! He turned around to see who called him. Oh what's up Malibu, Asia! Hey man, we're going to Nina's party, where is it? I'm heading up there now Asia, come with me. Ok cool! Did they block the streets off yet Malibu? Yeah, we parked on Flamingo and walked up. Damn; it's so many drunk people out there already and it's only 10 O'clock! That's every year on the strip ladies, these people come to party and party hard! Ding! Catch that elevator Asia, we're going up to the 46th floor. "What's up Las Vegas; Happy New Year, please be safe out there tonight." "This is Dj Shi C and that's my time, check me here tomorrow, same time, same station!" Ding! Ok this is our floor girls, make a right and it's the third door on the left.

Knock-Knock! It's open! What's the fuck up people! What up Looney! About to get my party on Capo! Happy New Year boy! Hey Sophie! Hello Loon! Everybody, you all know Malibu and Asia from Dolls right! Sure, hey girls you can put your coats in that closet behind you and just make yourselves comfortable. Food is on the table and the bar is over there. Thanks Nina, this is a bad ass crib! Thanks Asia! Oh girl, where did you get this white leather sectional? From Bradford's Malibu, over on Sahara! This view is breath taking, I love it! I was just telling Sophie that it was the reason I bought the place, it took my breath away too Asia. Knock-knock! It's open! Hey Neighbor! What's up Coop! Hey Brina! Happy New Year sis! Thanks bro! Where did you get these two? Oh we were playing spades at my place. Did you spank that ass AC? Nina, you know I don't lose sis! Man we won a game. Alright D; you and Remy won one, that's it though, out of like 12.

Derek you can put your coats in that closet behind you! Oh ok, thanks Nina. Denna, what's going on sis? Getting my drink on, you want something! Nah, not now, in a minute! See, you tripping bro! Brina you want a shot sis? Yeah Denna, I'll take a double! Yeah Chica! You heard her bartender, one double tequila! Yes Ma'am, double Jose' coming up! Remy did you want a shot? Hell yeah girl, pour it up! Bartender; make that another! Yes Ma'am got you covered! Knock-Knock! It's open! Hola Cuz! Hector; Chino, Que Pasa'! Happy New Year cousin, thanks cuz, come in, get a drink. Knock-Knock! It's open! Damn, Nina, this is sweet! Hey Will, thanks bro, you like it? Hell yeah; I'm jealous sis.

Hey Nina! Hey Monica, Happy New Year girl! Same to you babe! So; yall motherfuckers gone start the party without me! Duck what's happening bro, come in, check out my new crib! Wow, look at this view! Nina this is big time baby! Hey Karen, Happy New Year! Thanks Nina! Duck put your coats in the closet and grab some drinks the party is just starting. Ok everyone, can I have your attention please! First; I would like to thank all of you for coming to my very first New Year's party at my new place. Your Welcome Nina! Aww, thank you guys! Well, the food is on the table and the bar is open, so drink all you want and eat all you like. Let's party hard and bring 1998 in with a bang!

Yay! Turn the music on Denna; let's party! "Let's do it" "Workin all week" "9 to 5 for my money" "So when the weekend comes" "I go get live with the honey" Tone Loc baby, that's my song yall! Nina shouted as she pranced around the condo, drink in the air. Hey Monica! Yeah Denna, what's up? Come here chica and have some shots with us. Sure, what you guys drinking? Jose' girl, what else? I'm down; pour it up! Bartender, give me 8 more doubles for my ladies and keep them coming. Yes Ma'am you got it! Here you go ladies, drink up! The girls crowded over by the bar along-side the panoramic window, downing their Jose'. Damn Sabrina, that's a nice ring girl! Thanks Monica, AC gave it to me Christmas Eve night. Wow, that is gorgeous; is it an engagement ring? Yes it is; I will soon be Mrs. Cooper! Well damn, Congratulations bitch. I'm happy for you! Thank you Monica! You're welcome girl! Hey bartender; give me an extra shot and an extra one for the bride to be over here too! Yes Ma'am, no problem.

Here you go Sabrina, congratulations; drink up! Thank you! Whew hooo! Bartender; another round! Damn Brina, slow your roll baby; you want to be awake New Year's don't you? I'm good Denna; Jose' is my drink! Ok then chica, drink up! Monica, keep an eye on her will you? She's good Denna, I got her. "Introduce myself as Loc" "She said, "You're a liar" I said" "I got it goin on baby Doll and I'm on fire" Yo Coop, you want something to drink I'm headed to the bar? Sure Capo, let me get some Goose straight up! Alright, I'll be right back. Come on girls, let's go on the balcony! Nina led the ladies outside while screaming and dancing. "She loved to do the wild thing" "And I liked to do the wild thing" Happy New Year Las Vegas! The ladies leaned over the rail 46 stories up yelling down to the people on the strip. "She loved to do the wild thing" "Wild thing, Please, baby, baby, please."

Loon, the girls are wasted homie! I see that shit Hector; they drunk like 4 bottles of Jose' already. It's going to be a whole lot of hung over bitches tomorrow. Ha-ha! I sure hate it! Duck you're probably going to be hung over too fool. Oh congratulations AC! Thanks Hector! You're better than me homes, I fuck around too much to be married. I would be divorced the first week homes. Ha-Ha! Yeah it's a big step but Sabrina is cool, she's been there for me. I respect that homes; good luck with everything. What time is it Will? 11:05 Coop! Hey bartender; a round of goose please! Yes Sir; coming right up!

Whew hoooo! Viva Las Vegas! The ladies now drunk and rowdy, continued to shout over the balcony. Karen stood up on the bottom half of the rail, leaned over and joined in. Happy New Year! Sabrina followed suit and stood up on the rail beside her. Hell yeah, I'm about to be married! Yay! Happy New Year! Bing! Monica accidently dropped her glass on the balcony then slowly bent down to pick it up. She stumbled a bit, looked up, grabbed Sabrina's ankles and rose to her feet. The girls; still loud and rowdy were all hanging over the rail when she released Sabrina's ankles. Ahhhhhh! Oh shit! "Denna yelled" Sabrina! Sabrina! Ahhhhhhhhhh! Her screams faded the further she fell, while the on lookers down below watched in awe as her screams became louder. Oh shit; Oh shit! Come on, we have to go downstairs! The ladies stormed inside. AC! AC! Sabrina fell off the balcony! What the fuck did you say Nina! Sabrina fell! What! Are you serious! Yes! Come on, we have to get downstairs! Manny; dial 911!

To be Continued.....

Thank you for reading MADE II. Please check out these other titles by ANTWAN BANK$.

MADE is about Andy Cooper; a military vet, turned hustler, turned Gangster, turned Crime Boss. His marriage is on the rocks; fresh out of the military, AC finds himself broke and lost with a Wife and three kids to feed. Trapped in Sin City and working any job he can get from day to day, to make ends meet. Hating the state of mind he's in right now, a really fucked up way to be! Gone are the days when Uncle Sam paid for housing, day care and groceries. Now, all own his own again, with no idea of where life is going to take him. One thing for sure, Andy "AC" Cooper no longer wanted to wear that Army uniform another day. Coop loved every minute of it and would not trade it for the world but the next chapter of his life was about to start. It just so happen that he landed in Las Vegas, one of the hardest cities to make it in, it is truly the land of the

Hustler. What the outsiders don't know is that beneath the bright neon lights, the delicious buffets and luxurious casino's, lays a whole different world that would eventually suck him in.

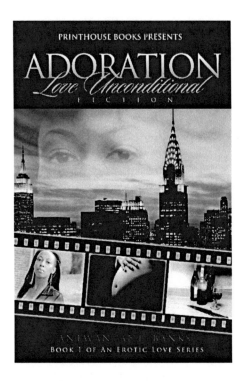

Adoration can be defined as fervent and devoted love or simply put; to worship. During our time on Earth we will all experience this powerful thing called Love. This novel will take you on a journey seen through the eyes of four couples and their relationships. For Love we endure amazing things and some of us will go to the limit to keep it.

Love can fill your heart with joy or leave it filled with hate. Adoration explores love at several levels; some of them good; some bad. In Book One of this Series; hearts will break, tears will fall, blood will shed and bells will chime; all in the name of love.

F.I.T.H. has a dramatic plot that sheds light on today's bullying epidemic. Take a look inside the mind of a bullied victim and how fear influenced his actions. *Inspired by True events*

Every School, City and County Library should have F.I.T.H (Fear Influences Thine Heart) on their shelves. It is a must read for any Parent, Teacher or Kid. F.I.T.H. is a Social Drama about a High School Freshman and a Bully. The situation becomes very intense when the bully does not let up. Although the victim tries his best to have tolerance and handle him accordingly, no matter what he tries, nothing seems to work. After several run ins and close calls, the victim is forced to become the Bully's favorite mark, influenced by an ever presence of fear, his life as he knew it; changed.

These collection of spirits; were some of my favorites to mix for the thousands of customers that I served as a bartender back in my 20's. During 1995 - 1996, I worked as a bartender in several Las Vegas Clubs and had a damn good time doing it! I've included a few recipe's; I picked up from fellow bartenders, some from customers and most I've learned from bartending school.

Mixology is an art and if mastered one can make a really good living serving spirits and conversing with the people you serve at your bar. If you're a bartender looking for some new drinks or you're just someone interested in mixing up some new drinks in your kitchen. This book of spirits is for you. Welcome to the Party Life and remember to drink responsibly.

The Cover Girl series is about, an Atlanta; Eye Candy photographer; name Malakhi Jones. Pronounced (*Mal uh Ky)*. This short story and many others to come; will take you inside a day in the life of a hot photographer and his daily encounters with several of the industries sexiest Magazine Models and Video Vixens.

While these events are Fiction; anyone in the industry knows; what goes on at the shoot; stays at the shoot! Malakhi is at the top of his game and is connected with every Men's Magazine Publisher, Casting Directors, Hip Hop Artist and Talent Managers in the industry. Getting a session with him is like winning the lottery; when it comes to being an eye candy Model, in the ATL. Any Model knows; that once the session starts and that camera flashes; all rules will be broken to obtain that success; if not! Then keep dreaming.

This title only available in ebook and sells for 99 cents.

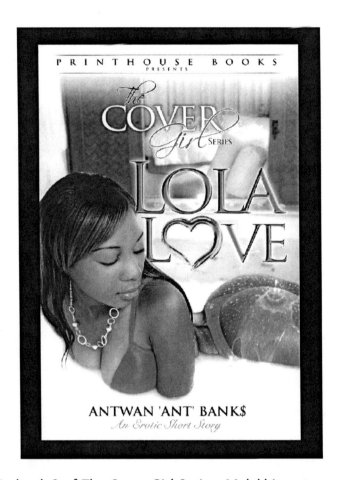

In book 2 of The Cover Girl Series; Malakhi ventures on an on location shoot, with the Sexy Chocolate, Video Vixen; Lola Love. Her enticing aura almost proves to be too much for the A List Photographer but in true Malakhi fashion; he prevails. The two meet up, downtown on Peachtree street Atlanta; at one of the Cities five star hotels.

Together, they will create magic for the camera and hot lustful memories in their Jacuzzi Suite. They say a picture is worth a thousand words but only the photographer and the model knows; what exactly goes on, between those poses.

This title only available in ebook and sells for 99 cents.

PRINTHOUSE BOOKS

Read it, Enjoy it, Tell a Friend.

www.PRINTHOUSEBOOKS.com

CPSIA information can be obtained at www.ICGtesting.com
Printed in the USA
LVOW131014090613

337652LV00002B/78/P